WORTH IT

S.M. SHADE
USA TODAY BESTSELLING AUTHOR
& C.M. OWENS

Copyright 2017 by S.M. Shade & C.M. Owens
No part of this book may be reproduced, or stored in a retrieval system or transmitted in any form or by any means, electronic, mechanical, photocopying, recording, or otherwise without express written permission of the author. This eBook is licensed for your enjoyment only. It may not be re-sold or given away to other people.

The story in this book is the property of the author, in all media both physical and digital. No one, except the owner of this property, may reproduce, copy or publish in any medium any individual story or part of this novel without the expressed permission of the author of this work.

Cover art by Cover Me Darling
Interior design by Cover Me Darling
Formatting by Athena Interior Book Design

CHAPTER ONE

Henley

Bright red boxer briefs in a tree, and a toothbrush and razor smashed into the dirt. Just a typical Sunday afternoon in my stellar life.

"Henley?" Kasha calls, standing in my yard and staring at the open second-floor window. She steps back just in time as a pile of clothing flies out and lands in the grass.

"Door's unlocked," I yell cheerfully. I may be enjoying this a little more than I should.

Fighting back a grin, she finds me in the bedroom, stripping the bed. "Not that I'm not thrilled you're dumping this loser, but isn't that your sheet?" she asks as I toss it out the window.

"It's tainted with skank. God knows what kind of crotch rot she has—herpes, scabies, Ebola. I don't want it."

I flop onto the bed and my best friend sits beside me. "Ebola isn't a crotch… um… I mean… tell me what happened."

"I took an extra shift at work today to cover for a friend. She ended up making it back a few hours early, so I left and came home to find Casey's naked ass in the air while some emaciated slut made porno sounds under him. Seriously, it was the fakest shit I've ever heard."

"Oh, hell. What did you do?"

"They didn't see me, and since the easiest way to get two rutting dogs apart is a garden hose, I figured a mop bucket full of cold water would do the trick. It did."

Kasha chuckles and helps me put a new sheet on the bed. "Well, you seem to be handling it well."

"I feel relieved. I guess that should tell me something. I mean, being cheated on after a year of living together, I should be a mess, but I just want him out of my house."

"At least you have good timing. A week away… where he can't find you."

I pull out my half packed suitcase and fold the last of the clothes I'm taking, tucking them inside. "Don't mention this to Lydia. This week is about her. She acts like she doesn't care, but you know that's bullshit."

Kasha, Lydia, and I have been best friends since we were kids. We've stuck together through high school hell, first heartbreaks, and family drama. I don't know what I'd do without them. Lydia has always been there when we needed her, so when she announced she was going to her ex-boyfriend's wedding, we didn't hesitate. She needs us and we'll be there to support her. Besides, it's also Kasha's family, so she sort of had to be there.

Kasha is right, though. The timing is perfect for me to rid myself of the loser who only drags me down. After a week on sunny Marco Island in Florida, I'll feel like a new woman.

"I tried to talk her out of going." Kasha shakes her head and follows me downstairs.

"Anderson was her first love and he royally screwed her over. I think she wants to go to prove to him she's over it. That she can be the bigger person."

"That shouldn't be hard," she states dryly. "Stay at my place tonight. I'll get Lydia over and we'll pig out and watch T.V. I just got the last season of True Blood."

"Sold. Help me grab my stuff."

My eyes flit down to her arm, and I notice she has a new prosthetic... if that's what you can call it. It's almost like part of the Terminator was robbed and attached to her. It's chrome and black.

"New arm? Looks like it was pimped."

She nods absently. "Dad's latest 'smart arm' prototype. Meet Jill." She waves her robot-like fingers. "Jack is still underway."

"The fingers move better. Hope it's smarter than the last one that caught fire when you tried to take a shower with it."

She groans. "It's waterproof. That's the first thing I checked. He's holding off with the synthetic skin because he can't get the sensors to work with the Nano patch on my neck yet. And I'm not having neurosurgery to have the chip implanted in my brain. I do draw the line somewhere. So, I have to think really hard about what I want the hand to do for now, but Dad says it'll get smarter as it goes, learning to pick up my thoughts easier."

"That's... cool? Creepy? Not sure which way to go with that."

She smirks before holding her hand up. "I'll be back," she says in a deep, Terminator-like voice.

We both giggle like it's the funniest shit ever.

And we're dorks. Should be an interesting trip.

Lydia shows up at Kasha's apartment with a huge box of donuts. Her strained smile betrays her anxiety over the next week. Kasha sits between us on the couch and opens a shiny brochure advertising Marco Island.

"Look at all the stuff we can do while we're there. Zip-lining, snorkeling, parasailing. They even have a huge family center with laser tag and an inflatable obstacle course." She puts the brochure in front of Lydia. "And look at the beach! We're going to drink, lie in the sun, and make a nice vacation out of it."

Lydia gives a half-hearted grin. "The beach sounds good. At least I've lost my winter weight."

"Like you aren't always skinny," I scoff. I'd kill for her metabolism. I can just smell food and my ass inflates.

We order a pizza and proceed to eat ourselves into a coma while watching hot vampires and werewolves battle it out on television. Lydia turns to me between episodes. "Aren't you a little concerned about leaving Casey alone at your house all week? Last time you left him for a few days, he burnt your new carpet."

I wasn't going to bring it up, but I'm not going to lie to her. "I kicked him out today."

Her eyebrows jump. "No shit?"

"Her yard and tree are full of his clothes," Kasha laughs.

"About damn time, girl. You can do so much better."

Sighing, I shake my head. "I'm starting to think they're all the same. Lying, cheating, scumbag losers."

"I agree. I'm just going to be like a nun."

"Yep. Screw it. Celibacy is the way to go," I agree.

Kasha snorts with laughter. "That'll happen."

"Wait. Vibrators don't count, right? Because Buzzy takes care of me just fine."

Lydia laughs, and Kasha winks at me. At least we cheered her up a little. "I'm going to bed. We have a long drive tomorrow."

"Even longer if you let Lydia bring that horrible dance mix CD," Kasha groans.

"I didn't bring it! I know you two have no taste in music," Lydia replies, throwing a pillow at me.

I hear them both go to bed right after me.

It's still dark out when we get ready to leave the next morning. Chilly air finds every tiny gap in my clothes and makes me shiver.

"Ugh, why do we have to leave so early?" Lydia groans, throwing her suitcase in the back of the SUV I rented for the trip.

"It's a long drive. We need to get started," I reply, hopping into the driver's seat.

"We should've flown," she grumbles, curling up in the back seat with a blanket.

"Last minute plane tickets cost a fortune. And you were the one who suggested a bestie road trip, remember?" Kasha tells her.

"Didn't know we had to leave in the middle of the night."

"So go back to sleep, you grouchy bitch," I laugh, and she gives me the finger. By the time we hit the nearest drive-thru for some coffee, she's snoring away. I make a quick detour past my house to see if Casey has been back. There are no more clothes scattered on my lawn, but the underwear still hang from the tree. Guess they were too hard to reach. The sight puts a smile on my face.

Kasha smiles and plugs in her iPod. The sun begins to show its face as we pull onto the highway, Kasha and I bouncing around to the upbeat sound of Imagine Dragons. "I hate you guys," Lydia mumbles from the back seat, and we dissolve into giggles. This might be fun after all.

Lydia perks up when we stop to stretch our legs a few hours later. By the time we hit the road again, dark clouds are moving in and the wind blasts against the side of the SUV, nearly pushing us into the next lane.

Rain pelts the window fast and hard, making traffic slow to a crawl, and I lean forward, struggling to keep my eye on the white line. The headlights are on, but it doesn't help much. It's gone from bright and sunny to dark as night within a minute or two.

"We should get off the highway," Kasha suggests. "Wait for this shit to pass."

"Next exit," I agree. I really can't see anything but the hazard lights of the car in front of me. A semi with a picture of a chicken on the rear flies past us, the blowback pushing us to the right and slamming us with more water.

"Fuckstick," Lydia blurts. "He's going to cause an accident."

The girl should be a fortune-teller. Less than five minutes later, just as the storm begins to let up, traffic comes to a halt. Flashing lights warn us we may be here a while.

We inch closer to the accident and Kasha laughs. "It's the dick weasel with the chicken ass!"

Sure enough, a semi lies on its side, blocking both lanes, the large goofy picture of a chicken prominently displayed. At least he didn't take any other vehicles out with him. A burly, bearded man who'd look right at home with an axe perched on his shoulder stands beside the rig, staring at it like the truck crashed itself just to piss him off.

A policeman stands by the side of the road, flagging the line of vehicles onto the exit ramp. Guess we're getting off the highway after all. Light rain falls as we find ourselves on an unfamiliar country road. Cornfields line each side of the twisting road, and there are no signs to lead us back to the highway.

"Update the GPS navigator so we don't get lost out here. Find a restaurant where we can wait this out," I tell Kasha. The rain may have let up, but ominous clouds are coming at us fast.

"I'm on it."

The GPS leads us to a small town nearby, and I pull into the Grab-a-Bite restaurant. "We may as well eat here while we wait for the storm to pass."

An elderly lady with a kind smile waits on us. She introduces herself as Dorothy, and proceeds to bring us more food than we order or could ever eat in one sitting. "Eat up! You girls are as skinny as a poor man's wallet," she says with a smile, putting a platter of fries in front of us.

She's so nice, which is more than I can say for the man in the corner booth. He's alone and obviously drunk off his ass. Apparently, saying please or thank you would mortally wound him. He barks orders at Dorothy and yells for her every couple of minutes. Nothing is good enough, and his shouted complaints fill the small restaurant.

Dorothy seems to know him—small town, I guess everyone knows everyone—and does what she can to keep him from bothering the other customers, who turn a blind eye. I can't do it anymore.

As we get up to leave, he yells at her again. "This coffee tastes like shit! And it's cold!"

My eyes meet Dorothy's. "Let me translate. I speak asshole pretty well. He would like another cup of coffee, even though there's nothing wrong with his. What he really wants is to feel like a man, and since the tiny appendage between his legs won't let him, he gets off by being rude to women."

A woman sitting beside her boyfriend spits her orange juice across the counter, and he laughs aloud. Dorothy is trying her best not to laugh as the jerk turns to her and slurs, "I'm a paying customer!"

"So are they," Dorothy replies, refilling another customer's coffee.

"She-she called me an asshole!" he splutters.

Turning to Dorothy, I shrug. "I honestly thought he knew."

Everyone in the restaurant laughs, and the man's face burns red. I leave a large tip on our table, and Lydia tells Dorothy, "Thanks for the wonderful breakfast. I'm too stuffed to walk."

"You're more than welcome, girls. Be sure to stop in if you pass through this way again."

"We sure will," Kasha promises.

The rude man is grumbling under his breath when we leave. "That's his car," Kasha says, pointing out a sedan in the parking lot. "I saw him pull in."

"Okay, so?" Lydia replies.

"So, I have an idea. Watch for him to come out." He's parked at an angle, so there's no way he can see her from his booth. Kasha grabs a handful of ketchup packets from the console of the car and tears them open.

Lydia and I play lookout while she tucks a few under each of his windshield wipers. The other she uses to coat the driver's door handle. "How old are you?" Lydia asks, giggling, as we pile into our car.

"You're never too old for revenge. Look! Here he comes!" It's sprinkling, and his windshield is just wet enough for him to have to use the wipers. We watch, holding our breath as he grabs the door handle. He must just think the handle is wet because of the rain, since he instantly rubs his ketchup-covered hand across the front of his white T-shirt.

The look of horror on his face is hilarious. It's a good thing we're parked far enough away from him so he doesn't hear us. He grabs a paper towel from the back-seat and attempts to clean his smeared shirt, just rubbing it in worse. Cursing, he gets in his car.

The engine starts, and we hold our breath, just waiting for it. Finally, it happens. The wipers sweep across the windshield, squirting ketchup in all directions. It takes him a second to shut them off, so they drag back and forth across the red mess a few times, covering the middle of the windshield.

This time, he must've heard us laugh, because his eyes fall on our SUV. His face is so red, it's a wonder steam isn't pouring from his ears. "Uh-oh," Kasha says, locking the doors. Just as I start the engine, a police car pulls in behind him. Busted. Maybe Dorothy called them. I don't know, but either way, he's obviously drunk and was going to drive.

He yells and gestures to his shirt and his car until the cop puts him in handcuffs. It's hard to appear innocent when you're shitfaced and covered in ketchup. As we pull out of the lot, Dorothy stands outside the front door of the restaurant and gives us a surreptitious thumbs up. "She saw it!" Lydia squeals. "Awesome!"

The rain has stopped and the sun beats down on the sparsely populated highway. The rest of our drive isn't nearly as eventful. We take turns choosing the music and singing along to our favorites. As much as I'm looking forward to the beach and all the activities, driving with the windows down and the warm breeze through my hair, while belting out my favorite song with my best friends, will still rank high in my week.

"You are so going parasailing," Lydia tells Kasha. "Don't be chicken shit."

"I'm not chicken shit! I mean, have we met? I'm accident prone on dry land. Who knows what I'll do five hundred feet in the air? I'll probably throw up, then crash into it."

A two lane concrete bridge carries us across the water to Marco Island, and a few minutes later, we're parking at the massive Anderson estate. "I just want a long, hot shower," Lydia says as we grab our luggage and head inside.

"We should have just enough time. There's a little get-together at seven for all the wedding guests, and I suppose we should be there."

Kasha slings an arm around Lydia's shoulders. "Are you all right?"

"So far so good."

"You let us know anytime you want to make a quick escape and we'll get you out of there," I promise.

Our room is huge, spotless, and frankly, too damn comfortable to want to leave. After a day of driving, I just want to eat and crawl into bed.

My dread of the approaching evening is nothing next to Lydia's. Though she's putting up a brave front, worry is written on her pale face. "Don't worry," Kasha tells her. "You've got this. Just keep reminding yourself he's the selfish dick who cheated on you."

"And he had a small one," Lydia adds with a grin. "Seriously, it was like a pimple with a pulse."

"Let's get this party started and show him what he gave up," Kasha announces. "I can promise no one will forget us, and no one will remember the bride by the time this week is over."

CHAPTER TWO

Kasha

Face down, ass up... No, it's not as sexy as it sounds. Humiliating would be a more accurate word to describe this moment.

This is *not* what I meant about not being forgotten.

Just a few hours ago, all my concerns were with Lydia—who has to face her ex at the wedding from hell—and Henley—who just lost her one-testicle asshole of an ex. Sure, I had my own problems with being here, but they were overshadowed by my concern for my friends.

Right now... right now, I no longer give a damn about them, because I just went for the *epic fail award* of all time by tripping into the party.

Silence is even worse than riotous laughter, because I feel all the eyes burning against my Superman underwear, while my flowy dress rests against my back. I'm thankful for the mud that is suffocating me, since it prevents me from seeing the gawking.

The first strangled sound resonates in my ears, seconds before the heckling of male laughter and a few feminine snickers.

I was wrong. Silence is better than riotous laughter.

Despite contemplating the benefits of drowning in a mud puddle at this moment to avoid the mortification, I decide to continue breathing. I pull myself up to my knees, feeling someone behind me jerking my skirt over my immature underwear. Superman was supposed to be my secret. The little cape over the back door is no longer as funny as it was this morning.

Fuck my life.

I wipe the muck out of my eyes—or try to. My "smart arm" struggles to read that I'm trying to wipe away the disgusting stuff, and instead, the robotic hand only smears it in worse. Stupid arm.

I stick to using my right hand, since it's my actual hand and understands what I'm trying to do. I also spit out a hellacious amount of metallic-tasting mud. That taste is never leaving my mouth. It's even in my nose, which is… not good. Not good at all. It's not like I can blow my nose in front of an entire wedding party. It'll look like my face took a shit in a napkin.

What a great way to start the week.

At least Lydia won't be the one everyone is whispering about anymore. Guess that makes me a team player. *Yay*.

"Kasha," Lydia hisses, seconds before I feel two sets of hands lift me under my arms and help to right me completely.

The hyena laughter around us definitely hasn't ceased, but there's still too much mud in my eyes to see, despite my attempts to wipe it away.

Something soft is pressed against my face, and I clutch it, using it to wipe away the rest of the mud. Then immediately regret seeing when I realize I'm literally in the center of the party. People have congregated around me like I'm a street performer at the peak of my show.

I'm tempted to grab a hat to toss down so people can throw in some money.

"Need a drink? I've heard vodka pairs nicely with sludge," Henley quips, her lips twitching like she's doing all she can not to laugh.

I glare at her like it's somehow going to scare her.

"Yes. But I think I'll shower first."

She smirks but has the grace to cover her mouth when it turns into a mocking grin. Lydia is also suppressing laughter. Her small frame is shaking from the internal war.

I flip them both off before walking inside… and getting shoved back out by my mother's evil head maid.

"Ah, hell no," Susie says with a scowl on her pasty face. I swear she's part vampire. I don't think I've ever seen her in the sun. "Servants' entrance is out back. Go in that way if you think mud-wrestling is sexy, Ms. J. I just waxed these damn floors."

More laughter ensues the scolding.

Someone kill me now.

It's been a long time since I've come to this house. They've added another floor, which is where I'm staying. My mother demanded I come here, and considering I got tired of her showing up at my apartment twice a week, I finally caved. I'm weak like that. I also wanted to be here for Lydia when I found out she'd decided to respond to her invitation. And since my apartment is over my father's garage, I didn't want to risk his heart breaking when he eventually ran into my relentless mother.

After finally finding the "servants' entrance," I head up the servants' elevator and drip mud all down the shiny hallway. I have a feeling someone will be kicking my ass later. Or searching for Big Foot.

Is my foot really that big? No. It's just because the mud is squishing out from under it. I only wear a size seven shoe, so it can't be that big…

This is so not the time for footprint examinations... Definitely not that big.

Finally, I find my room in the maze of unmarked doors. Who really needs a house this size?

My pretentious mother and her obnoxious husband. That's who.

I head straight to the bathroom and lock the door. I also lock the door across from me. Why does it have two doors?

Again, this is not the time...

Starting the process of peeling off my once-white dress, I step closer to the shower, cursing when the damn dress gets hung up in my hair. Life sucks sometimes.

After a few more twists, turns, and a couple of near-falls, I finally get the dress over my head and in the trashcan. I flip on the shower and peel off my Superman undies that now shame me instead of making me feel quirky.

Damn it.

My father recently made me a new arm, which looks like something he stole from a robot. While it may not be pretty, it's hella functional. It receives messages and works like a fully functioning bionic arm, thanks to the patch on the back of my neck that carries Nano technology and communicates the messages between my brain, spine, and fake arm.

Because my father is a genius. He could be on the path for some award once I find all the kinks with this prototype before he goes public.

Right now, I'm just glad it's waterproof. And I really like washing my hair with two functioning hands. I forgot how nice it was.

My dignity washes down the drain, while the mud cakes up on the sides, forcing me to move it around to keep the water from standing.

After a while, I finally give up and climb out, hoping I'm clean enough. The bathroom is nothing but a haze of steam, and I curse the slippery tiles that try to take me down. This is hell.

Pushing the bathroom door open, I stumble into the bedroom, and... scream. Because there's a boy in my room. No, no. Not a boy. There's a very tall, very sexy, very... amused *man* in my room.

He cocks an eyebrow when he sees me, pausing his fingers over the buttons of his undone—or half done, if you're an optimist—shirt as he stares.

"You're in a towel," he states with no emotion.

"You're perceptive," I bite out, then clutch the towel closer to my chest.

He deliberately rakes his eyes over me, letting them scale down my wet chest, to my towel-clad middle, down to my legs that are still glistening with water. When he bites his lip, I try not to find it sexy, because he's a perverted asshole who is in my room. Being sexy does not make any of this okay. Besides, his eyes linger for far too long on my 'smart arm.'

"Funny," he says, bringing his eyes back up to meet mine as his lips twitch. "I don't remember ordering a wet stripper."

Heat rises in my cheeks, and I glare at him—because that's what I do best.

"What the hell are you doing in my room?"

His eyebrows go up, and his smirk turns into a grin. "I was going to ask you the same thing."

"You were going to ask me what you're doing in my room? I have no idea. Hence the reason I asked you!"

Why is he still smiling?

"This is my room, toga girl. Are you a present, or are you seriously lost?"

And he's definitely an asshole.

"I'm not a freaking 'present,' and I'm definitely not lost," I growl.

Stalking to the closet, I cast a snarl in his direction. I sling open the door with one hand, using my 'smart arm' hand to keep a firm grip on the towel. The last thing I need to do is flash him.

"See?" I snap, then immediately grimace. Those aren't my suits, ties, or T-shirts hanging up. What the hell? "Where did my dresses go?" I ask quietly, wondering if it would be weird for me to hide in the closet until this week is over.

It can't be any weirder than showing everyone my Superman undies and hanging out in a towel in front of a stranger. Inside *his* room.

Slowly, I turn around to face the cheeky bastard who is covering his smile with his fist, but the amusement is clearly there.

"So, not a stripper present then?" he asks, clearing his throat while trying to rein in his laughter.

"I'm not a stripper," I grumble. "When I went into that bathroom, I walked through my room. Obviously there's a vortex or something that spit me out in here somehow."

"Obviously," he agrees patronizingly, still fighting that damn smile. "Or," he says, smirking, "you came through the wrong door after you left the bathroom. After all, we're sharing a bathroom that connects our rooms. It's not as likely as your vortex theory, but it's always best to explore all possibilities."

Any other time, I'd find him funny, possibly even charming. Not so much at this moment, because I'm sort of in the middle of praying for a hole to open up and swallow me.

Inky black hair, icy blue eyes, tall, sexy, designer everything, *and* he's gorgeous… This would be better if he was ugly. Much better.

Turning around, I head back toward the bathroom and slam the door behind me like a surly teen would do. It's really the only card I have left to play at this moment, aside from dying.

The second it's shut, I hear his deep rumble of laughter barely penetrate the barrier, and a slight set of goosebumps pebble my skin.

He even laughs sexy.

I hate him.

I hate this wedding.

I really, really hate the mirror that is showing me my towel isn't covering all my ass and he just saw more of my body than I realized.

Fuck my day.

"What took you so long?" Henley asks with a ghost of a taunting smile when I finally find them at a table outside. I sit down with them, making sure to cross my legs so no one sees the latest pair of underwear I'm donning.

Are there really people playing glow-in-the-dark croquet? I don't understand rich people. This is why I lived with my father. We did normal shit. Well, that's a lie. We did weird shit, like build robots that clean out litter boxes, and machines that dispense food for pets on automated timers.

I mentioned my father is an inventor, right?

"It takes a minute to wash ten pounds of mud out of your hair," I say with a bitter smile, deciding to omit the naked-in-a-stranger's-room bit.

Lydia and Henley both snicker, and I roll my eyes while grabbing a glass of champagne from a passing tray. At least rich people serve alcohol all day. I don't care that I haven't even eaten in a while.

"Did you know our bathroom is hooked to another room?" I ask them, wishing I had done a more thorough inspection of the room before we came out here.

"Yes," they both answer.

"Why?" Henley asks.

"No reason," I mutter.

My eyes flick around, discreetly searching for the face of the mystery man who saw me at my worst. Well, not my worst, but definitely not my best. Hmmm… There are very few men out here at all.

"Most of the guys seem to be missing," Lydia points out, as though she knows I'm noticing the lack of testosterone. "I think they're exploring the property."

At least my mother also seems to be missing. Thankfully something is going right today.

The girls playing croquet start squealing, and I roll my eyes. We don't even like the bride, so it feels weird to be hanging out with thirty other women who are here to celebrate the homewrecker and my cheating asswipe of a stepbrother.

I told Lydia not to date him. No one listens to me…

Pink decorations are pretty much everywhere. There are even pink couches outside, and I swear there are pink chandeliers hanging from the trees—the trees aren't pink.

Pink candles are lit as a centerpiece for our table, and I'm surprised the flames aren't pink. Pink flower petals are all over the pink tablecloth, and pink chair-covers are dressing the seats, and pink… Fuck it. You get the idea. It looks like Pepto exploded out here and rained down on the decorations, creating the pink apocalypse.

Even Barbie would cringe at this setup.

"Shit," Lydia groans.

"What?" Henley and I both ask at the same time.

"He's here," she says as though she can't believe it.

My eyes follow her gaze, and I see Anderson walking up and putting his arms around his bride-to-be under the glow of one of the pink, outdoor chandeliers.

"Well, it is his wedding," Henley reminds her. "Did you think you wouldn't see him?"

"I just didn't expect to see him so soon," Lydia says quietly.

She frowns while looking away, and I decide to do something stupid.

"I'll be back," I tell them.

"Do that in a Terminator voice next time," Henley quips, swirling her own glass of champagne. "It works for you."

At this rate, we're going to be wasted before the party even truly gets started. Getting up, I head toward the daffodil-embroidered pink buffet table, and grab a bottle of whiskey and a bottle of vodka from the bar on the way, tucking the vodka under my arm.

The buffet table is under a large canopy and abandoned. The food isn't out yet, but the beverages are still in use. It's far enough away from the festivities that people don't seem to notice me. Not to mention, it's a little darker over here.

Without even glancing around, I twist the cap off and pour the entire bottle of whiskey into the punch bowl. Then, like a sweetheart, I pick up the water pitcher and pour it out before grabbing the vodka and dumping it into the lemonade pitcher. Smiling, I toss the two empty bottles under the table, glance around to see no one is looking at me—other than my curious friends—and merrily skip back toward my table.

Well, I *try* to skip. I end up stomping the front of my shoe against the ground and toppling forward, sucking in a sharp, painful breath seconds before a body stops my fall. My head slams into a hard chest, and two strong hands grab my hips, steadying me.

This is so not my day.

"Easy there, toga girl," a familiar, deep voice says, chilling me to the bone.

My head snaps up, and my eyes widen at the man who is grinning down at me. He winks, and I stumble backwards, almost falling again. Fortunately, he's still holding onto my hips, and jerks me back toward him. Unfortunately, that has me slamming up against his hard, incredible body again.

How did my life get so embarrassing?

"Are you always so graceful?" he taunts.

"Are you always such a stalker?"

His eyes narrow as the smile falls from his lips. "You do remember that you walked into my room naked, right?"

"I had on a towel," I remind him, as though that somehow makes it all better.

"You ran over me," he goes on.

"You're holding onto me," I point out.

Being angry when you're humiliated… It's called a defense mechanism. Get over it.

He drops his hands from my sides, his lips pursing as he steps back. Under the glow of the candlelight, he looks even sexier. Why me? Why did he have to be the one I made an ass of myself in front of?

"I'm glad you ran into me," he says, leisurely sliding his gaze down my body.

A flurry of contradicting feelings bud in the pit of my stomach, and I'd be lying if I said I don't have a squeal-like-a-girl moment of smugness. Obviously I stay a mask of awesomeness and cool on the outside though.

"Oh?" I muse, and maybe I cock a hip while smirking. "Why's that?"

His eyes flick back up, and something akin to a wicked gleam lights his gaze.

"We'll be here a week, right?" he asks rhetorically.

Heat, excitement, and nervousness tries to claw its way to the surface, but I stick with the cool-girl exterior. I tend to test the waters with guys who don't mind the arm thing. Believe it or not, not all guys seem to overlook the fact I only have one arm. Some of them actually have an issue with it.

Shocker, I know. They apparently missed the memo where one-armed chicks are rarer than the ordinary ones with two arms. Who wants normal these days?

"Right," I drawl.

"And we'll be sharing a bathroom," he goes on, biting down on his lower lip as his gaze flicks down my body once more.

I like the no-subtlety, direct approach he's going with.

"Yeah," I say with a breathy tone that doesn't go with my be-awesome attempt.

When his eyes come back up, he smirks. "Given how disgusting the shower was after you left, I'm assuming it's rare that you bathe. Do me a favor and clean up after yourself if you do shower again this week. I'm not a neat freak, but I do draw the line at gross."

He flashes me a mocking grin as a new form of heat floods me. It's sure as hell not arousal anymore. And what can I possibly say to that?

No matter what comes out of my mouth, I'll only embarrass myself worse.

"Oh," he goes on, not finding the ability to speak as difficult as I do. "And I think these are yours."

He pulls my Superman underwear out of his pocket, and I hiss out a breath before snatching them out of his hands. I half picture myself stabbing him with one of the little shrimp forks near the buffet table. Dad told me my hand could crush balls with the same force as a baby alligator's jaws. I'm curious about the accuracy of that assessment at the moment.

Wadding my underwear up, I tuck the embarrassing fabric under my arm, considering my dress has no pockets, while he laughs like the dick he is.

"Stay away from me," I grumble, trying to walk by him, but he moves to block my path.

"We share a bathroom," he says, still smirking as his eyes dance with endless humor.

"Then lock the door so I don't *accidentally* come in there when you're taking a shower, and *accidentally* trip while I'm holding a knife, and *accidentally* stab you fifteen times through the shower curtain. I'd really hate for something like that to *accidentally* happen."

I give him what I hope is a creepy, scary smile, but he doesn't look the least bit intimidated.

"There's a shower door. Not a curtain," he chirps.

Is this guy for real?

"Accidents still happen." My eyes narrow as the threat leaves my lips.

"Don't worry. I won't *accidentally* leave it unlocked."

I'm not sure why that sounds like something dirty, but it does. He winks before walking away, and I go back to praying for that damn hole to open up again.

When I reach my table, Lydia and Henley are both staring and in attack mode, pouncing in unison.

"Who was—"

"I don't want to talk about it," I interrupt, waving my hand for emphasis before guzzling down the rest of my champagne.

Hey, my robot hand can hold the glass without breaking it. Dad really pulled out all the stops with this one. It's soooo much better than the one that caught fire and broke all my pencils.

"Did he give you your underwear?" Henley asks.

"I said I don't want to talk about it," I grumble, grabbing Lydia's champagne and downing it as well.

Their eyesight is too good if they could tell that was my underwear.

"O…kay…" Lydia bites back a smile.

"What was with spiking all the drinks?" Henley asks, redirecting the conversation.

I sag in relief when they drop the mystery asshole encounter, and I let a dark grin emerge.

"This party has a stick up its ass. I just made things more interesting. Or it will be soon, rather. Henley, you have the next shift. As soon as they refresh the refreshments, you're on."

At least I won't be the only one who has made an ass of herself by the end of the night.

Should be a hell of an evening. Good times. Good times.

My eyes discreetly find Mr. Asshole as a girl loops her arm through his. He casually disentangles himself from her, and I watch like a stalker as he moves toward a couple to speak to.

Shit. I don't know if I want to stab him or fuck him.

When he looks up and catches me staring, he smirks again, smugly gazing at me like he owns me.

Stab him. Definitely want to stab him.

"Okay," Henley pipes up. "This party is seriously painful. I've seen coma patients with more enthusiasm than this crowd. It's time to mix it up."

CHAPTER THREE

Henley

This may be the most tedious party I've ever been to. Snooty people, dressed to the nines, mingle and chat before moving on to talk shit about the person they were just trying to outdo. I feel as out of place as a nun at a strip club. Kasha is right. We need to liven it up or die of boredom.

No one seems to notice that she upped the octane of the punch and lemonade. Classical music plays through the outdoor speakers while people move about the dance floor as if they're at a formal ball. I can't take any more. "Do you know where the sound system is?" I ask Kasha, gesturing to the speakers overhead.

Kasha points to a small building adjacent to the pool. "It's in there, why?"

"Does it play CDs or will an iPod work?"

A smile climbs across her face. "Plug the iPod into the auxiliary slot and hit play."

That's all I need to hear. It only takes me five minutes to rush back to our room and grab my iPod. No one pays any attention to me as I slip inside the fence surrounding the pool and into the small building. It's a pretty simple setup. I find my "shake your ass" playlist of all my favorite dance songs and hit play. The music switches from symphony to sinful in an instant.

I sneak around the back of the building and return as if I'm coming from the house. The looks of confusion on the guests' faces are priceless. Kasha doesn't hesitate to grab Lydia and meet me on the dance floor, which has cleared out for some strange reason. We don't care.

"Let's show them how we do it." Kasha grins, rotating her hips and getting into the music. Lydia giggles, and we join in. Guests surround the dance floor, watching like we're putting on a show just for them. So, we do. We dance with each other, laughing and having a great time. A few others filter onto the dance floor, mostly young men and women like us, probably dragged here by overbearing parents.

The party is on. I keep expecting someone to switch the music back, but Kasha's mother—who I'm sure chose the soundtrack—is still inside barking orders at the staff. I take a short break to guzzle some more of the hard lemonade before returning to the dance floor that's now mostly filled with dancing bodies.

I can hear Kasha's rowdy laugh as the next song starts. Okay, maybe it's a little raunchy for the occasion, but it's not like I planned ahead. The thinning circle of stuck-up onlookers gape in horror when the crowd reacts. There's some serious grinding and humping going on as the alcohol drains inhibitions, and everyone *gets low*.

Two warm hands grab my hips from behind and I go with it, grinding my ass into him, my eyes closed, just feeling the music. "I'm sure Monica Harper did not choose a song where sweat drips from balls," a deep and strangely familiar voice murmurs in my ear. I may not immediately recognize it, but my body does. My face flushes with heat and a knot forms in my stomach. Holding my breath, I turn and come face to face with him. Davis Lane. Holy fuck.

My first love and only true heartbreak stands before me, grinning that familiar lopsided grin that always knocked me off my feet. Apparently, it still does since I'm standing frozen, my mouth opening and closing like a goldfish. "What the hell are you doing here?" I ask, finally pulling my head out of my ass.

He laughs and his eyes roam over my body, stopping when they meet mine. "It's good to see you, too, Hen."

My first instinct is to run, so I do, well, I walk fast. This night suddenly requires a lot more alcohol. On my way past the refreshment table, I grab a random bottle which turns out to be bourbon. Ew. Not my favorite, but tonight, I'll drink anything.

My feet sink into sand as I make my way down the trail to the beach, the full moon lighting my way. Davis is here. I can't even wrap my mind around it. Eight long years I've thought about this moment and how I'd react to seeing the man who took my virginity, then ran like hell. I was eighteen and in love the way only an eighteen-year-old can be. He was my brother's best friend, and for two years, we hid our relationship. I lived for the day when we wouldn't have to keep it secret anymore, the day I was supposed to leave for college. I was an idiot. It was never about him being two years older than me, or my brother's friend. He was just ashamed to admit he slept with the skinny nerd.

Kicking off my shoes, I flop into the sand, letting the small waves just brush my toes. It's such a beautiful setting, and here I sit. Alone. Pathetic as always. Some things never change.

"You're still beautiful when you pout."

Shit. Of course he followed me. Staring at the ocean, I sigh, "Why are you here?"

"The bride is a distant cousin." He sits beside me, and I do my best not to look at him. I'm drunk, and he looks even better than he did when we were kids. Those dark eyes are the same, and that crooked smile still makes me weak, but he's grown up. His jaw is sculpted and covered with a light scruff. Even through his suit, I can see he's far more muscular than he used to be. This could end badly.

He grabs the bottle of bourbon from my hand and takes a drink. "Since when do you drink bourbon?"

"Since I'm not a teenager anymore."

His gaze sweeps over me and his lips curl into a grin. "You've definitely grown up."

I'm still skinny, but my body has filled out. I still don't have the big boobs I used to hope for, but they're not tiny, and my hips and ass are curvy. The glasses have been traded in for contacts and I finally outgrew the acne breakouts. Light brown hair falls in waves just past my shoulders. I know I'm not beautiful, but I don't exactly scare kids on the street.

When he scoots closer, offering me the bottle, I relent and take another shot. His scent is killing me and I can feel the heat from his body. Desire surges through me, and blood rushes to color my cheeks. I only slept with him once, and the first time is never exactly fun. It hurt and it was awkward, but I wanted him to be my first.

Even though I've bounced between missing and hating him all these years, I've also thought about that night and wished I could have him again. Maybe I'm a glutton for punishment, but part of me wants to drag him back to his room and show him I'm not a pathetic, ugly kid anymore.

"Do you think if you just ignore me, I'll go away?" he asks.

"Guess that's too much to hope for."

His hand goes to his chest as he feigns offense. "Ouch! Are you trying to hurt me? Because the Henley I remember could do much better."

My anxiety over seeing him again starts to wane, and I try not to smile. Same old Davis. He could always make me smile no matter how pissed or upset I was. "That's better," he says, grinning at me.

"What do you want, Davis?" I take another drink of bourbon. I can feel it rushing through me, giving me strength and courage.

"More than I have a right to ask for, but for now, I just want to see you again." His eyes meet mine, a thin slice of moonlight reflected in them. "What do you want?"

I want to tear off his clothes and ride him like a stolen bike, and not just because the attraction is still there between us, that magnetic pull we couldn't resist when we were kids. It's clear from the way his gaze travels over me that he feels it, too. I always wondered if he left me because I wasn't pretty or because I wasn't good in bed. I mean, it was my first time. What did he expect?

My one big regret has been that I didn't get another chance, that I never got to show him I could please him in bed. A small, hurt part of me never got past that. Now, I kind of want to fuck him just to show him what he's missed out on. I've certainly never had any complaints. I want him to try to come back for more so I can be the one to leave and he can wonder what the hell went wrong.

You know what? To hell with it. One time. One night of out of this world fucking and I'll never speak to him again. It'll be like closure to help me put that part of my life behind me.

His eyes widen when I shove him back onto the sand and straddle him, grabbing his lips with mine. There's no hesitation on his part, though, and he wastes no time slipping his tongue into my mouth. His hands run down my back to grip my ass as I devour him. God, he tastes good.

"Your room," I mumble against his lips.

"Good idea," he gasps, lifting me off of him and getting to his feet. His hand wraps around mine and we practically sprint back up the trail to the house. I feel like a kid sneaking in after curfew and I can't help but giggle as we hurry through the decadent halls. He's a man on a mission.

Of course, his room is right across from mine. Maybe this isn't a good idea. It's going to be hard to avoid him the rest of the week, not that I expect him to pursue me. If there's one thing I've learned, it's not to expect a morning after with Davis. Or a kiss goodbye.

His hands sliding up my thighs kill any second thoughts. I need to get laid. God knows Casey couldn't get me off, and I can't remember the last time I had sex that was even decent, much less as good as I know this will be. I don't have to let any feelings get involved—love or hate. He's not the ex-love of my life, just a guy I'm going to have a rare one night stand with. I pull my dress off while he shoves his jeans and underwear down at the same time.

His muscles aren't the only things that have grown. He's going to tear me apart. He pauses to grab a condom from his wallet and slips it on.

The chemistry between us hasn't dissipated over the years, and we go after each other ravenously. I fist his hair, kissing him long and hard while he yanks my panties off. A yelp jumps from my lips when he bites my nipple, then sucks away the sting. My back collides with the wall, and he hesitates for a second. "You'd better be sure you want this, darlin'. Once I take you, you're mine."

I know drunk sex talk when I hear it. "Are you going to fuck me or keep blabbing?" I demand, wrapping my hand around his cock.

"Don't say I didn't warn you." With a chuckle, he dips a finger inside me. "Fuck, Hen, you're soaked." His hands slide under my ass, lifting me, and I wrap my legs around his waist as he drives himself deep inside me.

The line between pain and pleasure blurs while I struggle to take him, and I bite down on his shoulder, eliciting a growl and another hard thrust. Christ, he wasn't even all the way in. Pain fades and mind-numbing pleasure takes its place as he rocks in and out, his lips exploring my neck while he holds me against the wall like I weigh nothing.

Pressure builds fast. My whole body tightens to the breaking point, and I try to hold off. Even drunk and out of my mind with lust, I don't want to give him the satisfaction of knowing he got me off so quickly. His deep voice is raspy in my ear. "You can't fight me, girl. Give it to me."

His words set me off, and I lose all control, a garbled version of his name falling from my lips. Three hard thrusts later—it's like he's trying to nail me to the wall—he stills and a long groan rumbles his chest. He rests his forehead against mine while we catch our breath, and my lips are met with a soft, sweet kiss that surprises me.

It's not the sort of affection you show a one night stand, and I get a quick flash of the sweet boy he used to be. Images of him walking home from school between me and my brother, eating at our kitchen table, giggling over cartoons, and running through the yard during the warm evenings. We had six years of innocent fun before we started messing around. It was stupid, but what the hell did I know at sixteen?

I need to get out of here. I need to think of this as a random one-time thing with a stranger, because that's what we've become. Strangers. When he goes to the bathroom to dispose of the condom, I grab my dress and jerk it on. With my balled-up panties and shoes in one hand, and my phone in the other, I dart across the hall to my room without being seen. Classy.

Kasha and Lydia aren't back yet, and I haven't had any texts or messages from them, so they must be having a good time. Wincing at the delicious soreness between my legs, I take a hot shower and crawl into bed. Just when I'm dozing off, the room is filled with giggles and cursing as Lydia and Kasha stumble in.

"Shut up," Kasha says, rubbing her foot. "Table jumped right in front of me."

"Henley," Lydia says in an extremely loud whisper. "You awake?"

I can't help but laugh. The people in the room next door could probably hear her. "Nope."

"Why'd you leave?"

"Too drunk," I lie. "Just wanted to pass out." I'm sure I'll tell them at some point, but tonight when we're wasted isn't the best time.

"Ugh, me, too," Kasha replies, falling into her bed. "None of these debutants better wake us up early."

It's nearly noon when we drag our asses out of bed and down to the beach. Avoid Davis. Lie in the sun. Those are my two goals for today. So far, I'm two for two. Kasha, Lydia, and I are stretched out on a large blanket on the beach, soaking in the gorgeous day. There are plenty of offered activities, but after our drunken night, all any of us wants to do is guzzle water and juice and lie around.

"You should've seen Mrs. Harper when she came out and saw everyone dancing," Lydia says.

"I think it was the twerking that sent her over the top," Kasha replies, rolling onto her belly.

"I wasn't the only one doing it!" Lydia cries, making me laugh. I guess I missed out on quite the party.

It was worth it. Even having to avoid Davis the rest of the week is worth the orgasm I had last night. It was hands down, the best sex I've ever had. The way he took me, shameless and brazen, made me feel like he was as desperate for me and as turned on by my body as I was his. If it was anyone else, I'd be going back for seconds, but I know better. I barely managed to keep my feelings out of it last night. I can't look at him as a stranger after growing up with him, loving him.

"Kasha has a sexy stalker," Lydia remarks, sipping her water.

"What stalker?" I ask, sitting up.

"I don't have a stalker," Kasha sighs.

"Tall, dark, and handsy? Followed you around the dance floor all night, humping and grinding like an oversexed dolphin? Ring a bell?"

"Dolphin?" Kasha snorts.

"Dolphins are highly sexual," Lydia informs us. "And they're sexually aggressive."

Oh my god, that sounds familiar. Images of Davis nailing me to the wall invade my mind until Kasha starts making dolphin noises. Now I can only picture Davis opening his mouth in ecstasy and "eh eh eh eh" coming out.

Fighting back laughter, I turn to Kasha. "Spill it, chick. Who is he?"

"Just some dickwad I ran into… in my towel." She mumbles the last part.

"No wonder he was panting after you, you tease," Lydia says.

"It was an accident. We're sharing the bathroom with him. I went to the wrong room after my shower. It was no big deal."

"That would only happen to you," I laugh, and she swipes at the sand, making it land on my leg where it sticks to the sunscreen.

"You're in a better mood today," I tell Lydia. She's actually smiling and relaxed.

"I've decided you're right. I'm not going to think about why we're here. As far as I'm concerned, I'm just here on vacation."

"Maybe we can find you a dolphin," Kasha says.

"We should go to that club down the street tonight!" Lydia says, excited.

Kasha glances at me and shrugs. If it keeps her mind off of Anderson, another night of drinking it is.

Pulsing music and sweaty, gyrating bodies surround us as we make our way to a table with our drinks. The last thing I want to think about is anything pulsing. Or sweaty.

"Now will you tell us why you've been so quiet and moody today?" Lydia asks.

I don't want to. I want to pretend it never happened. Somehow, I don't think Davis will exactly shout it from the rooftops, either. He never thought I was good enough for him when we were young, and I doubt that's changed.

"Come on, it can't be that bad," Kasha encourages.

"I slept with Davis." The words tumble out, and I rest my forehead on my palm.

"With who?" Lydia asks, straining to hear over the music.

"Davis! I slept with Davis Lane!" If you can consider being fucked against a wall "sleeping with."

When I look up, I'm greeted by two horrified expressions. Seriously, it isn't that bad. It's not like they've never screwed someone they shouldn't.

"No need to shout about it, love. There's plenty more where that came from." NO. I didn't hear that. I especially did not hear that in Davis's deep voice. And that is not his laugh coming from behind me. Lydia covers her mouth, muffling a laugh, and Kasha shakes her head, trying not to smile.

Alcohol. I need copious amounts of alcohol. Without a word to anyone, I leap to my feet and make a beeline for the bar. I rarely drink and now I'm getting trashed two nights in a row. This man is going to make me an alcoholic. Margaritas just aren't going to cut it. The bartender nods when I order two shots of tequila and places them in front of me. They last about three seconds. I can sense Davis behind me, his scent unmistakable.

His hands land on my hips as he puts his lips against my ear. "What? You can brag about fucking me, but you won't talk to me?"

My face heats and it pisses me off. Turning, I plant my hands on his chest and shove. Yeah, that didn't work. He's solid muscle. It's like trying to shove a boulder. "I wasn't bragging, you narcissistic ass! I was confessing."

His brows furrow. "Confessing?"

"Yes, so they could tell me it was okay to screw up and sleep with a self-centered dick. I wasn't bragging and I won't be telling anyone else. Now, I'm trying to scrounge some kind of dignity, so if you don't mind."

He grabs me as I try to shove past him. "I fucking mind," he growls a second before his lips land on mine. I'd like to be able to say I pushed him away, or stomped his foot, maybe bit him. All of that would be preferable to my real response. I shoved my tongue in his mouth and kissed him like he was hiding winning lottery numbers in his throat.

His hands grip my ass, nearly lifting me off my feet, and I don't even care that people are watching. Until they start hooting. After a random shout of "fuck her, buddy!" I get control of myself and step away. An insufferable grin tilts his lips, and I'm not sure whether I want to strip him or kick him in the junk. I know I can't let this happen again.

"I'm not sleeping with you again."

"Don't remember us sleeping together. I recall a lot of cries of 'yes!' and 'don't stop!' Don't think I could sleep through that."

"Ugh!" I stomp my foot in frustration which makes his smile widen. "Just find another victim tonight." I head back to the table where Kasha and Lydia are trying to act like they weren't watching.

"Uh… you want to explain?" Lydia asks.

"It was a giant mistake."

"Sleeping with him or kissing him just now?" Kasha asks, sliding me a drink.

"He kissed me."

Lydia snorts. "The whole bar watched you try to climb inside his mouth. Try again."

"I-I don't know why I did that. He drives me crazy."

"Maybe because he's hot as hell. Look around, Henley, the women in here can't take their eyes off of him."

Kasha grins and tilts her glass toward the bar where Davis sits. "But he's too busy eye-fucking you to notice. I don't get it. What's the problem?"

Sighing, I shake my head. "He's been my brother's best friend since we were kids."

"And?" Lydia presses.

"And we screwed around for two years… and he might've been my first," I mumble quickly, draining my drink.

"Whoa, back it up. He's the one who left you right after?" Kasha asks, now glaring in his direction.

"He didn't leave me. We weren't really together. I was his friend's dorky little sister who was willing to take the scraps he threw me, while he made it clear he'd deny it if I ever told anyone. The last time I saw him was just before I left for college. Like I said, we were kids. It's long over. I'm not going to be his dirty little secret again."

"Didn't look like he was keeping anything secret," Kasha scoffs.

"I just want to avoid him. Can we talk about something else?" I look up at Kasha. "Tell us about your stalker."

"Nope. New subject."

Lydia's eyes widen before a sad expression steals over her face as Anderson appears, leading his bride-to-be to a table. "I didn't think they'd last," she murmurs. "He dumps me for her, and a year later they're getting married."

Kasha reaches over and squeezes her hand. "Once a cheating scum, always a cheating scum. She'll find out the hard way."

"Uh… Kasha? Your stalker's here," Lydia says, pointing toward the doorway.

At least I'm not the only one with guy issues. This should be interesting.

CHAPTER FOUR

Kasha

Instead of being cool and waiting a few minutes to turn around, I jerk around so fast that I fall out of my chair. Really. No joke. Who the hell falls while sitting down? This stupid girl.

My side hits the floor, and the music plays as laughter rings out. Why me?

I can feel my skirt tickle the backs of my legs, letting me know it's not up and showing off my boy-cut "exit hole only" undies. The front says "one at a time." I really need to buy adult underwear.

I lift my head and my eyes land on a set of amused ones near the doorway as Mr. Mysterious stares me down. A pretty blonde girl from yesterday is on his arm, looking immaculate and annoyingly sexy. Her warm smile and sympathetic eyes hold no mockery for my current situation, since she's staring at me too. She doesn't even seem like a bitch, which sucks. It'd be easier to ignore the pang of jealousy if she was a bitch I could hate and talk shit about.

One song. Lydia acted like he followed me around all night, but it was one fucking song and one drunken dance where I humped his leg like a dachshund going after a stuffed bear. Spiking the punch didn't work out so well for me, since I kept drinking the damn punch.

It takes me a minute to realize I'm still sprawled on the floor, extending the humiliation for longer than necessary, and I jump to my feet, only to sway and have two large hands settle on my hips in the next second to steady me. I turn my head to see who is holding me, and smirk at what I see.

Tall, dark, and sexy. Just like I like them. And this one hasn't seen me in a towel, or had me hump his leg like a pro, and he doesn't have a blonde on his arm. He's seen me sprawled on the floor, but I can overlook that since he seems fascinated with my robo arm.

He smiles, and I ignore the fact he's missing one tooth. I can live with one missing tooth for a night. No biggie. I mean, he has plenty of other nice teeth, after all. And how can I be annoyed with one missing tooth when I'm missing half an arm? It sounds like a double standard.

I need to quit with the inner ramble thing.

"You look incredible," he says in a sweet tone, blushing.

Aw. He's a sweetheart.

Shit.

"Thank you," I say with an obligatory tone as I turn to face him fully.

Looking over my shoulder, I cast a glance at Mr. Mysterious, surprised to find him still staring. His eyes move from me to the hand on my hip, and he looks back down at his sexy date. They were together most of the night—dancing, laughing, talking. They didn't seem too passionate, but that might have been my fault—yes, we're back to the leg-humping situation.

"You want some fuck?" the guy holding onto me asks, and I choke on air while whipping my head back in his direction with wide eyes.

"What?" I squeak.

He grins again, and I decide he's cute without that front tooth.

"You want some luck?" he asks, holding up a napkin.

I settle down a little, feeling a bit flustered. "A napkin is lucky?" I ask him, confused.

He moves to start twisting the napkin, and after a boringly long amount of time, he finally holds up a U. I think I'm supposed to be impressed. My impressed face isn't emerging though.

"It's a whore's shoe."

Damn this music. "A what?" I yell.

"A horseshoe!" he yells back.

Yeah. No. Can't do this.

Smiling, I turn and walk away, and I move to the center of the dance floor where my friends are both biting back laughter. I flip them off with my robo hand and pass by, because my bladder demands relief. I really love my smart arm. It's nice to flip someone off with my left hand again. Yes, it's the small things that count.

The line is short, and I make my way in and out quickly. A few breaths are audible even over the music, and I look back to see a group of guys grinning openly at me. That's right. I might not be little miss perfect blonde, but I've still got a little game. My hips don't lie, after all.

I wink at them, and they waggle their eyebrows, but when one laughs and turns away, I frown. Deciding not to dwell on it, I move back toward the dance floor, getting a little annoyed with how everyone seems to be staring at me.

They can't seriously be gawking at me because of my arm? Surely they've seen an amputee before…

Ah. That's right. I'm the chick who fell in the floor. Actually forgot about that since my head was preoccupied with thinking about Mr. Mysterious and Mr. Boring.

Lydia and Henley are dancing, and Davis is boring holes through Henley like he's seconds away from giving chase. Henley is doing the thing where she's pretending not to stare, but she's discreetly glancing at him from the corner of her eye. Lydia is hands-up-in-the-air dancing like a… I don't know how to describe something that embarrassing.

People are giggling and snickering in our direction because of poor Lydia's hideous dancing. I try to dance a little sexier, hoping to make them stop pointing and laughing. Apparently I'm not sexy enough, because the laughter and attention only seems to grow.

Suddenly there's a warm body pressing against the back of mine, and I jerk my head around to see the smirking face of Mr. Mysterious.

"You really are a stalker," I grumble, looking around at how all eyes are on us. What the hell? Why is he laughing now?

"I think it was you who attacked me on the dance floor last night," he tells me, smiling and pressing closer against my back.

His hands stay at his sides, and he makes no attempt to actually touch me with anything but his front.

"I didn't attack you," I hiss. "I fell on top of your leg and got stuck. All that movement was me trying to free myself."

He laughs harder, and I actually smile. His smile transforms his face, and he looks a little less arrogant when he's laughing.

My eyes move to the pretty blonde, but she doesn't seem to be paying us any attention as she orders drinks from the bar. When I look back, he's smiling down at me. I start to turn, but his hands shoot out and grabs my hips, pulling me back against him even more.

Heat washes over me, and I bite down on my lip when I feel a little more of him. But his eyes… He doesn't look like a man who is turned on—even though there's proof he is against my back. He looks like he's mocking me…

"You don't want to do that," he says, struggling not to laugh again.

"Why?" I ask him.

He leans over, and my breath gets caught in my throat when his lips brush my ear. "Because you have fucking terrible taste in underwear."

My eyebrows go up in confusion when he leans back and winks, and he steps away. Just as he does, I feel a breeze where no breeze should be, and my eyes widen as he walks away laughing.

My hand that has the ability to feel wraps around and grabs panties. Not skirt.

Oh no.

Panicking, I start struggling, and realize my skirt is tucked into my underwear! No! Everyone sees "exit hole only" right now, and they're dying laughing as I wildly flail and finally manage to get my skirt shoved down into place.

My cheeks burn, but Lydia and Henley are clueless. Henley is distracted, and Lydia is getting better at dancing—which means she's halfway drunk now.

Leaning over, I curse as I grab the phone I dropped in my haste to get my skirt lowered, and walk away while texting Henley's phone. They won't notice I'm gone for at least a little while, and I don't feel like explaining why I'm leaving. I just want to die in peace.

When I reach the doorway, I spot the asshole who loves watching me feel like a fool, and I cut my gaze away as he grins at me. Just as I get outside, I hear someone coming up behind me, and it's him. Of course it's him.

"Go stalk your date and leave me alone."

"You mean my sister?" he asks, smirking.

Sister? She's his sister?

Doesn't matter. I hate him for real now.

"Why is it you get off on being an ass?" I demand, stepping closer.

His eyes narrow in challenge as he shrugs. "You seriously don't remember me, do you?"

My eyebrows knit in confusion, and the humor vanishes from his face as he takes a step back. I have no idea what he's talking about.

"I have to admit, I didn't recognize you at first either," he says, letting his gaze dip down the length of my body. When his eyes come back up, he smirks. "You were way hotter in school."

That wasn't a dig at my arm either. That was a dig at me. The hell?

With that, he turns and walks away, but I'm too confused to really give it much thought. Nate, one of Anderson's friends, walks up just as Mr. Mysterious turns and gives me one last look before disappearing inside.

"You need a lift?" Nate asks me.

I turn to face him, still feeling confused and rattled. "Who was that guy?"

"Who? Roman? He works with Anderson, and I think they were friends in school too. Why?"

"Thanks, Nate. I'll take that ride, if you're still offering."

Oh shit. Roman Hunt. *The* Roman Hunt. And the chick? That's really his sister. His freaking sister is Sicily Hunt. She was gorgeous and popular, but she's so much prettier now. Roman was a major star in basketball until his senior year—my sophomore year.

What did I do as soon as I got back? Dug through the study until I happened upon a few yearbooks, then grabbed one I needed.

He looks so much different that it's insane. His hair was shoulder-length and lighter back then, and his body was stacked with bulky muscle.

Senior year was the year he was hurt, and he lost his place on the team, as well as a chance to play college ball. The injury didn't happen on the court, though. He picked a fight with a rival team—the whole team. He tried to take them on by himself after a cheap shot they took at one of our guys during the game.

I don't know the details firsthand, but he ended up with a messed up knee after that night. He also ended up at my stepbrother's apartment, crashing with him after his parents kicked him out. Basically, they punished him for not being able to be a big college star, due to his injury. And yeah, my stepbrother had his own apartment senior year—spoiled brat.

Anyway, I don't know what he's pissed at me about. Is his ego really so inflated that it insulted him I didn't recognize him right away? It's not like I went to Anderson's too often—unless I was too drunk or stoned to know what I was doing.

I only went to Mom's when she forced the issue, which was more often than I wanted.

I stayed with my father, and I hung out with my unpopular friends. I never even spoke to Roman. Hell, I never even met him, other than a few accidental brushes in the halls of school.

Sighing, I turn over in the bed and stare up at the ceiling, pushing the yearbook away. This week has been terrible, and it's only just the beginning.

Oh, and by the way… The peril of boy-cut undies is that you don't always realize when they're on backwards, like mine were tonight. Found that out when I got back. Instead of everyone seeing "exit hole only" on my ass, they all saw "one at a time" back there.

Lovely.

I'm totally buying some adult underwear that don't make me look like an anal whore. This is getting ridiculous, and I mean—

My inner ramble shuts off, and I'm bolting upright in the next second when the light comes on in the bathroom and creeps under the crack of the door on my side.

Lydia and Henley are still at the bar, and I'm here alone. Judging by the silence on the other side of the door when the water comes on, he's alone too. I have questions, and I want answers.

I move to the door quietly, and I hold my breath as I ease it open, happy to find that he didn't bother locking it.

Oh… my… uh-oh.

Naked, tan, incredibly firm flesh is in front of me as Roman tosses a towel to the rack, and I watch like a creeper as his ass muscles flex when he walks back toward the shower. He opens the shower door, steps in, and I watch his backside, wondering if he'd notice me creeping on him through the crack if he turned around.

Unfortunately, an unbidden, embarrassingly loud moan leaves me when he bends over, and his entire body goes rigid as he turns and straightens, snapping his head in my direction.

Fuck. My. Life.

My eyes drop, and I sway on my feet as the door opens wider. Shut the door! Walk away! Run and scream an apology! Just stop staring at his penis, you idiot!

My brain continues to scream at me, while I mindlessly gawk at the hard flesh sticking straight out in front of him. Holy big penis. That's a lot of man.

"Getting an eyeful?" he asks, sounding bored.

He's as hard as a rock, and I'm… still fucking staring.

My head finally snaps up, and I meet the cold stare in his eyes as he tilts his head, studying me as the water sprays against his back. Wet… He's wet and hard and… *I'm staring again!*

"Sorry!" I yell much louder than necessary, then cringe.

He doesn't react at all, and I continue to stand in the doorway when my feet cement themselves in place. Instead of acting uncomfortable, Roman grabs the shampoo and starts working it into his hair. I remain a true pervert and watch. Hey, when you commit to something, you stand by it.

"I-I don't remember you... I mean, I do remember you, but I don't remember what I would have done to piss you off... We... um... never spoke... Different circles and all," I ramble.

His hands pause in his hair, and he sticks his head under the spray of the water to rinse it off before his eyes come back to mine. He studies me hard for a minute, but he finally shakes his head as if he's disgusted.

"Figures," he mutters. "Do you remember anything about the Halloween night you came to party with Anderson and his friends?"

My eyebrows hit my hairline. "Now I know you have me confused with someone else. I never went to one of those parties. I spent most of my time hating him, or calling him names." *Or avoiding his noogies, his smelly feasts, and his constant snot rockets he tried to hit me with.*

"Yet you're here at his wedding?"

My eyes drop to that naked penis again. Having a conversation with a man built like an Adonis while he's naked... Yeah. Tell me you can do that without looking, and I'll shut up.

"My eyes are up here," he says, amused.

Again, my gaze jerks up to see a small smirk playing on his lips.

"I'm... um... here because my mother is relentless. Also, my friend Lydia... For some reason, she needed to be here and have her heart surgically cut from her chest."

He looks confused, but he doesn't comment on that last bit before slathering some sort of gel on his body. A dark, arousing scent washes over me, and I half wonder if he's practicing witchcraft on me or something.

"Senior year for me, you showed up at your brother's Halloween party drunk *and* stoned. Too drunk and stoned to stand."

"Stepbrother," I correct, then frown. "I really don't remember that."

"He spent the night trying to sober you up because he knew his dad and your mom would blame him and he'd lose the apartment. Then you decided to be a bitch to me for no reason."

Again, I frown. I have no idea what he's talking about. This is soooo not in my memory bank. Then again, high school was just my time to get high—pothead—and drunk.

He sighs as he cuts off the water, and without any modesty, he opens the glass shower doors and steps out, taking his time to wrap the towel around his waist and cover that massive, still-hard penis.

"Are you always hard?" I ask, then realize I said that aloud when he cocks an eyebrow at me. "I mean, um, how was I a bitch?"

"I believe I tried to hit on you, and you told me I was an arrogant prick, and it served me right to lose my scholarship, since I had no right fighting anyone. Violence isn't the answer and blah blah blah—insert more hippie speak."

I really, really, *really* don't remember that.

"I never would have said that," I tell him, even though those weren't exactly the best years of my life and I might have actually said that. He might have just been in the wrong place at the wrong time. But really, violence isn't the key, even if I am internally violent. It's not like I ever act on my thoughts.

He looks at me like I really am an idiot. "It's not exactly something a guy forgets."

"And now you hate me?" I surmise. "Because I was a stoned teenager who said something hurtful to you one time?"

His jaw tics like I've now said the wrong thing. "Like I said, it's not something a guy forgets."

"Well, I apologize for the scholarship thing. That was uncalled for. But you have to admit you were an arrogant prick. You thought you owned the school and looked down your nose at everyone until your injury."

Wrong thing to say, I decide when he stalks toward me like a rabid wolf going for my throat. I flinch and tense, even stumble back, but he grabs my hips and lifts me, tossing me onto the sink counter.

When he steps in between my legs, I consider angry sex. I mean, I consider slapping him with my super robo hand. Not angry sex.

His eyes drill into mine, and his jaw clenches as he glares at me. So… I finally react by grabbing his shoulder and crushing my lips to his, surprising him enough that he parts his lips to exhale his shock, and I slip my tongue into the opening.

It's like kissing a statue at first, but then those fisted hands beside my legs open and grab my hips, jerking me against his body as he kisses me back. It's all harsh, and mean, and brutal…

It's the best kiss ever.

I moan against his tongue, and my skirt hikes up higher on my waist. Just as it's getting good, he tears his lips away from mine, and he glares at me like that was all my fault while jerking back. Shaking his head, he stalks out of the bathroom and slams the door.

Cranky much?

"Sounds like you need to get over some teenage bullshit, Roman," I call out sweetly, but there's no response.

Maybe I used to party too much, because I have zero memory of that night. I really think I should remember a guy like Roman hitting on me…

"I'm over it," he finally says back, sounding more amused than angry now as he pokes his head back through the door and smirks at me. Ahhh, so this is whiplash. Now I get why people gripe about it so much. "I just think I need to make you work for it."

He winks and shuts the door again, and I stare at it in disbelief. Is this a game? Is he for real? Am I actually feeling bubbles of excitement and smiling like an idiot?

I really hope Lydia and Henley are having a better night than I am at this moment.

CHAPTER FIVE

Henley

This night sucks. I'm trying to have fun, dancing with Lydia and a few random guys, but my heart's not in it. I can feel his gaze on me, and a surreptitious glance shows me I'm right. His eyes brush over me, removing every stitch of clothing in the process—at least that's how it feels.

Ignore. Ignore. Ignore.

Kasha has already called it a night, but Lydia is going strong, having a great time as one man after another claims a dance with her. It hasn't escaped Anderson's attention, and I'm sure she's playing it up, trying to keep that frown on his face.

Men. Even when they don't want us, even when they throw us away, they don't want anyone else to take their place.

I'm more than ready to go, but I don't want to leave Lydia, or drag her out of here when she's getting a bit of revenge. My last drink was over an hour ago and I'm starting to sober up. After Davis ambushed me, I decided getting smashed tonight is not a good idea. I don't want to be vulnerable when he's anywhere near me since I seem to be prone to attacking him with my vagina when drunk Henley is in charge.

"I'm going out for some air," I yell to Lydia, who nods and smiles before returning to grinding on the man in front of her.

There's a small park across the street from the club, and the gazebo in the center looks like a good place to escape for a while. I kick off my shoes and carry them, enjoying the sensation of the cool, damp grass on my sore feet. Two nights of dancing in a row. What was I thinking? The sound of running water piques my curiosity and I pass the gazebo in search of the source.

A narrow path, dimly lit by moonlight, winds into a thin line of trees. Maybe it's not the smartest move, but I push any reservation aside and follow the sound of water to a small gurgling creek. It's beautiful here, a small clearing hidden from the street by trees and brush. With a sigh, I sit on the bank, dangling my feet into the cool water.

Approaching footsteps make me leap to my feet. What the hell was I thinking coming back here alone? It's probably a rapist, or a serial killer. I grab one of my shoes, prepared to use the heel as a weapon, when a deep chuckle fills the air. It's Davis. Damn it. Where's a serial killing rapist when you need one?

"What were you planning to do with that?" he asks, grinning at me.

"Smash a serial killer in the face."

"Sorry to disappoint you."

"I should go check on Lydia," I mumble, stepping around him.

His hand grips my arm. "Whoa, stop running from me."

"I'm not running!"

"You snuck out last night while I was in the bathroom."

"We were done," I reply with a shrug. It's not like I was going to hang out until he started making excuses to get rid of me. I saved us the awkward after sex dance, so why is he complaining?

"We are nowhere near done, darlin'," he growls.

Yep. The man actually growled. Before I can say another word, I'm scooped up and my legs wrap around his waist. Traitor legs. They weren't supposed to do that. My back lands against a tree, the bark scraping my skin, but it doesn't even register. Nothing does but his mouth on mine, his hands on my body.

"I want you under me this time," he says, turning and placing me on the soft grass. He has my panties off in record time. I'm going to let him fuck me here, where anyone could catch us. I must've lost my mind. That's what he does to me, the effect he's always had on me, and I don't know whether to love or hate it.

I've never seen a man get into a condom so fast. My hands grip his ass when he slams inside me, my fingers digging into his flesh, driving him faster, harder. "We're not done, Henley," he says. "Do you understand?"

Apparently, the inarticulate noise I make isn't what he wants to hear.

"Understand?" he insists, pausing until I moan out a "yes." I'd tell him anything as long as he doesn't stop. There's no slow buildup this time. I'm struck by a bone-jarring orgasm that races through my body for what seems like minutes. If anyone is nearby, they're getting an earful, because I couldn't be quiet if my life depended on it.

Davis groans long and loud seconds later. His whole body tenses, then relaxes on top of me and we lie there for a few moments, panting into the cool air. The night suddenly seems so still and quiet. "God, I love it when you scream for me," he murmurs.

Regret seeps in. I can't believe I did this again. No matter how determined I am to avoid him, all he has to do is get me alone and I go full-on slut. Cue the little devil on my shoulder telling me I could just use him for the week. Just have my fun and more great orgasms until the wedding week is over, then forget it ever happened. There's no little angel to argue restraint or chastity; I killed that little bitch long ago. There's only the ghost of pain past to remind me how he tore my young heart out and stomped on it.

"Let me up," I order, and he rolls off of me. Sitting on the ground, he watches me try to straighten my wrinkled dress and mussed hair. A smug smile rests on his face while he enjoys my attempt to wipe away the evidence that I've been rutting in the grass like a dog. There's no way it isn't obvious, since I can feel the damp dress against my ass. I need to get Lydia and get out of here.

Of course, she won't answer her phone. It's probably tucked in her purse, and even if it isn't, the music is way too loud to hear it. Davis approaches me, still wearing that smile I'd like to slap off of him. "Are you going to run off again? I'd like to spend some time with you, Hen. With clothes on."

"Uh-huh, save the smooth bullshit for a woman who doesn't know you. I have to check on Lydia."

"You can't run forever," he calls as I rush back down the trail and across the street to the club.

It's late and the crowd has thinned a bit. It isn't hard to spot Lydia sipping a drink at the table. She giggles when I approach. "Looks like you're having more fun than I am."

"That obvious?"

"The leaf stuck in your hair kind of gives it away. And you have mud on the back of your leg." Damn it. Damn Davis. She reaches up and plucks the leaf from my hair. "Let's get out of here."

We're on our way out the door when Anderson and his bride step into our path. Lydia steels herself, lifting her chin and pasting on a strained smile.

Anderson gives a shit-eating grin. "Hi, Lydia, Henley. I'm sorry I haven't had a chance to introduce you to my fiancée. Jane, this is Lydia and her friend, Henley. Lydia is an old friend of the family."

Lydia's jaw tightens. An old friend of the family, like she's some dusty old aunt they invited out of pity, and not the ex he cheated on. It occurs to me that Jane may not know Anderson was seeing Lydia when they first got together. Maybe she isn't to blame for falling for his shit any more than Lydia was. My attempt to sympathize with her is short lived.

Her smile is plastic as she extends her hand to shake each of ours. "It's nice to meet you. I'm so glad you could come. Anderson told me he wanted some diversity at our wedding. I'm happy to see he succeeded."

Diversity? The four of us are the same race, so I have no idea what she's talking about. "Diversity?"

"Yes, he didn't want the only invitations to go to the upper class, you know." If her nose goes any further into the air, she'll tip over backwards.

Bitch. I know her type. Born with a silver spoon up her ass. Probably never had to work a day in her life. Perfect makeup and nails, an expensive dress wrapped around her bulimic body. I had to deal with these catty rich bitches in school, and I'm sure not taking any shit from one now.

I fall into a thick Southern accent. "Well, it's so kind of you to invite the riffraff." I bend my leg up behind me so I can swipe a handful of mud from my calf. "Just because we're peasants doesn't mean we don't enjoy a good shindig, you know." Before she can react, I throw my arms around her in a hug and smear mud up the back of her white dress.

Anderson sees it, but she doesn't realize what I've done. "If you'll excuse us, we've got to find an outhouse. Afraid I ate too much, so I need to give birth to some food babies."

I grab Lydia's hand and walk away, leaving Anderson standing there with his jaw agape. I know what he was trying to do, that they were both trying to rub it in Lydia's face. Anderson wants her to think he's done better, found someone above her, like she's the one who dumped him. I'm so pissed I could go back and beat both their asses.

"Thank you," Lydia sighs, as we wait out front for a taxi. "I just couldn't think of what to say. She's so—"

"Vapid?"

"Beautiful," she says, wiping her eye.

Ever want to shake the shit out of one of your friends to make them see reason? Yeah, I'm tempted. Instead I grab her arms and look her in the eye. "No, you're beautiful, and you don't need a ton of makeup or the thousand dollar dresses she hides behind. You can put sugar on shit, but that don't make it a brownie. You're better than her in too many ways to count."

Lydia dissolves into tears and wraps her arms around me. "Thank you. I hate him. He always gets what he wants."

Our taxi pulls up and we settle into the back seat. "This time I think he'll get what he deserves." An idea occurs to me and I grin at Lydia. "But maybe we can help that along. Let's talk to Kasha. I'm sure she'll be happy to cause some trouble. That girl is the queen of pranks and sabotage."

Ugh! Why does he have to be here? It was setting up to be such a beautiful day. It's bright and sunny with a gentle breeze. Warm water laps at my feet as I wade in. I'm just going to ignore him. After all, the beach is filled with wedding guests, along with a few others from the nearby hotels. If I don't draw attention to myself, he probably won't even notice me.

I sit down in the sand, letting the waves wash up to my waist. Eyes closed, head tilted back, I'm soaking in the rays and enjoying the peace. Until a shadow falls over me. I know who it is before I even open my eyes. "Don't you have other women to harass?" I groan.

"No one as fun as you." His slanted smile makes my stomach knot. "A group of guests are headed to the zip lines. Want to go?" He gestures down the beach where two lines descend into the water.

"No thanks."

"Scared?"

"Oh, don't double dare me, then I'll have to do it."

Kasha is calling my name and when I look back, she points to the zip line tower, jumping up and down and waving for me to come. Damn it. With a sigh, I get to my feet. "Fine, let's go." It's not that I have any problem getting on a zip line, I just don't want to spend time with Davis if I don't have to. I don't trust myself.

It's bad enough Kasha's mother has two days of events planned she's dubbed the Wedding Olympics. The first activity starts this evening and I doubt I'll be able to avoid him.

Kasha, Lydia, and I get in line with everyone else and make our way up a ton of steps to the top of the tower. Davis is right behind us the whole way. Riders go two at a time, one on each line. Kasha and Lydia go together, which of course leaves me with Davis.

"Race you," he says with a grin as we're strapped into the harnesses.

I can't resist. "Prepare to get your ass handed to you by a girl."

The two women who fasten us in laugh and both give Davis a "come get it" smile. "Count of three," one of women says, and we're pushed off at the same time.

I don't move as fast as I thought, and it's not scary at all. It gives me time to soak in the gorgeous view. The wide expanse of ocean with its different shades of blue, the shoreline winding back and forth, dotted with swimmers and sunbathers. The sun on my face coupled with the wind in my hair feels amazing, and I forget we're racing until Davis hoots as he hits the water.

The attendant helps him out of the harness just as I crash into the water a few feet away. Another attendant rushes to undo my harness while Davis treads water, grinning at me. A sudden intense stinging shoots across my upper thighs and the lower curve of my ass cheeks. Without thinking, I shove my hand down my boy short swimsuit bottoms and my hand lights up in pain as well.

Noticing the grimace on my face, and probably the way I'm thrashing around like I'm being electrocuted, Davis swims to me. "What's wrong?"

Shit. He's the last person I want to know, but the pain just keeps getting worse. "I don't know. It really hurts. I think something is in my suit." When I bring my hand above the surface of the water, a thin layer of slime rests across my palm.

Davis curses and shoves my hand underwater, rubbing his palm across mine. The sting lessens, but it isn't my biggest problem. My ass is on fire. "Take your bottoms off," Davis orders, and I look at him in horror. "It's a jellyfish, Henley. It's going to get worse. We have to take care of it."

Kasha must notice something is wrong since she starts to wade back out. "Towel!" Davis shouts to her. "Bring a towel!" He grabs my hand as I go to touch my ass again. "Don't, you'll just get more stingers in your hand. He tows me over to where we can touch the ocean bottom with our feet, away from the attendants and zip line riders, and yanks my bottoms down. "Step out of them."

Not seeing any other choice, I obey. It can't get any worse than this. He stands behind me and rubs his hands over my thighs and ass, washing them with the seawater. Okay, it can get worse. I just want to dunk underwater and stay there.

"Jellyfish leave stinging cells behind. We have to get them off of you. I'm sorry, sweetheart. I know it hurts."

Kasha wades out with a towel and Davis submerges it, wrapping it around my waist. "I can walk!" I insist when he scoops me into his arms. It probably would've been more convincing if tears weren't starting to run down my face.

"I've got you." He turns to Kasha. "She needs some vinegar and baking soda. Can you see if the pharmacy has some?"

"Of course!"

"And hydrocortisone cream!" he calls when Kasha runs off to gather supplies.

Davis carries me toward the house. I don't have the strength to argue. The sting is horrible and unrelenting. It strikes me how lucky I was it didn't get further in my suit. Jellyfish sting on the vagina? At the moment, I can't imagine anything worse.

Of course, that was before Davis laid me on his bed face down and started dragging the edge of his driver's license across my bare ass cheeks. "What are you doing?" I twist out of his grasp.

"It got you pretty bad, over a large area. This helps remove the stinging cells. When Kasha gets here, we'll wash it with vinegar and baking soda. It'll deactivate the remaining stingers we can't get out. It's going to burn and itch for a day or two though."

Yeah, this isn't humiliating at all.

Davis throws a sheet across my ass when there's a knock on the door. I'm relieved it's only Kasha. This isn't exactly how I like to be seen. I'm already going to be the laughingstock of the wedding, the girl who got stung in the ass by a jellyfish.

Kasha sits beside me on the bed while Davis removes the sheet and bathes my behind in vinegar. "Does it hurt bad?" she asks.

"It's getting better." I peek up at her and roll my eyes at the sight of her trying to repress a laugh. "Go ahead, bitch. Get it out of your system. I'm going to be the laughingstock of the wedding anyway. Your face plant in the mud has nothing on this."

Giggling, she shakes her head. "Come on, Henley, you know I'll do something to top it before the week is over." Davis finishes covering my ass and thighs in a paste of vinegar and baking soda and heads to the bathroom.

"My sort-of ex—who is still way too damn good looking—just scraped my ass and covered it in goop. I think I win this round of most embarrassing wedding moments."

"Stay still and leave it on there for a few minutes," Davis says, returning with a tube of cream. He tosses it on the bed and proceeds to wash my stinging hand with vinegar, then coats it in hydrocortisone cream. It's then I notice his hands are red and swollen.

"Your hands," I point out.

"I'm taking care of them." He coats them with the paste. I was so mortified, I didn't even think about what he did when he removed my suit and scrubbed at my body. He used his bare hands, knowing he'd get stung as well.

"Will you please grab me some clean clothes? My black running shorts are on top of my suitcase," I ask Kasha. They're my loosest piece of clothing. Something tells me panties aren't happening either.

"Sure." She glances from me to Davis and smiles before leaving.

Davis gently lays a sheet across my body and settles into a chair next to the bed. "Thank you," I murmur.

"You're welcome."

I rest my head on the pillow and gaze at him. "I mean it. Your hands are all stung because you helped me."

"It was worth it. You still have a great ass. A little bigger now it's swollen, but…" He shrugs, a smirk on his face.

"And you're still a pig. If you tell any of your bachelor party buddies about this, I'll tell everyone about the time our dog bit you in the nuts and you cried until your mom picked you up."

"I was eight!"

"Not the way I tell it."

Laughing, he sweeps a lock of hair out of my eyes. "I've missed you."

"Couldn't tell from my end," I grumble.

"I know. I was twenty years old, Hen. I shouldn't have left you, but I had to go. I knew you were too young. Your parents and brother would've killed me."

I don't want to talk about this anymore. I know why he left. There's no nice way to say "I realized I could do better than a skinny nerd," so he's coming up with excuses. I don't have a right to be pissed just because he couldn't love me back, right? Although, running the day after taking my virginity was a dick move.

"Let's just let bygones be bygones. A few more days and we probably won't see each other for another eight years." He smiles as if he knows better, but his reply is cut short as Kasha returns with my clothes.

After I shower off all the paste and coat my ass with the hydrocortisone cream, I feel better. It's more annoying than painful now. I feel bad watching Davis do the same to his hands. They're really swollen.

On an impulse, I hug him and plant a kiss on his cheek. "Thanks again." I glance at his hand. "And if you need help with anything, just call me."

A mischievous grin cracks his face. "Well, since you offered, I like to jerk off every night, and since I can't…"

Kasha laughs aloud, and I shake my head. "Still a pig."

CHAPTER SIX

Kasha

After changing out of my bikini, I pull on a shirt and my most awesome panties... that no one will be seeing, damn it.

They say "Danger Zone" right across the ass, and I give myself a little pep talk in the mirror. My favorite part about my mother's obnoxious lifestyle? The Wedding Olympics.

That's right. I actually love this part.

I pull on a pair of "Duck You" socks and crank up my music as Henley lies on the bed—on her stomach, since her ass isn't fully back in commission just yet. Good thing she's not into anal.

She rolls her eyes when I slide across the floor and start singing "Danger Zone" in nothing but my panties and T-shirt. And socks, of course.

I even turn and point to my ass for good measure, which earns me a small snort from Henley.

Lydia giggles as she walks in, watching me sing the lyrics word for word, getting pumped up.

WORTH IT

I continue to sing, still dancing like a lunatic. Maybe there's even a little air guitar going on.

Someone bangs on our door, and I squeal while diving beside the bed before the door opens.

"Game on in ten!" Anderson calls into the room.

"You son of a bitch! You don't come into a girl's room without being invited!" I yell.

"Too late to gripe about it now."

Asshole.

Game on is right.

"I really shouldn't have come," Lydia says quietly when he leaves, shutting the door behind him.

Sadly, I agree, but I don't point that out right now. Best friends don't give the *I told you so* speech.

"It'll be fine," I tell her, still unsure how much damage I want to do to his wedding. I know I said we'd sabotage it, but… Shit. I've gone and grown a conscience like an adult these days.

She clears her throat while standing up. "I think I'm going to sit out the Olympics. Maybe read a book or something."

My mouth falls open—because the Olympics are the best part of the wedding—but I close it immediately. Obviously she needs a second. I wouldn't be here if I was her, but Lydia and I are two different people. She needs this. Even though I'm not sure why.

Never mind. I'd go to the wedding of the guy who crushed me just to be a part of the Wedding Olympics. Totally worth it. Especially the obstacle course—which is first.

After pulling on a pair of athletic shorts and tucking some laxatives into my pocket, I toss on my sneakers and leave as Henley waddles behind me. When we get outside, Henley winces.

"Need a pillow or something to sit on?"

She grimaces, but nods.

"I'll get it. Stay put."

I jog back in, but before I track down a pillow, I hear hushed voices and giggling. Because I'm nosy, I lean in and listen as my mother is speaking.

"I can't say that I understand it," my mother states, sighing heavily, "but at least she brought my daughter with her. Lydia has always been a mouse, but she's usually more sensible than this. Surely, she has to see how incredibly uncomfortable this is making people."

Anger prickles my spine at hearing that. Is she really going against Lydia right now? After everything?

"I'd never be caught dead at an ex's wedding," someone remarks, snorting derisively.

"I have more self-respect. I mean, it's pathetic."

Jane—my sister-in-law-to-be—adds to the bash-Lydia party. "I'm glad she's here, though. You have no idea how hard I had to work to get Anderson to realize he deserved better. She'd be wearing this ring if I hadn't stepped in. Imagine how miserable my Andy would be with her."

Heat sizzles up my neck, and I bite my tongue—literally. I might need a robo tongue if I don't release my grip.

Lydia came here under the pretense my family was still close with her. We grew up together, after all. My mother was like her mother—until the divorce. Then it was like she wasn't even my mother anymore. But Lydia was there for her when I refused to have anything to do with her; she constantly tried to broker peace between my mother and me. Lydia is the *only* reason I ever went to my mother's house at all after the divorce.

Lydia got me through the hell I went through with accepting the fact I lost my arm. She was the first person who looked at me without pity and told me to get my ass up and off the pity train. She's always been there. Yet, this is how she's repaid.

Fuck the wedding. Fuck my conscience. Fuck my mother. Fuck the bride. And fuck my stepbrother.

I'm about to turn fourteen again. And I won't do something as pointless as spiking the punch. In hindsight, that really was weak. Anderson has unleashed prank hell on me over the years. I can return the favor in the name of Lydia.

Right now, I have some games to win. Yeah… I might have entered all of them.

Just as I walk back outside, I realize I forgot the pillow. But, it looks like Henley already has one, and Davis is walking away.

Grinning, I head toward Anderson, who tosses me a red jersey.

"You're on my team, sis," he announces, acting like he isn't a twatwaffle dick weasel.

I toss it back just as Roman walks by in a blue jersey, smirking at me before cutting his eyes toward his sister and heading toward her. She's in a red jersey.

"Actually, I'm going with blue. Sorry, *bro*."

I grab a blue jersey from the pile as he glares at me, and pull it on before knotting it on my side to keep it from hanging past the top of my shorts. I tie it one-handed out of habit, and my robo arm twitches to remind me it works just fine.

Anderson is glaring because he knows I'm a badass on the obstacle course, hence the reason he wants me with him.

"Oh, we added a new obstacle," he says, a taunting ghost of a smile on his lips. "In honor of your memorable arrival to my wedding."

It's not even embarrassing anymore. When you're clumsy, you shake shit off quicker than the average person.

"I'm sure I can beat you with one hand tied behind my back… Oh wait! That's right! I've beaten you one-handed numerous times! Now that I have two hands, you're so fucked."

He rolls his eyes while looking away, and I wiggle my robo fingers at his horrified friends. They dart their eyes away like they can't believe I'm making jokes. I mean, how dare I have a sense of humor about a missing limb instead of mourning its loss years later.

There are five types of people around me.

Type One: People who pretend they don't notice my arm because it's not politically correct to address it.

Type Two: People who stare at my arm unabashedly. Sometimes staring is all they do. Sometimes they ask probing, personal, somewhat awkward questions.

I'll never forget the time some guy old enough to be my father asked me if I ever tried to masturbate with my prosthetic since it didn't have feeling. He seemed to think it would be like getting some foreplay from someone else. Sheesh.

Another guy asked me if I had to wear the prosthetic all the time. When I told him I usually took it off at home, he asked if he could lick my 'nub'—his word, not mine. This was on a date. Obviously there was not another date with that freaky fetish boy.

Anyway, back to what I was saying…

Type Three: People who really don't give a damn if I have an arm or not.

Type Four: People who accept the fact it's not there, but can't help but notice. Those people are usually curious, but not in an offensive or creepy way. Those are my favorite people.

Type Five: People who think missing limbs are contagious. Seriously. It's like they're going to catch a case of amputation if I accidentally graze them on my way by.

Anderson's sports bottle is on the ground, and I snatch it up without drawing attention while he talks with a group of his friends.

After unscrewing the cap, I squirt the liquid laxatives inside, replace the cap, and put it back where I found it. Then of course I act like I'm stretching when he turns around right as I'm bent over.

Yeah, I totally play it off. He's still clueless when we start moving.

As we walk around the side of the house to the massive backyard, I see what Anderson was talking about—my entrance involved mud, and so does the new obstacle course.

I… can't believe my mother allowed them to make gigantic mud holes back here. But sure enough, there are two trenches about five feet wide and a few inches deep. Muddy as hell.

Rope squares are above it, meaning they expect us to crawl through this damn thing. That's really going to piss Susie off when a slew of muddy people come traipsing through the house.

"Here are the rules!" Heath—my stepfather—has a voice that booms across the yard as he lifts his glass of champagne into the air. "Every man must pair with a woman from their team. The teams must be divided evenly with the genders. Any missed obstacle results in disqualification. All obstacles must be completed *with* your partner before you can start a new one, or you'll be disqualified. Crossing the finish line without your partner results in disqualification."

He rattles on about the rules, and I look around to see one lone blue jersey not paired off. Trying not to smile, I sidle up next to Roman as Heath finishes all his rules, and Roman looks down at me with a cocked eyebrow.

"Alright! Starting in five!" Heath announces to finish up his speech.

"Looks like we're the only two not paired up," I tell Roman as he continues to stare down at me. He really is hella tall.

Damn that smirk he keeps giving me. It makes him sexier.

"Is that your idea of wooing? Because it really sucks," he states flatly.

Smiling sweetly, I step a little closer, invading his personal space as I crane my neck up to keep eye contact.

"The guy is supposed to woo the girl. Just sayin'."

He releases a mock sigh while shaking his head. "The guy once tried, but the girl called him an arrogant prick. She also said some pretty nasty things after that."

"The girl has already apologized for her very young, very inebriated self. The guy should really let it go, considering they're both adults now."

His lips twitch, and he takes a step back before stretching his arms above his head. My eyes drop when the hem of his shirt rides up just enough for me to get a peek of that V. Maybe my gaze lingers on the front of his loose shorts for much too long, because he clears his throat.

"My eyes are up here," he drawls, sounding so damn amused when my eyes snap back up. "You seem to have a problem remembering that."

He winks at me while moving around me, and I feel like an idiot as I follow him. Especially when my gaze drops to his ass. Even in those shorts he has a nice ass, and I know full well what his body looks like naked.

Which is incredibly distracting. And hot. Very, very hot.

Fanning myself, I take my place beside him on the blue side of the obstacle course starting line. There are two obstacle courses to separate the teams and prevent sabotage. Ironically enough.

My long, dark hair is tied up in a knot on my head, and my sports bra is strapping back my oversized ladies as I stretch some more. My tank top hangs loosely under the jersey, the orange peeking through the mesh blue.

"Think you can keep up with me?" Roman asks as my mother moves toward us.

She smiles when she sees me, but I cut my eyes away. She just stabbed Lydia in the back for the woman who not only stole Anderson from her, but also ran her mouth about Lydia—who was the one wronged.

Arrogant asses.

"Ignoring me?" Roman asks as I look up from the ground.

His smile falters when he sees my face, but I force a smile.

"Hunt, you'll be staring at my spandex-clad ass all day. Don't worry. I'll wait up for you when you get too far behind. But only because I don't want to be disqualified."

His throaty chuckle leaves me awash with tingles like some preteen moron, but I smile in spite of myself and look back toward the course. The first obstacle is the trampoline jump, and Heath is now explaining how to do it, along with every other obstacle.

You hit the trampoline, and bounce over the large plastic tubs of goo to hit the mat on the other side. If you hit the goo, you have to do it again until you don't hit the goo. Not too difficult to understand, but it is a much wider jump than usual.

"Kasha!" Mom says, smiling openly when I turn to see she's almost right beside me. "I've been missing you all over. Everyone keeps telling me I just missed you at every single turn. It's about time I found you."

I'm tempted to slap her, but I wasn't raised to slap my mother. My father would still be pissed to this day if I did it.

Damn conscience.

"Maybe you should go find Lydia, since she's the real reason I decided to come, and thank her," I state while glaring at her.

Her smile slips, and she clears her throat while looking over my shoulder at Roman. Just like that, her sugary sweet smile is back in place, and she's in control again.

"Roman, dear, I'm so happy you made it. I've barely gotten to speak to you this week. Anderson said you closed the Harbin deal you were discussing with us last week. You two make quite the team."

Ugh. So Roman hangs out with my family?

That obsessive attraction? Yeah, it's gone now. Well, for the most part. As long as I don't look at him. You're only as good as the people you surround yourself with, and Anderson is not choice company.

Neither is my superficial mother.

"Yeah, it was an easy one to close," Roman replies, and they get engulfed in their conversation about shit that doesn't appeal to me, so I tune it out.

Roman just lost a lot of sexy points because my mother seems to love him. Which means he's loaded. It also means he's part of this grand socialite world she's so obsessed with.

It's not like I wanted to date him, but I did have thoughts about what it would be like to play for the rest of the week. And because of that kiss last night, I haven't thought of much else. My fingers absently trace my lips, and maybe some throbbing starts in all the wrong places.

Even the memory of him standing between my legs hits a strong chord, making my body sing with a lot of really unwanted desires. And… I'm going a little crazy. I barely know the guy.

"You look lost in thought." Roman's whispered voice is suddenly really close to my ear, and I become painfully aware of the fact he's pressed against my back.

My hand falls from my lips and I swallow hard, but before anything else can be said, the loud whistle blares, and the race is on.

My eyes widen, and I feel like an ass for forgetting what the hell I'm supposed to be doing. I manage to race toward the trampoline after another girl clears it. My feet hit the surface hard, and a sick feeling hits when I sink just before I feel it launching me into the air at the perfect angle.

Someone screams, almost distracting me, but I land painfully on my side on the pad next to some guy, who rolls onto his feet and races with a girl to the next obstacle. An ungraceful grunt leaves my lips on impact, but I'm across. No one can land that thing gracefully. Most importantly, no goo for me!

I roll off the mat and turn in time to see Roman defy all laws of nature and land feet first, bending his knees just barely before straightening to his full height and winking at me.

I thought he was supposed to have a bum knee!

All he does is wink and smirk. I'm starting to think my younger self called it right about the arrogant prick thing. Rolling my eyes, I turn around and start toward the wall, when I hear a burst of laughter coming from the asswipe behind me.

"Something amusing?" I ask him, looking over my shoulder.

He covers his mouth as his body shakes with laughter and his eyes dance with humor, but he doesn't answer me. Resuming my original task, my eyes scan the wall we have to climb, and I tighten the harness that goes around both my shoulders to keep my arm in its socket. Time to give Dad's sport harness a good tryout.

Just as I get to the wall and grab the rope, I hear Roman laughing again.

A few whistles sound out around me, and I turn to see a couple of guys laughing and clapping. What the hell?

That's when I feel a little breeze… somewhere there should be no breeze. A-fucking-gain.

No. Not possible. There's no way people are seeing my freaking underwear three days in a row.

I drop the rope and reach behind me, feeling the proof against my good hand when I realize I've split the back of my short, athletic, spandex shorts right up the ass crack. And it's a wide split, because it's spandex, and that shit doesn't stay together if it isn't stitched together with a seam, damn it.

"Do those say… Anger Zone?" Roman asks between his guffaws. "All I can see is 'GER' and 'ZO.'"

Oh shit.

Really?

"They say Danger Zone, asshole." As if that makes him laugh any less. In fact, I swear he's laughing harder.

It's not like I can go change right now. There's a freaking race going on.

Grabbing the rope and ignoring the laughter, I start up the wall. When he starts humming *Danger Zone* below me, I roll my eyes. It was way cooler when I was singing it this morning.

"You're so immature," I call over my shoulder, still climbing and hearing the sound of my shorts tearing more with each inch I gain on the wall.

Just great.

"Says the girl who doesn't own a single pair of normal underwear."

I scowl at the vacant air above me while continuing to climb.

"I can't help it that I'm not a boring person," I quip, trying to play it off. By this point, people seeing my underwear is getting freaking old. I'm definitely buying some plain Jane undies now.

Roman laughs and starts actually singing the song, while I heave myself over the wall. "Wait on me, Goose!" he calls out, and I glare down at him while he mockingly grins up as he makes quick work of the wall.

As soon as he crosses the top and joins me on the platform, he grabs the pole in front of us and slides down like a fireman on duty. I wait until he clears it to do the same.

The second my feet hit the ground, I start running, flipping off some guy who joins in on singing that damn song with Roman. The next part is the hard part, since we have to crawl through the mud. At least that will hide my underwear, seeing as I'm about to be a mess.

As much as I hate to take the time to do it, I don't want to get my smart arm muddy, so I grab the plastic bag I had stashed in my sock and unwrap it, making quick work of it.

I notice Roman is silently observing me, but not in a creepy, I-want-to-lick-your-nub kind of way. Once I have it secured on my smart arm, I start belly crawling under the netting, and Roman joins me at my side, still grinning, but at least he's not singing anymore.

"Didn't expect you to dive right into the mud pit," he says as we make our way through the slop.

"Unlike some *boys* I know, I'm not afraid of getting dirty."

I smile sweetly while keeping my head low but away from the mud. Just as we reach the end, I reach over and grab his hair—no, not with my ball-crushing robo hand. He looks confused for a split second until I use my grip to slam his face into the mud.

I'm the one laughing when I scurry out before he can retaliate, and I dance from foot to foot, waiting on him to climb out. All I can see are two slits when he opens his eyes and narrows them on me at the same time.

"I can't move on to the next obstacle without you," I remind him, hurrying him.

He glares as he pulls himself out of the pit and grabs one of the hand towels that are off to the side to wipe his face. There are still remnants of mud, but for some reason, the whole dirty boy thing is sexy on him.

I must really need to get laid.

I grab a towel and clean off my left arm above the bag, then I pull the bag off as I jog with him toward the next obstacle. I drop the towel and bag onto a table.

Mud runs down my legs as I rush to the line of the three mile run's starting point, still waiting on him. He grabs two blue batons with our names on them, and he tosses me mine before we start jogging side by side.

"Was that really necessary?" he asks as I grin bigger.

"Yep," I say in a sugary sweet tone, batting my lashes at him as I peer in his direction.

His lips twitch, but he shakes his head and keeps running, staying with the pace I've set.

"That's no way to woo me," he states with a heavy sigh.

"Woo you?" I ask incredulously. "I'm not trying to woo you. If anyone should be wooing, it's you. You're the guy."

"That's very sexist of you," he points out, smirking while staring ahead.

"That's very arrogant of you."

He slants his eyes in my direction, and I stare at him, smiling like I'm winning something. Until I'm suddenly yelping and being slammed into… No, not slammed into. *I* just slammed into a damn pole.

I clutch my head that took the brunt of the impact, waiting on the riot of laughter that never comes.

"Shit!" Roman says, cupping my chin and tilting my head back. "We should probably take you to see a doctor. That was a hard hit."

No amusement, no laughter, no joking at all. He's serious.

Aww.

I rub my head a little more, feeling a touch of a knot forming. Great. Now it'll look like I have half a horn forming on the right sight of my head.

"It's fine. After being clumsy for so long, your body grows resilient."

He doesn't look convinced and he studies my eyes, probably looking for signs of a concussion. I've taken much harder hits to the head and not gotten one of those. I really need to walk around in bubble wrap all the time.

"We should seriously have that seen about," he goes on.

"No way," I tell him, batting his hands away. "I'm not losing this race."

I turn and start jogging again, and he groans while running to catch up with me.

"You're stubborn as hell, you know."

"That's no way to woo me," I tell him, but I keep my eyes facing forward so that no more poles can jump out in front of me without my knowledge. "If you want to get laid this week, then you're really going to have to step up your game."

He mutters something under his breath, and I smile to myself.

"I like flowers," I add, keeping with the banter. "And chocolate. And fruit. Give me chocolate covered fruit and you may even get laid twice."

I can feel him smiling without seeing it as we turn the corner toward the empty golf course, running down the sidewalk that surrounds it.

"I could get you some new underwear. Maybe something with Batman?" he muses, forcing my smile to spread wider.

"I have a few of those already."

He snorts derisively. "I'm not surprised."

"They have a cape too," I decide to point out, because really, it's only embarrassing if you can't joke about it.

"Why are you here?" he asks me, shifting gears in the conversation and taking it from fun to real without any preamble.

I almost don't answer, but then I do.

"Because my mother is relentless and far more stubborn than I am."

"Why is Lydia here?" he asks, prying into things too real to share with someone I don't know or trust.

"Because she's my friend, and for some reason, she needed to see this. Me? I want to fuck this wedding up."

"You're going to ruin the wedding?" he muses, not sounding overly surprised. I guess my crazy is showing too much if people aren't surprised by it anymore.

"No. Not the wedding. Just some of it. You going to tattle on me?"

"Tattle? I swear you're fucking five." He doesn't sound annoyed. If anything, he sounds like he's enjoying this. "But no. Jane is terrible," he groans.

"See?!" I exclaim. "I know! She's worse than him, and I didn't think that was possible."

"That's because you see the worst in him, and you've never really given him a chance."

"Too deep for a conversation while running with mud on you," I tell him, deciding to shift gears again.

"Fine. Then let's skip back to the wooing shit. What kind of fruit?"

My smile spreads again, and I turn to face him for a second before returning my gaze to where it should stay—straight ahead.

"Strawberries are good. Oranges in chocolate are my fave."

"Noted," he says, doing something with his phone.

"So you work with Anderson? And have dinner with my mother?"

He smirks before putting his phone back in his pocket, and glances over at me.

"You really hate her, don't you? Little long to hold onto a grudge." I don't like it when people throw my words back at me.

The light air around us loses some of the fun as seriousness comes into play again.

"My father is an inventor," I say randomly, shrugging.

"And that makes you hate your mother?"

"He's also an artist."

"So *that* makes you hate her?" he asks, confused.

"No. She left him because he was a starving artist and his inventions weren't exactly getting offers either. She wanted more. He didn't start making money until after she cheated on him with her current multi-millionaire husband. Dad's a true artist who just also happens to be incredibly smart with robotics, and I swear people like him feel things on a much deeper level. All these years later, and he's still painting pictures of her for his private collection. She didn't just break his heart when she cheated, Roman. She broke *him*. And she never even cared."

He grows quiet, and I try not to act affected. Word vomit is real, and I just threw up my past for no certain reason. But it's out there now and there's no taking it back.

"Sorry," he finally says. "I didn't know about all that."

I don't know why, but that makes me laugh a little. "Not your fault. My dad kept it quiet, so he wouldn't tarnish her shiny new reputation in this world. Despite how she treated him, he still loved her and didn't wish her anything bad. I wouldn't hate her if she'd just left him. People fall out of love. I get that. What I don't get is why she cheated on him instead of just leaving him."

"People make mistakes," he offers gently.

"That's not a mistake. That's a choice. A mistake is falling into a mud puddle. You don't 'accidentally' fall onto another man's cock with your vagina."

He groans, and I angle my head to the side as we slow our pace a little more. Talking and running is not easy, and I'm getting breathless. He doesn't seem to be as out of shape as I am, since his breathing is just fine.

"That's not what I meant," he grumbles, his cheeks a twinge of red.

Aw, did I embarrass him? That's a little adorable.

"At the end of the day, I have a zero tolerance policy for cheaters," I add. "Hence the reason I hate Anderson. He used to just annoy me. Now I wouldn't drive him to the hospital if his dick was rotting off."

He grunts and reflexively covers his crotch as though he's shielding it from the hypothetical dick rot.

"Okay, fine. I really would drive him to the hospital, but I wouldn't feel sorry for him."

He shakes his head and shudders at the same time.

"On to less painful topics. What do you do for a living?"

"My, my. You just shift subjects like I change underwear." He arches an unimpressed eyebrow at me, and I shrug. "I make jewelry, and before you laugh or say that's not a real job, you should know I'm good at it and I make a decent living."

"I wasn't going to say anything. That's actually pretty cool."

I give him a suspicious glance, and he holds his hands in the air, palms up. "I really think it's cool," he adds.

"What do you do?" I ask him.

"Marketing. I land accounts and such that want new commercials, in short. I help them run a fresh campaign or coin a slogan. That sort of thing."

Puppy Monkey Baby starts playing in my head after that, but I decide not to share that with him.

"You going to be my partner for the egg toss too?" he asks as we come up to the final half mile marker.

"Is this wooing?"

"Back to that, are we? I feel like we're just talking in circles," he sighs, but he's smiling this time.

"My panties might get shown a lot, but you do have to work a little bit to get into them."

To this, he laughs, and it's a sexy laugh again. I really should be worried about the effect he has on me, but I'm not. After all, I won't see him again after this week is over. If he works with Anderson, he's almost a six hour drive from me, and long distance things never work out.

"Can I ask a personal question?" he asks.

"It's a run. Not a psychology session, but sure. Let's get deep again," I quip, aiming for light.

"What the hell kind of arm is that?"

That has me laughing, and I lift my robo hand, squeezing it into a fist. "This is my father's newest baby. Her name is Jill. So far, she's amazing. I just hope she stays amazing. If I think about something hard enough, she understands the command. Climbing the wall back there was a breeze, which is phenomenal. Dad hopes that soon it will be as natural as using my flesh arm and hand. There's a Nano patch on my neck that helps send and receive signals from the brain to the arm. When he gets neuro testing approved, there will eventually be a chip implanted in the brain. I'll stick with the patch, but the idea of having a usable arm for the rest of my life… It's a good feeling. It connects to wifi twice a day and sends all the data to my father, who is probably geeking away in his lab, sifting through said data as we speak."

He purses his lips, but stares straight ahead. "That's one thing that threw me off on day one when you stumbled into my room half naked—I mean, it's one reason I didn't recognize you at first. I wasn't aware anything happened to your arm."

Pretty sure that's code for "what happened to your arm?"

"Anyone related to my mother pretends it doesn't exist. She refuses to accept that I'm less than perfect. You should see her face when I make one-arm jokes. She thinks I'm being insensitive. Um… it's me who's missing an arm, so I'm not sure how I'm insensitive."

His lips twitch. "So it doesn't bother you?"

I shrug, still jogging—a little slower. "Not anymore. Well, it's annoying to do things one-handed, for sure, but this new arm may solve all that. The stares used to bother me, but they don't anymore. Mom wants me to wear a fleshy, realistic prosthetic and a long-sleeved shirt to keep others from being uncomfortable. She also wants me to nix the jokes because of the discomfort it causes too. You only get one chance to live. Why waste it pretending to be something you're not for the comfort of others? It's easier to love the things that make you different, than to be miserable over the things you can't change."

"Good philosophy," he says without looking at me.

"I'm awesome like that," I remind him, smirking when he snickers quietly.

The finish line comes into sight, and we both pick up our pace, turning it into a sprint. I can tell he's holding back, but I'm running with all I have. The red team is coming in from a different angle, but we beat Anderson by at least thirty feet, and we both toss our batons into the basket before I crash to the ground.

Roman drops beside me, sitting down while I heave for air, but I notice Anderson is sweating profusely as he zips by and keeps running toward the porta-potties that are placed outside on this end of the property. We're pretty far away from the house, and a slow grin creeps over my face when he leaps into one and slams the door.

The laxatives have done their job.

"Want some water?" Roman asks me.

"Sure," I tell him, but my eyes are on the large tractor and chain, probably what they used to haul the porta-potties out here.

Honestly, I'm surprised my mother doesn't have gold-plated restrooms down here just for the wedding.

As soon as Roman goes to the refreshment table, I jump to my feet and hook the chain to the back of the blue beast that Anderson is inside of. Since I can't have this tied to me, I eye the Mulder kids, who are probably plotting someone's murder. Everyone knows they're evil.

Skipping over to them, I smile over at the oldest, who glares daggers at me. "Have you kids seen the guys who run that tractor?" I ask innocently.

"What'll you give us if we tell you?" the twelve-year-old boy asks, crossing his arms over his chest.

"Nothing. I just wanted to let them know they left the keys in the ignition on that tractor."

I point at it, just in case they're stupid. Something sinister flashes in their eyes as they all exchange a look, and I hide a shudder. Seriously, these are the creepiest kids ever.

"We'll let someone know," the boy lies, and I thank them like I buy it.

I make it back just as Roman walks over with a bottle of water, and he eyes me like he's suspicious this time. Probably because I'm smiling like a little girl with a big fat secret.

"What have you done?" he asks me.

"Nothing. Thanks for the water."

I snatch the bottle from his hand, but he tugs me back to him. When I look up at him, confused, he cocks an eyebrow at me.

"About that wooing," he says, reminding me we've been playing this game.

"About that, you see, I was just kidding. You're too close to my mother for me to play with, and I don't really see us being compatible," I tell him, patting his chest gently with my robo hand.

Just as I'm about to pull away, he shoves a hand in my hair, and his lips are on mine, silencing every thought in my head. My lips part on their own accord, and his tongue takes advantage, sweeping in and stealing the rest of my sanity.

Those butterflies I've been ignoring burst into flames as everything on my body starts to ache and crave more, and I drop the water to wrap my arms around the back of his neck and pull him closer. When I moan into his mouth, he smiles against my lips and pulls back suddenly.

My eyes are still closed, and I'm leaning forward against vacant air when he releases me completely. Slowly, my eyes peel open, and I see him smirking at me. Again.

"Yeah. Not compatible at all. I totally agree," the cheeky prick tells me before turning and walking off.

Everyone is gawking, but I'm still cemented to the ground, trying to keep from falling. I definitely need a change of panties now. His tongue is amazing, and I bet he could give some majorly awesome orgasms with it.

While my head goes to all kinds of sexy thoughts, I barely recognize the sound of a loud engine roaring to life until there's a louder, masculine screaming sound—if there's such a thing.

My head darts around just as the Mulder kids start dying laughing, driving off on the tractor, and the porta-potty rolls five or six times before Anderson manages to break free and roll on the ground, slathered in something that might look like mud, but isn't.

Covering my mouth, I rein in the laughter that tries to break free, and my eyes land on the familiar blues as Roman turns to give me the *did you really just do that?* look.

And the sabotage has begun.

A whistle and some chuckling behind me remind me that I've also been sabotaged. Time to change into something that will *not* show my underwear by the end of the night.

CHAPTER SEVEN

Henley

I'm tempted to hide out in the room for the rest of the day and nurse my stinging backside, but it's clear Lydia would like to be alone, so I reluctantly take a seat outside to watch the Wedding Olympics. I ignore the snickers and murmurs from the guests seated around me. No one has asked me what happened at the zip line, but it's clear from all the nods and smiles I'm getting that everyone knows. Whatever, they can all kiss the fattest part of my red, swollen ass.

"Hey, Little Chicken, how's your ass?"

Davis takes a seat beside me, and I try not to grin at the nickname he gave me so many years ago. Henley got shortened to Hen, but Davis had to take it a step further. I always pretended to hate it when I was a kid, but secretly I loved that he had a special name for me, no matter how ridiculous.

"Don't call me that, and quit thinking about my ass."

His dark eyes are alight with humor as he grins at me. He may have grown up, but that boyish, crooked grin hasn't changed a bit, and apparently it can still send butterflies scattering through my body. I want to hate it, to hate him after all the pain he put me through, but I can't seem to manage it.

"I thought you might need this." He produces a thin cushion for my chair.

Great, I feel like an old woman who has to carry a donut pillow around. It's not a donut pillow, but still. "Thank you," I mumble, dropping it onto the chair and sitting back down. "Why aren't you running the obstacle course? Scared to get dirty?"

"I thought you could use some company."

"What are you doing, Davis?"

"At the moment, I'm sitting next to a grouchy, beautiful woman."

"You know what I mean. There are plenty of available women here."

"That's true," he says, restraining a smile as he lets his eyes sweep across the crowd. "And I'm sure they'd fall at my feet if I gave them a chance."

"Glad to see you haven't developed a self-esteem problem over the years."

"Confidence has never been an issue."

"No, your head has always been swollen with self-importance." I can feel him looking at me, but I keep my eyes on the obstacle course.

"It only swells for you, baby. And from the noises you make when it does, I know you appreciate it."

A grin creeps onto my face. "You're impossible."

"You're beautiful."

"Stop saying that." I decide to cut through all the bullshit. "Look, we only have a few more days and we'll both go back to our lives. If you want to do the fuck buddy thing while we're here, I'm game, but stop with the compliments and lines. I'm not as gullible as these plastic women."

His long fingers brush a lock of hair behind my ear. "I call it as I see it, Hen." I squirm, trying to get comfortable. It has to be ninety degrees and the heat isn't helping the prickly feeling on my ass cheeks. My discomfort doesn't escape his attention. "Let's get out of here. I know something that'll help."

I'm in no position to argue, so I take his offered hand and let him lead me toward the back of the house. "Where are we going?"

He gestures toward the pool. "Everyone is at the obstacle course. We'll have it to ourselves."

"I'm not wearing a swimsuit." Or panties, for that matter. The chafing was just too much to bear, so I settled for a silky pair of running shorts. I feel half naked with nothing underneath, but it's much more comfortable.

"Really? What happened to the crazy girl who jumped a fence to swim in the closed county pool, fully clothed?"

Laughing, I shake my head. "That girl was drunk and under the influence of my stupid brother and his persistent friend." It was one of the best nights of my childhood. We snuck out and Davis swiped a bottle of vodka from his father. We mixed it with some horrible canned fruit punch, and I got drunk for the first time. The county pool was right down the street and nothing sounded better on that humid August night. We got to swim for about twenty minutes before a security guard ran us off, cursing us and promising to call the police. Good times. Almost all my best childhood memories include Davis.

"I'm still persistent." And apparently, I'll still follow him anywhere. To hell with it, my T-shirt is dark blue, and I'm wearing a bra, so it shouldn't show through.

After tossing our phones on a lounge chair, we wade into the shallow end. Cool water washes over my hot skin and the relief makes me sigh. So good. I dunk underwater, wetting my hair, before swimming toward the corner of the pool. Resting my arms on the ledge, I lay my head back and revel in the sensation of the sun on my face, the chilly water washing over my skin.

Davis surfaces right in front of me, and my eyes are drawn to his chest where drops of water dance across his sun-kissed skin. The boy I loved was attractive, cute. The man in front of me can't be described as cute. Handsome, gorgeous, extremely attractive? Absolutely. But not cute. His dark hair appears black when it's wet, a wild, overlong mess that somehow works for him, and coupled with the scruff on his jaw, gives him a dangerous look. And I know he's dangerous to me, to my heart that took years to get over him.

Just for the rest of the week, I remind myself. I'm going to enjoy him until the wedding is over and then go back to my life. It occurs to me that while we've reacquainted ourselves with every inch of each other's bodies, I know nothing about his life now.

"What do you do for a living?" I ask, as his hands rest on my hips.

"I'm a physical therapist at Nashville Community Hospital." Nashville. That's where he went when he left Pensacola? And we both ended up working in the medical field.

"I still live in Pensacola. I'm an x-ray tech."

"I know," he replies with a teasing grin. "Your brother and I still talk."

Great, I wonder what else he's told him. "Any kids? Ex-wives? Gay lovers?"

"No to all three. How about you? Are you seeing anyone? And if it's a gay lover, please be as detailed as possible."

"Sorry to disappoint you, but there'll be no muff diving in my future. I just broke up with someone a few days ago, actually."

His hands wander up my sides. "I'm sorry to hear that."

"No, you aren't," I laugh as his fingers run over my ribs.

"Still ticklish, huh?" he teases. His rough palms travel around to my lower back and when I peek up at him, his lips land on mine. I can't feel the cool water anymore as heat rushes through me, setting my skin ablaze. Why is it always like this with him? We can't just kiss. We devour each other, our hands groping and caressing. We probably would've gone at it right there in the pool if a tiny voice hadn't interrupted.

"I want to swim!"

"Okay, Nicky, I'm coming. Put your floaty on." A young mother chases after her toddler, finally catching him and wrestling him into a lifejacket.

"Guess that's our cue," I laugh, pulling away from Davis and climbing out of the pool. "Let's go see how the obstacle course went, then I need to get cleaned up. I told Kasha I'd do the egg toss and three-legged race."

I try not to stare when Davis pulls himself over the edge of the pool, every muscle tightening, water pouring over his skin. I need to get a grip. I toss him a towel from the bathhouse and wrap another around me as we make our way to the large area roped off for the events.

We've just reached the end of the course when Davis exclaims, "What the hell?"

A scream that barely sounds human seems to be coming from a blue porta-potty a few yards away. A blue porta-potty that has somehow ended up on its side and is now rolling across the yard. "Someone's in there!" I cry.

Davis points to a tractor being driven by a couple of kids. "They're dragging it." Before he can say anything else, the potty rolls again and the door pops open, leaving a thoroughly shit-soaked Anderson lying on the grass.

Giggles turn to uncontrollable laughter as Davis gazes at me with a confused look, a careful smile on his face. Kids or not, I know who did this. Kasha is officially my favorite person. "Christ, I can smell him from here," I exclaim, trying to quell the laughter and catch my breath.

A small crowd gathers, but Anderson doesn't seem to hear the laughter around him. Careful not to be seen, I take a quick picture with my phone, preserving the look of disgusted horror on his face forever. Davis can't help but chuckle when I show him. "I take it you aren't a fan of his?"

"He's an asshole who screwed over my friend." Glancing around us, I see Kasha heading away quickly. "I'll talk to Kasha later," I decide, tugging him back the direction we came.

He slips his arm around my shoulder and we start toward the house, Anderson running ahead of us like he stole something. "Remind me never to make you mad."

"I didn't do anything to him," I point out. "Now, his stuck up bride, she may want to beware of me."

"What did she do?"

"Just let us know how charitable they were being, inviting us lowly middle class peasants."

"Uh-oh."

"Speaking of, I wonder where they're keeping the eggs for the egg toss?"

A mischievous look crosses his face and he grabs my hand. "Get cleaned up, and we'll find out."

After a warm shower and another coat of hydrocortisone cream, my ass feels much better. At least I'm able to wear panties. I throw on a pair of light cotton shorts, a sports bra, and tank top, and head to Davis's room. We make our way to the massive industrial kitchen in search of eggs. The plan is to try to switch the hard boiled eggs meant for the egg toss to raw ones. Juvenile and not that creative, but funny nonetheless.

We locate a fridge stocked full of egg cartons, half marked *For Egg Toss*. As I pull out two cartons sitting on the bottom shelf, the little elderly lady working in the kitchen makes our devious idea ten times better with the following words. "Oh, not those, honey. They're rotten. I meant to run them to the gardener since he uses them for fertilizer, but I haven't had the chance. Stuck them in there so they wouldn't stink the place up."

With a smile, I grab the cartons. "I'll drop them off for you. It's on our way."

"Why, thank you."

This is lining up to be the best egg toss ever. We form two parallel lines and the aim of the game is to toss an egg to your partner across from you. If your partner catches it, you both take a step back and toss it again. If the egg hits the ground or cracks, you have to start over. The first team to cross the finish line behind us, wins. Since they're using boiled eggs, it isn't meant to be messy and would probably be boring as hell, but Davis and I have livened it up a bit.

A bucket sits behind each team, filled with eggs. I was surprised we weren't met with suspicion when we volunteered to fill the buckets, but no one really seemed to notice. Anderson is on my right, paired with one of Jane's snooty friends, and on my left is Jane, partnered with a guy I don't recognize. While we filled everyone's buckets with raw eggs, we saved the rotten ones for Anderson and Janes' teams. Their partners are collateral damage. Sorry about their luck. I didn't have a chance to let Kasha in on my plan, and she's way at the other end of the line with Roman. I hope she at least gets to see it.

Davis seems to be as excited as I am when someone blows a whistle for us to begin. We're using raw eggs as well, since it would be obvious who switched the eggs if we were the only ones with hard boiled. Davis tosses it to me and I catch it easily, taking a step back before tossing it back to him.

After a few more steps back, I hear Jane squeal as she fumbles an egg and it ends up cracking on her knee. Whew, I can smell it from here. To her credit, she must think it's a mistake, and carries on, choosing another egg and starting over. Trying not to laugh, I throw mine just a little too hard and it splats into Davis's hand.

He raises an eyebrow at me, and I shrug as we both go back to our starting positions. "Not so hard," he warns with a crooked grin.

"Is that what she said?"

"It sure isn't what you said last night," he retorts, and I resist the urge to throw an egg at his head.

We start to catch up with Jane and her partner, and it must unnerve the guy because his next throw is far too high and hard. The egg bursts against Jane's neck, and the putrid smell instantly fills the air. She screams as the stinking goo drips down her top between her breasts. I can't help it. Laughter leaps from my throat, stealing my breath, and I don't even notice when Anderson approaches from behind me until I hear him demand, "What the hell is going on?"

"It's not funny, bitch!" Jane cries, and throws another egg at me. I duck, though it was so high it may have missed me anyway, but it doesn't miss Anderson. It explodes like a rancid hand grenade right on Anderson's big forehead. His face goes from red to purple as he sputters and the slime oozes down to his lips, giving him a nice taste.

I can barely see him turn and throw up, the tears of laughter in my eyes making the world blurry. My sides hurt and every time I try to take a breath, a squeaking sound accompanies it. I'm not sure I've ever laughed so hard in my life, and if I don't get a grip, I'm going to pee myself.

Through Jane's outraged cries and Anderson's retching, an amused voice says, "Time to go, baby." A strong arm wraps around my waist, and Davis leads me away, toward the beach. I manage to run and grab a quick picture of Anderson bent over holding his stomach with egg still smeared on his face. Jane is in the background, grimacing as her friend wipes at her chest.

Best Wedding Olympics ever.

"Where are we going?" I ask, finally catching my breath.

"Away. Anderson looked like he was ready to kill you."

"You mean after he was done puking?" I giggle.

The beauty of his smile rivals the multicolored sunset happening behind his back. "Again, I hope I never cross you."

"And again, I never touched him. We have to go back soon. The three-legged race is going to start."

He pulls me down beside him in the cool sand. "They'll lynch us."

"Aw," I tease. "Are you scared? They don't know we switched the eggs. As far as anyone knows, all we did was laugh at them."

"Fine," he agrees, pulling me into his lap. "I'll run the race with you, then I'm taking you straight back to my room and stripping you naked."

"No complaints here."

The next few minutes are spent in comfortable silence while I sit on his lap, his fingers wandering through my hair the same way they used to when we were kids. Part of me is trying to forget, to block that out, but a stronger part is soaking up every second, knowing no matter what I do, I'll miss this when the week is over.

The sky turns a brilliant red, fading to violet and pink before the sun gives up the fight for the day. "We should go. The race will be starting," I say, hearing the reluctance in my voice. I could stay right here forever.

My stomach growls and Davis laughs. "When was the last time you ate?"

"Breakfast, I guess. It's been a busy day, what with getting stung in the ass and playing with rotten eggs and all."

"Come on," he chuckles, slinging an arm around my shoulder as we start toward the lawn where the race is being held. "Let's get this over with so I can feed and fuck you."

"Such a romantic," I sigh.

Floodlights have been set up on the decadently decorated front lawn. Again, there's pink everywhere. "Ugh, I feel like I'm inside a vagina," I grumble. A woman I don't recognize hands me a scarf—

pink of course—printed with Jane and Anderson's smiling faces and the date of the wedding. "I think I'm going to puke."

Davis laughs and ties the scarf around our calves. God, his is as hard as a stone. Kasha waves at me from a few feet away where she's tied to Roman and is obviously happy to be there. I don't understand why she loves this Olympics thing so much, but at least she's getting some fun out of this trip. I wonder how Lydia ended up spending the day and hope she hasn't been cooped up in the room since this morning. I'll have to check on her.

"On the count of three, you may go!" the man behind us announces. "First team over the finish line wins. One, two, three!"

I don't have a chance to take a step. Davis wraps an arm around my waist, lifts me off my feet, and darts across the yard. He's so damn strong. "Davis!" I laugh. "This is cheating!"

"Team three is disqualified!" a voice declares from behind us, and I hear Kasha's snort of laughter.

Unfazed, Davis keeps going, carrying me past the finish line and toward the house. "Put me down, you crazy ass!"

Laughing, he stops, tearing off the scarf and tossing it aside before taking my hand. "You think you're really funny, don't you?" I ask.

He smiles when I punch him on his shoulder. "I'm a damned delight and you know it. Let's get out of here and grab dinner in town."

"Fine, but I want to check on Lydia first and change into some jeans. It's getting chilly and I have sand in my crack."

"Leave it overnight, maybe you'll make a pearl."

"Ass," I scold, trying not to smile.

His arm snakes back around my shoulders. "And a damn fine one, too."

"Mine or yours?"

"Oh, yours, too." Some things never change. He always could make me laugh. We spent half our time tossing insults back and forth, and neither of us was ever hard up to find a comeback. In smart ass language, we're complete equals.

Davis agrees to meet me in ten minutes, and we part ways while I get changed. Lydia is curled up in a chair in the corner, her tablet in her lap.

"Hey, what are you doing?"

"Reading." She shrugs, setting the tablet aside. "How did the Olympics go?"

"I have *soo* much to tell you, but I have to get changed. Davis will be over in a second. We're going out to dinner. Have you been in here all day?"

"Seemed like the best idea."

"Come with us," I order, tugging on my jeans.

"Nah, I'm fine here." She moves to the bed, stretching out on her stomach.

Before I can respond, there's a knock on the door and Davis walks in. "Hi, Lydia, how have you been?" he asks.

"Fine," she replies.

"I'll just be a second," I tell him and close myself in the bathroom. I quickly clean my face and fix my hair. I'm sure the restaurant we choose won't be fancy, but the beach bum look is not what I'm going for. When I return to our room, Lydia is pulling on her shoes.

"I invited Lydia to join us," Davis explains with a smile.

"So did I. I'm glad you changed your mind," I tell her.

"Your guy is extremely persistent." Lydia glances up at me, shaking her head.

My first impulse is to deny he's my guy, but I don't want to sound like a bitch, so I let it pass. "Sometimes it's a good thing. You need to get out of this room and have a little fun."

A small smile lights on Lydia's face as we make our way down the hall and Davis moves between us, linking an arm with each of us. He escorts us to his car, and a few minutes later, we park outside an

Italian restaurant. "I have almost no control when it comes to Italian food," I remark. "I'm going to gain ten pounds."

Davis smiles and wraps an arm around my waist. "Yeah, I remember how pasta crazy you were." He turns to Lydia. "Do you like Italian?"

"Doesn't everyone?" she asks.

It's a nice, cozy place and we're seated at a booth in the corner. It's nice to get away from the ritzy mansion and bitchy crowd for a while. If Davis pulls me any closer, I'll be in his lap. I'm not sure why he's so affectionate. It's weird. Fuck buddies don't spend so much time together, or hang all over one another, but it feels too good to complain. It'll probably come back to bite me in the long run. Right now, I just can't summon a shit to give.

After way too much pasta and bread, plus multiple glasses of wine, Lydia's mood seems to have improved. Maybe it's because Davis is filling her in on some of the things she missed today.

"You're kidding!" she cries, drawing a few looks from other customers.

"Ask Henley. He spent the day covered in shit and rotten eggs."

I hold up my palms. "I had nothing to do with the porta-potty. That was some bratty kids."

"Uh-huh. That was Kasha," Lydia laughs. "Only she would think of something like that."

"And all we did was give them the rotten eggs. I didn't make them throw them at one another."

"Oh god, I should've gone. I would've loved to have seen his face."

With a smile, I produce my phone and hand it to her. "I may have taken a few pictures after he crawled out of the potty, and after the egg hit him."

Lydia dissolves into giggles. It's good to hear her laugh and sound like her old self. "Is he throwing up?"

"Apparently, rotten eggs do not taste like strawberries," I reply, and we both break into hysterical laughter. The waiter smiles as he brings us our check, but it's clear he'll be glad to see the back end of us.

Davis sweeps up the check, looking offended when we offer to split it, and we head back out into the cool night. Even though we're a few miles away, I can smell the ocean in the air, that light, salty scent you can almost taste.

Davis points out a little ice cream shop, and Lydia and I both groan. "No way. If I eat one more bite, I'll pop like a tick," Lydia says, and I agree.

I spot an arcade just down the street that's closing for the night. "Hey! They have Skee Ball. We're totally coming back here before we go home."

Lydia laughs. "You're a big kid sometimes."

"You're just mad because you can't beat me."

She beams at Davis when we climb out of the car back at the mansion. "Thanks for inviting me. I had a good time."

"Anytime," he replies with a grin.

"It was really nice of you," I tell him, after she walks away. "It's a hard time for her. Anderson is her ex. He cheated on her with the bride, and now Kasha's whole family treats her like some home-wrecking slut for showing up here."

"Why did she come?" he asks, his hand traveling to cup my nape as we walk.

"I'm not completely sure. All she'd say was she needed to be here. Kasha and I knew she would be upset and need us, so we're here for moral support. I was half hoping she'd meet someone to hook up with, wipe the memory of that asshole from her brain."

"She's lucky to have you two."

"We're lucky to have each other."

"Well, I hope they can do without you tonight." His hand moves to lightly squeeze my ass. "Because you're coming back to my bed. I'm not done eating."

"Again with the romance."

"I also want to fuck those amazing tits."

"Anything else?" I giggle.

"Too much to list, baby."

We've arrived at his room, but before we can enter, I spot Kasha and Roman making their way up the stairs together. Looks like she found her dolphin after all, and I can't resist making the "eh eh eh eh" sound at her.

Then, for some weird reason, she tosses up a peace sign with her robotic hand while scowling at me… "Why are you giving me a peace sign?" I ask, confused.

"Damn it," she hisses. "Piece of my mind. Not *peace!* You're supposed to be flipping her off," she harps at the arm before disappearing into our room.

Davis's expression is as confused as Roman's was. "Did you just make a dolphin noise at them?"

"Inside joke. According to Lydia, dolphins are very sexual and sexually aggressive."

The room tilts as I'm scooped up and tossed on the bed. "A dolphin would be in awe of the things I'm about to do to you," he warns, stripping me faster than I ever thought possible.

True to his word, the next three hours are filled with too many orgasms to count.

CHAPTER EIGHT

Kasha

"My hand just gave my bestie a 'peace' sign instead of flipping her off. First warning sign I've found," I tell my father over the phone.

"I'm not sure how it got those commands mixed up," he says to me as Lydia watches me with an amused smile.

"I was thinking about giving her a piece of my mind. I hadn't decided if I was going to flip her off or not, though, when robo arm decides to give her the universal hippie sign."

His breath catches. "You didn't command it? It worked on its own reflexively? This is great news!"

"Um, no it's not. It didn't do what I wanted it to do."

"Obviously there are still some kinks—"

"Obviously," I interrupt dryly.

"—but this really is a major breakthrough."

It's pointless to argue with him when he's geeking this hard. I'm stuck listening to a thousand scientific details that make no sense to me, but I'm probably the only human contact he's had since I left to come here, so I endure it. Unless his interns have shown up. But they usually don't actually speak to him. They spend hours geeking too.

It's approaching the midnight treasure hunt for the Olympics when I finally get off the phone, wondering if he even heard me say "goodbye."

Lydia is right where I left her earlier after I came back to change my split shorts. Stupid shorts showed my stupid underwear to that stupid Roman who kisses me stupid.

"You want to treasure hunt? Nate Dukes needs a partner."

She shakes her head while settling down on the bed, still smirking at me.

"Lydia, why'd you come? This is making you miserable."

She blows out a long breath. "Trust me. I need to be here."

I opt for yoga pants now that the sun has set, since bugs will be a bitch. Lydia returns to reading from her tablet, and I sigh while shaking my head. I wish I could understand what exactly she hopes to benefit from this entire, painful reunion.

"Okay, last chance, I'm leaving," I tell her, hoping she gets up.

Instead, she grins and shoots me a 'peace' sign.

"Wench," I mumble as she laughs at my back.

As I jog down the stairs, a bloodcurdling scream erupts from the massive study that has been turned into bridezilla central. My feet stumble over themselves as my heart kicks my chest, and I dart inside the room to see several horrified faces as Jane screams again, clutching a pink dress as she sobs.

What the... Uh-oh. That dress isn't supposed to be pink...

"Jane, we'll figure something out," my mother is telling her, patting her awkwardly on the back as Jane strings together incoherent sounds she thinks are words through her sobs, clutching the bright pink fabric as she rocks back and forth on the ground.

Heh. The dress matches the decorations now.

"Who would do this?" one of the bridesmaids hisses.

WORTH IT

Gretchen, the maid of honor, shrugs. Then... they all cut their eyes to me.

"Her!" Jane shrieks.

"Me? Hell no. I wouldn't touch your dress!" I really wouldn't. Jane's a bitch, but my primary target is Anderson.

"No," Jane seethes, getting control of her sobs as anger takes over like a red rage. "Lydia," she adds.

Now my anger bubbles. "Lydia wouldn't touch your fucking dress. She hasn't even been anywhere around this room!"

Mom steps between us, as unruffled by the tense air as ever. "I'm sure Lydia had nothing to do with the dress. The Mulder kids are here. Please remember that. They are indeed your family, Jane," Mom says softly. "But we know how they love their pranks. Those pranks veer toward the vicious."

Jane starts sobbing uncontrollably again, and I turn and walk away with twitching lips as my anger dissolves. Someone dyed her dress pink to match the hideous decorations. It wasn't Lydia—she's too mature. It wasn't me; my focus is my stepbrother.

So I do the obvious and text Henley.

ME: Did you paint the wedding dress pink?

HENLEY: WTF????? Her dress was painted?!!! Lmfao!

ME: Painted or dyed or whatever. Not really sure, but it's hella pink. It's not so lmfao down here. Screams. Sobbing. Mourning like someone just died... Wasn't you?

HENLEY: I wish. I'm texting Lydia right now.

Um... Where is she? Never mind, I don't want to know.

Smirking, I put my phone away, silently thanking the Mulder kids for being hellions right now as I head outside.

"What have you done?" Roman's voice has me snapping my neck to the side as he approaches with a worried look on his face.

He's not covered in egg anymore, and his hair is a little damp, as though he's fresh from the shower...

Not an image I need to conjure up at the moment, since I'm done trying to play with fire. Roman is definitely fire. And I'm gasoline.

"I haven't done anything. But someone turned Jane's dress pink." Yep. I smile. I'm evil like that.

He tries not to smile, but secretly he's evil too, and he basically admitted he didn't like her earlier.

"So, we're doing this treasure hunt together?" he asks as I start walking toward the starting sections.

I notice Anderson going on his own, which is totally against the rules. Male and female pairs only. And yes, I will tattle on him like I'm five or something.

"Unless you have another girl you want to hunt with," I say as I turn to face the current bane of my existence. His disheveled dark, damp hair is really tempting to touch. His icy blue eyes dance with amusement as he studies me.

"First you berate me, then flirt with me, then you act like you can't get away from me fast enough. Do you always play so many games?" he asks, catching me off guard.

"First you flirt, then you push me away over something I said when we were young and dumb, then you expect me to flirt with you, then you flirt with me again. Yes, I play games and keep score. So far, you're winning on the wishy-washy event."

His lips lift in a smile instead of creasing in a frown the way I expected. He really is grating on my nerves by never doing what I expect.

His eyes dart down to my robo hand, and a trickle of insecurity washes over me with unbidden surprise. I push it away, refusing to let anyone wiggle that self-doubt back into me.

When his eyes meet mine again, my breath catches in my throat. He moves closer, cupping my chin in his hand, eyeing my lips like he's about to go in for the prize. He leans down, and my eyes flutter shut like I'm some teenager who can't help herself.

"Tonight the games stop," he whispers across my lips, teasing me by staying a hairs-breadth out of reach with those taunting lips.

My eyes open as he backs away and grins. Asshole. He knows what he does to me.

I snatch a map off the table, ignoring the tingling sensations in my core. Roman reads the map over my shoulder, and I roll my eyes when he presses his body much closer to mine than necessary.

"Here are the rules," my stepfather announces. I'm tempted to tell him his son has already broken the rules and headed into the woods alone. "Male and female partners, of course. You use the first map to find the second map's location. Then the second map will take you to the third. And so on. Only one flashlight per team! The first to find the treasure will be the event winners, and you'll also win the booty!"

That just sounds so wrong coming out of his mouth.

A few snickers ring out, as always. Goodness forbid *booty*-winning be taken any other way.

Roman even snickers, and I flip him off—with my good hand. I don't trust my robo hand with that gesture.

As we head toward the woods, he takes the lead, flicking on his flashlight. The moonlight is bright enough for me to appreciate his ass in those jeans... Damn. I really want to touch it just to see if it's as firm as—

A shriek leaves my mouth when my arm darts forward, and my robo hand actually grabs a handful of ass. Roman jerks, looking over his shoulder as my hand kneads said ass like it has a mind of its own.

"I swear that's not me!" I bark, grabbing my robo arm with my good hand and tugging like crazy to get it away.

"Sure looks like you to me," he says dryly.

It continues to massage his ass, and I close my eyes to concentrate. *Let go of his ass!*

It finally drops away from his ass, and my eyes pop open to find Roman watching me with undisguised mockery in his eyes.

"That wasn't me," I repeat, glaring at him. "My arm is malfunctioning."

"And turning into a pervert?" he quips, his lips barely restraining the smile he wants to taunt me with.

"No it's—" My words die in my throat, because the damn hand only reacted to my unfiltered thoughts of grabbing his—

The hand shoots out again, cutting my stupid thoughts off as it wraps around him and grabs his ass once more. Roman is knocked into me, and his arms go around me to keep from knocking us both over.

His laughter only adds to the heat on my cheeks as mortification sets in. *Let go of his ass!*

It finally does, but Roman doesn't stop laughing, nor does he release me. He fingers a lock of my hair, and I close my eyes, trying my damnedest not to think pervy thoughts.

Cats dancing on a table. Dogs playing a piano. Squirrels hiding nuts.

No!!! Do not think of nuts!

"What are you doing?" Roman asks me as I try to turn off my arm. It doesn't work. The link between my patch and my neck seems to be keeping it up and running, and the manual switch isn't going to cut it off. My father said this could happen.

"Skipping the treasure hunt before my hand decides to grab something else."

He grunts and turns away like he's reading between the lines, and he cocks his head as I start walking away.

"Because you grabbed my ass?" he asks in disbelief.

"Because my hand grabbed your ass twice without my permission. Imagine what else it might do and tell me you still feel safe." I toss an evil grin over my shoulder, and he grimaces while covering those jewels of his.

"Let me take you back. It's late and dark."

"I can see the house from here."

Maybe I'm not insecure anymore, but I really don't want to walk around without my arm in front of people. The faux arms draw enough attention when they're obvious. But no arm at all? I get gawked at, and the whispers that follow really annoy me.

Besides, Roman may not seem fazed by my robo arm, but he might be a little taken aback when the whole thing is just vacant space. Seeing the pity on people's faces is worse than seeing the grimaces.

And no way in hell am I taking off my patch without putting it in its case. That's hundreds of thousands of dollars in that little rectangular thing.

Roman follows me despite my protests, and I glare over my shoulder at him. He just winks back at me like it's no big deal I have a rogue arm that may or may not kick his ass at any given moment.

My eyes flit up just as a guy nears. I remember that jerk. He's one of Anderson's friends who told his girlfriend I lost my arm because of an STD. I wanted to slap the hell out of him that—

A yelp leaves my lips as my arm jerks out, shoving the guy hard. He curses and stumbles to the ground, and I grab my stupid arm, jerking it back against my chest.

"You crazy bitch!" he snaps as he stands.

Roman is suddenly in his face, and the guy pales as he steps back. Even in the moonlight I can tell Roman looks like he's on the verge of snapping.

I'm not really sure why… I mean, I've been called a hell of a lot worse.

"Roman," I hiss when his fists ball at his sides.

I snatch the flashlight from the ground that he must have dropped, and I clutch it in my robo hand. Suddenly, he grabs the guy by the shirt and slams him against the tree.

"Roman!" I snap again, louder this time.

He turns to face me, and I arch an eyebrow. "Are you taking me back or staring at the prick all night?"

I know he plans to do more than just stare, given the pissed off stance he's holding. The guy pinned to the tree casts a helpless glance in my direction.

Roman once fought an entire team, busted his knee up too much to play sports again, and he gave as good as he got from seven guys.

I'd rather not see what lies beneath the surface of the Roman I've been getting to know. One thing is definitely for sure; he's still carrying around a lot of rage.

He stares at me like he's trying to decide, and he finally shoves the guy to the side, knocking him to the ground as he turns to walk to me.

Silence ensues, and his dark mood seems to be firmly in place. I'm not sure what just happened, to be honest. And it's a little… unnerving.

"In all fairness, I did knock him down with my rogue arm," I remind Roman as we walk back to the house.

He pockets his hands and clears his throat, still avoiding looking at me.

"Sorry. I didn't mean to scare you," he says quietly.

"Want to talk about it?" I ask, staring around at all the lights disappearing into the woods. The flashlight I'm still holding isn't really helping us anymore, so I turn it off as we reach the bright yard.

"Not out here," he says on a sigh.

I glance around at all the faces hanging out in the yard, seeing some of the bridesmaids on their phones, and hearing them desperately trying to find a dress to replace the pink one. Who are they calling after midnight?

He walks into the house, and I follow him. He's so tense that it's swallowing up the air around me, and I tense in response. Something akin to metal crunching draws my attention, and I look down, horrified when I see the crushed flashlight in my robo hand.

Roman turns, looking at it with the same expression, and his eyes meet mine.

"That's totally stronger than a baby alligator," I say in awe.

"What?" he asks, confused.

I shake my head and drop the remnants of the flashlight on the stairs.

"Nothing. As you were," I tell him, ushering him on.

Dad is going to have to fix this damn thing before I accidentally hurt someone.

As we top the staircase, I debate going into my room. Roman just showed he has a violent side still. I'm not sure how smart it would be to follow him into his room. Apparently my feet don't get the memo, because they follow him anyway.

He turns to me as he reaches his room, and he blows out a breath.

"Don't back out now. I'd like to know why you almost kicked a guy's ass for calling me a name. I did hit him first."

"He raised his fist. Anyway, why did you hit him?" he counters.

"My arm did it. Not me."

"Your hand grabbed my ass, but it didn't hit me. What's up?" There's not even a hint of playfulness in his tone right now.

I really don't want to explain in the hallway, so I reach over and open his door, walking in before him. He follows, and I take a seat on the bed, feeling on display as I shift awkwardly.

Roman stands, leaning against the large dresser as he crosses his arms over his chest. I'm not sure how this flipped from him to me, but I shrug.

"Jill is a prototype. She's a smart arm, meaning she's learning with each passing day. She reads projected commands and reacts accordingly. Unfortunately, now she's gotten too smart, and my inner thoughts are being acted on."

"I figured as much. What'd he do to you to make you hit him?"

I roll my eyes. "He made a wiseass remark about how I lost my arm. No, there were no STDs involved. Is that really what people think?" I ask, peering over at him.

"I haven't discussed it with anyone but you, so I don't know what people think," he says, still watching me.

"Anyway, I was thinking back to how I wanted to slap him the day I heard him talking not too quietly about it. And… my arm reacted. Jill needs an upgrade."

He relaxes like I've said something he wanted to hear. I'm not sure why.

"I thought he might have done something worse. I'm on edge. I snapped without thinking."

"Why is that?" I pry.

He heaves out a breath. "How'd you really lose your arm?" he asks instead.

He's a master at deflection.

Since there isn't a heaping ton of choking pity in his eyes, I decide to tell him.

"I'm a bit accident prone, as you might have noticed," I say, keeping the tone light. His lips twitch. "Anyway, Dad had this machine he was creating to crunch metals for the heating process. I'd just turned twenty, and had decided to launch my jewelry business. We didn't have a lot of money at the time, so he made anything he needed from junkyard scraps—yes, there's a junkyard in our backyard. We're that kind of trashy. Still are. I used those scraps to create gems. I learned to heat the metal and bend it to my will. I also used his metal crunching machine when the pieces were too big to stick directly into the melter. No, I don't know the technical terms, and never wanted to know them."

He adjusts, getting more comfortable against the dresser, and I sigh as I think back to the scariest day of my life.

"There was a piece stuck, and I turned off the machine so I could reach in and dislodge the jam. However, I tripped, and my hip slammed into the power button while my arm was inside. Long story short, I pulled back a mangled limb, and my father called 911. I lost everything up to my elbow, and making jewelry one-handed became one hell of a learning curve."

He flinches, and looks away. I'm not sure if it's the vivid imagery that has him averting his eyes, or if he's hiding the pity he knows I don't want.

"Some good came out of it though," I go on, shrugging. "Dad got into the prosthetic field. He received his first grant for an arm he made for me. He made one that allowed me to hook my jewelry while I worked on it with my good hand. Then a very realistic 'going out' arm. Then a swimming arm. Little by little, he's made his way to the smart arm. Legs have come a long way, but arms… You have to be ultra rich to afford a good arm. Dad is trying to clone the technology from Jill with more affordable methods so that every arm amputee can have one. He's made a lot of money in this field, and he loves inventing new arms for me. I started making the arm jokes for his sake. His guilt always crushed him after the accident, and I hated seeing that pain in his eyes… Like he'd failed me. At first I faked being okay with it. Then, with the help of Lydia and Henley, I really was okay with it."

He studies me, like he's soaking it all in.

"When my knee got crushed in that fight, they told me I'd walk without a limp again, but that I'd never be able to play sports. Some days it hurts worse than others, but losing basketball… It hurt worse than the physical pain I endured to get back to walking," he says quietly.

I nod slowly. "You don't know how much you use a limb until it's suddenly gone," I say, acknowledging where he's going.

"At least I got to keep my leg," he says on a sigh. "I spent a long time wallowing in self-pity. Here you are being awesome with it."

"I wasn't always so awesome. I wallowed in my own pity pit too. It's part of the healing process," I say with a shrug. "You mourn the things you *will* lose more than anything. I just learned to want new things. Not to mention, I was lucky to even survive the blood loss, so that put things into perspective for me. Acceptance heals all."

He smirks, nodding again while absently staring over my head.

"Do you regret that fight?" I ask him, pulling my knees up to my chest.

I really want this arm off, but I want to know more about him even worse.

"Not even a little bit," he says on a sigh while meeting my gaze again. There's nothing but truth there. "If I had it to do all over again, I'd still end up in that fight."

"Why? Because they hurt that guy on your team? He was fine."

"Wick was fine. Just had a concussion," he agrees. "When they took that cheap shot and knocked him to the court, I played the game of my life that night. I threw up garbage and sank buckets with it. Everything I tossed up was good for at least two, sometimes three. I ended up with triple doubles and left as the highest scoring player in a game in Trojan history that night. We went on to the state championship because of that game. The fight had nothing to do with Wick. I handled that on the court."

Confused, I purse my lips. "Then why fight?"

"We were all at the after party that night, celebrating. A friend of ours had a massive cabin we partied at a lot. Wick was there, even though he couldn't drink. I was three shots in when I noticed my sister was missing. Long story short, I found her in one of the bedrooms, and she was screaming when I kicked the door down. The bastards had her tied down, but she was still fully clothed. I barely made it in time. They were going to punish me through her, since I ended their season with an embarrassing blowout. I lost it. Seven fucking guys. I was holding my own when they came at me two at a time. It wasn't until they all jumped me at once that I ended up on my back, and the baseball bat came down. It's a sickening sound to hear your own bone crunch, to actually hear the sound of all your dreams being shattered."

He blows out a heavy breath, and I nod. If anyone understands that last part, I do.

"I was wrong," I say quietly. "Violence was definitely acceptable."

He clears his throat, shifting his weight a little.

"I haven't told anyone about my sister besides Anderson, my parents, your mother, and now you. That's why I'm here for Anderson. He was there for me. It's why I can excuse his womanizing ways, because my parents kicked me out when I was no longer a prime candidate for college scouts. They refused to let my sister go to the police because she would have been labeled a slut. That's how things work, according to them. And when I needed the money for college, your mother paid my way, not expecting a dime back, even though I paid back every cent."

That's definitely the mother I used to know… before she left my father in a thousand tiny pieces to go be a wealthy woman. It also explains why Roman spends any amount of time with my twerp stepbrother and my superficial mother.

"I was dating Emily Lawrence at the time," he goes on, grumbling a little. "She dumped me once I no longer had an athletic future ahead of me."

I'm a bobble-head doll, nodding once again, remembering Emily. She was definitely a jock bunny, but it sucks to hear that there wasn't more to her than that.

"Some people want what we have, instead of what we are." It sounds philosophical, but it's all I can think to say.

"Anyone in your life?" he asks, clearing his throat.

Is he suddenly nervous?

"No. Single. Last guy I was serious with decided he couldn't handle the one-arm thing. He didn't mind it when I was wearing a prosthetic, but it eventually weighed on him having to see me without an arm. I take it off to sleep, and, with the exception of this one, I only ever wore the arm when I went out."

My robo hand twitches, as if it knows it's being talked about. Damn rogue arm. It's caused enough problems for the night.

Roman looks confused.

"Most of the arms are just for aesthetics," I explain, shrugging. "If they weren't just for looks, then they weren't really functional past certain tasks they may have been designed for. If I wasn't doing those tasks, it was annoying to keep the arm on."

He shakes his head. "Just trying to see what the problem was. How long did you date?"

That's... not what I was expecting. "A little over six months. Not all guys can handle an awesome girl with just one arm," I quip, keeping my tone light so he doesn't start to pity me.

"But your tits definitely make up for the fact you only have one arm," he deadpans.

Grinning, I make a show of glancing down at my perky, slightly large ladies. "Funny, I said the same thing. Guess he wasn't a breast guy." I shrug, still grinning.

My eyes meet his when he flashes a full smile at me, and I feel a weight off my chest when there's not an ounce of pity in those blues.

"I'm all about tits and ass. Legs are next. Eyes are after that. Then the mind... Arms are last on the criteria," he goes on, pushing away from the dresser as his grin broadens.

So much for not giving in to Roman Hunt.

"Quite the charmer," I say, even though it doesn't come out with as much snark as I want. It sounds more breathy, giving me away.

His eyebrows bounce. "So you've been wooed?"

"I never got those chocolates," I reply, still hoping to delay the possible fireworks. If his sexing is anywhere nearly as good as his kissing... I'll be in love by the morning.

Sexing? Did I really just think sexing?

My robo hand suddenly grabs and cups my... sex. *Oh no. Oh fuck me.*

"No!" I shout when robo hand starts trying to pull my pants down, probably to actually fuck me with those damn metal fingers that are *not* meant for masturbation. "Don't you dare!"

Robo hand hesitates, still shoved halfway down my pants, and I start unstrapping the harness frantically. "What are you doing?" Roman asks me, reminding me that he's witnessing this horrifying moment.

"I have to get it off!" I snap. Robo hand hears that command all wrong, and it starts shoving down my pants again, and my eyes watch in horror as it tears my underwear off.

"No! Not you! I have to get you off! I don't want you getting me off!" I shout at the rogue, bitch arm.

Loud laughter snaps me out of my panicked haze, and my eyes dart to the closed door. At least ten people are laughing on the other side of it, which means they're totally hearing this all wrong.

"Have fun with that, Hunt," someone calls through the door, causing my cheeks to warm even more. "Sounds like she's a giver and not a taker. Lucky bastard."

The arm is still again, but I'm far more frozen, as Roman stares at me with his fist over his mouth, his body shaking with silent laughter.

This. Is. Hell.

Cursing, I finish undoing the harness, thinking of anything and everything to keep my damn hand from violating me. As soon as it's undone, I freeze. One step left, and I can remove my arm, but that means Roman will be seeing me without it. Even though I've overcome my insecurities for the most part, I still feel too vulnerable when there's nothing but my true arm.

"You need help or something?" Roman asks.

He's kept his distance until this moment, and now he's walking closer.

"I... should probably go back to my room," I say on a soft breath.

"Why? Because your arm is going crazy? I thought you were taking it off. I sure as hell don't want that thing anywhere near my balls after what it did to that flashlight. Hence the reason I'm over here."

He points to where he's standing, smirking like he finds this amusing. As much as I appreciate the fact he doesn't seem to mind, I also know how it feels when a guy sees me without my arm for the first time. We're only here for a few more days. There's no reason to leave myself that exposed to him.

"I have another arm in my room," I tell him, even though the moment is pretty much lost and sex is no longer as appealing to me. "But I think I should just call it a night."

I stand and start walking to the door, when he calls out, "Why?"

I don't answer. Instead, I cut through the bathroom, and thank mercy that our door is unlocked on the other side.

As soon as I'm inside, my eyes flit to where Lydia is snoring in the bed, sprawled across it like she's the only one who has to sleep in it.

I could be in Roman's bed right now. I'd probably be working on an orgasm instead of just thinking about what it would have been like. My mood was soured, and his would have been too if I'd taken the time to go change into another arm.

I bet Henley is getting fucked right now. Two-armed girls have all the fun.

Blowing out a frustrated breath, I finish removing my arm, my socket, and my liner, then send dad a message.

ME: My arm violated me tonight. To be more precise: It tried to fuck me. I'm not wearing it again until you fix it.

Even though it's closing in on two in the morning, it's likely he's still awake. I don't wait for a response from him.

Instead, I stare out the window, watching the flashlights flicker from all around as everyone closes in on the elusive treasure as I pull off my clothes. My ripped up "Fun Zone" panties fall to the ground with my pants that they were caught in.

Stupid savage arm. I liked those panties.

Just as I get changed into a long T-shirt, someone knocks at the door. Damn Henley.

"Forget your key?" I ask as Lydia snores on, and I open the door to—

A squeal leaves me when I'm suddenly being jerked out of the room by my hips and slammed against a wall in the hallway. My wide eyes lock with Roman's a second before his lips come down on mine, and I'm lost, kissing him back as his tongue slips in and demands all my attention.

I moan against his mouth as he essentially devours me, because it's definitely more than a kiss. The fingers of my right hand find silky hair to hold onto, and his hands slide down to my ass, jerking me closer until I feel every hard inch of him straining through his pants.

He tears his mouth away from mine, leaning back enough so that his hungry eyes sear a hole through me.

"Pretty tired of you taking off when I'm not finished," he says before his lips seize control of mine again.

I'm still holding onto his hair, and I don't let go, using my grip to pull him even closer. His hands roam over my body until he suddenly bends and lifts me, never breaking the kiss. I don't fight him when he lifts me. Nope. I wrap my legs around his waist, forgetting all about the fact I'm not wearing panties under this shirt until his hands grab bare flesh on my ass.

He groans against my lips and stumbles as he grips me tighter. I grind against him like a shameless girl with one thing on my mind. So much for that mood being soured.

I try to reach for him with my other hand, and it isn't until then that I remember I removed it. He's too busy kissing me stupid for me to think about it for too long. When I hear a door shut somewhere, I realize we've made it back into his room, and my breath catches when he drops me to the bed.

His eyes are trained where my shirt has risen up. I'm damn glad I got that wax job before coming here, considering he seems to be intent on getting an eyeful.

"I feel underdressed next to you," I say, leaning back on my elbows. Well, what little bit of elbow I have on one arm, that is.

His eyes flick up to meet mine, and he stumbles as he starts ripping his shirt over his head. A grin flits across my lips as he curses his pants. One thing is for sure; I could stare at his body all day, so I don't get annoyed with how long it takes him to finally battle his pants down. I also don't point out that I can do it quicker with just one hand. It seems a little bit like bragging, after all.

I do, however, go ahead and toss my shirt aside, since I don't want him to take all day getting me the rest of the way naked.

My thoughts cease when he finally shoves his jeans and boxers down at the same time, because I think he really does stay hard all the time. My eyes glue themselves to that part of his body as he starts moving toward me. It's not until he grabs my legs and jerks me down to the end of the bed that my eyes pop up to find him smirking at me.

Before I can ask what he's doing, his head disappears between the V of my thighs, and my hand grabs and twists in the sheet. My eyes roll back in my head when his lips fasten onto that bundle of nerves, not playing games as he flicks his tongue and sucks in unison.

I think I call him amazing, or perhaps I call him a fucking clit-owning legend… Not sure. I'm too busy moaning to keep up with what praises I'm dealing out. Something loud thumps from somewhere distant, but nothing matters besides Roman and what he's doing to me.

My stomach muscles tighten, and I can't decide if I want to push him away or pull him closer when it starts to feel too good. When it hits, it crackles across my body and rolls through me like a euphoric tidal wave. My back arches, and another string of random praises release from my loose lips as I cry out his name. Yes, I really just freaking screamed his name like a porn star.

I'm panting, and writhing, and begging him to stop or never to stop... Not really sure which. He breaks away, slowly climbing over my body as I watch him, unable to move.

When he finally slides over me fully, he reaches past me, grabbing something from the nightstand. I smile when I hear the distinct sound of paper crinkling.

He brings the condom to his mouth, uses his teeth to help tear it open, watching me the entire time. My hand comes up and discreetly slides into his hair, checking to make sure I didn't leave him with any bald patches.

His hand moves between us, and my legs slide up higher, my skin rubbing against his as I move them. He shudders like the motion is driving him insane, and that seductively powerful feeling uncoils inside me.

I've always liked sex. However, feeling sexy isn't as easy as it used to be. But right now... with the way he's looking at me and reacting to me... I've never felt sexier.

You can't fake that kind of lust, and I really like it.

Something thumping in the background dully registers as Roman shifts, keeping his eyes fixed on mine like he wants to make sure I see him and only him. My breath catches in my throat when his hips rock, and I feel him right where I want him.

With an agonizingly slow pace, he starts to push in, and I whimper while trying to rock my hips, urging him to move faster. Unfortunately, he has me pinned with his body, and all the control is his when he grabs my one hand. Our fingers interlock, and his eyes stay on mine as his jaw stays tight.

Suddenly, he thrusts deep, and my entire body feels full. I fight hard to keep my eyes open, because I can't help but love that look in his gaze. His lips brush mine, but he doesn't kiss me as he slowly rocks in and out, taking his time, and driving me insane.

He lifts up, barely separating our bodies, and his pace quickens as he starts driving in from the perfect angle, hitting everything just right until that knot balls up in my core, just waiting to explode.

My eyes finally shut when I can't take it any longer, and it snaps something in him as the pace becomes punishing, almost too good all over again. He doesn't make a sound, but I'm making enough noise for the both of us.

And then, that thread breaks, and that explosion really does happen twice as powerfully as before. My body seizes, stiffening like I can't take all the pleasure at once, as it washes over me and weighs me down.

Roman releases some guttural noise, and his hips jerk harder until he suddenly stills inside me. A slow grin crawls across my face as he collapses to me, and I stroke his hair with my fingers as his head rests against the crook of my neck.

He's breathing heavily as he pulls out of me, and one of his hands glides down my side, tickling me enough to make me giggle. I can feel him smile against my neck before he lifts his head and peers down at me.

"Just think," he says, sounding a little breathless, "you almost missed out on that."

"I was just waiting on chocolates," I say with a long sigh.

He rolls his eyes while lifting off me, and I watch as he stands and gets rid of the condom in the trashcan next to the door. His muscles flex in his ass as he walks over and grabs two bottles of water from the mini fridge, and he cocks an eyebrow at me when he turns around and catches where my gaze has been.

I don't even pretend that I wasn't appreciating the view of his ass as he moves back toward me, completely naked. He's incredibly comfortable with his body, and I really like that.

WORTH IT

When he sits down and hands me a bottle of water, I take it. His eyes drop to my missing arm, and I tense. "Shit, I can open that," he says, looking up and reaching for the bottle.

I ignore him, since I already have the bottle between my legs, and I twist the cap off with my hand and lift it to my lips. "Not my first rodeo," I remind him, smirking when he fidgets like he's nervous.

His eyes drop to my missing arm again, but I pretend to not let it bother me. At least until he lifts his hand like he's going to touch it.

I back away, and he lifts his eyes to mine. His look is questioning, as if he's asking for permission. Instead of speaking or moving, I just drink the water like it's vodka. Is there any vodka? Vodka would be awesome.

His hand glides over the sensitive flesh, and goosebumps pebble my skin. A slight tremor racks my body, but he doesn't seem to notice. When he leans down, I tense for a new reason. The last thing I need is another guy with that freaky fetish. But Roman just places a sweet kiss on the inside of my elbow before leaning back up.

His eyes drop to my bare chest, and he blows out a long breath. "I didn't even take the time to show them the attention they deserve," he sighs.

My lips twitch, and I open my mouth for some witty retort, when a scream pierces the air.

Roman's eyes widen and freeze on mine, and I stare right back. Neither of us move until the second scream.

"Lydia!" I squeal, scrambling off the bed and grabbing the sheet, wrapping it around me the best I can as Roman dives through the adjoining bathroom, and crashes into the bedroom—still naked. Yep.

I barge in behind him, flipping on the light. But I get tripped up in the sheet, and stumble into Roman's back. I bounce down to the ground, landing right on my damn ass.

Lydia screams again, but her eyes are wide in her head as she stares at Roman's cock.

He curses, and grabs a random shirt from the back of a chair, and he covers his dangling man with that. It's a pink and purple shirt, which makes this entire situation that much more awesome.

When color darkens his cheeks, I start laughing, but then my laughter dies when I remember why we came in here.

"Why the hell are you screaming?" I ask Lydia, struggling to get up and keep the sheet in place.

Her eyes dart away from Roman, and her gaze rakes around the room until it lands on… robo arm.

Damn it!

Robo arm is on the floor, flopping around like it's chasing something. It's then I remember hearing a constant thumping while Roman and I were… *Oh…*

"That damn thing scared the hell out of me!" Lydia says as she covers her heart with her hand. "I got up to pee, and I heard something thumping, then it hit my ankle. I didn't know what it was. Sorry." Her eyes move between the two of us as robo arm continues to flail on the ground. "Really sorry," she adds, grimacing.

I reach back and feel my patch on the back of my neck. Damn. I forgot to remove it.

"Oops," I say, peeling it off and holding it up at Lydia, who is as red as a tomato right now and doing all she can to not look at Roman again.

"I… um… yeah. Clothes. Room. Bye," Roman says, turning and walking toward the door. "Join me after you lock up your arm," he adds, quickly retreating the second the bathroom door opens.

I bet he's never had to say those words after sex before. I'm totally memorable now. He'll forever remember the time he fucked his friend's stepsister at the wedding, and she had to lock her arm up before rejoining him.

I'm legendary status now.

Heh.

Lydia turns and gives me an I-know-you-didn't look. "Really? So that arm was reacting to you two having sex because it thought it was still connected?" she whisper-yells.

I shrug, trying not to laugh.

Holding the sheet under my left armpit, I use my right hand to put the patch in the metal box dad sent for recharging. The second it's inside, robo arm goes dead still.

Lydia sighs while picking it up, and I smirk as she glares at it like the arm has wronged her.

"Sorry," I say as she puts it down.

"You know, for a metal arm, it doesn't weigh very much."

"I'll tell you all about it later," I say, watching as her face turns redder.

"Right. Yeah. Well, I'll just pee and...er...go back to bed," she says, scrambling into the bathroom.

I snicker as I plug the motionless arm up to its charging port, and I glance at my phone to see if Dad has messaged back.

He has.

Three times.

He usually does everything in threes. He once overshared and told me he made it his goal to give my mother three orgasms every time they slept together, which is why he couldn't understand her cheating on him.

Ewwwwww!

DAD: That's...I have no words for that. Were you thinking of masturbation?

DAD: Don't answer that. The scientist in me needs to know, but the father in me can't stomach the answer.

DAD: I'll meet you in town tomorrow if you can get away from the house. I'm driving out now. Just message me a time, and I'll give you my hotel information.

Lydia walks back out of the bathroom, and I put my phone down as she glances over her shoulder then back at me.

"I really think I need to get laid. The most action I've had since Anderson was your sex hand brushing my ankle," she groans.

My lips twitch as she shakes her head and collapses on the massive bed. I stare at the bathroom door, wondering if his invitation was sincere or just—

"Get your ass in here, Jensen," Roman says through the other door, ending my internal struggle.

Grinning, I head back inside, shut and lock the door, and lean against it as my gaze rakes across a very naked, very amused man on the bed.

"Is your life always so entertaining?" he asks.

I push away from the door and slowly walk toward him. No words seem necessary when he pulls me down on top of him, and his lips seek mine in a kiss that has all the craziness of the past few minutes melting into a distant memory.

For now, it's just us in this little bubble. I'll worry about tomorrow… tomorrow.

CHAPTER NINE

Henley

Sunlight beams through the curtains, and I reluctantly drag my eyes open. My whole body aches in the best way. A few more days with Davis, and I might never walk again. I had every intention of going back to my room last night, but we kept at it until dawn, and then I couldn't summon the strength to put my underwear on, much less go anywhere.

My bladder is screaming at me, and the sound of the shower kicking on doesn't help. I dress quickly and creep out of the room, hoping to make it across the hall without being seen in my walk of shame clothes from last night. So, of course, not only is Gretchen, the pucker-faced maid of honor standing in the hall, but Kasha's mother, Monica, is right beside her.

"What do you mean the decorator didn't show?" Monica shrieks, and Gretchen winces, recoiling.

"I-I called them weeks ago. They were supposed to be here yesterday. I don't know what happened," Gretchen cries.

"This was the only thing you had to do! Just plan the Ladies Night. And you couldn't even do that! Ugh! Fix it!"

Ladies' night is snooty code for a bachelorette party. Because strippers and booze would be so uncouth, a night of wine and god knows what boring activities are planned for tonight. I can't say I'm too disappointed something screwed it up.

Gretchen glances at me with a pleading look, and I sigh. There's no reason she should expect me to intervene with Monica chewing her ass out.

Roman's door pops open and Kasha steps out. Looks like I'm not the only one who spent the night under a hot guy. The look on her face when she's confronted with Gretchen and her mother makes me snort with laughter.

"What the hell are you yelling about?" she asks, while her mom's gaze sweeps over her with disdain.

"Ladies' night is ruined. The decorator didn't show and now the entertainment has canceled." Kasha rolls her eyes at Monica's dramatic reaction.

It strikes me this may be a perfect opportunity to cause some trouble and have some fun. "Kasha and I can handle it," I volunteer.

I don't know who looks more shocked, Kasha or her mother. A weird smile flashes across Gretchen's face, but she quickly reins it in. Or maybe it's a Botox side effect, I don't know.

Monica looks doubtful, but turns to her daughter. "We want to have a classy get together for the women. Nothing inappropriate or raunchy. Do you think you can handle that?"

I nod behind her back, and Kasha sighs. "Where are we holding it?"

"The ballroom. I've had a stage erected on the south side. The cases of pink champagne have arrived, and the caterer is set. We need a decorator and an entertainer... today."

"We can take care of it," I blurt, and Kasha raises her eyebrows at me before turning to her mother.

"We'll handle it."

A bright smile, faker than spray cheese in a can, blooms on her mother's face. "Thank you, dear. The guests should arrive around eight." She hands Kasha a credit card, and her face crumples into a scowl as she regards Gretchen. "You need to come with me. Jane needs us to help her find a new dress."

"Yes, ma'am." Gretchen gives me and Kasha a grateful smile. "Thank you."

Not exactly what I expected from a well-known harpy, but I dismiss my instant suspicion and turn my attention to Kasha, giving her an exaggerated head-to-toe inspection. "Have fun last night?"

"Three orgasms' worth," she replies, leading the way back into our room. "Why the hell did you volunteer us for that lame party?"

"So we can jack it up. Get with the program, girl. Did he fuck your brains out? We can have a real bachelorette party. Strippers, dirty games, penises everywhere."

Kasha grins. "If we're going to get it together in time, we'd better get going."

Lydia comes out of the bathroom, smiling and shaking her head at us. "You sluts," she teases. "You both look like you've been rode hard and put away wet."

"I'm not a slut. I just have a friendly vagina," I toss back, and head off to shower, leaving Kasha to tell our plans to Lydia.

Kasha solves the entertainment problem with a few phone calls. "You seriously hired strippers?" Lydia asks, giggling.

"I'm sure there will be no shortage of half-naked dancers at the bachelor party tomorrow night," I point out. "Fair is fair."

Kasha snorts. "No way. My mother had her hand in that, too. It'll be as dull as Anderson's personality." She smiles and adds, "Maybe I should call the entertainment company back."

"One sabotage at a time," I laugh, leading the way into a shop called Scarlet Toys. We've come to the right place for penises. It's cocks galore. Dick city. Weiner haven. You get the picture.

Kasha grabs a huge inflatable strap-on penis and fastens it around her. Complete with two furry balls, it hangs down, nearly touching the floor. Lydia isn't paying attention, she's too busy perusing a shelf of edible underwear until Kasha runs up behind her, thrusting her hips and shoving the giant balloon cock against her ass.

Lydia squeals, and the salesperson on duty approaches, laughing with us. "Hi, I'm Sandy. Can I help you find something?"

"We need to perv up a prissy bachelorette party," I reply, trying not to laugh as Kasha chases Lydia down the aisle, still thrusting.

"Well, we have plenty to choose from." The young woman gestures toward Kasha, who is now sneaking up behind an unsuspecting man looking at the porno movies. No... she wouldn't.

She does. Just starts dancing behind the guy and humping him from behind with her big blue penis. Why is she singing *Danger Zone*?

"Those inflatables are made to joust. You each wear or hold one and try to knock down your opponent. They're heavier than they look."

I can imagine the look on Monica's face at that competition. "Perfect. Do they come in pink?"

"Absolutely."

"We'll take two."

Lydia and Kasha return while Sandy is showing me a massive penis fountain. I don't mean it's a fountain that sprays penises, although that'd be something to see. It's a large punch bowl with a thick, peach-colored cock rising up from the middle, and I have to admire the attention to detail, tracing the veins with a fingertip.

It's set up in a corner of the store, already filled with water, and when Sandy turns it on, water spurts out the tip and runs down the shaft into the bowl.

"We could use this for the champagne, surround it with those wine glasses," I suggest, pointing out a set of glasses with a man posing in a thong.

"The thong disappears when you pour in a cold drink," Sandy informs me.

"Sold!" Kasha cries, moving on to the next aisle.

We spend the next hour sorting through all types of dirty toys and party favors, finally emerging loaded down with bags.

"Your mom is going to shit a brick, Kasha. Are we taking this too far?" I ask, sliding into the driver's seat.

"She needs to pull the stick out of her ass. Besides, she'll be dress shopping all day. By the time she sees the ballroom, it'll be too late."

"What time are the strippers supposed to show?" Lydia asks.

"Ten. Everyone should be nice and drunk by then." She turns to look at Lydia in the backseat. "You're coming, aren't you? I'm sure Anderson won't be there."

"I wouldn't miss it."

As soon as we return, we carry all of our purchases into the ballroom, then lock the massive doors behind us. I know Kasha's mom expected us to hire a decorator, but we've got this covered.

Half the room is filled with round tables, covered by pale pink tablecloths, and Kasha wastes no time trimming the edges of them with a string of tiny, glow-in-the-dark ball sacks. I set up the long tables meant for the food and place the penis fountain in the center, surrounding it with the vanishing thong wine glasses.

I can't resist filling one with cold water to see if the thong will really disappear. "What the hell?" Lydia comes up from behind me as the guy's limited clothing dissolves, leaving an oddly shaped dick. "It's bent. It looks like he's been fucking around a corner."

"What are we going to do about music?" I ask. "I'm sure whatever your mom planned to pipe in would put a speed freak to sleep."

"I'll take care of it," Lydia volunteers. "Simon Carr is an A/V tech. He owes me a favor."

Kasha grins. "And what did you do to earn a favor from Simon?"

Simon Carr was a year behind us in high school. I don't remember much about him, other than he was a geek who hung out with the other geeks. I noticed him at the obstacle course yesterday and... whew, he's grown up. If I wasn't busy being nailed to the bed by Davis, I'd have given him a go.

"I blew him under the table."

Kasha's jaw drops and Lydia bursts out laughing. "I pretended to be his girlfriend for a few minutes to get rid of some chick who was flirting with him. Get your mind out of the gutter."

"Her mind lives in the gutter," I laugh.

The catering company shows up just after Lydia rushes off to find Simon. The man in charge approaches us, glancing around at the myriad of cocks with a barely restrained smile. "Should we go ahead and set up?"

"The kitchen is right through that door and down the hall," Kasha informs him, pointing to an ornate door now covered with a "Pin the Penis on the Hunk" game.

Deep, rumbling laughter draws my eyes to the other doorway where I'm greeted by Davis's brilliant smile. He's dressed in only shorts and running shoes, a towel slung over his shoulder, sweat drying on his chest. He picks up one of the inflatable dicks and holds it up as I close the distance between us. "If you wanted a big cock, you could've just come to my room."

God, he fucked me half to death last night and I already want him again. His dark hair flops over his forehead and he shoves it back absently, his oil-drop eyes seizing mine. "Later, marathon man. I have every intention of getting wasted tonight and taking advantage of you."

The room rotates as he spins me, pinning me against the wall. "You have no idea what you do to me, do you?" His hand clutches the back of my neck, tilting my head up until our gazes lock. I'm imprisoned by six feet of hot, sweaty male. His hips roll against mine, showing me he's hard as a stone.

"I have a general idea," I reply, slipping my hand between us to skim over his bulge.

His eyes fall shut and open again, full of fire. "No, you don't. You don't have a fucking clue, but you will. I'm going to spend hours kissing every part of your body so I can hear you whimper and moan and beg while I watch you writhe under me."

Damn, that's the hottest thing a man has ever said to me, and it takes a second for my brain to re-engage. He smirks and murmurs, "Speechless, I like it." His lips land on mine for a brief second and then he's gone, striding out of the room with a wave at Kasha.

Shit. I'm in trouble.

Kasha and I make our way down to the ballroom a few minutes before the first of the guests are due to arrive. Kasha's mother informed her by text that she'll be late, and Kasha assured her that Ladies' Night was well under control.

We meet Gretchen in the hall and she gives us a reluctant smile. "I barely made it back in time. Did you manage to find a decorator? And the entertainment?"

"It's all taken care of," Kasha says with a fake smile. "See for yourself."

Kasha throws open the doors and saunters in, Gretchen right on her tail. The room is dimly lit, allowing the glow in the dark balls trimming the tables to stand out, along with the penis shaped candles that burn in the centerpieces.

The elaborate spread of fancy finger foods and hors d'oeuvres are a wonderful backdrop to the penis now spurting pink champagne out of the tip. Gretchen turns and shoots daggers at Kasha, who just smiles.

"You bitch! Monica is going to lose her shit!" She looks around as if she's still trying to convince herself she just walked into dong central. Her gaze returns to Kasha, her eyes narrowing. "It's been you. Anderson and the porta-potty, the rotten eggs, destroying the wedding dress, all of it. You're trying to sabotage the wedding."

"You're being ridiculous," I intervene, grabbing a wine glass and holding it under the fountain. "Here, have a drink. It'll loosen you up." Her lips snarl at the offered glass. "Look, the guests are arriving," I add as women begin to flow in, dressed for a black tie event that obviously... isn't.

"You're both going to pay for this," she threatens and stalks away.

Club music suddenly fills the air with a pulsing beat, and I grin at Kasha. "Guess Simon came through."

"Guess so," she agrees. "Lydia better show up. She promised to get here before the strippers."

"Well, guess we better play hostess since Gretchen split." I grab two glasses and fill them from the fountain. "Welcome to the party, ladies! Jane will be here soon. In the meantime, have a drink!"

A group of women head my way, a few trying to hide their smiles. "Drinks are also available at the bar," I add, gesturing to the tiny bar set up in the corner.

Jane has obviously invited women outside the wedding party because there are more than fifty women now milling around with drinks in their hands. A few have even opted to use the dick-shaped test tube necklaces, which proves my suspicion that these ladies aren't all stuck up prudes, no matter how they behave in polite society.

We saw it that first night when Kasha spiked the refreshments and I hijacked the music. They just need a little alcohol to strip away those inhibitions, not to mention years of conditioning.

By the time Lydia shows up over an hour later, the ballroom is filled with laughing, chatting women, a few showing off their moves on the dance floor, despite their fancy attire. Gretchen is seething over by the dick fountain, watching the fun with a hateful glare.

"Wow," Lydia exclaims as more women make their way inside. "I can't believe Jane invited so many people."

"She didn't," Kasha admits with a devious grin. "I may have tweeted about a big party tonight."

That explains why most of the new guests aren't dressed to the nines like the others. It doesn't explain why some of them are holding vibrators, and even comparing them.

"And why did they bring their sex toys?"

Kasha shrugs. "Vibrator race. First place wins the dick fountain at the end of the night."

Lydia giggles. "How the hell do you race vibrators?"

"Easy. Put them on the floor and see which rattles across the finish line first. Mom and Jane will love it."

I sling my arm around Kasha's shoulders. "We have to be friends until death. I'd be completely terrified of you otherwise."

"Best bitches until the end," she agrees, pulling Lydia in for a three-way hug. "Now, let's have a dick fight."

Laughing, I down another shot and poke her. "You're on."

A few minutes later, the ballroom sounds more like a frat party. A circle of drunk women cheer us on as Kasha and I don the huge inflatable dicks and do our best to knock the other over. I finally get the best of her, and she falls on her stomach. After what she did to the guy at the toy shop, I can't resist jumping on her back and humping her to the excited cheers of the crowd.

Raising my hands in the air as if I've just won a boxing match, I dance around, the big dick flopping against the floor. After helping Kasha to her feet, I turn and come face to face with Monica.

You know all those cartoons where smoke sprays from the character's ears and the top of their head shoots off? Yeah, that's exactly what she looks like.

Jane stands beside her, her mouth open in horror as I remove the dick, and a woman dressed in an evening gown straps it on. Kasha hands hers to a skinny chick with blue hair, and jogs over to us. "Mother! About time you showed up. You can go next," she says, gesturing to the women now beating each other senseless while the guests egg them on.

For a few seconds, I don't think Monica is going to answer, but finally she speaks through gritted teeth. "I can't believe you. I expected more from you, but I guess I should've known better. This is it, Kasha. Don't you dare show your face at the rehearsal dinner. I'm not giving you another chance to embarrass our family."

She stalks off without giving Kasha time to reply, and Jane sneers at us before making her way over to Gretchen. Gretchen lays a sympathetic hand on her shoulder and gives her a glass of champagne.

"Are you all right?" I ask Kasha, and she grins, pointing to the door. "I'm great. About to be better. The strippers are here."

Lydia snorts. "Oh hell, your mom might have us thrown out of here."

"Monica make a scene? Never. Come on, let's show the men where to go."

"I know where I want that one to go," Lydia says, tilting her head toward a big, beefy blond.

"How long did you hire them for?" I ask.

"Three hours. They'll put on a show, then stay to do lap dances."

"Dibs on the Jesse Williams lookalike," I tell them, as we make our way to the doorway full of muscle men.

"Holy shit, he does look like him!" Kasha exclaims.

Kasha places two glasses of pink champagne on the table in front of Lydia and me. "Drink up, girls. The show is about to start."

Kasha drains her glass, but Lydia scoots hers across the table. "I've already had a few shots and I want to remember this tomorrow."

A young, lean man walks onto the stage and taps the mic, causing a flood of liquored up women to stampede, trying to be in the front row. "Well, hello, beautiful ladies! Is everyone excited?"

The response is deafening and Kasha beams at me. Yeah, maybe her mother and the bride don't consider this a proper Ladies' Night, but it's a kick-ass bachelorette party.

"Now, before I introduce the men, we have a couple of rules. First, since this is a private event, you are allowed to touch."

Again, an ear-splitting cheer rolls across the room. "But, please, let the guys decide what clothing to remove. No stripping them."

"Not even with my teeth?" a woman yells.

"Sorry, pretty lady. No teeth. Now, are you ready to meet the men of Ravage?"

Christ, these women are going to bust my eardrums. Lydia, Kasha, and I make our way through the crowd to the edge of the stage just as four too-gorgeous-for-life men stalk onstage dressed as firefighters. My heart starts to race and I feel my face getting hot while we watch the choreographed seduction playing out before us.

Shirts are ripped off and thrown into the audience, revealing sweaty, rippled abs. Breakaway pants go next, leaving them in tiny thongs and bikini briefs. They said we could touch, right? Fuck, do I ever want to touch! Especially the Jesse Williams lookalike dancing right in front of me.

Caramel colored skin and light green eyes. A chilling tingle races down my spine, and for a second I'm struck with a hint of nausea before a rush of sensation overtakes me. What the hell? And suddenly, I recognize the feeling.

I grab Kasha's arm. "Oh shit. I'm rolling!" Still dancing, she takes a break from screaming at the guys to "show her some stripper dick."

"What?"

"It's molly!"

With her eyes still glued to the stage, she asks, "Who the hell is Molly?"

"No, ecstasy! I took it a few times when I was a teenager. This is how it feels!"

"Where the hell did you get ecstasy?"

"I didn't! Someone must've dosed me."

Now I have her attention. "Are you serious?"

"Yes!"

A look of realization washes across her face. "I've never done it. Does it make you feel sort of jumpy? Excited?"

"At first," I reply with a nod, and her eyes widen.

"Shit. I think someone drugged us both. Who the hell would do that?"

My gaze sweeps around the room, taking in the scene from a new perspective. These normally uptight pageant girls aren't just screaming and dancing. They're all over the strippers who have now made their way off the stage. They're grinding on them, slapping and grabbing asses, and not just on the men, but each other as well.

"It's not just us." I grab Kasha's head and turn it toward the near orgy taking place on the dance floor. Damn, her hair is soft.

"Why are you petting me?" she laughs.

"Sorry."

"Everyone is fucked up on E?" she asks, looking for Lydia, who has taken off somewhere.

"Oh fuck. Look!"

Kasha follows my finger to where her mother has her hand down the back of the blond stripper's banana hammock. Her dress is hiked up high on her thighs and she's grinding against his leg that's bent between hers. "Phone!" she demands, snorting with laughter. "Where's your phone? I left mine in the room."

Rushing back to the table, I grab my phone and hand it to Kasha, assuming she wants to call someone to get her mother out of here. Instead, she jumps onto the table and starts videotaping. "This is the best day of my life!" she crows, filming her mother grinding on the heavily muscled man. When Monica shoves her hand down the front of his underwear, he smiles and shakes his head. Pouting, she pulls it back and goes back to kneading his ass.

"These bitches are crazy!" Lydia cries, joining us. She looks up at Kasha. "What the hell?"

"Her mom," I gasp, trying to get my laughter under control. "Look at her mom!"

About the time Monica drops to her knees and licks the guy's bulge, the MC taps the mic again, drawing attention, and the guys retreat back to the stage. I give Kasha a hand getting down from the table. I swear I have never seen her laugh so hard.

"Oh god. I've got to go before I piss myself!" she cries, handing me my phone and darting off.

"Do you feel it?" I ask Lydia, who looks at me like I may have eaten paint chips as a kid.

"Feel what?"

"The ecstasy! I'm rolling my ass off."

Her jaw drops. "You took ecstasy?"

"No! Someone slipped it to us… to everyone, apparently."

Understanding fills her eyes as she surveys the crowd of women now surrounding the stage again. "Who would do that?"

"I don't know. You don't feel anything?"

"No, maybe it's in the champagne. I didn't drink any."

"Well, have a glass! This is the most fun I've had in years!" I crow.

"Uh-huh," she agrees, a patronizing smile on her face. "I'll be right back."

As soon as she walks off, I head toward the stage, practically elbowing my way to the front. God, it's hot in here. Kasha returns to my side, followed by Lydia, who thrusts a bottle of water at both of us.

"I'm good. I'm going to get another shot," I tell her, and she rolls her eyes.

"Drink the damn water before both of you dehydrate," she insists.

To avoid arguing, I drain the bottle and Kasha does the same. Ahh, that's better. Since when does water taste so good? "How many glasses of champagne did you have?" she asks Kasha.

"Just one," Kasha replies, not taking her eyes off of the stage.

"Henley?"

"Uh, three, I think."

Kasha and Lydia's eyes lock and they laugh together. Great. I guess I'm the only one who's this trashed. All concern about being too high fades when a dark-skinned stripper with a lean, swimmer's body walks to the center of the stage with a chair.

His smooth voice fills the room. "I hear we have a bride-to-be in the audience."

The crowd roars, pointing to Jane. I haven't seen much of her, but one look at her face and I know she's rolling as hard as me.

"Get your sexy ass up here, sweetheart," the guy calls, and two of Jane's friends drag her onstage.

Kasha smacks me, and I hand her my phone. I almost feel sorry for Jane, knowing every second of this will be caught on video. Almost.

Jane is seated on the chair and the audience hoots and cheers when he takes her hands and starts to roll his hips, putting his bulge right in her face. She licks her lips and grabs his bare ass cheeks, nearly tearing his thong, and jerks him closer. He shifts so she ends up licking his stomach instead of her target.

"Oh my god!" Lydia laughs. "Look at Ms. Proper!"

Two more men walk out, one on each side of Jane, and place two more chairs on stage. They walk to the edge and their gazes sweep over the crowd, trying to decide who's next. The Jesse Williams lookalike eyes me. I've never really understood the expression "my heart's in my throat" until he grabs my hand and tugs me onto the stage.

Kasha and Lydia are yelling and urging me on. Like I need it. I'm high as hell, and a near-naked, perfect specimen of a man is dancing on me. My hands have a mind of their own. Shut up. That's my excuse and I'm sticking to it. How else did they end up running over the hard planes of his sweaty abdomen?

His skin is baby smooth and warm. He leans to whisper in my ear, pushing my temperature through the roof. "I've been watching you, sexy. Your eyes have been on me all night."

Can't find words. My brain is frozen. He catches my earlobe between his lips for a moment before pulling back and gazing down at me with a naughty smile. All I can do is stare at those thick, luscious lips while I run my fingers over every inch of skin I can reach. Can you kiss a stripper? He ends my indecision by kissing the corner of my mouth before planting his lips on mine. The tip of his tongue traces my lips, and suddenly, the room tilts, sending a slight wave of nausea through me. What the fuck?

"That's enough of that," Davis growls, and I'm carried off stage over his shoulder. What's he doing here? Why did he grab me, and how does he always smell so damn good? I reach down and resume my night of feeling up hot men by grabbing two handfuls of firm ass.

An upside down Kasha waves as I'm carried out of the ballroom. "Put me down!" I laugh, still squeezing his ass. His lounging pants are smooth and silky, so I start running my fingers over them instead.

"Shut up." A sharp smack on my ass makes me gasp.

"The party's not over!"

"It is for you. What did you take?"

I wobble for a second, trying to regain my equilibrium when he sets me on my feet in his room. "I didn't take anything. Someone spiked the champagne with ecstasy."

His face softens. "Are you okay?"

"I'm fantastic." I know he's done E before, since I did it with him.

My hands sneak under his shirt, and he looks at me, raising his eyebrows. "Oh, *now* you want me?"

"Mmm hmm." I shove my hand down the front of his shorts and wrap it around him.

A string of curses fly from his mouth, but he doesn't stop me. "I should spank the fuck out of you."

"Then I couldn't suck you," I argue, kneeling and pulling his pants and underwear down together. I love the way his hairy thighs feel and I rub my hands up and down them, savoring the raspy tickle on my palms.

His head falls back when I lick around the head of his cock, a pained groan echoing through the room when I take him to my throat. His hands crawl into my hair, and I love how it feels, the tingles zipping through me. The noises he makes spurs me on, and I can feel him growing thicker.

Abruptly, he steps back and pulls me to my feet. "Hey! I wasn't done with that!" I cry.

"No, you're not. It's going to be inside you all night." He grabs my chin and his eyes burn into mine. "You hear me, Hen? All night. I'm going to fuck you until you can't think of anyone but me."

"Turn around." His voice is gruff and demanding. He unzips my dress, and has me completely naked in a matter of seconds. My feet leave the ground again—what is his thing about carrying me?—and I'm tossed face down on the bed. Strong hands grip my ankles, pulling me until I'm bent over the edge.

His thick fingers plunge into me, and I groan. "So wet from sucking me. This belongs to me now, Henley. Do you need a reminder of that?"

"Yes." I'll say anything to get him inside me.

Apparently, yes is the correct answer.

CHAPTER TEN

Kasha

There's a whole lot of penis in this room. And I'm a whole lot of wiry. I want to dance, sing, and hump a chair leg all at once.

The strippers have been into the champagne. The ecstasy champagne. Hence the reason I'm seeing a lot of penis and not a lot of thong...

Whoa!

My world tilts upside down. Did I fall? No, no. I'm just tucked under some dude's arm. And there's a naked ass right by my cheek.

He bangs on *my* ass like it's a bongo drum, as a Conga line forms behind him. I don't know whether to giggle or hurl. If I hurl, it could end up in his ass crack. Probably not very nice.

Oh! Balls! I see balls! Where did we get bouncy balls?! They're huge!

Huge balls... That has me snorting to myself.

I wish I had my robo arm right now. Holding true to his word, Dad stopped in and got a hotel room. He also brought his tools with him to fix my baby. Jill is with him, since I dropped her off earlier to get worked on.

So now, I'm wearing my very pretty, realistic looking arm, but it's useless as far as functionality goes.

I'm trying to move up on Dude's hip, since my cheek keeps thudding against his ass cheek. It's a hard ass cheek. Not a squishy one.

A bruise on my cheek from a cheek… Snorting again.

The room is obnoxiously loud, and my ass is still a drum to Gorilla Hands. It's starting to sting a little.

My mother is the caboose of the Conga line, and *oh my damn*. Is she really waving her panties in the air like a freedom flag? My brain is still hurting from what I saw her doing earlier.

Trying to focus, I push up with all my strength, but Man Hands is still holding me effortlessly.

I'm seriously going to puke. His ass will be forever desecrated.

By some miracle, he finally swings me up on my feet, and I sway a little, somewhat dizzy. He grins when I glare over at him, and then he grabs my hands and jerks me to him like we're going to dance.

One problem: My pretty arm is not meant for being tugged. It has no harness. There's nothing keeping it in place if pulled hard enough.

So… he rips my arm off, and then stares in horror as I fall down to my ass.

Screams erupt, and all the intoxicated/drugged partiers start scattering away from him and me, as he starts shaking, eyes widening more and more. Sheesh, those things are going to pop right out of their sockets if his eyes get any wider.

Things can get a little awkward or super awkward from here.

I go for super awkward.

"My arm!" Insert dramatic scream of faux agony here. "You ripped off my arm! How could you!"

The look on his face is priceless as he drops the arm like it's on fire, and staggers back while turning a precarious and concerning shade of pale. You'd think he'd notice there's no blood or anything. And I'm not even close to being a good actress.

I feel bad when he suddenly turns and hurls… all over the floor… and on one girl's bare leg. It sets off a chain reaction, because the girl who gets some on her leg turns and heaves like she can't stop. From there… total ripple effect. It's like a group exorcism orgy has just spontaneously combusted, complete with mass projectile vomiting.

I've got to get out of here before I cave to peer pressure and join the new cult of lost guts.

Scrambling to my feet, I start to run, but turn around and grab my arm. Leave no body part behind, and all that.

After tucking it under my armpit, I run away from the brutal upchucking session, and rush right into the hallway. I'm looking over my shoulder like a stream of vomit is going to chase me around the corner. Just as I turn around, I slam into the body of a surprised Anderson. Who is with Roman. And about five other guys.

I stumble backwards, glaring at him like it's his fault for being in my way. No doubt I look like a crazed madwoman on the loose, given their curious expressions.

Suddenly, it's like a synchronized game of eye tennis. They all look at me, then up to my hair that is probably a hot mess, then down to my missing appendage, then over to where the fake appendage is nestled under my armpit, then back to my eyes.

Roman is the only one who looks like he wants to laugh. Everyone else looks like they're so lost and confused.

"There's ecstasy in the champagne," I blurt out randomly. I have no idea why I felt like spewing that juicy morsel. "At least I think that's what it is."

Anderson's eyebrows hit his hairline, and the humor in Roman's eyes dies as he steps closer.

Anderson barrels around me, and Roman tugs me closer, inspecting my eyes. It's really hot in here. I need water. So thirsty. So hot.

"Shit," Roman says under his breath, taking my good hand and tugging me along as my fake arm stays wedged under my armpit.

The other guys shuffle toward the ballroom as well, and Anderson runs back out of the ballroom just as we reach it. He's gagging. Oh no. It's going to happen all over again.

Roman's nose wrinkles as he peers in.

"Ecstasy makes you puke?" some guy asks.

"That... is a whole other story," I tell them. Then my eyes widen. "Is your sister in there?" I ask Roman, horrified.

"She had to leave early because of a work thing," he says, shuddering as he walks back over to my side.

Good. She can't tell him I started all that craziness in there. Morbid arm-losing theatrics are usually something that gets a few chuckles or major crickets. Projectile vomiting epidemic is actually a first.

"Come on. You need water and... a shower."

I sniff myself, but all I can smell is stripper sweat and not puke.

Then... Then I get dizzy. The last thing I remember is Roman scooping me up, and my world goes black.

Groaning, I sit up, looking around at the hella bright room... Not my room.

My eyes widen as I dart up, panicking. I reach down, feeling my lack of underwear under—*Hey!* Whose T-shirt am I wearing? Please let me be in Roman's room. This is his room, right? Did I have sex—

"No, we didn't have sex." The masculine voice has me snapping my eyes over to the doorway where an amused Roman is staring back at me. I hope I wasn't rambling aloud.

"What time is it?" I ask, so confused.

Oh! Oh no! Champagne, Puke Gate Scandal, Stripper palooza… It's all coming back to me now.

I totally witnessed my mother touching a penis. Ewwww.

"It's a little after three."

Roman's words break me out of my horrifying, scarring, traumatic memories. Losing an arm was easier to cope with than remembering my mother's nails grazing stripper penis.

"Wait… What?" I ask, looking around again like I'm magically going to hear him differently. "In the afternoon?"

He grins over at me before walking toward me. He pauses and grabs a bottle of water that looks chilled, and he hands it over after removing the cap. I guzzle that thing like I've been in the desert for eighteen years, while he climbs onto the bed, coming to sit next to me.

"Yeah. You didn't go to sleep until after four this morning. I think you should just say no to drugs in the future."

Slowly, I shake my head. "No. No. Last thing I remember is you taking me away from the… madness." I choose my words carefully. I think I've embarrassed myself enough for the time being.

He looks like he's barely holding back his laughter.

"Well, I carried you out, and I thought you'd be down for the count. However, when I got you back to the room, you were still awake. After forcing you to drink a bottle of water, I got to hear you chat about the strippers and your mother—"

"I'll be sick if you continue with that line of conversation. My stomach isn't that tough."

His grin spreads, and he chuckles lightly while getting closer, running his hand over my shoulder and up to my neck.

"Then you stripped and got naked," he says, clearly loving the way I get confused.

"I thought you said we didn't have sex."

"Really glad we didn't, since you obviously don't remember this. How could you forget making my cock sing *I Will Always Love You* to your vagina?"

My eyes widen as he bursts out laughing. "I didn't," I groan, but I bet I did. It wouldn't be my first dick chorus. Usually that comes a little later in a relationship though. You know a guy is a keeper when he lets you use your fingertips to make his pee hole move with the words like the little guy is the one belting out those awesome lyrics.

Try it. It's epic.

It's also a great way to find out where his tolerance level stands on the weird-o-meter. Usually I don't bring my vagina in for a duet though. That makes me sound like a crazy girl.

"You did," he sighs, trying to sound putout, but he can't stifle his mocking grin.

Apparently his weird-o-meter tolerance level is really high.

"How did you get naked?" I ask, trying and failing not to sound flustered.

"You made me get naked, because you demanded that my cock sing along with the music on your phone. Obviously I had to oblige just to find out what the ever-loving fuck you were talking about."

I look around aimlessly for that pesky, absent hole that never seems to swallow me up when I need it to.

His soft rumble of laughter only makes me burn a little hotter with embarrassment. One-armed girls gotta have a few more awesome attributes than those damned two-armed girls. Making his penis sing too early on is not smart. Then again, it's one week. He lives too far away for this to turn into more. Which sucks. Because I kind of like him.

Sighing and pulling myself out of my own head, I slide back on the bed so I can get comfortable against the headboard. I take in the fact he looks showered, dressed, and incredibly sexy in his jeans and collared shirt.

"Where are you going?" I ask, as though I have the right.

I don't remember what's on the docket for the wedding week today, but I'm pretty sure I'll be banned from all further festivities once my mother wakes up and remembers she had her hand on an unknown man's penis. I'm sure she also won't be too thrilled with the fact she was drugged. It was probably one of the randoms who showed up—thanks to me—but she'll blame me. I guess it is my fault, if you want to get technical about it.

"I've been helping the guys get things set up for the bachelor party tonight. You missed brunch. So did most of the other women, your mother included."

He grins, and I groan while covering my face with my hands.

"She's probably bleaching her hands."

"So, there was more to the story about your mother? Do I want to know?" he muses.

"No. Definitely not. Save yourself, because I'm already doomed to the memory being seared into my brain forever and damning me."

"I have to meet the guys in a few. The party starts at six, but we've got to go into town. Thanks to your ecstasy champagne and gross-a-thon, everything we had planned suddenly pales in comparison to your bachelorette party."

A slow smile spreads across my lips. "Want me to handle the strippers for you?" I ask innocently. "The place we used has a great variety."

"I doubt they'll come out here after last night," he says, smirking.

"I doubt they'll drink the champagne, but I still have my mother's credit card, and anyone will come if the price is right." I pause and think about that. "Anyone will *work* if the price is right. Not sure *come* is appropriate for that sentence, given the events of last night."

His eyebrows go up, but I hold my hand up, stopping him from whatever he's about to ask. "Never mind. I need to get ready and go get robo arm from my dad. I dropped it off with him at his hotel yesterday. Have you seen my pretty arm?" I ask, cringing at how ridiculous that question probably sounds to a normal person.

"I put it up in your closet last night. Stacked it next to the other two you had in there the same way they were stacked."

"Awww," I say, drawing out the word as I bat my lashes like a grateful damsel he saved from distress. "My hero."

He laughs while rolling his eyes. "Handle the strippers. Anderson said he gets some since Jane did. Drink water. Rest up. I'll come find you tonight as soon as I can slip out of the party."

A challenging grin forms on my lips. "Who says I want to see you later?"

He's suddenly on me, tugging me under him so fast that my breath catches in my throat. I open my mouth to gasp, but he seizes that opportunity to kiss me, stealing every indignant word and curse I planned to spew. And I melt like I have no brain cells as the lustful animal in me takes control.

I moan into his mouth as he lowers against me. His belly is right against the bare skin of my desperate lower half, and I grind against him. My fingers tangle in his hair, and my other arm comes up, resting against his chest as he makes my mind go completely blank.

Suddenly, he pulls back, and I kiss the air for a second before the motion registers. When my eyes open, he's staring down at me. Then, the jackass winks as he smirks and stands up, and my jaw falls open as he starts walking toward the door.

"What are you doing?" I ask, jerking the T-shirt back down into place.

"Reminding you that you want to see me later. Bye, Kasha." He turns and faces me after he opens the door, and he grins like he enjoys seeing my glare. "Lay off the drugs. I like you sober."

With that, he shuts the door, and I mutter a few curses before using the bathroom doors to go back to my room. Lydia is missing, but I find my phone easily enough.

After dialing the number, someone answers on the third ring.

"Yes, I'd like to order five strippers for the night. And I have a really special request."

As soon as I get off the phone, my door flies open. I swing around, and blow out a breath of relief when I see it's Roman stalking toward me.

"What are you—"

My words are cut off when he grabs me at the waist and drags me to him. His mouth is on mine in the next instant, and I grin against his lips as I kiss him back.

"Thought you had somewhere to be," I mumble against his lips.

"Fuck them. I can be late," he says, lifting me enough to carry me back through the bathroom and toward his room.

I giggle against the kiss as my toes swing in front of his shins.

"You never give me any warning that you're about to kiss me," I mumble, still kissing him.

"Because I never want you to try to stop me," he mumbles back.

I decide talk is overrated when his tongue starts doing mind-numbing things against mine, sending my mind into the gutter as I imagine that tongue somewhere else.

My feet touch the floor at the same time the bed touches the backs of my knees. Roman lowers me down, sliding me onto it ever so gently as he comes down on top of me, never breaking the kiss.

It's slow and savoring, and I can't stop worrying that I taste like death, because I never got to brush my teeth.

Dental hygiene gets forgotten as he slides my shirt up around my hips, finally taking advantage of the fact there's nothing on under the shirt.

His fingers brush sensitive flesh, and I shudder against him. He groans against my mouth, and then I hear the rustle of his jeans being moved down. That has me grinning again, because I love the way he seems to want me as much as I want him.

Pushing up, he sits back on his knees, his jeans hanging down past his hips, and I lick my lips as I watch him roll the condom down, slowly covering all that sexy. It's mesmerizing.

"Where the hell have you been?" he asks as he comes back down on me.

Before I can ask him what he means, he's kissing me again, and I'm getting lost in him, which seems to be too easy for me to do.

When he starts pushing in, my legs slide up, giving him better access.

I lose track of time as he draws out each thrust, slowly taking me like we have all the time in the world. Our bodies are slick with sweat in no time, and my lips are tingling from the deep, hungry kiss we've been lost in.

My fingers find his hair, and my other arm slides up his arm, gripping it the best it can. All it does is make him kiss me harder, and his thrusts get a little rougher.

When I'm crying out his name, my body is thundering like a boulder of pleasure has just rolled through it, hitting every single bit of my flesh on its way down.

It's the most powerful and most vulnerable I've ever felt in my life. Roman whispers something too soft for me to hear before he's suddenly thrusting in one last time, and his body jerks before he drops to me, breathing heavily as I grin at the vacant air in front of me.

My eyes are too heavy to open, and I'm too comfortable to move. So I wrap around him like a one-armed spider monkey and savor the moment while it lasts, trying not to fall too deep before I have to let him go.

"What are we doing?" Lydia hisses as I adjust Jill—my now fixed robo arm, according to Dad.

So far, so good. Jill hasn't tried to *Jill* me off, and I've purposely thought about masturbation without directly insinuating intent.

I pet my robo arm. "Good girl."

"What? Seriously, Kasha, stop petting Jill and answer me. What are we doing here?" Lydia says again as Henley walks away from the side. You'd think Lydia was scarred from her experience with the ballroom or something, since peering into the windows is freaking her out.

"Definitely in the pool house. I guess the ballroom wasn't clean enough to use."

"Probably smelled like thirty different varieties of vomit," I state dryly.

"So sorry I missed all that fun."

"Hey! Hello! Someone tell me why we're here, because I *still* smell like thirty varieties of vomit."

I cringe as I turn to face poor Lydia. Apparently she got caught up in the crosshairs. She really doesn't smell too pleasant. I blame all that hair. It's hard to get all that out of your hair, and, according to her, she was covered in it. I don't know, because I bailed out of there and spent the night making sweet penis music with Roman that I can't remember making.

Henley and I both got berated earlier when Lydia finally found us. Henley spent all day with Davis. I was in Roman's room until some of the guys came to drag him down. Then I had to go find my dad and get back my arm. Just a typical day in the life of Kasha Jensen.

I like Jill when she behaves.

I go back to petting my arm. Henley is giggling at a text she just got. Lydia groans.

"It's like I'm dealing with puppies!" Lydia hisses.

"Puppies?" Henley and I both ask in unison.

"Yes. Puppies. One second you're chasing your own tail, and the next you see a ball. Answer me without getting distracted. Why. Are. We. Here?!"

"Shhh," Henley and I hiss in unison. "You're going to get us caught."

"Caught doing what?" Lydia whisper-yells.

Music starts thumping from the direction of the pool house, and Henley and I share an excited look.

"Think they're here?" I ask Henley.

"Who is here?"

"Let's find out," Henley says, as we continue to annoy Lydia by purposely evading her questions.

Lydia is the good one. We're both the devils on her shoulder, versus her one angel on the other. That angel doesn't get much talking in, because we're pushy. Two to one odds run in our favor.

"What are we finding out?" Lydia whisper-yells.

"Did you already tip?" Henley asks me.

"Who?" Lydia groans.

"I tipped majorly. Monica really should ask for her credit card back. I paid for several extras."

"Extra what?" Lydia asks.

"Nipple clamps?" Henley asks seriously.

"What the actual hell?" Lydia gasps.

"No clue. I didn't really read the list. Just told them I wanted all the extras they could throw in with their most popular package. They overlooked the ecstasy fiasco."

"Who?" Lydia hisses.

We tiptoe over to the back of the pool house as the guys toast their beers. Unfortunately, no strippers yet. My eyes search the room like they can't help themselves until I find Roman. He's in a black button down shirt now, and a pair of darker jeans. We might have wrinkled his other clothes a little.

With his inky black hair, his cool blue eyes, and that devilish little smirk, he looks like gift-wrapped sin.

Yes, I'm licking my lips. Get over it.

"Why are we here?" Lydia hisses, ducking down beneath the window while her eyes widen wildly.

"To see the show," Henley says, grinning when her eyes zero in on Davis. I go back to eye-fucking Roman as we wait.

He's talking to some guy, and the guy is laughing about whatever he's said. I really hope he isn't telling him the singing penis story. Surely that would be just as embarrassing for him.

Lydia peeks over the edge.

"What are we waiting for?"

As if cued, the door swings open and in walk five women wearing trench coats. Their hair is up on their heads, bound tightly in a knot, and their lips are all wickedly red.

Game on.

My eyes flick to Roman as the guys break into a fit of cheers. He smirks but sits down in the back, watching it from a distance as the girls start walking through the room, their eyes sizing everyone up.

A woman's lips move, but I can't hear what she says. Everyone starts looking around as she steps onto a table. I look down as Henley raises the window just enough to let the sound carry better.

"Who's Anderson?" the woman asks loudly as one of the big men who came with them starts unlatching a trunk.

Someone cuts the music, making the whispers of excitement hiss louder around the room.

"I'm here!" Anderson yells, walking toward her with a massive grin on his face.

Her dark smile curves her lips, and I swallow hard. She looks seriously menacing—hot, but scary. Like she might enjoy beating the shit out of his ass and then shove her fist in it.

Maybe I should have looked at those extras I bought…

Anderson seems oblivious to the cold, ruthless look in her eyes, but Henley's eyes meet mine, and we share a panicked breath.

Lydia gasps when Mr. Security walks over and hands her a black leather thingy. Is that a riding crop? No. No, it's not. It's a cat o' nine tails.

That's not good. That's not good at all.

"You ready to play?" she asks Anderson as the other girls start picking guys.

One picks Roman, and I tense, but he shakes her off, distracting himself with his phone until she moves on to pick someone more eager. My phone buzzes in my pocket, and I snatch it out, frowning when I see Roman's name on the screen.

When did he put his number in my phone?

ROMAN: Really hope this isn't what it looks like... You didn't seriously call in dommes, did you?

Should I be worried that he spelled it correctly?

I grin like an idiot and decide not to respond, because Anderson is watching Queen Evil Eyes as she disrobes. She's wearing a black leather, lingerie-nightie thing that fits every cliché vision of a dominatrix I've ever had. And wow. She's fit. Her muscles aren't bulky, but they aren't hidden either.

Anderson's smile wavers a little. He likes his chicks soft, not muscular.

Gross. I've retained information about Anderson. That's important brain space! What if I ever need to tell someone what those plastic thingies on shoelaces are and can't remember because Anderson's female preference checklist is invading space?

Wait?! What are those plastic thingies? No!!!

"Ah fuck. Why the hell not," I hear Anderson say in amused resignation, drawing me out of my head.

Gross! When the hell did he get down to his boxers? Why is he in his boxers? No strippers asked us to undress last night. And I would have totally remembered that.

"Definitely a double standard," Henley sighs. "No one asked us to undress," she adds, echoing my own thoughts because she's as crazy as I am.

He turns and smirks as he bends over, putting his arms against the wall. One of the other girls grabs something, and four more guys from the party are lined up against the wall after that.

Evil Eyes smirks. It's super creepy too.

She suddenly rears back with her cat o' nine tails, and a loud *pop* slaps through the air. Anderson's high-pitched scream rattles around, Roman leaps to his feet, and then four more shrill screams join it behind familiar *pops* that sound off in uniform sequence.

"Silence!" the women all command at once.

Roman's eyes are wide in his head. I keep looking from him to the craziness to him again just to watch his reaction.

"I *kiiill* you," Lydia says in a small, weird sounding voice.

Henley and I both look down as Lydia's body shakes with silent laughter, tears forming in her eyes.

"Silence!" the women inside snap again.

"I *kiiiill* you," Lydia says once more, snorting, then covering her mouth like she's dying on the inside from so much laughter.

"What the hell?" Henley whispers, which forces Lydia to snort again as her body shakes harder.

Another series of loud pops, and some louder curses follow, and I look up as Anderson gets restrained by one of the security guys. Evil Eyes grabs his crotch, and his eyes widen as he gets held immobile. "I said SILENCE!" she roars.

"I *kiiill* you," Lydia says again, this time laughing and then choking to stop the sound from escaping.

She's lost her motherfucking mind.

"Did you go drink the tainted champagne?" Henley hisses.

Lydia shakes her head, but she can't form words because of her internal riot.

We go back to watching as Anderson is restrained and now he has a ball gag in his mouth. Oh dear fuck. What did I buy?

His eyes are wide in his head, and there are totally nipple clamps on him right now. Four other poor guys are stuck in the same position, the security team too buff to be toyed with.

I quickly pull up my phone to figure out what I bought. Scrolling through my email, I finally find the contract with the list of specifications. It's when I get to the extras that I cringe.

Forceful roleplay for the ones who fake resistance and want a dark experience.

Bound and gagged.

Little Bow Beep. What the fuck is a Little Bow Beep?

My question is answered, unfortunately, when a massive dildo is pulled out, and it has a bowtie at the bottom. My eyes widen when the thing beeps loudly, and vibrations start. That's not *little* at all.

"Whoa," Henley whispers. "That escalated quickly."

Anderson tries to speak around the gag, his voice squeaky despite the muffled state of it.

"Silence!" The woman barks again.

"I *kiiill* you," Lydia says from the ground, now heaving. She's laughing so hard that she literally can't actually make a sound as she flops around like a fish. Her face is turning red because she's so silent and yet laughing.

None of the guys in the room are moving. I think they're all too stunned. Quickly, I go back to reading, panicking now.

Anal play. *Applies to the client only. Our employees are not to be touched.

Oh, no! No, no, no, no!

If at any time the client wishes to stop, the safe word must be used. It's Llama.

"Llama!" I shout just as she starts tugging at Anderson's boxers.

Everyone turns to look at the window as I push it up, desperately trying to stop this before things go too far. Are they seriously just going to watch him get mauled by a vibrator? "Say llama!" I yell to Anderson. "It's the safe word!"

His eyes are wide and panicked, and all you can hear is a muffled, "Yama! Yama! Yama!"

He's going to fucking kill me.

The woman frowns as the guys unclip the gag, and I drop down as Henley grabs Lydia's arm, tugging her hard. It takes the both of us to pry her up from the ground before anyone catches up to us.

Just as we round the corner, two strong arms clamp around my waist, hoisting me in the air, and I scream like the first whore to die in a slasher film.

Loud laughter follows my scream, and I relax when I realize it's Roman holding me. *Whew.* Made my throat sore for nothing. Guess he won't be getting a blowjob now.

Lydia sobers when she sees Davis and Roman, since Davis is eyeing us but trying hard not to laugh.

"Llama?" Davis asks.

"I didn't pick the safe word," I explain, still hanging over a shoulder.

Roman drops me to my feet, and I turn toward Lydia.

"Why the hell did you keep saying 'I kill you' back there?"

"Jeff Dunham? Achmed? Silence, I *kiiill* you? It's like his greatest piece of work ever," Lydia says, then dissolves into a fit of giggles.

Henley and I share confused looks, and the guys look equally confused.

"You guys are so lame," Lydia sighs, a big smile on her face. "But thanks; I needed the laugh."

She turns and skips—like, literally starts skipping—away. *Well, that's not creepy at all.*

"Care to explain why you ruined the strippers for us?" Roman drawls, but he doesn't look the least bit disappointed.

I grimace, because that so did not go the way I expected. Strippers don't touch you, right? I mean, they do, but not like *that*.

"Can we have this discussion far away from here? Like before Anderson gets on his clothes and comes to kill me?" I ask, wondering why he's laughing at me.

I'm serious. Anderson may actually hide my body after this one. I'm already missing most of one arm, so that makes dismemberment easier on him.

He takes my hand, and I wave over my shoulder at Henley as Roman drags me toward the house. I'm practically running to keep up with his long strides.

"I see you got robo arm back," he notes, smiling down at me as we hurry through the house.

"I did. I'm sleeping in your room tonight too, by the way."

"So you *do* want to see me, after all."

"You may be strong enough to keep Anderson from slitting my throat in my sleep."

He barks out a laugh. Again, I'm not being funny.

"Why didn't you try to stop it?" I hiss.

"I would have. I was just trying to figure out how far they planned to take things."

"*Too far* is the answer," I grumble.

He laughs harder as he puts his arm around my waist, and we finally make it to his room. Where I will stay until it's time to leave, because I'm seriously scared for my life. So far Jane, Mom, and Anderson want me dead. This could end up being a live episode of Clue.

I can see the editorial pieces now: Monica in the ballroom with the wrench. Or Anderson in the pool house with the revolver. Or Jane in the study with the knife.

My inner ramble is silenced when Roman decides to take my mind off everything, using his awesome mouth. I moan against his lips, happy for the distraction. When my hands come up to his shoulders, he breaks the kiss and steps back.

"Jill has to go," he says, eyeing my robo hand like it's going to attack at any moment.

"She's good now. She hasn't tried to molest me all day."

It's weird that statement sounds like bragging rights.

"Anything that can 'accidentally' crush my balls is not going to be near them." He crosses his arms over his chest like he's taking a stand.

Laughing under my breath, I turn and start the tedious process of removing it all, unstrapping one section of the harness.

"Fuck it. Just think happy thoughts," he says, apparently too impatient to wait, and I grin as he spins me around and crushes his lips to mine again.

Weirdest night ever.

Just as we reach the bed, excitement hits me. "Aglets!" I say against his lips, grinning now as I kiss him.

He pulls back, eyeing me like I'm crazy.

"What?"

"Aglets! Those are the plastic pieces on the shoe strings. I didn't lose the brain space!"

He shakes his head and kisses me again, silencing me once more. The second we drop to the bed, a loud scream pins us in place. The last time I heard that scream, Jill was fucking the floor like I was fucking Roman.

Jill is on my arm. So why is Lydia—

Another scream has Roman cursing, and we both dart through the bathroom.

"What the hell?" I hear Lydia demanding.

My feet skid to a halt right behind Roman, and my eyes widen as a seething Anderson scathes me with a murderous glare.

"You!" he growls, pointing his finger at me just to make sure I know it's me he's here to kill.

Roman moves to be a little more in front of me like he's going to protect me. Awww.

"Too fucking far this time, Kasha!" Anderson snarls.

"Calm down. We can handle this in the morning—"

"Stay out of it, Roman," Anderson bites out, his eyes never leaving me. "That was my bachelor party, and that crazy bitch almost—"

"I know!" I shout, groaning thereafter. "That was *not* what I was expecting. I swear I never would have paid for that. I'll even throw you another bachelor party with pretty strippers who wear too much glitter. Let me fix this," I say, honestly feeling like an ass.

He relaxes a little. "I hate glitter," he deadpans.

Roman relaxes upon hearing that, and he shifts a little as Lydia swallows like she's fighting to get a ball down her throat.

Poor choice of words...

"I also want them to dance and shit. No violence," Anderson adds, mellowing much better than I thought.

"Can do," I tell him, smiling happily.

I really thought this was going to be much worse.

Roman's phone rings in the other room, and he looks between us.

"All good?" he asks me, casting a wary glance at Anderson.

"All good," I tell him.

He looks between us one last time, before walking toward the other room. As soon as he's out of sight, Anderson's expression changes, and I suck in a breath just before he lunges.

Bruce Lee movies flick through my mind, and suddenly Jill shoots out, connecting with Anderson's chest just in time. A painful grunt/yelp leaves his lips as he flies backwards and slams into the wall.

"Holy shit! I'm a total badass!" I cheer, throwing my hands in the air like I'm Rocky Balboa. "I'm the bionic woman!"

Roman rushes back in as Anderson heaves for air, clutching his chest. Hope I didn't break anything.

"The hell?" Roman snaps.

"Anderson attacked!" Lydia tattles, reminding me she's in the room and she's actually pointing at Anderson like she's five again and the playground bully is my stepbrother.

"You were going to hit her?" Roman asks, an icy edge to his tone.

"No, and fuck you. I'd never hit her, asshole." Anderson coughs, wincing like he's in pain. "I was going to give her a smelly feast."

Poor Roman looks so confused. That fucking dick stepbrother of mine needs another ass kicking.

I go into my crouching-tiger, hidden-dragon stance, totally showing off my badassness.

"Bring it!" I snap, ready now that I know I'm awesome. "Jill is loaded with thirty different combat styles."

It's a total lie. But Anderson has no clue what my father has done with this arm. He pales a little.

"That's cheating!"

"You can't be a bully anymore, so fuck your smelly feast."

"What the hell is a smelly feast?" Roman groans.

"It's where Anderson holds her down and farts in her mouth," Lydia says dryly. "It's disgusting."

I shoot her a horrified glare. Now Roman will kiss me and think of fart breath from now on.

Roman chokes back a laugh, shaking his head. "I... I can't do this right now," he says, his body shaking with suppressed laughter.

Anderson narrows his eyes at me.

"Hiiii-yaaa!" I say, slicing the air with Jill, then going back into my awesome, fuck-with-me-I-dare-you stance.

Anderson rolls his eyes before slowly dragging himself to his feet.

"You won't have Jill on all the time."

"You won't have sexy strippers at your make up party."

He bats his hand. "You really think I'd let you order my strippers ever again?"

"Can you please get the hell out of my room now?" Lydia growls. "And don't *ever* barge in again."

Anderson tenses, and he clears his throat without looking at her.

"Right. I'm gone," he says, walking away, still not looking in her direction.

"It's not over, *sis*," he says just as he shuts the door.

I slice the air again with Jill, even though he doesn't see it. "I'm ready for you! I'll make your smelly hole clench in fear!"

I cringe when Roman doubles over, losing it. Yeah, he so can't find me sexy anymore.

When he straightens again, he motions for me to come to him with a come-hither finger move that sadly works for me. My feet move without any hesitation until I'm right up against him.

"I hate being interrupted," he says, bending and kissing me.

I swoon like a dope, and he holds me to him as the obnoxious throat-clearing reminds us we have an audience.

Roman snickers while breaking the kiss, but his expression sobers in less than a blink.

"Jill has to go," he says, gesturing to her charging port.

"She doesn't really have combat training," I sigh.

"Bye, Jill," he quips, causing me to laugh.

I should have hit Anderson harder for interrupting us. Next time.

Yep. Next time.

CHAPTER ELEVEN

Henley

"So, how much of a hand did you have in that?" Davis asks, dragging me away from the scene of the world's worst bachelor party.

I hold up my palms. "I had no idea what Kasha ordered."

"That would be a little more convincing if you could wipe that grin off your face."

"Probably not going to happen. The look on Anderson's face when that vibrator was coming for him." My sides ache as I crack up again. "Yama! Yama! I should get him a T-shirt made."

Davis chuckles, shaking his head. "I knew crazy Henley was still in there somewhere." He slings an arm around my shoulders, leading me toward the house. "Since you and your friends sabotaged the bachelor party, it's your responsibility to keep me entertained tonight."

I'll entertain the fuck out of him. "What did you have in mind?"

"Let me take you on a date."

WORTH IT

A pang shoots through me like a hot dart at the realization we only have a couple of days left together before we head our separate ways again. I know the only reason I let myself get involved with him was because it would be temporary, but now it seems a little too temporary. It's stupid to be upset about it. It could never be anything more even without the years and miles between us. I could never trust him not to run off on me again.

Two days. We may as well have as much fun as we can. "Ice cream and Skee Ball?" I suggest, remembering the arcade we saw in town.

"If that's what you'd like to do," he laughs, his dark eyes sparkling.

We make a pit stop at Davis's room so he can grab his wallet, then we're off.

What I dubbed an arcade is actually a family fun center complete with laser tag, mini golf, an array of inflatable bounce houses, and a pizza parlor, in addition to the arcade of games. "What would you like to do first?" he asks.

"I could kick your ass at laser tag," I boast, and he grins.

"Oh, sweetheart, I almost feel sorry for how badly I'm going to beat you." He pays and we get strapped into vests.

While a young man fiddles with his vest, letting out the straps to fit over his wide chest, I can't resist taking a quick shot. A piercing sound rings out and the vest lights up. The guy turns to give me an exasperated look, and Davis shakes his head, grinning. "Sorry, didn't realize the safety was off."

"There's no safety," the guy growls.

"Oh, guess it wasn't my fault then."

A group of guys are going in with us, and we're divided into teams by the color of our vests. Davis is on the yellow team while I'm on the red. "All right, boys, help me teach this guy a lesson," I say, nodding to Davis.

"Sorry, baby, but I'm going to have to wipe the floor with you," Davis taunts.

"No firing until the buzzer sounds," the man in charge warns, shooting me a look. Geez, one little shot; you'd think I used a real bullet.

We're let into the arena, which is actually just a large room glowing with black lights. Partitions stand here and there, turning the area into a maze of obstacles. Everyone runs to find a good hiding spot, and a few seconds later, the buzzer sounds. My vest instantly lights up as I'm shot from behind by a guy who managed to climb his monkey ass up one of the partitions. Laughing, he's just picking people off.

Another member of my team crouches down beside me and grins. "Help me knock him down?"

"Hell yeah."

While monkey boy is turned away, shooting away from us, we run at the partition, ramming into it, then shaking it with all our might. He topples at our feet and we both shoot his vest point-blank a few times, before my team member high-fives me and darts off on his own.

Now, I have to find Davis.

It's hard to make out who is who from any significant distance. The only way I know who to shoot is to aim for the yellow vests. I trade fire with a couple of yellow vests before finding the one I'm looking for. Davis is crouched down, facing away from me, and it's all I can do not to giggle as I sneak up behind him. Just as I start to aim for him, he turns and fires, laughing his ass off.

The asshole was using his phone camera to watch behind him. "You cheater!" I cry, tackling him.

He lets out an *oomph* as I land on his stomach, and his arms wrap around me. "You're just mad because I'm winning," he taunts, before slamming his lips to mine.

My body softens into his and I succumb to the amazing way his kisses always make me feel. As usual, the world around me shrinks to nothing, and we lie there, making out like a couple of high school kids while the battle rages around us.

When we finally break apart, I notice the time clock projected onto the ceiling is almost at zero. I press my lips softly to his again, and shoot him in the chest. His vest flashes and I get to my feet, darting away before he can get me back. If I can shoot him one more time, we'll at least end in a tie.

Unfortunately, I'm not the only one who sees time is running out. As the last seconds count down, Davis runs to the door, zigzagging, and steps through it just as the buzzer sounds, ending the game. Damn it. "No fair!" I yell, exiting the arena. "The buzzer hadn't sounded! Premature evacuation!"

Davis stands just outside the door when I emerge, and the sight of him laughing at me is tempered by how gorgeous he looks with sweat pasting his hair to his forehead, a smirk on his face. "I won," he gloats, stripping off the vest.

"Your team won," I correct. Petty? Yep. I hate to lose.

"Which means I won."

"You won because one of those asswipes climbed up on a wall and kept shooting us."

The asswipe in question waves, laughing with his buddies.

"Do you want a rematch?"

"No," I grumble. "I want to kick your ass at something else."

Still chuckling, Davis grabs my hand and we head to the arcade. "Skee ball?" he suggests.

"Only if you really want your ass handed to you."

"I believe I've heard that before. Maybe right before I beat you at laser tag."

Fine. He's asking for it. "Care to make it interesting then?"

His eyebrows reach for the sky. "You want to make a wager?" He stands behind me, and his arms snake around my waist. "What did you have in mind?"

"If I win, you're my slave for the day. You have to do whatever I tell you to tomorrow."

"Are we talking sexual favors?"

"Well, I wasn't planning on making you clean my room."

"And if I win, you're my slave for the day?"

"Sure, why not?" I can't keep the smile from my face. I rock at Skee Ball. It's like a damn superpower. I can't miss.

His lips brush my ear as he murmurs, "Oh, Hen, you screwed up now. I could watch you blow me for hours."

I could too, but I have much better plans in mind for him. "You're up first. I want you to think you at least have a chance."

Laughing, he plunks in the quarters and nine balls roll into the slot. "No cheating," he warns with a grin, and I step back, holding up my palms.

I snort when the first ball falls into the ten point ring.

"I'm just warming up," he grumbles. He actually does pretty well after that, hitting the fifty pointer a couple of times, and even one of the one hundred point rings once. When he steps back and smirks at me, his final score is four hundred fifty.

Stepping aside, he pokes his tongue into his cheek, and grins. He's real sure about that blowjob. I almost feel bad. Almost. The truth is I've played this game so much it's not even a challenge anymore. I can hit the one hundred point ring every time. Granted, it's a skill I haven't found much use for… until now.

I shove in the quarters and grab the first ball. "Should I make this quick, or would you rather I draw it out?"

"Your mouth is writing checks your ass is going to cash," he warns, trying not to grin.

We'll see about that. I decide to screw with him. I only need four hundred sixty points to beat him, so I have four balls I can waste. I purposely roll the first one too slow, and it falls into the slot at the bottom. No points. Pretending to be frustrated, I chuck the next one way too hard and it bounces off the top, falling into the ten point hole.

Yeah, just keep smirking, buddy. The next ball goes into the ten point hole again, and he looks almost giddy with excitement. "Ready to back out yet?" he taunts.

"Actually, I was thinking we should raise the stakes. The loser has to be a slave in and out of the bedroom."

"You're on. I had no idea you were so determined to be submissive."

"No worries, I'm just going to hit the hundred pointer with the rest."

"Okay," he snorts, crossing his arms. God, he looks sexy as hell. I'm tempted to let him win because the thought of him bossing me around actually sounds sexy as fuck, but my competitive nature just won't let me do it.

I angle my hand and throw the fourth ball, watching it roll and jump smoothly into that corner one hundred ring. Without looking at him, I quickly do the same with the fifth and six. I can't help taking a peek at him when I grab the seventh ball.

The corner of his mouth is tucked in and he's glaring at me. Awesome. Ball seven easily finds its way to the one hundred ring, and I turn to grin at him. "You had four-fifty, right?" I ask innocently. "So, I need forty more points to win."

I decide to give him one last sliver of hope and toss the next ball into the thirty point ring, tying the game. His hot body presses against my back as I prepare to toss the final ball, and I feel his tongue on my neck, sending goosebumps racing across my skin. Dirty cheater.

"That feel good?" he asks in a low voice, pressing his crotch into my ass.

"Mmm hmm. You realize we're in a family fun center." He's practically humping me.

"I'm more concerned with your fun center."

Before he can mess me up, I chuck the ball, then turn and throw my arms around his neck. I don't even have to look to know it fell in the one hundred ring. Dark eyes burn into mine. "You hustled me."

"By telling you over and over I was going to win?" I reach into my pocket, then ball up my hand and hold it out as if I want to give him something. On instinct, he opens his hand, and I pretend to drop something into it.

"What the hell was that?"

"Your ass. I told you it was going to be handed to you."

His hands grip my jaw and I'm shocked by the intensity of his gaze. "You have no idea how much I've missed this."

My voice comes out in a whisper. "Me kicking your ass?"

"Just you, being your smartass, funny self." Soft lips take mine in a gentle kiss that feels way too intimate. "I missed you, Hen."

I don't have a response for that. I don't want to get too serious or discuss our past when we only have a couple more days together. "Let's go get that ice cream," he says, stepping back to grab my hand.

On the way to the ice cream shop, I spot a custom T-shirt store and drag Davis inside. The young guy working gives me a strange look, but proceeds to airbrush the shirts as I specified. "Okay, I get the llama shirt. You're an evil little thing, but why did you have a shirt made with a dolphin?" Davis asks as we leave.

"You'll see."

We get waffle cones at the ice cream shop across the street and walk around the town a bit before heading back to the house. After sharing a long, hot shower, in which I gave him that blowjob he was so desperately wanting, we go to bed where he returns the favor. This time when he slides inside me, it's different. Slow and gentle and heartbreakingly sweet. He makes love to me as if there's nothing else he'd ever want to do.

When he falls asleep with me cuddled in his arms, I lie awake, staring at the ceiling and trying to make sense of the emotions churning inside me. It wasn't supposed to be like this. We're just supposed to fuck around, then say goodbye and go our separate ways when the week is over. No regrets and no strings. God, there are strings and they're wrapped around my heart, trying to yank it out of my chest at the thought of going home and not seeing him again.

There's no point in dwelling on it. We live in different states and have our own lives to lead. Even if he agreed to something more, I don't think I could trust him not to change his mind and leave. He said he loved me before and didn't hesitate to run. Maybe I'm judging him too harshly for something that happened when we were kids.

Forcing my eyes closed, I try to block out the warring voices in my head. I don't want to ruin the time we have left, and tomorrow should be a lot of fun. I fully intend to spend a large chunk of the day in bed, but I'm also looking forward to seeing just how far I can push him. Will he really obey my every command?

The smell of bacon wakes me the next morning. When I drag my eyes open, Davis stands in front of me with a tray full of food. "Just thought I'd get a head start on the whole slave thing today."

God, I love that crooked smile. "Such a good minion," I tease, sitting up.

"Minion?"

"Would you prefer servant? Serf? Lackey?"

"Minion it is," he growls, placing the tray full of food between us on the bed. "So, plans for the day?"

"Before or after you pleasure me countless times?"

"In between."

"There's a bonfire party on the beach this evening for all the guests, since the wedding party members will be at the rehearsal dinner."

"Want to go get some alcohol?"

"Of course."

Both smiling, we look at each other, and I feel that little ache that's starting to become familiar. Sitting here having breakfast together just feels so damn domestic, so... right. I need a distraction. "Get naked."

His fork stops halfway to his mouth. "Excuse me."

"Get naked so I have something pretty to look at while we eat."

"Pretty?!"

"Sexy," I correct, and he cracks a smile, stripping out of his clothes.

"Hope I don't spill hot coffee on myself."

"You'll be all right," I giggle as he sits his bare ass back on the bed. Damn, he's a distraction all right. No matter how bad my heart is going to be torn out, it's worth it.

"I could damage parts of my body you've expressed appreciation for."

"Yeah, it's kind of pointing at me." I nod at his cock that's growing bigger by the second.

Davis shrugs. "I'm naked in bed with you. He's got a mind of his own."

I'm done eating. Reaching between his legs, I run my fingers down the silky skin. "Maybe we should show the poor thing some attention."

"If that's your command, my liege."

"My command, huh? I command you to bend me over the bed and fuck me good."

His gaze instantly heats, and I'm jerked down the bed, my clothes yanked off in seconds. He grabs my ankles and pulls them apart, making me stumble a little. His warm hands feel huge as they settle on my hips. I brace myself for the burn of him entering me with no foreplay, and a shocked gasp escapes my lips when his tongue slips between my folds.

Holy fuck! I've never been eaten from behind like this, and the man is damn good at it. His fingers slide inside me, teasing with slow thrusts as his mouth continues to torture me in the best way. "Fuck, Davis, yes, God, your mouth," I babble, drowning in pleasure. I'm right on the edge when he stops, and I groan in frustration.

"Just waiting on instructions, my queen." The mischievous smile on his face when I look back at him does nothing to quell the lust in his gaze.

"Fuck me!"

The condom is rolled on in record time, and his hands grip my hips hard as he slams into me with no warning. There's no buildup or pause after he sinks deep. He thrusts into me hard and fast, and I vaguely register the sound of the bed scraping across the wooden floor. He fucks me. It's rough and ruthless and demanding. My hands fist the blankets, my feet hovering a few inches off the ground as he takes me harder than I've ever experienced, and I fucking love it.

My ass stings when his palm strikes one cheek and then the other, making me cry out. An unexpected orgasm rages through me with no warning, and I barely recognize my own voice when I babble an incoherent form of his name.

I hear him come, that mix of a groan and growl that's so fucking sexy, then his body drapes over mine. We're soaked in sweat, and my back sticks to his chest as he brushes the hair off my neck and replaces it with his lips, still breathing hard. "Any further orders?" he murmurs.

I know without looking there's a smirk on his face. Any illusions I had of being in charge during sex are long gone. I can insist on whatever, but he's going to take charge and own my ass just like that. But it's not like I'm complaining.

"You might have to carry me around today. Not sure I can walk."

Chuckling, he kisses my ear and pulls out of me, walking to the bathroom to dispose of the condom. My legs shake when I stand and grab his shirt, pulling it over my head. I have my panties and shorts on when he emerges from the bathroom.

"Going somewhere?" Self-satisfaction is written all over his face. He thinks he's won, but I have plenty in store for my minion today.

"I'm going to take a shower and try to appease my angry vagina."

"She's angry?" He laughs and pulls clean clothes out of the dresser.

"Livid is more like it. She really doesn't like you."

His arms wrap around me, his chin resting on my head. "That's too bad. I'm pretty fond of her. But, as long as you like me, I can deal."

Oh, I like him way, way too much.

When I let myself in our room, Lydia stands at the mirror, fixing her hair. "Hey, what are you doing today?"

Lydia shrugs. "Drinking and avoiding people."

I know how she feels. After the bachelorette and bachelor parties, I'm sure my name is on multiple shit lists. "The wedding is tomorrow, then we can get out of here," I assure her, and that unwelcome weight is back in my chest at the thought of leaving. "I need to make another trip to Scarlet Toys. Want to go with?"

"Oh hell, what are you planning now?"

"This revenge is years in the making, girl. Davis lost a bet and now he's my slave for the day. I need some torture items."

A smile brightens her eyes. "Make him wear vibrating underwear. You can fuck with him all day."

"They make those for men?" I laugh, loving the idea.

"I saw them last time we were there while you were busy getting molested by Kasha and her big blow-up dick."

"You're an evil genius. Kasha must be rubbing off on you."

"I'm not the only one," she snorts, picking up the T-shirt I had made. On the front is a cartoon llama with a ball gag in its mouth, its eyes bulging comically. "Yama! Yama!" is printed in a bubble above its head. When she spins it around, the back reads #YAMA.

Kasha bursts through the door, her hair a mess, wearing the same wrinkled clothes she had on last night. Her gaze lands on the shirt and she cracks up. "What do you plan to do with it?"

"Hadn't really thought about it."

"Let me wear it to the bonfire party tonight."

"I thought you were going to the rehearsal dinner." I toss her the shirt.

"I'll meet you at the beach after." She crawls onto the bed. "Right now, I need a nap. Roman is wearing me out. The man's relentless."

Lydia laughs. "Henley is walking funny, too. You two have turned this week into a fuckfest."

"Don't forget there's a luncheon today for all the guests to mingle," Kasha says, rolling her eyes.

Lydia's gaze locks with mine and we both laugh. "I'll liven it up. Just keep an eye on Davis," I tell her.

Lydia and I return from Scarlet Toys and I can't wipe the smile from my face. On top of the vibrating boxer briefs, I bought a huge strap on, just to scare the hell out of him. Tonight is going to be fun.

I text Davis that I want to meet in his room before the luncheon, and by the grin on his face he thinks I asked him there for sex. Well, he's not far off.

A black tailored suit is laid out on the bed. "Figured I'd wait for you. No reason to get dressed twice." His dark eyes run up and down my body, taking in my little black cocktail dress. "You look beautiful."

"Thank you. I brought you something," I tease, swinging the bag as I approach him.

His hands run up and down my sides. "Yeah?"

"First, here's your shirt. You have to wear it to the bonfire tonight."

He cocks an eyebrow at me. "The dolphin shirt? You want me to wear a powder blue shirt with a dolphin on it? And what the fuck does 'eh eh eh' mean?"

"It's the sound a dolphin makes, duh." I toss the shirt on the bed. "But that's for later. I have something more fun for now. Get undressed."

"So bossy."

"I only have until midnight, and I plan to take advantage of it."

He strips and stands naked in front of me, a cocky expression on his face. We'll see how long that lasts.

His eyes narrow when I pull out the underwear. "You bought me underwear?"

"Special fun underwear. Put them on." I checked them out when I opened the package. There's an elastic band that wraps around the balls and base of the penis, holding a small vibrating bullet in place so that both areas are stimulated. What's really going to freak him out is the smaller, softer bullet that is sewn into the back. It protrudes just enough to press against his hole when he sits.

His jaw hits the floor when he examines them. "You are out of your fucking mind if you think you're sticking anything in my ass."

"It doesn't go in your ass," I reply, trying so hard not to laugh. "It's too soft to penetrate."

"Not happening."

"I won the bet, Davis. Are you a man who keeps his word or not?"

If a gaze could cut a person, I'd be in ribbons on the floor. "You're going to pay for this," he warns.

"For giving you a day of orgasms? Don't worry, there's an absorbent panel in the front."

When he slips on the boxer briefs, I reach in and fondle him a little before wrapping the band around his cock and balls, securing the bullet to him. "Is that too tight?" I ask sweetly, and he shakes his head, glaring at me. "Good, don't want to choke the little guys."

I press my body to his and reach around to slide my hand down the back, adjusting the tiny rear vibrator so that it juts between his cheeks in just the right spot. He'll feel it even when he's standing, but it'll really get his attention when he sits. "This isn't what I had in mind when you said slave," he growls.

"What's the matter? Can't take it?" I taunt, giving him a smack on the ass right over the rear vibrator, making him jump.

"Enjoy yourself now, Hen. When I get a hold of you, you won't be able to sit for a week."

"Promises, promises. Now, get dressed before we miss the luncheon."

He tries to look unaffected as he gets dressed, but I can see a slight wince when he sits. As he bends over to tie his shoes, I remove the tiny remote from my purse and turn on the rear vibrator at the lowest speed. He lunges to his feet and reaches back to pull at the seat of his pants. My hand cracks against his. "Ah-Ah, leave it."

He breathes a sigh of relief when I switch it off, but it's short lived because I hit the button to turn on the bullet. His hands instantly grasp the dresser. "Is that better?"

"Fuck! Henley! Turn it off!"

This is awesome. I have this cocky, arrogant, bossy man under my control. With a push of a button, I can bring him to his knees. "You expect me to walk around with a hard on all day?"

The front of his pants are loose enough that it doesn't really show. "Button your jacket. That'll cover it." I toss the remote in my purse and grab his hand, leading him out the door.

"I'm driving," he insists, when we get outside.

"Whatever blows your skirt up."

He's trying to look pissed, but the corner of his mouth keeps twitching up. His confident demeanor returns as we exit his car. He lays a hand at the small of my back and holds his head high as we make our way to the patio Monica has reserved. It's going to be so much fun watching him try to keep up that sophisticated act while his balls and ass are being tortured by vibrations.

The restaurant Monica has chosen is beautiful; I have to admit that. It sits right on the beach, and the patio overlooks the ocean. We must be one of the last to arrive, because almost all the tables are full. Lydia and Kasha wave to me, and we take a seat at their table.

Ugh, of course Gretchen is seated with us. She's probably persona non grata after the bachelorette party too. If she hadn't screwed up in the first place, we wouldn't have had the chance to sabotage it.

Roman sits beside Kasha, looking at her like he'd like to throw her down on the table and maul her in front of everyone.

Davis acts as if nothing is out of the ordinary as we order and eat our meals, but every now and again, he shoots me a warning look. He knows it's coming. I wonder if he knows he'll be coming. He probably thinks I won't get him off in public.

It's like he doesn't know me at all.

Kasha and Roman are deep in conversation, and Lydia is reluctantly chatting with Gretchen, when I slip my hand in my purse and turn the rear vibrator on low. Davis grabs my thigh, but his face remains impassive. After a few seconds, he shifts in his seat, and I smile at him. He can't keep moving without calling attention to himself.

I bite back the laughter as I watch him try to ignore it, as Gretchen suddenly focuses on him. "So, Davis, Monica tells me you work in the medical field. Are you a doctor?"

I choose that moment to activate the vibrating bullet tucked between his cock and balls, and nearly lose it at how he sounds when he answers. "I'm a physical therapist." The first two words come out in a high squeaky voice, and all attention at the table shifts to him.

He quickly reaches for his glass of water and takes a sip. "Sorry, frog in my throat."

No, buzzing on your junk, I think, and a chuckle breaks free. His glare doesn't escape Kasha's notice, nor does the tight-lipped smile on Lydia's face. She knows exactly what's going on and is struggling not to laugh.

Kasha excuses herself to go to the restroom, and Lydia follows. Gretchen is flagged down by another guest and walks a few tables away to talk to her.

"Roman, there you are," Monica says, approaching our table. "I need to speak with you about the rehearsal dinner."

Davis turns to me as soon as they leave. "Turn it off," he growls.

"Turn it up?" I ask, increasing the speed of the bullet.

His teeth grit and his hand clamps tight onto my thigh. "You're going to make me come."

"Probably more than once."

Before he can respond, Lydia and Kasha return. One look at the gleeful expression on Kasha's face and I know Lydia told her why this impeccably dressed man is squirming in his seat like a hyperactive toddler.

"So, Davis, you've been awfully quiet. Not up for any *stimulating* conversation?" Kasha goads.

"Actually, I think we're going to go." His voice jumps on the word go, maybe because I turn up the bullet another notch.

"Not yet," I insist, running my hand over his crotch. Oh, he's rock hard and his cheeks are starting to get red. "I want a piece of that chocolate cake for dessert."

Monica and Gretchen return and Monica stands behind Davis, planting a hand on his shoulder. "Davis? Are you feeling okay? You're awfully flushed."

Sweat is beginning to run down his forehead. Monica rubs his shoulder as I switch the bullet to an intermittent setting. That does it. His eyes slam shut and his forehead crinkles. His lips press together so hard they nearly disappear as he climaxes in a restaurant full of people, all the eyes at our table on him.

Lydia snorts, trying to hold in the laughter, and quickly takes a drink, while Gretchen and Monica stare, completely confused. I give him a break, shutting all the vibration off and he gets to his feet. "Sorry, something must not have... erm... agreed with me. Thank you for lunch. I need to get some air."

He flees the scene like his hair is on fire and his ass is catching, and Lydia, Kasha, and I break into laughter.

"Excuse me, I should go make sure he's okay," I announce, giggling.

"Well, I don't see what's so funny," Monica huffs as I walk away, and I hear Kasha and Lydia dissolve into laughter again.

Davis stalks down to the shoreline, ignoring the fact he's in a suit, his shoes getting full of sand. I don't get a chance to say a word when I approach him, still giggling. His lips curl into a reluctant smile. "I underestimated you."

"You did say you'd like to see the old crazy Henley."

"You made me come in my pants like a teenager. In public."

"Didn't it feel good?" I ask innocently.

"With Monica rubbing my shoulders at the same time? No."

Oh, my God. I hadn't even thought of that. Gross! The glint in his eye makes me pause. His expression is full of bad intentions. Hmm... maybe I pushed him too far.

WORTH IT

"No, you don't," he exclaims, grabbing me before I can retreat. I'm scooped up in his arms and—holy shit, he's not really going to wade into the ocean fully dressed.

Yeah. He is. "Don't you dare! You have to do what I tell you today!"

"Guess I lose, sweetheart." I probably look like a cat afraid of water the way I'm climbing his body. Despite my attempt to hold onto him, I'm tossed in the air, plunging into the waves.

Fuck me. I'm glad I wore a bra, but my dress still clings to my body, showcasing more than I'm comfortable with, especially since we're being watched by everyone on the restaurant's patio.

"You son of a bitch!" I shriek, but Davis has problems of his own. He has waded in just far enough for the waves to wet him to the waist, and he's learning the hard way that a crotch full of electronics and water don't mix.

"Ah! Fuck!" he shouts as the vibrators turn into mini tasers in his pants. He darts out of the water, grabbing his crotch and pulling the wet material away from his body, which only presses the rear one against him for another shock.

"No! Fuck! My ass!"

"Did he just ask to get his ass fucked?" Kasha says, standing beside me to watch the show. When did she get out here?

Tears roll down her face from laughing so hard. More guests from the restaurant are starting to filter onto the beach to see why a man in a dripping suit is screaming and grabbing his crotch.

Finally, he reaches his breaking point and shoves his pants and the underwear down. It's about the time he's standing on the beach with his cock bobbing in the breeze that I realize I may have taken this too far.

He's going to kill me.

Completely oblivious to the gasps and hoots from his audience, and one cry of "damn, he's hung"—thank you, Kasha—he strips off the underwear and tosses them in the sand.

His dark eyes meet mine as he's pulling his wet pants back on. I step back, holding up my palms when he stalks toward me. "I'm sorry! I didn't know it'd do that!"

Without a word, he grabs my thighs and I'm over his shoulder again, being carried to the car.

I might be in trouble.

CHAPTER TWELVE

Kasha

"What I'd like to know is why all the villains usually have some handicap? Like Hook! He's missing a hand, and surprise, surprise, he's a villain. One-eyed Willie. Of course all the other bad pirates have a peg leg. It's like America is teaching people to automatically think that if you're missing a body part, then obviously you're a dark force just waiting to attack."

Roman grins, only amused by my random ramble.

"I guess Davis will be revered as a villain too if that shock took a testicle away. Oh! He'd be one-nut Davy!" I say too enthusiastically.

The laughter slips out of the man who has been trying not to laugh at the accidental electric shock therapy that took place back on the beach. What guy wants to laugh about crispy balls?

Roman's hand is holding mine, and his other is driving the rental car as we head toward the house. A smile curves my lips when I think about the shocking-penis device. The purpose of its design is actually intriguing, if you discount the minor electrocution glitch, of course.

"So, do you think you'd ever wear one of—"

"No," Roman says, cutting me off while giving a shake of his head, adamant on that stance. He's gotten to know me too well too soon if he knew what I was going to ask.

"But our last night is coming and—"

"No."

"It only shocked him because of the water, and if—"

"No."

"But—"

"No," he says firmly, eyeing me with no humor in his eyes, even though he's fighting to not laugh.

He returns his gaze to the road and shudders dramatically.

I mean, we just saw a penis getting shocked half to death, so I understand his reservations, but…

"What if—"

"No!"

"Fine," I grumble, still half laughing.

As we drive through the town, Jill rests under my right hand that is holding Roman's, still behaving like a good little smart arm. I'm turned in my seat because Roman won't hold Jill's hand, which had me stretching my right arm across my body for the sweet contact. For some reason he doesn't trust my robo hand.

"Rehearsal dinner is in a few hours. I thought we could just chill until then," Roman says.

"Chill is code for sex, right?" I muse.

He shakes his head. "I just saw another guy's dick and balls. I'll pass on the sex for a while."

For a while? The wedding is tomorrow. There's no more time. It'd be too weird to expect this to go anywhere further, since we both live so far away and it's not like we really know each other.

Great. Back on inner ramble mode.

"I need to head to my Dad's hotel room. He's leaving today, and he wanted to check Jill one last time to make sure all was good before his flight back out."

He cuts the wheel, and I frown.

"Where to?" he asks, heading back toward town.

"You don't have to go," I say quickly, realizing it did come across as me asking him to go.

"I want to."

My dad is three tiers of crazy past the normal tenth tier of crazy. I mean, guys don't usually know how to react around him. He's usually geeking out over some new invention. He's also surly and short, or too invasive and chatty.

And... that just seems a little too personal to do with a guy I only have today and tomorrow left to enjoy.

"But my dad is—"

"You really haven't figured out that I don't lose arguments, have you?" he asks, sounding really amused right now as he arches an eyebrow at me.

Has he been winning all the arguments? That cheeky bastard. He has!

"Where to?" he asks when I open my mouth to call him a few names.

I start to argue, then decide this will probably be the best way to ditch him. Obviously I have to ditch him by tomorrow anyway. Meeting my father usually ends a relationship quicker than anything else.

So, I tell him the hotel, and I sit back as he drives. He smiles like he's earned another merit badge or something. That smile won't last for long.

We park at the hotel, and Roman follows me as I head straight for my father's room. He gave me his spare key, and I use it without thinking.

Big mistake.

Huge mistake.

Mistake of epic proportions.

The sound of plastic squeaking and my father's ass pumping into the plastic really drills home just how terrible of a mistake I've made. The horror freezes me in place as my eyes try to catch up to what I'm actually seeing, forever searing this traumatizing scene into my memory.

I scream.

Dad screams.

Roman chokes on air.

Dad scrambles to jerk the covers over him, and in the process, knocks the doll off the bed. Yes. I said *doll*. As in a plastic blowup doll. As in a life-sized, plastic blowup doll. There's also a big tube of lube on the nightstand to notch up the level of grossness too.

I'm going to be sick.

"Kasha!" Dad gasps, his eyes wide and horrified.

I'm still frozen in place, and the door is still wide open. My eyes flit to the doll that has red lips forming an "O" mouth, as though this needs to be more disgusting. Fairly sure she's wearing a real skirt and it's pushed up around her plastic waist.

"Are you kidding me?!" I snap.

"I… uh… I'll wait outside," Roman says uncomfortably, darting out the door and closing it behind him.

Bye, Roman. It was nice knowing you. Take care of your penis, and have him sing to remember me.

I glare at my father, who has apparently finally lost his mind. "A blowup doll?" I yell, then shudder in disgust.

Dad wipes the perspiration off his brow, which has me gagging again. I guess he worked up a sweat with Dolly Dearest.

"Why wouldn't you knock?" he demands, flushed.

"Why are you banging plastic?"

"Why are you here?"

"Does my new stepmother have a name, or do I just keep calling her Dolly Dearest?"

"Kasha! For heaven's sake, why did you just barge into my room with some guy? Who was he? What will he say about this?"

"I don't think you should bring *heaven* into this right now. I mean, are you that lonely? I can totally set you up on some websites if that's the case."

"Kasha!"

"And really, couldn't you have at least gotten one of those silicone dolls that doesn't squeak like a balloon when it's getting twisted into a giraffe or something?"

"Kasha," he groans, pinching the bridge of his nose while thankfully remaining covered.

"Does she have a family? Maybe the balloon animals are missing her while you're desecrating her body."

"Now you're just being ridiculous," he says, exasperated.

"You're fucking Barbie's slutty, twice-removed, distant cousin, but I'm the ridiculous one?"

He glares at me, and I arch an eyebrow. This is just too much. Obviously it's time to move on to someone with a heartbeat if he's reached this level of desperation.

"Why are you here?" he asks calmly, still clutching the blanket. His glasses are warped on his face, but he doesn't attempt to straighten them.

"You said you wanted to see Jill again before you left." I hold up my arm. "But I think she's fine, and after what I just witnessed, I'd rather your hands weren't on an appendage of mine."

He mutters something under his breath and finally adjusts his glasses.

"I'll wash my hands first," he offers, as though that makes the past fifteen minutes suddenly okay.

He moves like he's about to vacate the bed.

"No thanks. I'll just take Jill with me. I'll be home in a few days anyway."

He tries to argue, but I walk out, casting one last evil glare to the inanimate stepmother I don't want, and head outside. Definitely not how I wanted to spend my day. Some things a daughter should never see, to be honest.

Why give me a key if you plan on sticking your dick inside a fake vagina?

Shuddering, I walk out, already dreading the awkward silence that will be thickly placed between Roman and me. I mean, I knew we were going to end, but like this? My father is hella geeky and rudely invasive with his questions. Sure that ends a lot of my relationships, because he's weird and people don't know how to take him.

Never realized quite how far off the reservation he'd wandered until this moment.

Now Roman will see me as the one-armed chick he screwed at Anderson's wedding, and it ended after witnessing my father piston into a squeaky bedtime toy.

My life should be a how-to disaster manual—1001 ways to become a social leper.

Roman is in the car when I finally reach the parking lot, but the sun is glinting against the glass just enough to obscure my view of the disgusted expression he's probably donning. I really don't even want to be in the car with him.

It's just going to be weird, awkward, and terrible to end things this way.

I can spend the quiet car ride planning out dating websites to put my father on before he buys Dolly Dearest a ring.

Breathe through the humiliation, Kasha. That's the only pep talk I give myself before swinging open the door and dropping to the seat, never once daring to cast a glance in Roman's direction.

He doesn't speak, and neither do I. That projected silence is suffocating as he backs away from the hotel and begins driving back toward the house.

At least he waited for me instead of leaving me here to call a cab.

Searching for the right words seems impossible. How do you apologize to a guy for making him an accidental voyeur to your father's squeaky kink?

Just as I open my mouth to utter the most bizarre apology of all apologies, he bursts out laughing. My eyes swing to him to see the tears falling from his eyes as he loses it, laughing so hard he has to pull over to the shoulder to keep from wrecking.

I watch in fascinated confusion as he doubles over, pressing his head against the steering wheel as his body shakes with the riot. I'm not sure what to say now.

"The hell?" I ask, feeling the infectious laughter creeping into my system, causing me to giggle against my will.

"That's... I saw his ass... before his face... Never happened before," he heaves out through his relentless guffaws.

"Seriously?" I ask, now laughing as hard as he is because it's impossible to not laugh when you hear someone else laughing that maniacally.

"Your face, though," he goes on, wiping tears out of his eyes, unable to form a word properly. "Just your face."

Totally not how I saw this going down. There was no laughter in my earlier projection.

Now my sides are in pain, and I try to catch my breath as his laughter slowly tapers off, allowing mine to also ebb.

We sit here, chuckling softer, staring at each other. He flashes me a grin before shaking his head.

"Your life is far more interesting than mine," he finally says, sighing wistfully while cranking the car back up.

"You find that interesting?"

"You just told your father off for fucking a blowup doll *after* barging in for him to check your arm, just to make sure it doesn't try to molest you again. The last conversation I had with my parents was something random about the weather. That's about as deep as we go. So yes, I call it interesting."

How does he make something so ridiculously mortifying sound so whimsical and refreshing?

After checking the traffic, he pulls back onto the road, grinning unstoppably.

"You aren't freaked out? I mean… that didn't turn you off?" I ask, then grimace. Gah, that sounds so freaking weird.

"I'm not in any mood to strip you naked right now, but that was already decided after seeing Davis's swinging boys this morning. As for your dad… Definitely the most insane introduction ever, but hey, chicks buy vibrators. A guy gets tired of his hand, and I imagine it's been a while for him."

"Vibrators and blowup dolls are nothing alike."

"Double standard," he points out, smirking.

"Vibrators don't have faces!"

He shrugs, still grinning.

"This is officially the weirdest conversation ever," I grumble to myself.

"Most interesting," he says, acting as though he's correcting me.

"Our definitions of interesting are not in alignment."

"Because your life is far more interesting than mine," he repeats.

Rolling my eyes, I try not to grin. That shouldn't be a compliment, but it feels like one. And I'm not sure how I feel about being complimented for these reasons.

"Where are we going?" I ask as we pass the road for the house.

"There's this quiet, private lake on your parents' property that's great for 'chilling,' which is what I said I wanted to do earlier. Maybe you can take some time to tell me what it was like growing up as Kasha Jensen."

"There aren't any other blowup doll fiascos, if that's what you're asking. That was a first."

He laughs under his breath while taking a road I haven't noticed before. I haven't been here in years, and when I was here, I spent the entire time sulking or doing typical rebellious teenager things.

My eyes take in my surroundings, and I smile when I see what has to be the most picturesque, if not somewhat cliché, lake setting ever. It's actually more of a pond, but I don't shatter the illusion for Roman as he steps out.

There's a massive hill on one side, and he takes my hand to guide me toward it, heading for the gazebo that rests at the peak. Our fingers stay locked, and I ignore all the girly feelings unfurling in my core.

Definite butterflies going on.

As soon as we reach the gazebo, he gestures for me to sit, and I do, unsure of what to say. He sits beside me and drops his arm around my shoulders like it's the most natural thing in the world.

A warmth blooms across my chest, slithering throughout the rest of my body with its calming effect.

A few swans glide gracefully around the pond—er, I mean *lake*. A small family of ducks seems to be peacefully coexisting with them, although they stay on the opposite end.

"I can't believe I didn't know this existed," I say softly, scared to break the tranquil spell around us.

I lean against him, and he kisses the top of my head. It's not a 'fling' gesture either.

Okay, so maybe long distance can work? I mean, if we're both interested in seeing where we can go from here, that is.

Not that I voice my crazy girl thoughts aloud. It could freak him out if he thinks I'm the type who is already planning our wedding or something.

"They actually haven't owned this part of the property for very long," Roman tells me in a smooth, relaxing tone. It's as though this place just washes out all the tension someone could have.

I totally get zen now!

Always wondered what all that fuss was about.

As a boneless calm washes over me, I start wondering if meditating gets the same results. If so, I'm in.

Sighing happily, I burrow into Roman's side a little more, watching the cute little ducks as they shake their little tail feathers and quack to a melody only they can hear. His phone buzzes, cracking our little fortress of perfection with the annoying sound, but he ignores the text.

"You need to get that?" I ask.

"Nah. It's just Anderson letting me know the wedding party pictures will be starting soon. They're going to play the shots on a slide with some other pictures while the wedding is going on."

"Where are the pictures being taken?"

"Don't know. Don't care. I'm not moving from this spot, so they can do them without me. I'm sure they won't notice I'm missing," he says, lifting my actual hand and kissing it.

"This is nice." Maybe I say that with a dreamy sigh.

"Mmm," Roman says. "Thought you were going to tell me more about being Kasha Jensen."

"Telling that story would harsh the mellow we're feeling right now. Tell me more about what it's like to be Roman Hunt."

He snickers softly, and I absorb the sound like I can bottle it up for later when I need a smile. Gah, I'm getting cheesy.

"I go to work, then I go home, then I eat, go over some work files, sleep, then start all over again."

I frown while gazing up at him as he stares thoughtfully over the lake.

"What about girls? I know there are lots of girls."

Yes, I'm doing the coy thing where I pretend like I'm totally cool with that, while secretly waiting to make a mental list of other women to kill and get out of my way. Hiding bodies is the most important part of plotting a murder. This zen ground would be an excellent burial ground.

No, no. I'm not really going to kill anyone. I'm not *that* crazy.

"I've been working where I am now since three days after I graduated college. In order to get promoted to my current position, I never took a vacation day in all those years. So the girls fell few and far between. This was the first time I've taken any time off, and I honestly don't know that I would have made it for the entire week if you hadn't stumbled into my room and accused me of being a perv."

A small smile curves my lips, but it dies as I think about what he's really saying.

"That's kind of harshing the mellow too. It sounds like you have no life."

He shrugs a shoulder, still staring out over the water that rests pretty far down below.

"It seemed fulfilling."

"Seemed? As in past tense? What changed?"

He clears his throat. "You going to the rehearsal dinner? I sort of have to, since I'm in the wedding, but… Are you coming with?" he asks me.

I know the signs of deflection, but I let it go.

"Depends on how much my mother wants me dead at this point. The bachelorette party already had me on her bad side. I'm sure by now she's heard of the bachelor party. And add that in with Davis showing his junk to everyone after my bestie shocked his balls… Well, I'm kind of killing the sophistication trajectory she was aiming for."

He smothers his laughter while groaning. "I've never seen so much chaos squeezed into a week."

"Hell, this has been tame compared to some things I've seen."

"You've seen more chaos than this week? Bullshit."

I lean back and hold up Jill, raising both eyebrows at him. "Yeah. I stumbled into a machine and my hip turned it on. Trust me. This girl knows chaos."

Why does it sound like I'm bragging right now? Because I'm crazy. That's why.

His grin spreads surprisingly, and I lean forward, unable to stop myself from kissing him. When his hand slips into my hair, I press into him more. When Jill lands on his thigh, he breaks the kiss.

"Fuck no. Take Jill off. We're all alone up here, and—"

"Say no more," I announce, immediately reaching up and unclipping the harness that's laced together under my shirt.

After the events of earlier, I never expected us to get our mojo back too soon, and I'm in a hurry to make sure it doesn't go away.

I start struggling, so Roman—the sweetheart he is—tears my shirt over my head to give me better access. After darting a quick gaze around to make sure we're actually alone, I finish unsnapping Jill, remove her, and toss her aside like she isn't worth a small fortune.

But… Jill doesn't stay where I toss her. Nope. Jill starts rolling down the massive hill, and hurrying toward the lake.

"Shit!" Roman hisses just as I start chasing after Jill, stumbling to a halt midway down when I see her stop right in front of the water's edge. She's waterproof, but I still don't want her dunked in a pond where ducks shit.

Blowing out a breath, I turn to see Roman doubled over, laughing so hard he can't stop.

"My prosthetic arm rolling downhill has you in a fit of giggles? You really need to get out more."

He shakes his head, straightening as he gets ahold of himself. "It's just…your arm's name is Jill… And Jill just went tumbling down a hill."

"But at least she wasn't chasing Jack! Now *that* would have been funny."

He laughs while I roll my eyes. I turn and hurry the rest of the way down. Just as I bend down to grab it, there's suddenly a loud squawking, and my gaze snaps up as the crazy duck from hell comes after me.

I scream and stumble backwards, and Duck McBeasty comes at me harder, those wings flapping like harbingers of death. The *wooshing* sound they make is disturbingly terrifying as I try to run away, only to get yanked back. That demon freak has me by the hair!

"Get the fuck off me!" I yell.

"Son of a bitch!" I hear Roman roar, and I struggle as the crazed, rabid duck pulls my hair, forcing me to the ground as it tries to drag me out into the water.

I look over to see Roman fighting three ducks, getting beaked all over. Yes, *beaked* is totally a verb.

With one burst of energy, I grab the duck attacking me by the throat and sling it as hard as I can into the water. It makes some loud, angry noise that sends chills up my spine, and I dive for Jill, grabbing her up and rushing toward Roman who is still fighting, even though he's been brought to his knees by the merciless, feathered fiends.

I start to put my robo arm on, but one of the rabid ducks charges me, and I barely kick it away in time. Instead, I use my good hand to swing Jill like a bat.

"Oh, you've gone and pissed me off now," I tell them as I start swinging Jill wildly, connecting with one that is on Roman.

He rolls away just before I almost accidentally hit him in the process, and I curse the next duck that attacks me, beaking my robo arm. Yes, I said beaking! What the hell else do you call it? It's far more vicious than *pecking*.

Roman curses, fighting his own two ducks now, as I take on the other two. They turn ducktail and run when I let out my banshee scream that comes straight from something dark and wild inside me, probably that handicapped villain I've been suppressing.

I chase them, waving my arm like a battle axe, and I stop right before running into the water.

My eyes lift across the pond, and staring back at me are several familiar faces, my mother's included. Her eyes are wide as Roman finally makes his ducks retreat. We're both panting heavily, and I've probably never been a bigger mess.

Well, other than the day I lost my arm. Lots of blood. Or the day that firework went off in my cake and made it explode. Or… You know what, I've been a mess plenty of times, so I'll stop there.

Anderson turns away as his body shakes with silent laughter, and I take a full moment to truly appreciate what they're seeing.

A one-armed girl who's coated in a few layers of dirt, standing in a bra and some shorts that used to be white, and holding her robo arm high in the air with her good hand. My hair is a twisted, tangled mess, complements of the rabid ducks. Roman looks just as flushed and mussed as I do, with his shirt torn in some spots and his hair sticking up in all directions. Dirt smudges are all over him.

It's not fair that disheveled is a sexy look on him.

I'm sure I look like something akin to the lake monster right now. Or Sasquatch's daughter.

Roman comes up, wrapping his hands around me, and actually tries to cover my bra-clad breasts with his hands. It just looks like he's groping me in front of everyone.

As if he decides this is the best moment in time to be captured, the photographer snaps a picture of us.

Lovely.

I could curl into a ball and let the embarrassment wash over me, or I could handle this the same way I handle all the humiliating incidents in life.

I cock my robo arm over my shoulder, holding it there like a bat, while posing as a slugger who just hit a homerun. Roman lowers his hands from my dirty ladies when he realizes he's not really covering much.

"Take my shirt," Roman hisses, reaching down to take it off.

"No," I whisper-yell. "It's too late for that. Show no weakness! Act cool."

The photographer snaps another picture.

Does he really think this is what Monica wants to have in the family albums?

"What?" I ask loudly, snorting derisively. "Never seen a topless, one-armed girl be a badass? We're not all villains!"

With that, I start strutting toward the car, keeping a wide berth from the demons who've possessed ducks. It's an excellent disguise. Sam and Dean will never look for them in those duck bodies… Unless they visit this pond and the ducks reveal their evil selves the way they did to us.

"We need to start carrying salt," I tell Roman, ignoring all the whispers as he snakes an arm around my waist like he's proud to stand next to me right now.

Awww.

"I agree," he says, not even questioning my random anymore.

I grin over at him. It doesn't go unnoticed that he's on the side where Jill isn't propped up on my arm. He doesn't seem to mind the fact I'm all pressed up against him either.

"What about pictures?" I hear someone calling out to Roman.

"I doubt they want me looking like this in their wedding photos," he says back, but he's grinning as though it's the greatest thing in the world.

He's not embarrassed. Everyone is embarrassed of me, except my girls and my dad. But not Roman.

"No one is going to believe me when I tell them about this week," he says on a long breath, still grinning.

"You can't make up this kind of crazy," I point out.

A loud squawking sounds from behind us, and screams pierce the air. Roman starts running, dragging me with him, but I don't need the urging to race toward the cars.

The demons are attacking again, and no one has a salt circle! Or is that for ghosts? Damn it! More head space has been stolen!

Several other screams and more angry quacks mixed with squawks have us both diving in the car and locking the doors like the ducks are going to open them. We both burst out laughing as we see the wedding party being picked apart by the same ducks.

They really don't like people around their pond. Looks like the swans have joined in on the ambush too.

That's going to leave a mark, I think, as Gretchen gets tackled by one of the massive swans.

"I bet they wish they had me out there batting ducks down right now," I say, turning to face Roman, who grabs my face, surprising me with a kiss.

My eyes widen until they close, and I relax into the kiss, savoring it, and melting against him. As chaos rages on outside, we stay in our little bubble, kissing, forgetting the rest of the world.

When he breaks the kiss, my lips are swollen, and I want so much more. My eyes feel heavy as I open them to see him staring at me with an intense look I wasn't expecting.

"I really like the crazy," he says, thumbing my lips.

A small shiver runs through me.

"The crazy really likes you too," I whisper.

CHAPTER THIRTEEN

Henley

Davis holds my hand as we walk down to the beach where a roaring bonfire burns. He's forgiven me for the shocking underwear incident, but promised to get revenge. I'm going to have to watch my back. Especially since he isn't exactly thrilled with my T-shirt choice for him.

"Don't worry," I smack him on the chest as we approach the fire. "Dolphins are totally manly."

"Just keep poking me, Hen. See what happens."

"You'll poke me?" I ask hopefully. "Or is Little Davis too sore?"

"First, never call him that again. Big Dave will be insulted. And the worst of the... erm, discomfort was from the rear device."

"Oh no, I singed your little brown berry!"

"Oh, God, please forget I said anything," he groans.

"What? You don't like that term? How about balloon knot? Poop chute? Don't worry, I'll think of a good one."

"If you don't want me to throw you into the ocean, you'll stop right now." Davis pulls me down onto one of the long wooden benches placed around the fire, waving at a few guests he recognizes. God forbid people actually have to sit in the sand. Everyone looks different dressed in jeans and hoodies for a night on the beach.

"Stop what?" Kasha asks, as she and Roman sit beside us.

"Nothing," he replies, at the same time I say, "Finding an appropriate way to describe his crispy man purse."

Kasha laughs, and Roman grins at him. "Ouch, the thought of getting nuts shocked is bad enough. You can't do damage to a man's shit winker. That's just wrong. Here, take the edge off," he laughs, handing Davis a bottle of bourbon.

Davis accepts and takes a long pull before handing it back.

"How did the rehearsal dinner go?" I ask Kasha.

"I'll tell you later," she promises.

Lydia is making her way down the beach, a man walking beside her. "Is that Simon Carr?" I ask.

"Sure is. They've been hanging out a lot. She swears she isn't fucking him, though. He's bulked up a lot since high school. I wonder what he's packing."

Davis looks at Roman, shaking his head as Kasha and I discuss what may be hiding in Simon's jeans. "I never want to hear that men are pigs again. Women are just as bad."

"There you are," Kasha exclaims as they approach. "I looked for you after the dinner."

"We went out the servant's entrance."

"Servant's entrance!" I cry, pointing at Davis. "That's another good one!"

"That's it!" Davis announces, grabbing me and throwing me over his shoulder. Kasha and Roman try to laugh themselves to death while Lydia and Simon look on in confusion. "Excuse us," Davis says, as if carrying a woman around is completely normal behavior.

He tramps up the beach, and I'm starting to get a little motion sick from bobbing over his shoulder. "Put me down!"

"Are you going to stop running your mouth?"

"I'll do my best," I giggle, and he places me on my feet.

His hand brushes my hair out of my face, and he chuckles, "No one can ever accuse you of being dishonest."

Moonlight illuminates his face, reflecting in his eyes and making him almost too gorgeous to look at. How many nights had I spent sitting beside him on our back porch, watching the moonlight fall across his features just this way? Only a few more than the mornings we spent in the front yard, gazing at the way the light crawled across the grass to reach us. It wasn't supposed to end the way it did.

We had dreams.

We had plans.

We were going to be together forever.

We were stupid fucking kids.

Twenty-six years old and I'm still stupid, dreaming of having more with him when it's just not possible. "What's that look about, Hen?" he asks, his voice soft.

"Just tired I guess," I murmur. One more day. I only have one more day with him.

"Let's sit down." He sits in the sand and pulls me down beside him.

"Why did you leave the way you did?" The words slip out before I can stop them.

He sighs, and I go on. "I know it's stupid, but I need to know. Was it because I wasn't good in bed? I mean, we only did it once. It wasn't fair to judge—"

His finger lands on my lips. "Stop. It had nothing to do with you, Hen."

Anger takes over. "Are you kidding me? It had everything to do with me. When you said we would be together after I graduated, I believed you. Did you even…" My voice cracks. "I loved you."

I'm pulled into a warm lap, and I lean back against his chest, reveling in the feel of his arms around me. Soft lips press against my temple before he says, "I loved you, too. You were my little chicken."

"But you left without even telling me goodbye."

"My mom overdosed."

Everything falls quiet at his admission, even the waves seem to fall out of their rhythm, holding their breath in anticipation and dread. Or maybe it's just me. "You went to your mother's?"

Davis spent a lot of time at our house when we were kids because he was being raised by a single dad. His father was a police officer who worked a lot, and didn't have much time to deal with a kid. His mother had left them when he was very young, and I didn't even realize Davis was in touch with her back then, since he never talked about her.

"She was living in Nashville and she used my dad as an emergency contact. The hospital left a message on our machine, and dad ignored it. When I pressed, he said to forget about her. He said she was a junkie who would never change and wasn't worth our time."

"I'm sorry," I whisper.

"I went home before you woke up, planning to be back by lunch, but I heard that message and got into it with Dad. He was pissed I called the hospital, and even more pissed I wanted to go to her." He squeezes me tighter. "The doctors didn't think she was going to make it. It didn't matter that she left us. I thought it was my last chance to see her, so I jumped in my car and went.

"She was somewhat better by the time I arrived, but it was still awful. She looked like she was going through chemo she was so skinny, but her face lit up when I walked in the room. I swore to her I'd stay and help her get better if she'd try, and she agreed." He rubs his palm across his face. "I didn't know what I was getting myself into."

"You couldn't have called me?"

"I wanted to, but I knew the life we planned couldn't happen. I was facing months, if not years of taking care of her, and I was right, Hen. Years of cleaning up puke and hauling her into the shower to sober her up. She drank and took any pill within reach. That was my life and I didn't want it to be yours as well, because I knew you'd join me if you knew. I went to school, studied, and took care of her while she got worse and worse. Rehab didn't help, even when I took out an additional loan to send her again. She died just after I graduated from college."

My mind is whirling with all the new information. "I'm sorry about your mom."

"I'm sorry I didn't tell you why I left. I wanted to call so many times, but I knew how hurt and angry you'd be, and I was chicken shit. Every second of my day was miserable and stressful and I just couldn't handle it. You had every reason to hate me, but I couldn't bear to hear it from you."

Turning in his lap, I place a soft kiss on his lips. "I never hated you. I couldn't if I wanted to."

Silence falls over us. I lean against his warm chest, listening to the music of the ocean. We share a few brief, soft kisses before he whispers, "We only live three hundred miles apart, Hen. Tomorrow doesn't have to be goodbye."

My chest aches with longing, but I know better. I'm not a naïve kid making plans that can't pan out. We were kids who loved each other, but those days are long gone. We have our own lives to live, and even if one of us was willing to uproot and move, they'd eventually resent it. It's better to leave the past in the past. "Let's just enjoy the time we have left together."

I can feel his disappointment in the rise and fall of his chest, but he agrees.

Hand in hand, we walk back toward the bonfire, where it becomes clear Roman wasn't the only one to bring alcohol. "No!"

Kasha shouts. "I'm not taking it off! Fuck off or I'll wear it to the wedding ceremony!"

Uh-oh. Anderson stands across from her, glaring at her chest. Davis chuckles when her llama shirt comes into view. She must've kept her jacket zipped up until Anderson and his buddies arrived. Everyone but Anderson seems to think it's hilarious, though I doubt half of them get the joke.

Every minute or two, someone shouts, "Yama!" and they all laugh again.

Davis slips his arm around my waist and angles us toward the house. "Let's skip tonight's drama."

"Sounds good to me."

"Join me in the shower," Davis offers.

"Nah, go ahead. I'll be waiting in your room."

"You'd better be naked."

He disappears into the bathroom, and I quickly whip out my other purchase from Scarlet Toys, a twelve inch dildo and panties designed to hold a strap-on. I can barely control my giggles as I strip down and put on the pink panties, threading the head of the huge cock through the opening in the front. I can't resist standing in front of the mirror to see how it looks, especially when I jump up and down a little.

It must be fun to have one of these all the time. Giggling to myself, I swirl my hips, making the dildo spin around. I'm so amused, I don't notice the shower has stopped running until I hear Davis exclaim, "What the hell are you doing?"

"Um...the helicopter?"

I've never actually seen someone do a face palm before, but he does, his shoulders shaking with laughter. "What's so funny? I have a huge cock!"

Running toward him, I shake it. "Fear my weapon of ass destruction!"

Grabbing my shoulders, he shakes his head, still trying not to laugh. "You are insane if you think I'm letting you anywhere near my ass with that."

Voices and laughter start to filter in from the hall. The bonfire must be over. I can hear Gretchen and Monica chatting about the decorations for tomorrow's ceremony. "Make sure the door's locked," Davis says, pulling his towel around his hips.

The man must move like a damn ninja because I don't hear so much as a footstep behind me when he comes up and yanks the door open, pushing me out into the hall. "Payback's a bitch, Hen," he calls.

Monica and Gretchen freeze, their jaws on the floor like they've never seen a woman wearing only a T-shirt and panties, sporting a huge dildo. It's not just them. No less than ten people are gaping at me, including Kasha, Roman, and Anderson.

"Uh… Henley? Trying a little role play, are you?" Kasha asks, laughing.

There's no graceful way out of this situation, so I'm taking that asshole Davis down with me. "Well, you know, Davis begged to try pegging, so I thought we'd give it a shot."

I hear him curse a few seconds before he joins me, fully dressed, in the hallway. "I do not take it in the ass!"

"Now, there's no reason to be ashamed. There's no judgment here… well, there's a lot of judgement, but not from me or Kasha. Right, girl?"

She's laughing too hard to respond, so I look at Roman. He throws his palms up. "Hey, whatever gets you off, man."

Davis fumes and tries to grab my arm, but I shrug it off. "Kasha, look, I can do the helicopter." Kasha holds her side, tears of laughter leaking from her eyes as I gyrate while making a whirring noise.

"Awesome. Love your cock," she says, stepping toward me.

I thrust out my hips. "Touch it. I know you want to."

"That's enough!" Monica exclaims, finally overcoming her shock and finding her voice. It was probably Kasha stroking the massive, plastic penis with her robo hand that pushed her over the edge. Or maybe the way I groaned when she did. Either way, the small crowd begins to disperse, and Davis pulls me back into his room.

"I can't believe you did that!" he huffs, locking the door behind him.

"Me? You threw me into a crowd of uppity bitches wearing a bright red dildo."

"Everyone thinks I want it in my ass!"

We glare at each other until a small smile cracks his lips. That's all it takes for both of us to lose it, laughing at how ridiculous we sound. His arms creep around my waist as I peek up at him. "I'm going to miss you."

"I'll miss you, too." He closes his eyes when I kiss his stubbly jaw. "I'm not letting you go again, Henley. I don't know what my future holds, but you're in it."

"No promises," I warn. "Just take me to bed and fuck me until I can't walk."

Kneeling, he removes my panties and looks up at me with a devious grin, the dildo in his hand. "No. No way. Get whatever thought you just had right out of your head."

"You made my ass sore, it's only fair."

"My ass has an exit only sign. Never going to happen."

Davis strips off his clothes and mine, throwing me onto the bed. His warm body covers me, and his words pull at my heart. "I'm going to make sure you don't forget me when you go home."

I bite my lip to stop the truth escaping from my lips. I could never forget him. He feels like home.

We make love until the early hours of the morning, and I relish every second I have him. Our usual desperation for each other is present, heightened by the knowledge that this is our last night together. He explores my body as if he wants to remember every inch of skin, and I lock the sound of his deep voice and low moans into my memory to pull out on the lonely nights I have ahead of me.

His chest rises and falls beneath my cheek when he finally falls asleep. I'm exhausted, but I hate to close my eyes when I know I'm opening them to a painful goodbye. I was stupid to think I could sleep with him and not become attached when I was never unattached. Eight years of no contact didn't change my feelings for him. In a little over twelve hours I'll be in a car, heading back to my life that seemed just fine without him in it until now. I set myself up to get hurt again, but everything in me is screaming it was worth it.

He was worth it.

Voices in the hall wake me a few hours later, and I creep out of bed. As quietly as possible, I get dressed and grab my stuff. I'll see him later in the day, at the wedding and the reception, but right now I need some space. I need to pull back a bit, distance myself, though I know it's too little too late.

Kasha looks as bleary-eyed as me when I enter our room, but Lydia is awake and alert, already dressed in a cute yellow dress.

"You look pretty. Where are you off to? The wedding isn't until this afternoon," I tell Lydia.

"Oh, I'm supposed to meet Simon for breakfast."

"Is that code for sex?" Kasha asks.

"How could that be code for sex?" Lydia replies, rolling her eyes.

"Anything can be code for sex. Seriously, give me any word."

"Ocean."

"He can dive into my ocean," Kasha instantly replies.

Lydia groans. "That fell a little short."

"That's what she said."

"I'm out of here," Lydia laughs, and makes a quick exit before Kasha really gets ramped up. She can do the "that's what he or she said" all day.

"So, who's walking funny today? You or Davis?" Kasha asks, turning her attention to me.

"He was determined to hold onto his virtue," I reply, forcing a smile.

Kasha sees right through it. "You're going to miss him, huh?"

I fall back onto the bed and roll over to look at her. "I don't want to talk about it. Talk about anything else."

"Roman and I walked in on my dad fucking a blowup doll."

See why I love her?

CHAPTER FOURTEEN

Kasha

Earlier...

Once upon a time, there was a one-armed princess who lived in a junkyard with a mad inventor. Her prince, Roman Hunt, came to rescue her from her life of blowup dolls and molesting prosthetics, but alas, life was just too fucked up to allow the two to be together... Unless they magically found a way to make the long-distance thing work, although it never worked for anyone else.

My fairytales officially suck, but I'm not giving up hope just yet.

"Don't pout," I tell the mirror as I tug the blue dress from the hanger that Mother Dearest insisted I wear today.

Heaven forbid I wear something I chose and disgrace the pedestal she thinks she's on.

I angrily fight my way into the stubborn dress that refuses to go down my body. My shoulders bend and weave like I'm a contortionist trying to squeeze through a tiny hoop.

This thing is at least a size too small. My left arm—yeah, the one that's half gone—gets stuck, and there's no way to budge it. My right arm is through the armhole, waving like a freaking flag, stranded in the upright position with no flexibility. Only my left eye can peek over the dress to see how ridiculous I look in the mirror.

Panicking, I rush over to the wall and start pressing against it like it's going to grow fingers and help me tug this condom over me. Yes, I called the dress a condom. A condom that's a size too damn small. And I'm the penis losing my circulation to the damn thing.

Desperate, I try to turn into the Incredible Hulk and bust through the dress, but the suffocating grip isn't allowing me to grow huge muscles and turn green. Even my pathetic little Hulk *roar* sounds more like an asthmatic wheeze.

"Kasha?" Lydia's voice is like a beautiful angel's blessing right now.

Okay, so maybe that's dramatic, but…

"Help," I strain, sounding like a ninety-year-old woman who has smoked for seventy years.

She rushes to my side, and starts trying to pull it off me, but that seems more impossible. I cry out when my shoulder feels like it's being dislocated.

"They make dresses in your size, you know," she grumbles.

Deciding getting it off is too hard, she starts tugging it down.

"Monica," I wheeze.

"This is a freaking size four. You're a six!"

"I… know," I hiss through labored breaths.

"We need butter," she decides, nodding her head once.

I glare at her.

"Got any lube?"

I glare at her harder.

"Got any better ideas?" she snaps.

This earns her a murderous glare.

"Cut it off," I manage to say through strain.

"It's a five thousand dollar dress! I'm not cutting it off."

She begins struggling with it again, slowly tugging it over my hips. It finally goes down, and even though I have no idea how I'm going to sit, the fucking dress is on.

"Can you breathe?" Lydia asks with a hint of a mocking smile.

I flip her off then move to the mirror. Surprisingly, I don't look like a can of biscuits about to bust free. The dress actually has a very slimming effect. Then again, there's no room for anything to bulge out. Not that I normally bulge out when I'm wearing a dress that actually freaking fits me, but you know what I mean. Squeezing into something a size too small usually means some serious lumps, humps, and puffs.

The green in the dress matches the green in my eyes, which has them popping. Usually my eyes are dull and not noticed. Mom did good in that respect. Too bad she wants me to be smaller.

Shrugging, I test out my walking skills in it. Walking isn't hindered, so I should be good. I'll worry about how I'm going to eat—since my stomach has zero room to expand—later.

A knock at the door sounds just as I finish re-fixing my hair, and Lydia pulls it open to reveal a very sexy man holding a single rose.

Holy hot guy in a designer suit. I never knew suits could look that good.

Roman flashes a grin as his eyes rake over me with definite lust sparking in their depths. Totally worth not breathing to see that look in his eyes.

I'll die looking sexy, at least.

Life goals. Gotta love them.

"You look…" His words trail off like he's at a loss, so I decide to offer a few suggestions.

"Awesome? Amazing? Angelic? Sexy? Skinny? Wicked? *Hawt?*"

"Definitely sexy," he says, clearing his throat while shifting his feet.

I grin when he walks toward me. It probably won't be sexy when I try to sit down, but I'll take the moment. With the hand not holding the rose, he cups my chin, using it to tip my head back, and his lips come down with one of the barest of kisses.

He pulls back, and I wobble a little. Let's just blame it on the heels.

He smiles again before handing me the rose. What do I do with it? Take it with me? Leave it here? What's rude or acceptable? No guy has ever brought me a rose or flowers of any kind before a date.

Deciding I can't carry around a rose, I kiss his cheek and place the rose on the table. "If you're being sweet, should I worry?"

He puts a hand over his chest, feigning hurt. "A guy can't use a romantic gesture without being suspected of something nefarious?"

I arch an eyebrow, and his grin returns.

"Come on, pretty girl. Let's join the party before the natives grow restless. I'm sure Monica is dreading what you might do tonight."

"I'll be on my best behavior," I say, drawing an "X" over my heart with my index finger.

I quickly pull on Jill and harness her. It takes away some of the prettiness of the strapless dress, but at the same time, it gives it a bit of a steampunk flair that sort of works.

I lace my arm through Roman's, feeling like a blushing girl on her first date, and he leads me down to the dinner. As soon as we reach the massive ballroom that has been turned into a dining room for the night, Roman releases me and pulls out a chair where my name is on the card.

But his card isn't on either side of me. There are a few people, including Gretchen, in here, but no one is paying us any attention as they carry on talking about whatever it is they talk about.

"You can't leave me here on my own," I tell him, scowling as he starts to walk away.

Instead of ditching me, he swipes a card, then he returns and swaps it with the card on my right. After he takes the other card down toward the end of the table, he comes back, and I stare at my seat woefully.

"What's wrong?" he asks.

Deciding not to tell him I'm packed in this dress like a vacuum-sealed ham, I blow all the air from my lungs and start the scary process of lowering myself to my seat. I have to angle myself just right, but I manage to get seated. And hey! I can still breathe… a little.

"Your sister back?" I ask, trying to find something to say in order to keep him from asking questions about why I may or may not be wheezing a little.

He settles down and puts his arm around the back of my chair with too much ease.

"Don't think she's coming back. She's a workaholic like me, and she had no reason to continue taking time off for a wedding she's not that interested in."

"Why'd she come in the first place then?" I muse, taking a sip of the water in front of me.

"Because I asked her to."

I grimace. "And then I stumbled into your room naked and have since occupied the majority of your time."

He flashes a grin at me. "She wasn't upset. She was relieved, if anything. She didn't want to be here, since she's not fond of Anderson either."

"I like your sister already, then."

He laughs under his breath while shaking his head.

People start filtering in, slowly filling the table until it's completely full. My mother frowns when she sees Roman beside me, and Mr. Bald Guy is now sitting where Roman was supposed to be. He's next to a seriously beautiful woman, so I'm wondering if my mother was planning sabotage against my budding romance by playing cupid.

Ms. Hottie glares over at Baldy, and he glares back. Okay… That's weird.

Ignoring it, I happily take a glass of champagne as the waiter starts bringing in various things, salads included. Roman's fingers start idly tracing circles on the bare skin of my shoulder, and I lean against him, keeping my slant just right, since a ninety degree angle is impossible.

"You okay?" Roman asks close to my ear.

I'm not okay. Breathing is getting harder and harder.

"I'm great!" I lie, forcing the fakest smile in history.

He doesn't look convinced, but my mother is standing and trying to get everyone's attention, taking the focus off me.

"Thank you, everyone, for joining us tonight." She takes her husband's hand, and he smiles while winking at her. It's the first time I've ever noticed him being affectionate publically. "We can't express to you just how much it means to us to have so many wonderful friends and family."

It's all *blah blah blah* from there, because I'm getting a little nauseated. Not because she's spilling sappy words out the ass, but because breathing has now become a hell of a lot harder.

I slant a little more, giving myself just enough room to breathe a hair easier, but my ass is just barely touching the chair now. Roman arches an eyebrow, but Monica is still talking about how wonderful life has been for our family and yada yada yada.

"You frigid bitch, it was your fault, not mine!" a man's voice yells, jolting me.

A hushed silence falls over the room, and all eyes move down the table to Ms. Hottie and Mr. Baldy.

Ms. Hottie wags her finger at him. "No! It was your fault! You stayed gone all the time! What was I supposed to do?"

"You were *not* supposed to fuck the pool boy!"

Wow… Cliché much?

"It was an accident!" she spits out, furious now.

Oh, this is getting good.

"Your vagina accidentally fell on his cock and you kept falling on it for seven weeks?" he snaps.

I burst out laughing, but then smother it immediately when I realize I'm the only one laughing. Not my fault this guy said the same thing I've said when people 'accidentally' cheat. That's hilarious!

Damn people need to grow a sense of humor, since no one wants to laugh.

"You shouldn't have hired him! I was lonely, and he wasn't more concerned with work than my body. I had needs!"

"I guess scooping leaves out of the pool wasn't quite as tiresome as defending criminals all day!"

From there, the woman dissolves into Spanglish that I can't follow, and he snaps a few more retorts at her. Monica pinches the bridge of her nose before casting a nasty glance in my direction.

"Oops," Roman says next to me, and I choke back a laugh.

The longer I sit, the more pain I find myself in. I'm starting to sweat now, and I lose interest in the heated argument I found so entertaining. That's when there's suddenly a loud scream, and once again I'm distracted from the suffocation I'm enduring.

"There are strawberries!" Jane shouts, frantically scratching her stomach and neck.

My eyes widen when I see all the welts forming on her face, neck, and arms. Her face is blotchy and red, and her eyes are bugging out in horror.

"Oh shit," Roman says under his breath before sniffing his salad. "It's the dressing!" he says loudly, having to speak over the arguing couple who still are not relenting about whose fault it is that she fucked the pool boy.

"His name was Justin! Stop calling him the pool boy!" Ms. Hottie shouts loudly.

"Help me!" Jane yelps as Anderson rifles through her purse in a panic.

"Like I give a damn what the help's name was? He was supposed to clean the traps and pool! Not flush your pipes!"

"She's allergic to strawberries?" I hiss, looking over at Roman. "Does she have an Epi-Pen?"

Not that I know what the salad tastes like, because there's no room for food in this dress! Strawberries sound really good right now, by the way.

"The help?! The help are people too!"

"He cleaned the fucking pool! That makes him the pool boy!"

"Not deathly allergic," Roman says, grimacing as Jane shrieks loud enough to pierce the ears of the dead.

I'm forced to stand when I can't breathe, but the dress takes one last stab at me. I end up slamming into the floor face first instead of standing when it refuses to give me even an inch of room. *Ouch.*

"Shit," Roman says, jumping up and racing to my side.

"He was hung like a horse! Unlike that teeny weenie you boast about so much!"

"Can't... breathe," I heave to Roman as he flips me over.

I think the dress has shrunk, or my body has grown since we came down the stairs. Or maybe I'm just out of strength to keep sucking in.

Roman panics, trying to turn me back over, possibly to reach the zipper. He stops before succeeding when I cry out, because the dress is digging into my sides now, as though it's shifted just wrong.

"My dick is not tiny! It's not! She's a lying whore!"

"I found the rash cream!" Anderson yells.

"I need the Benadryl!" Jane yells back.

"I specifically told them no strawberries!" my mother barks.

"Your dick is so tiny that I had to fake all my orgasms!"

All I can think about is tearing my dress off as the madness around me ensues. As Roman tries to scoop me up, Jill suddenly makes all my dreams come true. She comes at me like a horny caveman, and grabs the front of my dress with obvious intentions. Material tears, and I gasp as my robo arm hero rips it down the front, stripping it open and turning it into a robe that doesn't close.

Silence returns to the room, and I cover my eyes with one hand, as though I'll disappear if I can't see them. Roman coughs, and a few perverted whispers sound out from men far too close to the money shot. I groan loudly, which is the only loud sound in the room right now.

Even the Mad Hatter couple from hell have stopped talking about dick sizes.

I'm wearing a bra that has little bite marks on the nipples, along with drizzles of blood—no, not real bites or blood, people. All else is see-through on the zombie-inspired bra. Then my panties, oh my panties. They're white and in bold, red print, they read, "I like it rough," right on the front.

The back reads, "be gentle" but no one has seen that yet.

Bright side? I can breathe again.

"Really, Kasha?!" my mother snaps.

"It was a size four! I wear a six!"

"I thought you were a four! How did you gain so much weight since Christmas?"

"I was a six then too!"

I pull down my arm to see Roman is fighting with all his strength not to laugh, as he shrugs out of his suit jacket. I snatch it gratefully, and cover my front as he helps stand me up. As if covering my body from prying eyes has suddenly broken the spell, the craziness resumes.

"There's no Benadryl in here!" Anderson barks.

"There has to be! I always keep some in my purse."

"Maybe if you didn't let just *anyone's* dick inside you, nothing this big would seem so small."

Baldy totally jerks his pants down, and suddenly there's a penis in the room. A penis that isn't necessarily huge, but certainly not small either. It's also not circumcised.

I cock my head, staring at it while keeping my front covered. I've never seen one with so much foreskin.

"Eyes up here," Roman says, smirking when I look at him.

"See?! It's teeny!"

"It's not tiny," another woman says all breathy.

"Put your fucking penis away!" another man shouts to Baldy, then turns to the breathy woman who is fanning herself with her hand. "Stop looking at his penis!"

Things just devolve from there, and Roman bursts out laughing as the madness just gets madder. I sigh, happy this time that I wasn't the one who started it. Well, I sort of was, since Roman changed the seats around to be by me. How were we supposed to know a simple seat change would lead to a penis being thrust in people's faces to prove the size isn't under scaled?

Monica drops to a seat, and Heath squeezes her shoulder for support. He looks more amused than upset, but Mom looks like the apocalypse has arrived in the form of lewd behavior and strawberry allergies.

More arguments break out, and Roman starts guiding me toward the door. I've officially been a part of all the worst moments of the wedding so far. *Life goals*.

A few curious gazes meet us from people who have gathered around to listen to the craziness going on at the 'rehearsal' dinner. We never made it to the rehearsal part. Maybe they should have led with the whole rehearsal thing then moved onto dinner like a normal wedding party.

"By far the most interesting dinner I've ever attended, and we never made it to the entree," Roman says, laughing under his breath as I awkwardly shift his jacket to cover up the right side of my bra.

"What? All your dinners don't consist of two people arguing about the size of a dick and a pool boy? Or a little strawberry allergy chaos? Or maybe your girlfriend's robot arm stripping her dress off for everyone to see her embarrassing underwear yet again? Never happened before?"

I realize too late what I've said, and Roman's smile grows as his eyebrows go up. "Girlfriend?"

Annnnnd now I sound like the creepy chick who is designing a tattoo of his name for her ass. Awesome.

"Not... I mean... I didn't mean to... I just—"

He kisses me to stop the ramble, and I forget I'm holding onto the jacket when he pushes me against the wall on the staircase. In fact, I forget everything. It tends to be an issue, because his lips are laced with pheromones that make me stupid or something.

I guess I still haven't scared him away. His weird-o-meter is epically impressive.

When he finally breaks the kiss, I'm barely able to open my eyes. Now to make the impossible fairytale possible. Right?

"I'll order some pizza and we can go to the bonfire," he says randomly.

"Pizza sounds... great?" I'm not sure why that sounds like a question, but I do know why I sound confused.

He smiles and takes my hand. It's not until a guy almost falls down the stairs while gawking at me that I remember what I'm wearing and jerk Roman's jacket back over me.

The guy looks away quickly when Roman glares at him. *Awww. A guy glared at another guy for me.*

"I'll just... um... change clothes before the pizza," I tell him, still thrown off by how completely out of the blue that was.

"I'll wait on you in my room," he says, brushing his lips over mine again before walking away.

Sigh.

I opt for some jeans and the llama shirt because... *Yama.*

Snickering, I check my hair and happen to glance out the window. My eyes land on the lone figure who is walking toward the back with a bottle of champagne in her hand.

I shouldn't care. I really shouldn't.

Cursing myself for caring, I jog out the door, passing Lydia.

"What happened at the rehearsal dinner?" she calls out.

"A naked penis, more underwear viewing, and a strawberry breakout!" I say over my shoulder as I hurry down the stairs.

"So the usual," I hear her say through laughter.

As I make it past the ballroom—that is still in complete disarray—I shake my head. She's just going to yell at me and blame this all on me, so I don't know why I'm chasing after her.

It takes me a minute to find her, but I finally spot her on a gazebo that is near the edge of the woods. She doesn't even look surprised to see me as she sips her champagne from her flute, not saying a word.

"I just wanted to see if you're okay," I tell her, standing just outside the gazebo—out of striking distance and far enough away to have time to dodge the bottle or glass if she loses it.

"I'm just tired," she says on a sigh.

She sounds... defeated. But Mom never sounds defeated. Imperious? Absolutely. Obnoxious? All the time. But defeated? Not Monica. Never.

Cautiously, I move up the few steps and sit beside her on the wicker sofa. She hands me the bottle of champagne, and I arch an eyebrow.

"I don't have another glass."

Shrugging, I take the champagne, and very *elegantly* sip it straight from the bottle.

She sighs heavily while continuing to take hefty gulps from her glass before finally pulling the bottle back for a refill.

"For the record, I had no idea that couple would dissolve into a penis riot," I decide to point out.

I expect her to chastise me or huff some indignant answer, but instead, Monica—the humorless queen of stone masks and straight faces—suddenly erupts into laughter. In fact, she laughs so hard she loses her breath and has to wipe tears from her eyes.

She sighs long and hard when she comes down from her giggle-high. I'm staring at her like someone has invaded her body.

"I honestly expected as much. You've never failed to liven a party up."

She's drunk. Totally wasted. Or maybe that champagne has ecstasy in it too. No way would she say that otherwise.

"I didn't know they'd argue, and technically Roman did it." Why does it sound like I'm tattling?

"You hate me, don't you?" she asks abruptly. Like there's zero preamble. One second we're talking about the penis-arguing couple and card-swapping, and the next she's hitting me with that question.

"I don't hate you," I tell her uneasily, possibly lying. I've hated her a little over the years, after all.

"But you hate that I left your father and blame me for the mess he is today."

"You cheated on him, broke his heart, and then married Heath the second you could," I point out dryly.

"I wish I hadn't cheated. I wish I'd just left him without breaking up our home as terribly as I did. It cost me the relationship I had with you. It felt like I was forcing you to come see me. But I don't regret leaving him."

"Because he wasn't rich," I add, reminding her where her priorities lie.

"That's not why," she says, looking at me hard. "Your father never loved me until I was gone. He only thinks he loves me now because he lost me. Loss is a more profoundly beautiful thing to an artist than love can ever strive to be."

I shake my head adamantly. "That's not true. Dad loved you. I remember it."

"Do you?" she asks, leaning up as she takes another sip of her champagne. "What do you remember? Think hard about it, Kasha. Do you remember your father sitting down for the dinner I prepared? No. He was busy with a new project or a new art piece in the basement. Do you remember him holding my hand or kissing me goodnight? No. Because I went to bed alone every night, and the only times he touched me... They were all more of a conditioned reaction than affectionate ones. Do you remember him kissing me? Ever? Because I remember trying to rekindle the romance, and him always telling me he had a new project or piece he was busy with. That was our marriage, and it was killing me."

My mind goes back in time, trying to recall anything to counter what she's saying, but a pang hits my chest when the memories all seem to support her confession. But that can't be right. Dad fell apart when he lost her. Only love could do that to a person.

"And you're saying this now instead of then? Why?" I ask defensively.

"I never said a word then, because you loved your father. You were a child. A child's mind is easily manipulated, and despite what you think of me, I'd never want to turn you against your father. It wasn't his fault that I cheated. I own that. It was my decision—wrong as it may have been. But I love Heath, and he's *always* loved me."

I lean back in my seat, my heart hurting even more than it did a few seconds ago.

"And you let me hate you," I whisper.

"In a way, I felt like I deserved it," she says in a pained tone, then clears her throat. "I always had a lot of ambition, but no talents at all. Your father had all the talent in the world but no ambition. I tried to get his work the attention it deserved, and he'd pat my arm, dismissing me, as he told me he just enjoyed his work and didn't want more than he had. More than *we* had. I felt like if he made something of himself, it wouldn't be so hurtful for him to choose his work over me. I thought it'd be more like he was choosing to give his family the best of the best, instead of selfishly tucking himself away to chase his vision for no other reason. So I pressed him to be more. And he talked down to me. As you know, I'm not one for being talked down to."

No. She's definitely not. And I remember all those arm pats. I never thought anything about them. To me, it seemed like she was being greedy and petty, while Dad was just being true to himself.

I guess there really are two sides to every story.

And it sucks. It sucks balls.

"Heath hears me. Actually *hears* me. He argues with me when he disagrees. But it's respect he's showing by arguing instead of simply dismissing me. He loves me *and* values my opinion. In fact, my opinion means more to him than anyone else's. Never once has he ever talked down to me. And numerous times he's taken a business venture in the direction I suggested, because he appreciates what I have to say, and he listens with true interest. It's all I ever wanted from your father. I fell out of love with him after years of being patted on my damn arm."

Monica just cursed. She also just unloaded a bomb on me.

"Why are you telling me this?" I ask her as she drinks down the rest of her glass.

"Because I'm tired of being the villain. I respect your father because of the true dedication he's shown to you and your arm." She blows out a harsh breath. "I... I was lost when your accident... I had no idea what to do with... I just didn't know what to do. But he did. For the first time ever, he had a reason to be an inventor. And I'm proud of him for that. But I'm tired of him playing the victim when we were both in the wrong. And I think it's time you knew the truth. You're old enough now."

"There's a reason," I tell her, glaring at her. "There's always a reason."

She continues to stare at me. "Roman Hunt is a good man. He works a lot. I don't think he'd be like your father, but his career is very demanding."

"So you're trying to steer me away from Roman?"

"He can't relocate. If he did, he might resent you for it eventually."

"Um… we barely know each other, and certainly aren't talking about relocating."

"You design jewelry," she goes on. She tucks her hair behind her ear, and I suck in a breath. How did I not notice sooner? "Very nice jewelry," she goes on, gesturing to the cheap earrings Monica normally wouldn't be seen dead wearing. "But you can do that from anywhere."

"But Dad—" My words die in my throat as my eyes narrow. "That's why you're telling me. You want me to feel like it's okay to leave Dad all alone because he never loved you?"

"I want you to know your father will survive, and if you leave him, it won't be the end of the world. I want you to know that your father tends to forget that sometimes other people have needs as well. He'll let you stay there, because he'll be oblivious to the fact you want to be elsewhere unless you tell him. He truly is oblivious, Kasha."

Rolling my eyes, I snatch the bottle of champagne back, chugging a bigger gulp down this time.

"I can't believe you told me all that to convince me to move hundreds of miles away to be with a guy I just met."

"He makes you smile, and he's already falling," she says quietly. "He *sees* you. Most people fail to see the amazing person you really are. But not Roman. He truly sees you, and I don't want you to miss out on something because you're worried about a full grown man, who, by the way, is perfectly capable of taking care of himself."

The man can't even remember to eat most days. Has she seriously forgotten?

WORTH IT

I don't point it out. Instead, I drink my champagne, pretending as though nothing has changed. Even talking about relocating is ridiculous. I barely know Roman. Sure, it's been an amazing week, but… Yeah. Totally crazy.

"When did you start wearing a size six?" she asks randomly.

"Few years ago," I say, trying not to laugh at the ludicrous shift in conversation.

"I could have sworn you were still a four."

I'm not even sure what to do with this kind of weirdness, but now I'm starting to wonder if *random* is a hereditary trait.

"Do I want to know why you're wearing a llama shirt?" she asks, to which I snort.

I guess Anderson never filled her in. Then again, telling your stepmom that you were spanked by a dominatrix and almost fucked by a dildo probably doesn't rank high on share-time conversations.

"Probably not."

We sit in silence for a few more minutes, when there's suddenly someone walking by us like he's in a hurry or searching for something.

"Roman!" Monica calls, and he stops, turning and facing us with a quizzical brow until he sees me and his look softens.

"Sorry," he says, clearing his throat while running a hand through his hair. "Lydia said you took off this way, and I… got worried something was wrong. I didn't mean to interrupt."

"Good man," Mom says, smirking over at me. "Really good man."

"Did you order the pizza?" I ask, ignoring my meddling mother who actually feels more like a mother than ever before.

"Yeah. It'll be here in a few minutes, but you don't have to hurry. Like I said, I was just worried. I really didn't mean to—"

"It's fine," Mom interrupts. "We were just chatting about life and love. We're done now."

I cast a sidelong glance at her to see her smiling happily. Weirdest night ever—and that's saying a lot, coming from me.

Roman takes my hand as I step down, and he eyes my shirt before laughing, shaking his head. "Anderson is going to kill you."

"So I don't want to know?" Mom muses from behind me.

"Definitely not," Roman says, still chuckling as I grin.

"I think it's epic. Yama!"

He doubles over, and I hear Mom sigh wistfully. My eyes move up as Heath approaches us, his eyes looking over us with curiosity. I never gave him a chance. I was never mean to him, just indifferent. When all along he loved my mother for real, and she loved him.

I only wish she'd bothered to tell me sooner. Maybe… I don't know. I feel like life has somehow cheated everyone right now.

Roman's fingers lace with mine—no, not with Jill's. He avoids Jill. I'm not sure why he's so distrusting when it comes to her. After all, she did save my mouth from unjust trauma.

He tugs me away, and I look back over my shoulder to see Heath bending over and kissing my mom like he's been away too long and can't help himself. My heart does a little melting thing, and I wonder what else I've been too blind to see before now.

"You okay?" Roman asks as I turn around.

I lean into him, and he kisses the top of my head. I definitely don't want to give him up, but long distance relationships have an expiration date. Regardless of all I've learned, I'll have to be the junkyard queen until Dad has someone he can rely on. He's… I love him. He loves me. He *needs* me to be there.

"Ever had your mind blown?"

"Yeah," he says, smirking. "The day you stumbled into my room wearing only a towel and talked about vortexes was pretty mind-blowing."

"I mean, have you ever had the rug jerked out from under you because everything you thought you knew was utter bullshit and only half the story?"

He nods slowly. "Yeah."

"Want to know something else mind blowing?" I ask, deciding to shift the conversation to something lighter.

No way am I telling him all that shit that was just unloaded on me. Nor am I telling him that my mother pretty much suggested I leave everything I know in order to give this thing between us a real shot.

"Sure. What?"

"My name in the urban dictionary is defined as a blowjob."

He trips, curses, and almost falls as he loses his grip on my hand, and I skip happily along, snickering as he catches back up.

"You're making that up."

"Look it up. I'll show you why later if you're interested."

This time, he does fall.

"I find it amazing that you've never had one embarrassing moment in your life. And completely impossible," I tell Roman around a mouthful of pizza. Yeah, I'm totally a hottie right now in my llama shirt and packing in the pizza.

"I find it amazing that you've had so many," he tells me, grinning as he picks up another slice.

Clearing my throat, I decide to ask the tough question. "What's your work schedule like?"

I try to make it sound casual, but we both know why I'm asking. "Hectic. Busy. Demanding. Very—"

"You're a busy guy. Got it."

He looks down, and I decide to go with a different approach.

"You love your job, don't you?"

A smile graces his lips as he looks back up. "Most days. I like being challenged, and in marketing, you're kept on your toes."

He loves his job *and* he stays busy. Too busy to drive hundreds of miles to come see a girl he fooled around with at a wedding. Too busy to see a girl if she drove hundreds of miles to see him.

I suddenly feel stupid for trying to pretend like there's more. He hasn't once mentioned anything beyond tomorrow. Has he? Nope. Not one tiny little mention or hint of wanting to see me again.

"What are you thinking?" he asks, reaching up to tuck my hair behind my ear as he studies my eyes.

"I'm thinking we should have gotten extra pepperoni," I say, forcing a smile I don't feel.

"Liar."

"I'm thinking the camel toe is coming back in style, and I'm not sure how I feel about it," I say with a straight face.

He looks so confused right now. I'm good at this deflecting thing.

"What's your house like?" I ask, testing the waters.

He could always say I'd see it for myself if he wanted to see me again—

"It's nothing special, really. And it's an apartment, not a house. I live in the city so I can be close to work. My sister decorated it for me."

He shrugs like it's no big deal, and I smile like I'm not devastated. No invite. No future reference.

"What about your friends? Have many?"

Yes, and I can't wait for you to meet them, would be a great answer for him to give.

"Not too many outside of work. What about you?"

Great. He thinks this is casual conversation instead of a fishing expedition.

"Lydia and Henley are about it," I say tightly as I tug on the jacket I brought over from my room. "We should get to the bonfire."

He grabs some liquor, and I sigh at it wistfully. At least there's that. I'll need a lot of it.

I'm trying to make a relationship out of a fling. In my head, there was something past tomorrow. I was battling what to do all week, only to find out it was a waste of time. And I can't even be mad about it, because what person would expect anything any different? Well, what *sane, rational person* would think otherwise, I should say.

"You sure you're okay?" Roman asks, lacing his fingers with mine.

"Just perfect," I tell him, pushing all thoughts out of my head.

I won't pout or sulk. I won't ruin this last day by being the crazy girl who wants more. I'm going to enjoy every last second.

Then I'm going to eat ice cream, watch sappy love movies, and bitch to Henley and Lydia about how stupid I am for thinking I'm fling material.

Then I'm going to ask my family to never mention Roman Hunt ever again while processing the fact my monster mother may not be much of a monster. Tonight was the first time I've seen her as human.

And she kind of broke my damn heart.

"You seem a little distant. Did I say something wrong?" Roman asks, sounding genuinely concerned, which really kind of sucks. It's that concern and sweetness that reminds me why I'm struggling with this fling thing of ours.

"Nope. I'm really stressed out about this camel toe fashion epidemic," I tell him as we walk down the stairs.

He starts to speak as we pass the ballroom, but his words are halted by the fact Baldy is still yelling at Ms. Hottie, and now he's calling her nipples cracked and warped.

"Let's go before she flashes the room," I tell Roman, laughing.

He doesn't laugh, though. He's still studying me. I don't like feeling transparent, so I ignore his stare, fix my smile, and walk with purpose in my strides all the way out to the bonfire.

From now on, he won't know anything at all is wrong. Tomorrow, I'll kiss him goodbye and tell him it was fun. And then I'll move on.

"Why are you flipping yourself off?" Roman asks me as I glare at my robo hand.

"Bitch," I mutter to Jill as she lowers her bird finger. "Apparently Dad needs to fix her again." My smile brightens, and I cock my head. "Come on. It's Yama Time."

CHAPTER FIFTEEN

Henley

The wedding is a few hours away and Lydia, Kasha, and I take the opportunity for one last stroll on the beach. None of us is in the greatest mood. I know Kasha hates the thought of saying goodbye to Roman as much as I dread leaving Davis behind... again. Lydia actually seems to be in a better frame of mind than either of us, and she's the one who should be losing it today. It's her ex who's getting married.

We take the servant's entrance out of the mansion to avoid running into Kasha's mother, who would certainly find some task for us to do. She's bouncing around like a sugared up toddler, trying to make sure the wedding goes off without a hitch.

A group is busy outside erecting a massive tent for the reception, but it's the white crate sitting just behind the pool house that draws my attention. "What's that sound?" Lydia asks as we approach it.

"Cooing," Kasha replies, rolling her eyes. "They're doves. They're going to release them after the ceremony to celebrate their *lurve*."

We haven't planned anything to interfere with the actual wedding. That's just too cruel, and really, what's the point? Lydia seems to be working through her issues and moving on, and Kasha and I really couldn't give two shits what Anderson and Jane do. If anything, they're meant for each other. Better for two horrible people to end up together, than for one of them to ruin a decent person's life.

But the evil plan forming in my head won't be ignored, and it won't ruin the ceremony. "Help me grab it," I demand, lifting one side of the crate.

"What? Why?" Lydia replies, looking at me like I'm one twist short of a Slinky.

"So we can take it to the beach and replace them with seagulls."

A grin spreads across Kasha's face. "People will throw rice when the bride and groom leave the ballroom. I helped Mom tie up the little bags of rice this morning to hand out."

"Exactly, have you ever seen what happens when seagulls spot food? They'll dive bomb the crowd."

"I'm in," Kasha chirps.

"Doesn't eating rice make birds explode?" Lydia worries.

"Nah, that's a myth," I scoff as Kasha helps me lift the crate. It's surprisingly light. "Hurry, before someone sees us."

"How do you expect to catch seagulls?" Lydia chuckles as we make our way down to the beach, toting the crate.

"Easy, they're lured by food." We stop by a trash can that's stuffed full, two bags of old popcorn lying right on top.

"Ew! Henley! I can't believe you're digging in garbage."

"I didn't dig through it. It was right on top! Kasha, let the doves go."

Kasha backs up, shaking her head. "No way. I've already been attacked by ducks. Birds are evil."

"Fine, nervous Nelly," I laugh, unlatching the lid and flinging it open. White wings beat the air as the doves realize they're no longer confined. Despite Kasha's fear—she's ducked down and covering her head—they don't pay us any attention, instead choosing to escape into the sky.

"That was pretty," Lydia remarks.

I tilt the crate onto its side and grab the popcorn, heading toward a flock of seagulls. "This won't be."

All it takes is one handful of popcorn tossed into the air and I have their attention. They descend on it like they're starving, and I quickly deposit a trail back to the open crate. Kasha steps back, eyeing the birds with distrust as I throw popcorn inside the crate. This better work because I have no desire to actually catch the birds by hand.

As if they've been trained, the gulls follow the trail right into the crate. When we have enough, Lydia drops the lid and latches it. Voila! The doves have now become gulls. The ones that didn't fall for the trick wander around our feet, eating the spilled popcorn.

"See, they aren't so bad," I tease Kasha. I just want it on record that if I knew what would happen, I would never have tossed popcorn at her. I especially wouldn't have tossed it at her head where it would become tangled in her hair and cause not one, but two gulls to search through the strands while Kasha shrieks and beats at them.

"I'm sorry!" I cry, smacking at the birds as they dive and peck at Kasha's head.

I can hear Lydia's hoots and laughter behind me as Kasha runs up the beach, still slapping at her head. I chase after her and finally manage to distract the feathered demons by throwing popcorn on the ground.

Unfortunately, it attracts a lot of their friends as well. Kasha is in full freak out mode as they dip and dive around us. I point her toward Lydia, who's sitting on the ground holding her stomach as she laughs at us. "Run!"

I don't have to tell her twice. When we reach Lydia, tears are running down her face as she tries to talk through her laughter. "Y-you punched a bird! And their cries! They sounded like they were laughing at you! Ha-ha-ha! Ha-ha-ha!"

Kasha isn't the least bit amused by Lydia's impression of the seagull's cries. She flips her off before turning to glare at me. "I'm sorry! I didn't mean for them to come after you!" It's really hard not to laugh, but I manage to keep it in.

"What did you think would happen?" she says, throwing her hands up.

"I thought the popcorn would land around you and they'd peck the ground. I swear, I didn't think it'd turn into a Hitchcock movie."

"This is revenge for when I rolled your window down when we were in the middle of the car wash, isn't it?"

"No," I cry, the laughter finally bursting free. "But I think now we can call it even."

"Uh, I'm not so sure about that," Lydia says, pointing to Kasha's back.

"What? What is it?" Kasha spins around, trying to see her own back like a dog chasing its tail. She finally gets a peek at the smear of bird shit streaked down the back of her T-shirt.

Our laughter echoes down the beach as Kasha shrieks in disgust and rushes toward the mansion. "We might want to give her a bit before we head back," Lydia says, and we take a seat on the beach.

"How are you doing, Lydia? It's not too late to skip the ceremony. We can find something to do until it's over," I offer. I feel a little guilty for not spending more time with her this week since she was the main reason I came.

"I'm fine." She gazes at the rolling waves. "You know, I never really believed in karma, but I think sometimes things turn out like they're supposed to. Anderson was no good for me, and while I hate the way it ended, I'm glad it did. At first I was upset because I felt like Jane was getting everything that should've been mine. If I'd been the one marrying him, I'd be upstairs in that mansion right now, wearing a dress that costs more than I make in five years."

"But you'd also be marrying a cheater," I point out.

Grinning, she turns to me. "Exactly! It was my chance at a happily ever after I was mourning, not the loss of Anderson. I was in love with the idea of being with someone forever, having someone I could count on, and that's not him. I'd much rather find a man I can trust, someone who treats me as good as I'd treat him."

I wrap her in a hug. "You'll find it, girl."

"I wouldn't have missed this week for the world though," she laughs. "Killer ducks, dominatrix strippers, spiked champagne, you shaking your dildo at people, Kasha showing every pair of panties she owns, Anderson and Jane with rotten egg all over them."

"Don't forget a jellyfish sting on the ass," I add, dryly, and she giggles.

"See? Awesome week. I'm going to go to the wedding and watch, get drunk at the reception, then go home and get back to my life."

"Sounds like a plan." It'd sound like a better plan if Davis didn't live so far away from me. "We'd better head back and get dressed."

"So, are you wearing normal panties today, just in case?" I tease Kasha as we make our way to the ballroom.

"My dress is staying in place this time," she swears, flipping me off.

"Is Davis meeting you?" Lydia asks.

Kasha raises an eyebrow at me when I shrug. "I didn't ask."

"You mean you avoided him like the plague. You've been ducking him all day."

"We'll be leaving tonight. There's no reason to drag it out. It was a week-long fling and it's over." I try to ignore the spike of pain those words send through my chest. "What about Roman? Are you going to see him again?"

Kasha frowns. "I doubt it. He lives across the country." She pauses in the doorway, her gaze taking in the massive amount of white.

There's white everywhere. Gauzy white material covers the walls, a path of white rose petals leads up to an arch that's drowning in an array of white flowers. White chairs wait in rows, roped off with a soft cream theater rope linked to stone white stanchions.

"The white wedding dress was bad enough. She really wants people to think she's a virgin," Lydia snorts.

"Damn, it's whiter than a republican convention." Davis's voice comes from behind me. His hands fall on my shoulders, and his breath is warm in my ear. "You look beautiful."

His lips press to mine when I look back at him, catching me off guard. His arm wraps around my waist and he leads me inside, catching up to Kasha and Lydia, who took off as soon as he kissed me. "At least they don't have a groom's side and a bride's side," Davis points out as we sit by Kasha and Lydia.

"It's a wonder there isn't assigned seating," Kasha says, waving at Roman as he enters.

A scream from the hallway draws everyone's attention. "You never wanted to fuck me!"

"Maybe if you tried a little foreplay instead of just trying to stuff that little limp thing inside me, I could've gotten off!"

Kasha and I look at each other and crack up. "Is that the couple who were fighting at the rehearsal dinner?" I ask.

"Yeah, that's them. Apparently, he has a little dick, but don't say it aloud or he *will* whip it out."

"Is it little?" Lydia giggles.

"Meh," Kasha replies, tilting her hand back and forth. "He was uncut and kind of skinny. Looked like a bald anorexic in a turtleneck sweater."

Monica rushes in, wringing her hands, and Kasha stops her. "Mom! What's going on?"

"They're going to ruin everything! He's the officiant who is supposed to perform the ceremony and I can't even trust him to keep his meat in his pants."

My hand darts to my mouth to cover a chuckle. *Meat.* "Can't you just get rid of the woman?" I ask, covering my laugh by clearing my throat.

"She's supposed to play the piano for Jane's walk down the aisle."

Lydia gets to her feet. "Simon's running your music, right?"

Classical music plays from seemingly invisible built in speakers. "Yes, but—"

"I'm sure he can find a bridal march track. I'll take care of it."

Monica looks at Lydia in disbelief. She should since she's been bad mouthing her, and now Lydia is the one who's going to save the day. Or the song at least. "I… yes, that would work. Thank you, dear."

"No problem." Lydia rushes off as Monica hurries to break up the argument in the hallway.

"Did you see how eager she was to get to Simon? She's totally fucking him," Kasha says with a grin.

"Like you don't run to me when you get the chance." Roman taunts her before turning to me. "I'll bet she talks about me all the time. Right Henley?"

"I don't think she's mentioned you. What's your name again?"

"She calls me *oh god*, but you can stick with Roman."

"What are you laughing at?" Kasha challenges Davis. "We all saw your little red friend."

"I do not take it in the ass!" Davis exclaims, raising his voice. Two middle-aged women dressed like they're about to meet royalty quickly scramble away to find different seats. We'll be lucky if it doesn't look like we're in the center of a crop circle at this rate.

Our attention is drawn to the wall behind the arch as it lights up, displaying a picture of Anderson and Jane, their arms wrapped around each other. A general *Aww* fills the room from the guests. Most of the seats are now full, so it shouldn't be long. I just want this day over with so I can start trying to put this week with Davis behind me.

The picture changes to a shot of Anderson as a toddler, dressed in a tiny suit, then an image of Jane at about the same age in an Easter dress. "Ugh, I think I'm going to puke," Kasha grumbles.

Lydia returns and sits between Kasha and me. "Are you okay?" I ask, and she grins at me.

"I'm good. They're getting ready to get started."

"I guess I'd better go," Roman says, bending to give Kasha a kiss. The expression on her face as she watches his suit-clad ass walk away looks familiar. It's the same look I saw on my own face in the mirror this morning. She doesn't want to leave him.

The bald man, who was in the hallway yelling about fucking, strides in and takes his place behind the arch. I can't believe the man shouting about stretched-out vaginas and cracked nipples is presiding over the wedding. It's perfect. The woman is nowhere to be found, though, so I doubt he'll go into a tirade mid-ceremony.

The bridesmaids and groomsmen, including Roman, enter and walk down the aisle in pairs, taking their place on the altar, followed by the maid of honor and the best man, and an adorable ring-bearer and flower girl. Anderson makes his way down the aisle and waits for his bride. Finally, Wagner's Bridal Chorus begins to play, and Jane moves slowly down the aisle. The bitch looks gorgeous, I'll give her that.

I peek at Lydia to see how she's handling things and she doesn't seem upset. Sitting back in her seat with a small smile on her face, it looks like she's waiting for something.

WORTH IT

Pictures of Jane and Anderson continue to be projected above their heads as the bride and groom face each other and the officiant begins to talk. I try not to picture the penis Kasha described while he speaks.

I'm not really hearing them, my mind has wandered to Davis, who squeezes my hand and smiles at me. It's on the tip of my tongue to ask him about getting together again. I know it can't happen, we barely know each other and we live too far away to manage a real relationship. I don't know what I want. I just know the thought of not seeing him again is tearing me up.

A collective gasp from the guests brings me out of my head, and Kasha jabs me with her elbow, pointing to the image projected above the bride and groom. I have to blink and look again to process what I'm seeing. Anderson's naked ass faces the camera, two bare legs wrapped around his hips. A woman's head is tilted back as he fucks her against a wall.

Her hair gives it away, even before the next photo flashes on the wall, showing Gretchen's face, her mouth hanging open in ecstasy. Anderson looms over her, his sweaty chest glistening.

There's a cry as two women run to cover the eyes of the flower girl and ring bearer before leading them out. "This is the best wedding I've ever been to!" Kasha says gleefully.

"You bitch!" Jane screams at Gretchen, shoving her. About that time, the music changes to "It Wasn't Me" by Shaggy.

My gaze meets Kasha's, and we burst into laughter. We aren't the only ones. The entire audience erupts in a combination of laughter and irate shouts. Pictures of Anderson and Gretchen continue to flash on the wall. They're kissing, he's sucking her tits, one even shows her smiling up at him with his cock in her mouth.

"Get off me, bitch!" Gretchen screeches, clawing at Jane. "You've been fucking one of the gardeners since we got here!"

Anderson is talking a mile a minute, and oh, how I wish I could hear his explanation, but all I can make out is "Sorry."

Monica takes a seat behind Kasha with a sigh. "Fine, you're right. He's an asshole." She gazes around at the chaos taking place. "All of this for nothing."

Gretchen must take offense to whatever explanation Anderson is trying to use to save his ass because she yells, "You were the one who came to me!" She shoves him and he slams into the officiant. It's like watching dominoes as everyone stumbles and tries to catch their balance.

For a second, I think they've got a handle on it, until Jane grabs Gretchen by the hair. "Maybe if you sucked his dick once in a while he wouldn't have to come to me!" It's the girliest, prissiest fight in history, but they manage to knock the officiant off the altar and into the arch. The arch wobbles, pausing as if to build up suspense, then crashes to the ground, sending a spray of white rose petals raining down over the stunned guests.

Lydia pulls something out of her purse... Is that a pink microphone? It is! It's a child's microphone, and she's tapping it before pulling it up to her lips.

"And that, ladies and gentlemen," she says, her mischievous smile in place, "is why I'm fucking here."

Well I'll be damned.

She puts her arm out and drops the mic dramatically. A literal mic drop.

With all the chaos, most people don't even notice.

Monica stands on her chair and shouts, "If everyone could please move to the garden, a buffet is being served." She gestures to the door leading to the garden.

"Are you seriously trying to salvage this disaster?" Kasha asks, and Monica shakes her head.

"We should go," Davis murmurs, and we excuse ourselves. Lydia accompanies us out the door and we make our way to the tent, already filling with people. Grateful for a reason to escape, they line up, fill their plates, and sit at the tables scattered around the lawn.

"Oh hell." Lydia grabs my arm and points to the large white crate beside the tent. "The Mulder kids."

Before we can take another step, the Mulder boy opens the crate, releasing a flock of hungry seagulls. This is not how it was supposed to happen.

The birds go crazy, swooping and landing on tables, stealing food from plates as the guests scream and beat at them. Now, we only caught seven or eight birds, but apparently they have a way of calling their friends to join the party, because seconds later there are dozens of birds descending on the tables.

Food is everywhere, now mixed with bird shit, and tablecloths and dishes are sprayed across the grass. The cries of the gulls compete with the screams still going on in the ballroom, and the servers try in vain to shoo them away. They're no match for the gulls and everyone crowds inside the tent, watching as they tear apart the dining area.

Davis snorts and covers his mouth as a gull lands on an older man's head and proceeds to pluck off his toupee. The man grabs for it, but he's too late. "That should make one hell of a nest."

"I think I'm going to go pack," Lydia says, a smile on her face.

"I'll catch up with you." A quick exit wouldn't be a bad idea. As I watch her head inside, I can't help but wonder if she's behind this. All that time spent with Simon. Did she set this up? Simon was running the projector, so he has to have been the one to put those pictures up. If so, how did she get pictures of Anderson and Gretchen together? How would she even know about them?

No, too much has happened, and Lydia is far too good-hearted to ruin anyone's wedding, no matter what they did to her. Plus, there was the sabotaged wedding dress and the ecstasy in the champagne. She never would've drugged anyone, much less let her best friends drink it. We obviously weren't the only ones with a score to settle at this wedding.

"Come on," Davis urges, placing his hand on the small of my back.

"Where are we going?"

"Away from here. I want a few minutes alone with you. I've been trying to find you all day."

We end up sitting in a gazebo, far away from the bird attack, but close enough to hear the chaos still rampaging. I take a seat and he sits beside me. "Why were you avoiding me today?"

Shrugging, I try to find a place to point my eyes. "I'm not good at goodbyes."

His arm slides around my waist, pulling me to him, and I lay my head on his shoulder. "Neither am I, especially when I don't want to say goodbye."

"There's no help for it. We live in different states, and I have no plans to relocate."

"What if I did?"

His question catches me by surprise and I laugh. "You're just going to uproot your whole life and move to be with a woman you've only been seeing for a week? You don't even know me."

His large palm cups my cheek as his lips take mine in a long, devastatingly tender kiss. "I've known you since you were in grade school, Little Chicken. You haven't changed."

He's wrong. I don't take chances as easily as I once did. After he ripped my heart out, I learned not to get too close, and I tend to date guys I know are wrong for me to keep that vital distance. They never have a chance to leave me because I leave them.

"Yes, I have. I don't put all my hope in silly dreams like I did as a teenager. Happily ever afters only exist in stories. Things are much easier when I face reality. I loved you once, but that's over. I forgive you for the way you left me, but even if the distance weren't an issue, we couldn't be together. I'd just be waiting for the day I'd wake to find you gone again."

His chest rises and falls on a deep sigh. "I'm sorry, Hen. I never meant to hurt you like that. As much as I hated the thought, you were so smart and beautiful I assumed you replaced me without looking back."

How could he think that? I have to swallow a lump in my throat. "I don't have one good childhood memory without you in it. I didn't just lose someone I loved, I lost my closest friend." Peeking up at him, I ask, "Did you miss me at all? All these years, did you ever think about me?"

"Of course I did. I was so heartsick that first year I could barely function. And when I did finally ask your brother about you, he told me you'd moved, went to college. You were doing well and I had nothing to offer you. My mother was an anchor around my neck. I regret the way I left and not getting in touch before now, but I don't regret keeping you out of that mess. You deserved better. But there's nothing keeping us apart now."

But there is. My brain is telling me to run, that this is how it happened last time, the only time I've ever been in love. I don't want to set myself up for a fall like that again. Maybe we'd have a few good months before he got bored, then he'd move on and I'd be left in pieces again. My life may not be perfect, but I'm happy. I just need to get back home and into my routine to remember.

"I'm sorry. I want to stay in touch, but I can't promise any more than that. I'll always care about you, but I'm not the same person you left in that bed."

He sighs again, tightening his arms around me, and I turn to give him one last kiss before getting to my feet and heading back to the mansion. I shouldn't look back, but I can't help myself. The sight of him sitting on the gazebo steps with his tie in his hand, his sad gaze pointed at the ground makes my tears overflow. It'd never work. I'm doing the right thing.

Aren't I?

CHAPTER SIXTEEN

Kasha

"Give me that back!" I snap, fighting amongst the bird-pocalypse to pry my purse from the stubborn, relentless, vicious seagull.

It tugs. I tug. Jill tugs. And two against one finally wins, but when that winged beast releases its hold on my purse, the momentum tilts against my favor. A scream bubbles through my lips as I sail backwards, sliding across the ground in the eight-thousand dollar dress my mother bought for me overnight—one that actually fits.

I really like this dress too, damn it!

"I was sexy, you asshole!" I yell at the bird that is… "Is that motherfucker laughing at me?" I demand to no one in particular, pointing an accusatory finger at the offending asshole bird.

Roman is suddenly lifting me from the ground by my arms until my feet are touching firm soil again. He's trying to speak through his guffaws of laughter, but failing miserably. I glare at him when he finally gets his untimely outburst under control, and he doubles over, losing it again.

"No!" Mom shouts, wrestling for the ring bearer's pillow—that still has the rings tied to it—with a particularly shady gull that has an eye for fine jewelry.

Heath dives, tackling the bird and making my mother swoon with his heroics.

"This is not my fault!" I yell to her, just to make damn sure she knows it.

Totally Henley's fault. And the Mulder brats. Not my fault at all. I'm mostly innocent. I only aided in her quest to swap doves for seagulls.

It seemed like a good, harmless plan at the time…

Roman grabs me at the waist, saving me from being slammed into. It's like these things are starving, and they just keep pouring in. And Roman can't save me in time from the next attack.

Jill—I freaking love her—jerks up to guard my face, and the bird that crashes into her falls to the ground, stunned.

Roman takes my hand—obviously not Jill's—and starts tugging me through the throngs of frenzied people who are fighting for their lives. Okay, so maybe they're just fighting for their hairpieces, jewelry, and clutches, but this shit could always escalate!

As we weave, dodge, and stumble around, Roman continues to laugh like this is his first trip to the playground. Damn sheltered man.

Gretchen and Jane are still pulling hair as we round the corner, and Anderson is drinking a beer with two of his groomsmen. All three are watching the fight, though Anderson seems to be a thousand miles away.

"It was you!" Jane shouts, slapping Gretchen's hand like they're playing a game of hot-hands. Gretchen slaps her hand back, only cementing that observation.

"Of course it was me! That was the dress I wanted, and you bought it! You didn't deserve to wear it!" Gretchen roars.

"Where were you going to wear a wedding dress to? He let you suck his dick, but he didn't put a ring on it!"

So Gretchen was the saboteur? She dyed the dress pink? She spiked the champagne? Speaking of which, I have pictures of my mother I need to delete from my phone and Henley's. Yes, I sent all those stripper pics to my phone.

Since my mother went and opened her iron-clad chest to prove there's a heart inside, I feel bad about those. Damn conscience. I wanted those as blackmail.

Jane's face is still red and blotchy from yesterday's allergy outbreak, and the more she fights, the more the makeup gets smudged, revealing just how bad that rash has gotten. I take a step back like it's contagious.

"You like that salad dressing last night?" Gretchen taunts, slapping Jane in the face.

This is the most pathetic fight in history.

"You! It was you!" Jane screams like a banshee after a cursed soul.

From there, they dissolve into another slapping fight, which is still nothing more than an enthusiastic game of hot-hands.

Roman and I sneak by, but my eyes flick back to Anderson. He did this to himself. But the far-off look in his eyes actually has me worried about him. No. He's a dick. And a big boy. He made his own decisions and he can fix his own mess.

Just as we reach the house, Roman tosses his arm around my shoulders. "And to think I would have missed all this if you hadn't been here to keep me interested all week," Roman says, chuckling under his breath.

Interested enough to maybe see after the wedding?

I don't say that aloud.

We hurry up the steps, and I groan when I pass a mirror that shows this dress is full of dirt and grass stains. Stupid barbaric birds.

"Get changed and meet me outside in five," he says, pressing his lips against mine in spite of his grin.

"Why?" I ask, grabbing his shirt and pulling him back to me, forcing him to resume the kiss when he tries to break away before I'm done.

His tongue dips in, and I tilt my head back more, giving the tall bastard the room he needs. His greedy hands slide lower, clutching my ass with a possessive grip that has me arching toward him all the more. I'm like a cat in heat, and he's perfection and ruination with every single touch of his tongue against mine.

"Because I said so," he murmurs against my lips when he finally breaks the kiss.

I only allow the space so I can catch my breath, and he winks at me before ducking into the room next door, abandoning me to wrestle with my mindless stupor on my own.

Change.

Go outside.

Right.

Lydia is in the room when I walk in, and it looks like she's close to finishing up with her packing. Henley is face down on the bed, her bags open and half-packed as well.

"What's going on?" I ask them.

"We thought we'd leave tonight instead of in the morning," Lydia tells me, her eyes darting a glance to Henley who doesn't lift her head.

A heaviness settles on my chest. I thought I had a full night left with Roman.

"I can pack for you if… you need more time," Lydia says with a sympathetic smile.

"Yeah… um… thanks."

It sucks, but if I try to speak more, I'm afraid I might cry like an idiot or something. Roman still hasn't mentioned the future. To him, this still seems like just a wedding fling. I was hoping to have one more night… Hoping he'd be compelled to finally confess he wants to see me again… Now it feels like I've run out of time, and the harsh reality is that I want to keep living in this week's bubble, to hell with the real world.

Lydia pats my shoulder, and I blow out a heavy breath.

"How'd you know about Anderson cheating?" I ask Lydia mildly, less intrigued than I was five minutes ago.

I change quickly into some sexy jean shorts with all the rips and things and a T-shirt that has a pair of lips on it, removing the ruined sexy dress that I planned to keep forever and ever.

"Saw him and Gretchen together a couple of months ago. I only assumed she wouldn't let him walk down the aisle with Jane. I came to bear witness, needing to see them fall apart after what they did to me, bad as that may sound. I needed to know karma existed on some level. I got worried for a minute. Then Simon sort of spilled the beans about Gretchen's plan. So… yeah."

Nodding like that makes all the sense in the world, I change again, this time selecting a short denim skirt instead of the sexy shorts. Roman needs a memory seared into his brain, and a skirt holds more promise than shorts any day.

Henley mutters something into the pillow about dolphin problems, and I feel torn. It's obvious she needs a friend, but now I only have a couple of hours left with Roman. And now I sound like a selfish, shitty friend.

Just as I move toward the bed, Lydia steps in front of me. "I've got this. Go. We have an entire road trip for us to vent our frustrations."

She's right. It'll take forever to get home. That alleviates some of my guilt for bailing right now.

I start to walk into Roman's room via the connected bathroom, opening the door, but I see him on the phone. His back is turned as he talks, and I pause, my hand still holding onto the doorknob as I remain in the bathroom.

WORTH IT

"I'll be back tomorrow... Yes. Positive... No, I'm not leaving you hanging. You knew I was off this week, and I have a shit-ton of vacation time left... Nothing worth talking about."

I decide it's totally wrong to keep listening, especially since I'm vain and worry that last comment is about me... about this week. Nothing worth talking about? Was that about me?

I mean, I thought I was so crazy that he couldn't ever forget me. A one-armed girl who has fucked you in numerous positions, fought alongside you in a battle against demonic ducks and psychotic seagulls, and scarred you for life by making you a voyeur to her father's perversion is certainly someone who leaves an impression of some kind. Something definitely worth talking about, right?

I walk away, swallowing down the nonsensical insecurity. It's stupid to even dwell on a one-sided conversation that could have been about anything else.

"I'll be back soon," I say absently, not even hearing whatever Lydia says to that as I walk out the door, still mulling over what I heard.

It sounded like he was frustrated and talking to his boss, and a boss that was frustrating him wouldn't be asking how his week was or anything.

A smirk crosses my lips. I'll give him something worth talking about, alright.

As I strut down the stairs and form my devious plan, my eyes shift through the windows at the end of the foyer. Anderson is walking, head down and hands in his pockets, and I frown. Anderson never looks like he's upset. It's one of the most infuriating qualities about him. Mad? Yes. Bored? Too often. Cocky and arrogant? Almost always. But devastated? Never.

I jog out, looking around, and I spot him taking a seat at the gazebo from my last heart-to-heart conversation. Mom went there last night when I found out she'd visited Oz and hid her fabled heart all these years.

Groaning and silently cursing that bothersome angel on my shoulder that is louder than the devil on the other, I head toward Anderson. He's slumped in the chair, his eyes on the wooden ground beneath him.

As I step up, he doesn't even move or acknowledge me. When I sit down, he blows out a long breath.

"Not now, Kasha. Just… Just not now."

His voice is tired and strained, and I actually feel like shit. Though I shouldn't. Sure, I didn't want him to ride off into the sunset with Jane after the way the two of them did Lydia, but I was actually giddy to see it ruined. And now I feel guilty.

"I hate having a conscience," I grumble.

He snorts derisively. "Then share it with me. I could use one," he says with a harsh exhale before sitting up and staring blankly in front of him.

Our shoulders brush, and I recline back, staring at nothing with him.

"Why do you do it?" I ask quietly.

"Cheat? Fuck shit up? Offer to marry girls I don't love?" he deadpans, his eyes not moving from their spot on the yard. "You'll need to be more specific, Kash."

"All the cheating," I say, considering most of that other stuff is woven around that.

"Hell if I know. I keep thinking I'll be missing out and always wonder 'what if' if I pass something up that I really, *really* want. Then things get complicated, messy, confusing, and… I end up not knowing what I want. Then it feels like I'm stuck, and nothing I do makes it any better, so I don't do anything at all. Things carry on until they finally blow up in my face, sort of like the shit with Lydia and now with Jane."

"So it's not just the thrill of doing something wrong? I'm genuinely trying to figure you out right now, and this is my non-judgey tone for once."

After mom's upheaval of insight, I realize I've been too judgmental and only seeing things on the surface. Cheating is wrong—and I'll never waver on that—but what compels someone to cheat? Could it happen to anyone?

That's not a fun thought to consider. I always labeled cheaters as cold and callous, uncaring and selfish... but Mom was just overlooked and starved for attention, desperate to feel as though she mattered to someone. What's Anderson's real story?

"I don't know," he finally says. It's the quiet pain in his tone that has me worried for him.

It's a first. I've never been an Anderson fan. It's pissing me off that I now care.

The look on his face is vulnerable, as though he hates himself as much as Jane hates him. Even though, if there's any merit to that gardener story, she has no right to hate him unless she hates herself too.

"So you didn't love her?" I ask. "What about Lydia?"

He shrugs. "I keep thinking I have to love them, because why else would I want to see them more than once, right? Dad and Monica have been together for years, and he found her when he shouldn't have. I just... I keep thinking I'll miss something better if I stop looking."

Underneath all that sliminess lies a hint of a romantic. It's buried way under all his faults and indiscretions, but it's there, collecting dust beneath the rubble.

"Can I make a suggestion?" I ask.

He snorts again. "Keep my dick in my pants when I'm with another girl?" he asks, though it sounds more hateful toward himself than me.

"Well, yeah. But I was thinking more about you just being single for a while. No sex. No women. Just focus on you and figure out what *you* want instead of trying to find it in someone else."

He stays quiet for a moment, then finally looks over at me.

"Did you poison my beer?" he asks seriously, confusing the shit out of me. "Am I dying?" he adds.

There's true concern in his eyes that proves he's not entirely joking.

"Why the hell would you ask that?"

He narrows his eyes. "Why are you being nice to me instead of dancing around in circles, wagging your finger, and mocking me for being a cheating bastard again?"

I cringe. "You paint a really nasty picture of me."

"I wasn't trying to. I was saying that's what I deserve, and you're one of the few who actually calls me out on my shit. So why are you being nice?"

Blowing out a breath, I shrug. "Mom. Blame her. She went and fucked up all my inner rage, so deal with the gooey version of me for a minute. Consider what I said. It's what I did after I lost my arm. It took me some time to come to terms with who I was and what I wanted in life. Dating someone during that time was impossible. If you're looking for some lost piece of you, you're not going to find it in an endless string of vaginas no matter how many you wiggle into or how deep you root around."

His eyebrows arch. "At least you haven't lost your ability to paint a vivid imagery."

"That, my fuck-shit stepbrother, will never fade." I pat him on the shoulder, and he rolls his eyes, but I notice the small smile that cracks his lips.

"How will I know when I'm ready?" he asks. The question is so quiet that I almost miss it. "What happens if this is just who I am?"

It's a depressing thought. I once believed Anderson was as deep as a teaspoon of rain during a drought. Now... Well, now I think I've been walking around with a veil over my eyes so that I only see things one-dimensionally. The truth is, I feel like I've only been seeing what I've *wanted* to see.

"My dad is a bit of a poet and romantic, as you're well aware." I don't feel like mentioning his latest romance was with candlelight and a blowup doll in a hotel room. "He always says that the sick and depraved will sell their souls to evil. But the rest of us are just flawed souls looking for the redemption we don't feel we deserve."

His lips twitch. "I can picture him saying that with those fucked up magnifying glasses he wears."

Laughing under my breath, I nod. "He says it every time I rant about someone who has pissed me off and he tries to tell me to give them another chance."

"Like Monica?" he asks, getting a little too insightful for his own good.

"Yeah. Yeah. Enough with the gooey bonding stuff. In short, keep your dick on a leash for a while, and maybe once you figure out that missing piece, then you can find just one vagina to stick it in and be faithful to that vagina."

"You're so fucking crass."

"Then you can pet the vagina. Show it all the attention it deserves. Be loyal to it. Take it on long walks on the beach…"

He snorts out a laugh and shakes his head, and I grin, feeling as though I've accomplished something good for a change.

I stand, and he looks up as I do. Roman has caught my attention and latched onto it as he runs a hand through his hair, looking around in search of me.

"Where are you going?" Anderson asks.

"I think you've got it from here. I'm going to get my vagina petted."

He groans, and I smirk as I walk straight toward my favorite wet dream.

"Kasha," Anderson says, causing me to look back over my shoulder. His expression is decidedly grim.

"Be careful. Most of us are just assholes," he says, his eyes dropping back down to the ground.

I refuse to lump him and Roman into the same group, so I turn back around and ignore that niggling thread of doubt he placed under the guise of caution.

Instead, I take a moment to fully appreciate the man who first surprised me this week. From here, I can view how tight Roman's lips are instead of relaxed in the easy grin I've gotten used to him wearing. His eyes are shrewd and perceptive, instead of kind and intrigued. He looks arrogant when someone says something to him, and he just responds with that dickheaded smirk he wears so well. He's still the same guy; he just seems different with me.

Roman turns just as I near him, and a smile breaks across his face when his eyes settle on me, raking down all the leg I'm showing—I have two of those fuckers to put on display. "Where have you been? When I said outside, I meant outside the room. I had a call to make, and I figured Lydia was in your room. I didn't want anyone holding us up."

Ahh.

"You weren't specific enough," I tell him, batting my lashes as I still consider the things I'm going to do to leave a lasting impression.

"Where were you?" he asks again, running a hand behind my neck and tugging me closer with his grip.

A small shudder ripples through me. I'm not sure why my body loves his so much, but I know why I'm having a tough time leaving. I love the way those eyes look at me. I love the way he smiles for me and only me. It's as though the rest of the world pisses him off, but when those eyes meet mine, he can't help but grin.

It's a foolish assumption, but it still makes me feel empowered.

"I was spreading around my profound wisdom and having a serious heart-to-heart about vaginas." I say this with a serious face, and he nods, his expression completely neutral, as though it's a perfectly natural response.

This is why I'm falling for the guy. Well, that and the fact he gives really good orgasms.

"What should we do with our last night?" he asks, and my heart sinks.

Our last night. Not, our last night *here*. That fleeting moment of feeling special gets brushed under the rug with lint and everything else anyone is too lazy to throw out with the actual trash.

"Actually, it's our last couple of hours. Lydia and Henley have decided we're leaving early," I tell him, my smile tight and forced.

His grin dies instantly. "What? Why? I thought you weren't leaving until tomorrow."

I shrug, my lips thinning. He's pissed. He's *definitely* pissed. So that means he wants to spend more time with me, and there's no doubt he's going to ask when he can see me again.

Hope shuffles through me with a renewed flutter.

He runs a hand through his hair, messing it up. "Well, I was going to see if you wanted to go into town and maybe have a night out, but I guess there's no time for that."

He looks like he's not happy about that either. Those butterflies of hope flap their little wings inside me like they just found their fix of crack and can't slow down.

"Well, if we only have a couple of hours left," he says, and those butterflies catch fire, turning to ash as they explode, "let's make it count."

In one swift move, he's tugged me to him, and I wage a war between pride and desire. I'll regret giving up one last time of being with him just because my pride feels like I'm worth more. I am worth more. But... fuck it. I'm tired of thinking. It's too exhausting trying to adult.

My good hand threads through the strands of his hair, as Jill slides over his shoulder. He's so into kissing me that he doesn't even complain about her being too close to his throat.

One of his hands slides down, grabbing my ass, and I moan into his mouth as he starts walking me back in, forcing my feet to blindly follow the path in reverse. He lifts me at the stairs, and my feet dangle, but our lips never break apart.

There's almost a desperation in the way he's kissing me, as though he's as opposed to leaving this as a fling as I am. Yet, he says nothing. He pours all his anger out into that kiss, and I taste it, because it's rougher… almost punishing me for leaving early.

Even the way he grips me is rougher, and I kind of think it's hot as hell too. Maybe I should have been pissing him off more this week instead of trying to make him fall for me.

When my feet hit the ground, he shoves both his hands into my hair, his fingers tangling into the strands without any finesse or care. We drop down to a bed with the same reckless abandon. I'm not even sure when we got into his room—I think it's his room.

I moan again when he grinds into me, his hips perfectly settled between my legs for the most contact. He swallows my sounds, reaching between us to shove my skirt up around my hips. But I have to leave an impression.

With Jill's help, I shove him off me, and he drops to the bed, his eyes blinking open in surprise. His surprise ends when Jill rips open his pants like a savage. Sheesh, I really need to remember how strong she is.

A breath hisses through his lips as he tenses, and I internally groan. It was supposed to be a lot sexier, and it was… in my head.

"Sorry," I tell him, grimacing at the mangled front of his pants.

"Bye, Jill," he says, amused.

No. No. No. I don't want amusement. I want hardcore sexiness.

Determined, I hurriedly strip out of Jill, and he watches me, never taking his eyes off my face as I drop her to the floor. She roots around on the ground, causing some noise, since the patch is still on my neck and commanding her without me meaning to.

In an effort to salvage my sexy, I bend, tugging his boxers down. He lifts his hips, helping me push them and his pants down his legs, and his very noticeable erection is suddenly in my face. I capitalize, taking him into my mouth without warning, bypassing all the teasing.

This time when breath hisses between his teeth, it's for a whole new reason. That breath is followed by a groan, and one of his hands digs into my hair as I take him deeper.

"What the hell are you doing to me?" he groans as I slowly come back up.

My eyes meet his as his cock pops free from my mouth, and I hold it with my hand as I speak. "Making sure you remember me," I say softly.

An unknown emotion flickers in his gaze, but I take him into my mouth again, ending the stare-down with sexy memories I intend for him to be stuck with every time he thinks about this crazy week.

For at least a couple of hours, I plan to replace every 'amusing' thought in his head with hot, dirty visions that he'll see every time he closes his eyes.

Roman is passed out, and I smile, proud of myself for wearing him out so thoroughly. Carefully, I disentangle myself from his body that is coiled around me.

After taking one last wistful look at him, I grab my arm from the floor and head through the bathroom and back to the room. Any goodbyes would lead to me possibly turning into a blubbering mess, and besides, we had a fuck-bye. And this was just a fuck-week fling, so a fuck-bye is appropriate.

Roman snores, and I grin, fighting back the few tears that are trying to leak out. I'll sob like a baby when I'm going through my withdrawals in the privacy of my own home.

Until then…

As I push through the door, I notice Henley looks as red-rimmed around the eyes as I am, but neither of us speak about it.

Strapping on my arm with quick, jerky movements, I study the empty room they've packed away.

Lydia hands me my bags, and I sigh heavily as I open up my arm bag. It's a habit to count them, and I frown when I count one missing.

"Is there another arm in the closet?"

Lydia goes to the closet, then shakes her head. "All empty."

"Shit. I'm missing one."

"Are you sure?" Henley asks, sniffling then masking it with a cough.

"Positive. It's the one with pretty pink nails." I curse as I zip the bag back up. I unzip my other bag and rifle aimlessly through my clothes. Not there either. "Someone must have stolen it."

"What kind of asshole steals a prosthetic arm from an amputee?" Henley asks, her face a mixture of anger and disgust.

"Who knows? Lots of dickheads in this place," I grumble, frustrated now that my prettiest arm is gone *and* I'm leaving behind a pretty boy with soft black hair and deep blue eyes.

We don't say another word as we make it down the stairs. Mom is dealing with the aftermath of the worst wedding ever, and Heath is helping her, working right by her side. It sucks that I've never noticed how they're always close to each other, facing whatever obstacle is in their path as a team.

Now it's like I can't see her without finding him nearby. And more memories surface of my mother in one place and my father in another, rarely ever finding them in the same spot at the same time.

Funny how our minds work.

We start walking toward our car as the valet brings it around. I guess Lydia or Henley called for it. Just as the valet hops out to take our bags, I turn and walk briskly back toward my mother.

She turns around, her smile forming when she sees me, but I don't stop until my arms are wrapped around her in hug that surprises us both. She gasps, but then her arms tighten around me almost painfully as she holds me to her. I'm fairly positive I hear her sniffle.

"I'll call you when I get home," I tell her, releasing her as tears mist my eyes.

When I pull back, I notice Heath wiping his eyes and turning away. I'm not in hugging territory with him just yet. "Bye, Heath," I call.

He clears his throat loudly as my mother grins. "Bye," he says with a gruff tone.

Henley and Lydia are staring at me with gaping mouths when I return to the car. "Let's get this awful drive over with," I tell them, hopping into the front passenger seat.

Lydia takes the driver's seat, and I lean against the door. The atmosphere is noticeably cooler as we leave, compared to what it was when we burned in. Henley is silent, lost in her thoughts. I'm the same.

Lydia plays radio roulette with herself until she's slapping her own face to stay awake. It's a quiet and uneventful ride. To be fair, it's easy to be underwhelmed after a week like ours.

By the time they drop me off, I'm ready to crash. But instead of falling into a sleep-deprivation coma right away, I finally brave looking at my phone.

There's a text, and my stomach flips over when I see it's from Roman. It's actually a picture message.

The picture confuses the actual hell out of me. My pretty pink nails on my pretty arm are cupping a not so pretty set of truck nuts. You know, like the truck nuts you find on the back of a redneck's truck, balls hanging from under the towing ball thingy… I have no idea why I've even retained this information.

I quickly type out a message to him.

ME: Why is my arm with you? And WTH with the truck nuts?

He doesn't respond back, and I frown. The message is just an hour old. It's possible he's already in bed. I'm not sure why he simply sent a picture of my hand doing something that random. And did he find it somewhere?

I wait for another thirty minutes for him to respond. Finally, I give up and go to sleep, dreaming about chaos, ducks, and orgasms. And not in that order. Also, not in the same dream, just for your dirty information.

CHAPTER SEVENTEEN

Henley

The drive home is a miserable blur. All I can think about is the look on Davis's face the last time I saw him in the gazebo. I know I've done the right thing, but that knowledge doesn't make it any easier. A part of me really wanted to encourage him when he talked about relocating, but it wouldn't be fair to him. I can't trust him and I'm not even sure what I want anymore. I need to be single and not worry about a relationship for a while.

It's late when I finally make it home, and sitting on my step is the last asshole I want to see. "Henley! I've been looking for you for a week." My loser ex, Casey, stands and approaches me. "Where were you?"

Seriously? "It's none of your damn business where I've been. What are you doing here?"

"I just want to talk. I miss you."

"You miss having someone to pay your bills. We're done, Casey. You need to leave."

"I-I just need somewhere to stay for a few days."

The fucking nerve. "I would suggest staying with the skank you cheated on me with." I shove past him to unlock my door and heave my heavy suitcase inside.

"I don't want her! I'm sorry. I've told you I'm sorry a hundred times." His tone of voice pisses me off even more. Like I'm the one who is being unreasonable. How did I stay with this man for a year?

"Fine. You're sorry. It doesn't change anything. You need to leave."

When I turn to go inside, he grabs my wrist and runs his hand up my arm. "Come on. Don't you remember how good it was with us?"

Anger floods through me. "You want to know what I remember? I remember having to pay for everything. I remember having to drive you to work—when you actually had a job—and then pick you up because you lost your driver's license for a DUI. And even if I could overlook all that, I remember having to turn over and get myself off after every time we had sex, because you couldn't get the job done."

Indignation fills his face and his nostrils flare. It makes him look like an angry hog. "It's not my fault you're fucking frigid."

"Well, the guy who gives me four orgasms a night doesn't think so. Now get the fuck out of here before I have you removed and add another line to your rap sheet."

I slam the door behind me, drowning out his tantrum. I'm not kidding. If he isn't gone in another minute, I'm calling the cops. I'm done taking shit from men. I'm officially swearing off them. Buzzy, my trusty vibrator, will be the only man in my life.

By the time I throw my dirty clothes into the washer and relocate my bathroom items to their rightful places, he's gone. Guess he knows I'm not screwing around. After a long, hot shower, I flop onto the couch and turn the T.V. to one of my favorite shows. Thank goodness for DVR. It's been a long, emotionally exhausting week, and though I have to admit, I had a blast, I just want to veg out on the couch and relax. I have to go back to work tomorrow and life will go back to normal.

My phone buzzes with a text from Davis just as I'm crawling into bed.

DAVIS: Just wanted to make sure you got home okay.

ME: Made it home fine. Just going to bed. Thanks for checking.

A lump rises in my throat and my finger hovers over the call button, but I restrain myself. As much as I want to hear his voice, it won't help me get over him. Plus, if he was really serious about relocating, he probably won't give up easily. He always was tenacious. I don't want to have to keep saying no, or worse, fall into an argument over it. We left things in a good place and I want to remember it that way. I just have to keep the distance between us, physically and emotionally.

DAVIS: Bed? What are you wearing?

ME: A frown. I'm not sexting you.

DAVIS: Just a frown? Not even panties? Another thong?

Nope, I'm not taking the bait. A few minutes pass and he realizes I'm not going to answer.

DAVIS: Do you have any idea what you do to me?

Before I can make the decision whether to reply, I get a picture. A picture of a hard, swollen cock.

ME: Did you seriously just send me a dick pic?

DAVIS: I prefer the term penis portrait.

ME: I'm posting this to the Men Seeking Men section of Craigslist. Now stop texting me. I'm going to sleep.

DAVIS: Good-night, beautiful.

ME: Good-night.

Ugh! Now I'm thinking about him. My memories of the last week get tossed and churned with memories of us as kids. I loved him. Part of me still does. He was my first love, though he didn't know it. Sleep takes me into dreams of us.

The sun wakes me before my alarm, since I failed to shut my curtains before bed. Oh well, since I have some extra time, I'll treat myself to my favorite coffee shop breakfast.

The coffee shop is right around the corner from the hospital where I work, so I'm not surprised to see Linda, the receptionist from radiology, waving for me to join her. Grabbing my coffee and blueberry muffin, I take a seat beside her.

"How was the wedding?"

"It was a long week, but I had fun." Especially being bent over by my childhood crush. "Did I miss anything?"

Chuckling, she shakes her head. "All the usual drama. Oh! Wait until you see the clinic they're running today." Once a month, the hospital holds a clinic to test for specific conditions. Diabetes, breast cancer, glaucoma. It mostly attracts elderly people.

"Oh no, what is it?" I groan, popping the last bite in my mouth.

"I'll let you see for yourself," she replies, as we walk to work. A banner just inside the lobby reads: *What's up your butt? Rectal and colon check clinic.* I'm a professional. Okay, I'm supposed to be professional, but I can't help giggling like a four-year-old. The people waiting in line don't seem to see much humor in it. I suppose I wouldn't either if it were my ass about to get probed.

I have a great job. Being an x-ray tech lets me work in the medical field and help people without having to deal with the whole bodily fluid thing. I'm just too squeamish. I know I'm lucky because I work with friendly people and don't dread coming to work like so many others. It can be stressful at times when I get an uncooperative patient, or have to argue with a parent who can't understand why they're not allowed to stay beside their child and soak up radiation, but overall, it's enjoyable work.

One broken arm, a fractured finger, and case of pneumonia later, it's time for lunch. I usually join Linda or one of the other girls in the cafeteria, but I don't feel real sociable today. Instead, I grab a salad and iced tea from the cafeteria and park my ass on a bench outside.

My phone rings and my mom's face grins at me from the screen. "Hey, Mom."

"Henley Dixon! You were supposed to call me when you got back! How was the wedding?"

Mom and I are pretty close, and we talk at least once a week since I moved away. "It was interesting," I laugh. We spend the next few minutes chatting as I fill her in on the week—minus the fuckfest with Davis—and the calamity the ceremony turned into.

"You always have the most fun," she laughs. "Now, do you want to tell me why I had a call from Davis Lane last night?"

Holy shit. He called my mom? "Uh, what did he want?"

"Your address."

"You didn't!"

"Of course not. He said he had your cell number, so I told him if you wanted him to know where you live, you'd tell him."

"Thank you," I breathe.

"You realize he can just use the Google, right? Do you know why he wanted your address?"

The Google. After multiple times of trying to tell her it's *just* Google, I've given up. But she's right. Why is he trying to find me? I told him I didn't want anything more. "No idea. We met up at the wedding, but he lives in Nashville."

"Hmm." It's the tone she uses when she doesn't believe me.

"Look, I'm at work, so I'll call you later okay?"

"Sure, love you."

"Love you, too."

As soon as I hang up, I text Davis.

ME: Why are you bothering my mother for my address?

His response is almost instant.

DAVIS: Would you have given it to me if I'd asked?

ME: No.
DAVIS: Well, there you go.

Shaking my head, I dig into my lunch to keep myself from responding. It was supposed to be one week of fun. What the hell is he up to?

It's hard to stay in a bad mood on such a beautiful day. A light breeze blows through my hair, and the sun warms my skin. When I finish eating, I remove my tablet from my bag and get lost in the latest romance novel. Someone sits beside me, but I barely notice until he slides closer. I turn to tell the creep to back off and look into black-as-ink eyes. Fuck me.

An amused smile curls Davis's lips while I gape at him. "What the hell are you doing here?"

"I work here." His smile widens and he reclines on the bench, extending his long legs and crossing his ankles like he's just chilling out at home.

"The fuck you do!"

"The fuck I don't," he laughs. "I got the job offer a few days ago."

"We cannot be that hard up for a physical therapist." Come to think of it, Mrs. Lenky retired last month. They probably were looking to hire someone.

"It's nice to see you, too. Dinner tonight?"

My stunned brain is still trying to process the fact that he now works at the same hospital. Just down the hall from me. It took everything in me to resist him the past week. Now I have to do it every day? And probably watch him parade every skank in the city around after he realizes we aren't happening? I can't deal with this right now.

"I have to get back to work," I mumble, and walk away.

"So, no dinner?" he calls, laughing when I flip him off without turning around. "In due time, sweetheart!"

I'm relieved to see I don't have another patient for an hour when I return to work, assuming no one comes into the E.R. needing a scan. My head is all over the place. Davis is here. Working here. Living here. The physical therapy suite is just down the hall and I'll see him multiple times per day.

One thing about him hasn't changed. He's obviously as impulsive as ever. He left our hometown and never looked back and now he's done it again. I'd be lying if I said I wasn't flattered and so damn tempted to jump into a relationship with him, but that same impulsive streak will come back to bite me in the ass.

When the next x-ray tech shows up to relieve me, I creep out of the hospital like he'll hear my footsteps and come running. It's been a week since I've had any exercise, so I hit the gym for an hour before heading home. All I want to do is take a nice, hot bath and try not to think about Davis.

Which would probably be easier to do if he weren't standing in my yard with—for fuck's sake—he's talking to Casey. Great, now I have two stalkers. As annoyed as I am that Davis has tracked me down instead of just calling like a normal person, I will use it to my advantage to get rid of Casey for good.

They both turn and look at me when I climb out of the car. "Making a new friend?" I ask Davis, who shoots me an angry look.

"Are you dating this loser?" Davis asks, and I shake my head. God, he looks good, standing there in dark jeans and a blue T-shirt that shows the outline of his amazing physique.

"Nope, I kicked him out before I left for Florida. Apparently, he's too dense to understand."

"Henley!" Casey glares at me, and I'm tempted to kick him in the balls. I know whatever comes out of his mouth is just going to piss me off. "Are you fucking him?"

"That would be none of your business, but since you asked, yes. Casey, meet Davis, the best lay I've ever had."

A wide smile stretches across Davis's face until Casey screeches, "You fucking whore! You were gone a week!"

Like a bolt of lightning, Davis is on him, punching him in the mouth and dragging him into the street. It's far from a fair fight since Davis has more muscle and height than Casey could ever dream of possessing. Davis grabs his fist as he tries to hit him back. "No-no! Time to go home, little boy. Henley has decided to start dating men. Now, run along."

There's still a smile on his face as if he's loving every minute of this. Casey is panting and blood runs down his lip while Davis appears completely relaxed, bored even. "She's frigid anyway!" Casey yells.

"She's plenty warm when my cock's inside her. Now go before I really embarrass you."

With a glare of blackest hate, Casey huffs off down the street, and Davis approaches me. "Seriously, Hen? Those are the kind of guys you date?"

Unlocking my door, I mumble, "It's all temporary anyway."

As soon as we make it through the door, he has me pinned to the wall. His lips kiss the soft spot below my ear that drives me nuts. "Not anymore. We're not temporary."

"We're not anything, Davis. You can't just barge in here and decide we're dating like the last eight years never happened."

His lips travel down my neck, leaving tiny kisses and I feel my resolve weakening. "I've missed you so much, Hen. Just give me a chance, spend time with me and I'll show you that you can trust me again."

Stepping back so I can think straight, I ask, "How did you manage to find a job here so quickly?"

"I applied at multiple hospitals and received a few offers before I went to Florida. After we reconnected, I realized this hospital was where you worked, and I emailed my acceptance a few days ago."

"You came here for me?"

"There's nothing left for me in Nashville. I only settled there for my mother. It's time to start over, and I want to do it with you."

I drop my head. "I need to think about it. I can't just jump into a relationship with you. I don't want to get hurt again."

His rough palm slides under my chin, tilting my head until our gazes lock. "I'll never hurt you, love, and we have all the time in the world." His lips tilt in a small smile. "I'll make you love me again."

If he only knew how much I already do. "I suppose you can stay for dinner."

His deep laugh follows me down the hallway.

So, dinner may have turned into an all-nighter with a handful of orgasms between us. Instead of leaving after, he curled up beside me in my bed, pulled me into his arms, and held me all night. I could get used to this, which is exactly what scares me.

"Mmm," he moans when I try to get out of bed, and I'm pulled back against his warm body. "I don't want to get up. Let's stay right here all day. We'll try to break our *Oh God* record."

"Oh God record?" I giggle.

"The number of times you call me God, or we can try to break the *Please* record, you know, when you beg me for it."

"Ugh, remind me why I let you spend the night again."

Rolling me underneath him, he runs his tongue up my neck. "I'm trying to."

"I just got back from a week's vacation and it's your second day at a new job. Don't think the hospital will be cool with letting us off," I laugh, wiggling out from under him.

"Fine." He slaps my ass. "Get dressed and I'll take you out for breakfast."

If I can walk. This man is going to be the death of me. I dress while he showers, and a few minutes later we're on our way out the door. A large pot of flowers waits on the top step with a greeting card stuck on top. What the hell?

Davis snorts. "What did he do? Steal this from a graveyard?"

"I wouldn't be surprised," I grumble, grabbing the card. Curiosity won't let me just tear it up, so I sit on the top step to open it, and Davis takes a seat right beside me, making it clear he's going to read it too.

My curiosity and his possessiveness backfire big time when I open the card and a puff of white powder floats into our faces. "What the fuck?" he exclaims, and a chill runs through me at the words on the blank card.

Have some anthracks, bitch.

It can't be. Where the hell would that loser get anthrax? He doesn't even have a car. Davis is taking no chances, though, and he knocks the envelope from my hand, brushing at me and then himself. "It can't be anthrax," I tell him. "Look, he isn't even smart enough to spell it correctly."

"We can't chance it, Hen," he says, calling 911.

Twenty minutes later we're bundled into the back of an ambulance with two men who look like they escaped from the Outbreak movie, headed to the hospital.

We're taken to the nearest hospital, which of course is where we work, so the humiliation is complete. We're led down the back hallway to a decontamination room. I was wrong. The humiliation isn't complete until we're herded into the tiled room where two shower-heads jut from the far wall, and ordered to strip.

A man, who looks around sixty-five, is led in after us. "What's going on?" Davis demands.

"The same white powder was sent to Mr. Hatten. We need to decontaminate the three of you, then you'll be housed in the isolation unit until we can be sure what the powder contained," a man in a hazmat suit explains.

WORTH IT

Mr. Hatten is led to the far showerhead and ordered to strip off his clothes while another hazmat suited guy wields a hose with a sprayer, waiting to scrub him down. Only a four foot high partition separates the showers. "Can't we use another room, or wait until you've finished with him?" I ask, dreading the answer.

"No, every second counts. We need to get the powder off of you now."

Shit. Fine. I jerk my shirt over my head and strip off my pants and underwear, keeping my eyes on the ground. Davis does the same, shooting daggers at the two men ordered to decontaminate us. I step under the shower first and then lather up while Davis takes his turn under the spray.

The guy in the protective suit begins to spray me down, starting with my hair, and working his way down, rinsing all the soap away. He hands me a bottle of some lemon smelling disinfectant and has me wash with it before turning to Davis. I can't help the snort of laughter that escapes when Davis snaps, "Dude, I've been washing my balls since I was four. I've got it."

As I finish rinsing the rest of the disinfectant away, Mr. Hatten speaks up, "You spray my ass with that one more time, son, and I'm going to ram it up yours." I can't help it. Laughter shakes my chest as I dry off and dress in the gown I'm provided. I'm going to have to call Kasha or Lydia to bring me some clothes. Kasha's going to love this. I'll never live it down.

Davis approaches me, shaking his head. "We've just been publicly decontaminated and quarantined. What are you smiling about?" He looks so funny in the little blue gown that doesn't quite fit around his chest. At least I'm thin enough to wrap the gown around myself so my ass isn't showing.

"You wanted in my life, buddy. This is what you get. Are you ready to run, yet?" I tease.

"What kind of man would I be if I couldn't handle a little anthrax?"

"It's not anthrax. The asshole is just pissed. You watch. It'll turn out to be flour or something." I was sure Casey did this, the handwriting even looked like his, but that doesn't explain why Mr. Hatten is here.

We're escorted to a long room with four beds and told that someone will be in to brief us on the situation soon. In the meantime, we're locked in. Mr. Hatten takes the bed nearest the door, while I sit on the far one by the window. "Mr. Hatten, how did you end up here?"

"Some shit for brains left me an envelope on my counter at work. I opened it up and powder went flying."

"Where do you work?" Davis asks, also trying to piece this together.

"Salvage yard on Fifth Street." He climbs onto the bed, his saggy, wrinkled ass hanging out the back of his robe. It's nothing I haven't seen before. Patients are sent to x-ray in gowns all the time, but Davis looks horrified.

"We're cool as long as he doesn't bend over," I mumble. "We don't want to see anything resembling a baby bird."

"Thanks for that image," Davis sighs, and grabs a sheet off the extra bed, wrapping himself in it to keep from mooning the guy back.

"Do you know a man named Casey Hillard?" I ask.

Mr. Hatten tilts his head back and thinks about it. "Can't say I do."

"Skinny, blond, with a bird tattoo on the back of his hand?"

Recognition dawns in the old man's hazel eyes. "That little punk! Begged me to hire him on, but I caught him sleeping in one of the cars on his second day. Fired him. You think he did this? Why did he target you?"

"I dumped him."

"Well, shit fire. Wait until I get my hands on that little shit weasel."

Davis and I both laugh, and he climbs onto the bed with me. We don't have a chance to discuss it further because hazmat man is back. I recognize him as one of the new doctors. He explains that we have to stay here until they can test the powder and see if it's dangerous. Hopefully, we'll be out in twenty-four hours.

"Can we have some real clothes?" Davis asks.

"If you have someone bring them."

Thankfully, he gives me my phone so I can call Kasha. She agrees to swing by my place and bring me some clothes, along with picking up some sweats for Davis. Now, all we can do is wait. Mr. Hatten turns on the television and seems to tune us out.

I lay my head on Davis's chest, and he plays with my hair. "Are you scared?"

"No, I'm pissed. The powder is going to turn out to be nothing, but he still managed to humiliate us."

"At least you didn't have a man trying to wash your balls."

"It turned you on a little, didn't it? You can admit it."

"No!" We lie together, talking and laughing as if this isn't an incredibly awkward situation. It doesn't help that Mr. Hatten keeps cutting farts as if he's the only one in the room. Finally, Kasha and Lydia show up. They won't let them in the room, so I have to talk to them through the window, but hazmat man brings in the bag of clothes.

"What the hell have I missed in the last two days?" Kasha asks, gesturing to me and Davis. "I leave you alone for two days and you're quarantined with your wedding fling."

"Casey happened," I reply.

"Are you going to be okay?" Lydia asks.

"We'll be fine, but her ex isn't going to make it through the week," Davis growls. He's pulling clothing out of the bag and his gaze darts to Kasha. "Seriously?" he says, holding up a blue garment.

"Are those pajama pants?" I ask, and he thrusts them into my hands.

Kasha grins at him as I chuckle, handing back the pajama pants covered in smiling dolphins. He jerks them on and pulls a white T-shirt over his head. "Smile, sexy," Kasha says, snapping a picture with her phone.

Kasha and Lydia don't stay long, and we spend the rest of the evening cuddled up together, waiting to hear the test results. A police officer shows up and talks to us through the window, letting us know Casey has been arrested.

We eat horrible hospital food for dinner, and about an hour after Mr. Hatten falls asleep, we get the full effect of the chili we were served. The room is filled with his increasingly fragrant gas, and Davis laughs, pulling the sheet over our heads. Forehead to forehead, we cuddle together. "The answer to your earlier question is no, Hen. I'm not ready to run. I'm not going anywhere. I'm right where I want to be."

"You want to be in a stinking hospital room with a man whose anus has a questionable shutter speed?"

"I want to be with you. I don't care where we are, or what we're doing. I want to wake up with you and fall asleep with you. And everything in between. I'm in love with you, Hen. I always have been. I'm sorry it's taken me so long to act on it."

A lump forms in my throat. When I was eighteen, there was nothing I wanted more in the world than to hear those words from him, and in eight years, that hasn't changed. Maybe I'm being stupid and reckless letting him back into my heart, but honestly, he never left. It's always beat for him. It's dim under the sheet, but I can make out his features and the way his eyes widen when I reply, "Fine, you win. I love you, too."

His lips land on mine in a ferocious kiss. "You do?"

"I never stopped. You grabbed my heart when we were kids and never let go." He pulls me close to him and kisses me until I can barely breathe. "But I'm not fucking you here, with an old man playing the butt trumpet a few feet away."

The door opens before he can respond and a doctor walks in without a hazmat suit on. "The tests are back. It wasn't anthrax or any other harmful toxin. You can return home."

"Thank fuck," Davis says, stuffing his feet in the slippers the hospital provided. "Do you know what it was?"

"Baby powder."

"I'm going to kill that asshole."

"Get in line, son," Mr. Hatten speaks up, climbing out of his bed and bending over to retrieve his slippers.

Davis groans as I giggle. "See? Baby bird."

CHAPTER EIGHTEEN

Kasha

Since being home, things just keep getting weirder. Then again, that's pretty much *my* normal.

The only time I've really gotten out is when Henley got quarantined. That's how pathetic I've become.

Dad has been a flurry of motion, and his two part-time interns have been here daily since my return. Apparently, they were here before my return too.

Emitt is propped against the wall downstairs, guzzling down a bottle of water when I walk into the main kitchen. My tiny studio apartment doesn't have a fridge just yet.

Emitt is the sexy intern I used to enjoy watching during his trips here. It was awesome to subtly drop things so he'd bend over and pick them up. Now I barely even notice he's a man. He could wave his penis and ask me to ride it like a drunk cowgirl, and I'd politely decline so I could go sulk over another guy, who… Don't even get me started. Roman sends things, but won't respond to any of my messages.

Stupid turd nugget.

"Your dad was just bitching about you signing him up on a dating website," Emitt tells me, his smile forming to flash a set of perfectly straight, white teeth.

"He can get over it. I want a stepmom with a pulse."

His eyebrows go up in confusion.

"Never mind," I say, waving my robo hand in a dismissive gesture before he can ask questions.

"Your arm and hand still working good? Your dad said it messed up and he had to leave to fix it."

"She hasn't tried to molest me again, so I'm not complaining right now."

Again, his eyebrows hit his hairline. He used to act terrified of speaking to me, as though he was worried I was some psycho chick whose sanity was bled out when she lost her arm. Now he's gotten used to me, and other than the occasional eyebrow raises, he shrugs off most of my crazy. Since his field of expertise is prosthetics, he's never been weird about amputees either, so bonus.

"I guess he didn't tell me everything," he says, grinning as he props up on the dining room table. "Fill me in."

I snort, then shake my head. "I'll let your imagination work out the details. But never again will I say 'fuck me' in my head."

My eyes dart down, watching Jill twitch. But she doesn't go after me. *Good girl.*

He bursts out laughing, and I force a smile while turning back to my task of fixing a sandwich. I thought once I was out of the intense atmosphere the intimate wedding week provided, my brain would start firing on logical neurons again. It'd point out how stupid it is to be that attached to a guy I've only been messing around with for a week.

No such luck. If anything, it's getting harder and harder to think of anything but him, even though he went and got incredibly weird since I left. The weird factor just intrigues me all the more, because I like weird. But it's also annoying to be ignored while he continues to be weird.

"You okay?" Emitt asks, reminding me he's still in the room.

"Hmm? I mean... yeah, fine. Why do you ask?"

I take a long sip of my water, still distracted, as he answers.

"Well, you've been back for almost a week and haven't once dropped anything for me to pick up so you could check out my ass," he says, causing me to choke, sputter, and spit out half my water, while the other half sprays from my nose.

Awesome.

Fuck my day.

Emitt is laughing as I wipe away my mess from the counter. I'm still coughing while my nose burns, and I'm fairly sure there's a spit string attached to my chin. Using my arm, I wipe it away, then rub my arm on my shirt. Yeah, I'm sexy like that.

I guess I'm not the queen of subtle like I thought I was.

Clearing my throat, I start to try and recover from that, when my phone dings with a text. I'm scared to look at it. I'm almost positive I know who it's from.

After that first picture, Roman sent another one the very next day. It was a picture of my hand holding a chocolate dove. Then there was a picture of my pretty hand holding a vibrator on a bed—whose bed? The sheets were white, and that was all I could see beyond the vibrator and hand. And whose vibrator?! One of my vibrators, that's whose. How he'd get my vibrator?

The next time it was palming the back of an ass—I hope it was his ass. Then it was beside a bouquet of roses, holding a card that I couldn't read, thanks to the blurry pixilation that occurred when I tried to zoom.

WORTH IT

Sure enough, the new message is from him, and again it's a random picture. He hasn't explained any of this. He won't respond to any of the questions I keep asking.

This time my prosthetic hand is groping the boob of a mannequin in a lingerie store.

Not sure how I feel about that. Well, I feel violated, though I'm sure it pales in comparison to how that mannequin must feel. For all I know, that mannequin may be related to my dad's blowup, soon-to-be ex-girlfriend.

"That would be an awkward family reunion," I mutter to myself while shuddering.

"What?" Emitt asks.

My eyes come up, meeting his as my lips purse.

"Can I ask you a question?"

He shrugs. "Sure."

"What does it mean when a guy steals your prosthetic, and has it touching random things like truck nuts, chocolate doves, roses, an ass, and mannequin boobs?"

His eyebrows try to jump off his face this time.

"I'd say that's really fucked up."

"On the weird-o-meter scale from one to ten, ten being the highest, where would—"

"Twenty," he says, shuddering.

"I said one to ten."

"I know. I still say it's a solid twenty."

Hmm. On my scale I was saying at most a four, but he seems firm on his number.

Before I can say more, someone is ringing the doorbell, and Emitt jogs over to answer it. Our house is set up oddly. The actual house bleeds into my dad's office, then his huge shop that used to be a garage. He expanded it to make it more like a ten-car garage, but it's just machines and tech stuff. Above it is my small apartment, but I spend almost as much time down here as I do up there, since my jewelry room is in the back in my old bedroom.

"Kasha, I think it's for you," Emitt calls out.

I head for the door, confused. When I reach it, Emitt is grinning, perched up against the door as a delivery man thrusts two vases full of roses at me.

Emitt helps me take them, and I sign the pad. "Who are these—"

The man walks off before I can finish my question, acting like he has more important things to do than deliver roses from the rose delivery van like he's paid to do.

"Rude much?" I grumble, trying to look for a card.

"No card on this one," Emitt says, apparently snooping in an effort to help me.

The only card simply reads, "*KASHA.*"

For a fleeting moment I consider Roman, but then remember my mother loves roses. Now that we've mended fences and have started talking regularly, I'm sure this is her sending me the rest of the olive branch... or maybe the whole tree or whatever.

Emitt and I both set down the roses, and I shrug it off.

"You coming back to work with us today?" he asks as I follow him through the labyrinth we call a home, taking my sandwich with me.

"Just letting Dad download all the info from Jill," I say absently, before taking a bite.

Dad has on his weird little spectacles that seem to grow longer with each passing year. They have that whole pointy-eyed thing going on. He lifts one layer of the magnifying glasses, swiveling it out of the way. Then another, and another, and... *Sheesh.* How many does he have now?

Finally, he makes it to a set that don't make his eyes look like alien fish eyes.

"Kasha! Make those damn messages stop!" he snaps, and I grin like a mischievous little brat.

"What? Don't know how to correspond with breathing women?" I muse.

Emitt chokes, and Jenny—Dad's second, young, and very sweet intern—drops her tools on the floor before stumbling. In hindsight, that does sound more like necrophilia than... what's the fetish called for humping plastic shit?

Dad is a wonky shade of red right now.

Too far, Kasha.

"It was just an experiment!" Dad hisses, only making that necrophilia rumor grow bigger.

Obviously a good daughter would clarify so that his interns didn't go around telling everyone that he's screwing the dead.

"Was the experiment to see how deep your dick could go inside an over-embellished balloon? Or were you testing your speed? Maybe your endurance?"

I stop there, because now I'm gagging. I also toss the rest of my sandwich into the trash, because my appetite is gone.

Dad's eyes almost bug out of his head, and Emitt turns around, his body shaking with silent laughter. Jenny's eyes are wide and horrified as she looks to Dad for confirmation. Poor girl. She's barely twenty and being ever-so-slowly corrupted by the madness that is the Jensen household.

"I think I'll just go stand way over there," Jenny says, walking toward the machine that has more bells and whistles than anything else in here.

Emitt follows her, raising his hands in a *what-the-fuck* gesture while grinning at me. I just shrug in response. A small grin graces my lips when Jenny fake-stumbles and drops one of the screwdrivers. As soon as Emitt bends over to pick it up for her, she eyes his ass. *Sigh.* She's definitely been corrupted. I hope that I'll enjoy that ass again one day.

"We're not discussing my love life anymore," Dad hisses.

"Says you," I quip, moving my eyes back to my infuriated father.

"How about your love life?" Dad asks, arching an eyebrow. "Your mother called and told me I'd better make sure you felt like it was okay to leave me if things worked out with Roland."

"Roman," I correct flatly. "But things didn't work out, so no worries."

I don't mention the cryptic messages, because I'm not sure I understand them.

"Is he the guy…" He lets his words trail off as his brow furrows.

"The guy who saw you balls-deep in rub-a-dub Susie? You betcha."

He groans. "You're never going to let that go, are you?"

The doorbell rings overhead, alerting us we have yet another guest waiting at the front door of the main house this morning. Emitt jogs across the warehouse to go answer it, while Jenny's eyes chase his firm butt cheeks the whole way.

"I was irrevocably scarred for life because of that. So no, I won't let you forget it any time soon."

I shudder dramatically, just to emphasize how truly traumatized I am, but he just rolls his eyes and starts turning his glasses back down, clicking the lenses into place one at a time. When he's finished, his eyes are nothing more than two giant pupils, and he faces his tiny work once again.

As he uses some buzzing thingy to make smoke on some wire thingy, I prop a hip against the table. "I thought you wanted to check on Jill."

"I do, but first I need to find the short in this—"

"More deliveries for you," Emitt says as he walks back in. "They said they'd put it wherever, so where do you want this stuff?" he adds.

"Me?"

He nods.

Sheesh. How many roses will Mom send? Dad will be sneezing his head off when he goes in there.

"Just send them to my room with it."

The doorbell rings again, and Emitt jogs back into action. Dad's phone pings with a new hit from his profile, and I respond to the woman.

"You have a date with a tantric sex trainer," I tell my father, then make a mental note to bleach my brain from the fallout of those words later.

"I'm not dating anyone."

My phone chimes, and I look down as I answer, flipping open the newest picture from Roman.

"You're going out with her. She's not your type since her lips are real instead of painted on, but she'll do."

He mutters something as I cock my head, trying to figure out what purpose it serves for Roman to send me a picture of my hand stuffed inside some orange peels.

ME: Are you ever going to explain this? I tried calling you. Why do you have my arm?

Unsurprisingly, he ignores my text, just as he's done all week.

"Everything upstairs?" Emitt calls from the doorway.

"Yes, please," I call back, then focus my attention on my stubborn father. "You're going out this weekend. Public place. No drinking anything without watching it mixed. And give me an exact time to expect you back."

He picks up a screwdriver and holds it out, pointing it at me like it's a weapon. "I'm the father," he says, looking utterly ridiculous since all I can see are those magnified pupils when he tries to glare.

"The *father* was found molesting a blowup doll. I'm tired of finding quirky ways to put it."

He heaves out a breath, and Emitt comes back in, shaking his head. "I left the door open," he says, walking on back.

"Why?" I ask as he passes.

"They're gonna be a while."

I fully mean to ask about that, but I get distracted. Jenny drops her pencil, Emitt bends to pick it up, and Jenny leans back to check out his ass again. My phone chimes during the show, and I look at it, frowning. This time the picture is of my hand on top of a box. That's all I can see too.

ME: Why won't you answer me????? What is your fucking defect?????

The infuriating asshole still refuses to answer my questions.

Putting my phone away, I glare at my father as he continues doing whatever geek stuff he likes doing. "You're going on a date. I think it's long overdue. You're going to get to know her, and if you're really lucky, she'll be worth a second date."

I pat him on the shoulder, then curse when my phone goes off with another text. What's his deal today? Why so many pictures?

This time my hand is stuck in between towels... Why does that look so familiar?

"If I go on this date," my dad says, drawing me out of my confusion as I tuck my phone away again, "you're going to take me off that website?"

He doesn't look over at me. "I'll take you off that site when you put a ring on someone's finger."

He opens his mouth, and I add, "Someone with blood in her veins instead of air. I mean, you can get an airhead if you want, just not *literally*."

He mutters a few curses, and I grin. This has gotten boring, and it's obvious he's knee-deep in his work. Deciding to come back later for him to do his thing with Jill, I head upstairs to my apartment.

As soon as I walk inside, I'm yelping, and falling, and yelping some damn more. What the hell?

A grunt slips through my lips when I pound the ground. Cursing, I look around at the insanity in my room. "What the actual hell?" I groan, shocked as I survey all the boxes in my room. There's barely a trail from my bedroom to my bathroom, and my living room is essentially buried. My bed is like the only thing without flowers or boxes on it.

Just as I'm about to call my mother, my eyes catch sight of a note on my bed. It's typed, and there's only one sentence written on it: *All the fucking woo.*

What the hell does that mean?

I start to open the box I tripped over, when the very distinct sound of a running shower registers, and my veins chill like ice. Stumbling to my feet and tripping over boxes, I grab the broom from the corner and start creeping into the bathroom.

Did one of those delivery fuckers decide to shower in my freaking bathroom?

I will so break a broom on his boundary-pushing ass.

Quietly, I walk toward the bathroom, then glare at Jill when she crushes part of the flimsy broom handle. Calming my breaths, I charge into the bathroom, my banshee war cry echoing off the walls as I swing the broom at the shower curtain.

The curtain is jerked open, and a gasp leaves my lips as a hand darts out and catches the broom before it can connect with a very wet, slippery, incredibly sexy, naked man.

"You always so violent?" he drawls.

"Roman," I hiss, shaking for some weird reason.

He rakes his wet, inky black hair out of his eyes with one hand, while his other hand tugs the broom free from my grip and tosses it aside. He arches an eyebrow, his face expressionless other than that.

"What the hell are you doing here?" I ask, finding my small bathroom a lot smaller than it was a few seconds ago.

"I walked into my bathroom, and suddenly ended up here. Obviously it was a vortex or something," he says dryly, amusement flickering in his eyes as he mocks my words from the day I stumbled into his room.

That feels like so long ago.

"Obviously," I say quietly, cocking my head. "Or, you drove five and a half hours to take a shower in my bathroom. It's not as likely as your vortex theory, but it's best to consider all options."

I'm talking on autopilot, mostly. My brain is still trying to process whether or not I'm awake or just having a seriously good dream where Roman is naked in my shower. He looks just like he did that first day—all brooding, cocky, and arrogant.

And sexy. Of course sexy.

And wet.

And all lean muscly.

And wet.

And *hawt*.

And wet...

"What are you doing here?" I ask him as he continues to study me, a smirk now on his lips.

He turns around, giving me a nice view of his ass. Now I know why Emitt's ass does nothing for me anymore. It's not Roman's ass. Damn, that's a nice ass.

"It's a long drive, and my air stopped working about an hour ago."

I snap my eyes up, trying to understand his answer. He acts like this was something we planned, and his tone implies it's perfectly natural for him to be all naked and soapy in my home. Not that I'm complaining, but...

"Why?" I ask, still reeling.

"Probably ran out of Freon," he says.

I'm so confu—Never mind. I sound like a broken record.

"I mean *why* are you *here*?"

He shuts the water off, and my mouth dries as he turns back around. I think he's always hard. The shock of actually seeing him in my home distracted me from that part of his body earlier. But now my eyes are honed in.

Holy big naked erection.

He steps out of the shower, his big feet looking so out of place on my "Rocker Chicks Do It Better" pink bathmat. My eyes slither back up, but don't make it past his waist. I'm just human, after all.

"You just gonna stare, or could you hand me a towel?"

Absently, I reach out for the shelf, feel the towel at my fingertips, then grab a wash-cloth from beside it and hand it to him instead.

His lips twitch.

I'd like to see him try to use that tiny thing to cover up Thor's hammer.

He slowly walks toward me, and my eyes settle on his, watching the predatory gleam in his gaze. Please, for fuck's sake, let me be the prey.

He reaches me, and my breaths go shaky as I crane my neck back to keep eye contact. His smirk is in place, along with those devastatingly serious eyes. I got used to him being more carefree and full of laughter, like the sheltered man he is. He's back to the original Roman right now.

But intense is still hot on him. Very hot.

When his arm comes up, I shiver, anticipating his touch, but he reaches around me, not accepting my wash-cloth, and grabs a towel from the shelf instead. His eyes never leave mine, so I take it all in with my peripheral as the wash-cloth finally falls from my hand.

As he wraps the towel around his waist, his smirk deepens.

"You're here," I finally say, sounding like a breathy sex hussy about to get her orgasm fix.

Oh, all the orgasms. I want *all* the orgasms.

He just continues to smirk that infuriating smirk, not speaking as he walks around me to head into my bedroom. You'd think he'd been here hundreds of times before, given how easily and comfortably he navigates his way. Then again, I have a small living room, a tiny bathroom, a barely-existing bedroom, and a half kitchen in desperate need of updating, so it's not like there's much to navigate.

He uses the trail between boxes, and my eyes narrow as he grabs a bag from the floor and opens it up.

"You have something to do with all this?" I ask, gesturing around me. "And why did you steal my arm? What was with all those weird pictures of my hand doing things like touching trucker nuts and mannequin boobs?"

He almost smiles. Almost.

"I didn't steal your arm. I retrieved it from the Mulder kids before I left there. Anderson and I had to work together to get the damn thing back in one piece, because those kids are fucking vicious. As for the pictures... Did it piss you off that I sent them and wouldn't respond when you were texting back?" he muses, his hands going to his towel-clad hips as he studies me.

"It was annoying. What was the point?"

"What was the point of sucking me off, then riding my dick like a rodeo champion before putting me in an orgasm-induced coma, then taking off without a word before I woke up?"

Well, that's some vivid imagery.

"I don't do goodbyes well," I grumble, picking at an imaginary piece of lint on my shirt, unable to look at him anymore.

"You suck at wooing," he sighs, causing me to look back up as my brow pinches together.

"What?"

"You suck at wooing," he repeats. "You were supposed to convince me to come see you after the wedding was over, but instead you chickened out. I expected as much though," he says with a careless shrug.

"What are you talking about?"

A ghost of a smile flirts with the corners of his lips. "You're the most fascinating contradiction I've ever met. You want to be cold and tough, but really you're the warmest, gentlest girl there is. You're confident and mock your insecurities, but really you're just guarding yourself from anyone using those insecurities against you. You're competitive and hate losing, but you can also swallow your pride and admit when you're wrong. You're strong, bounce back from adversity quickly, and want the best for everyone, but you won't go after anything you personally want because of the deep-rooted fear of rejection. You're as fragile as you are tough," he says, still studying me.

Is he trying to make me feel naked right now? Because it's working.

"It's as refreshing as it is maddening," he says on a sigh. "The ultimate contradiction."

"And that's why you took pictures of my prosthetic doing weird things all week?" I ask, trying to follow his logic and get off the seriousness where he's ripping me open and exposing everything inside.

"No. I did that because you pissed me off by just leaving without a word, while I was still sleeping off being drained. For at least a few days, I wanted you to feel a fraction of the frustration and craziness you make me feel." His jaw tics, and I stifle a grin.

I don't know why I find it funny when he's pissed, but I do.

"I drive you crazy?"

"Certifiably," he deadpans.

"And all this?" I ask, gesturing around the room at the boxes and flowers. There are a lot more flowers than I noticed when I stumbled in here. Like, every type of flower. Roses. Lilies. Tulips—fucking tulips? You name it, it's in my room. Fairly sure there's even a Venus Flytrap by my window.

He opens a box, pulls out a smaller white box, and tosses it to me. I catch it with my right hand, then stare down at the small box. It's chocolate covered oranges.

"That's supposed to get me two orgasms, by the way," he says, his lips fixed back in that smirk.

"What?"

He gestures around. "Did you not read the note?"

"All the fucking woo?"

He nods, his cockiness unwavering. "It's obvious you suck at wooing, so that left it all to me. I know how to woo. You wanted flowers, chocolate covered oranges and strawberries, and you like your weird fucking underwear."

He opens another box, and I drop the chocolates—*the horror!*—to catch a pair of panties he tosses at my head without warning. I laugh when I read the front of them. *Clit here.* There's even an arrow pointing to the part of the anatomy most guys need a map to find.

"You didn't specify what kind of flowers, so I just got a little bit of everything they had. Full disclosure: Some of the boxes are empty, but I thought it'd have a bigger impact if your place was loaded down with them," he adds, then looks around. "Didn't realize they'd take up this much room, though."

"It's a small apartment above a garage. Not a house."

He turns his gaze back to me, while I struggle not to let my legs turn to rubber. I've never been wooed before.

"This is crazy," I say, even though my breath is shaky.

It's getting realer by the second.

"So are you," he says without an ounce of humor. "Turns out it's what I've been missing in my life."

He takes a step toward me, and I feel like gravity is kicking my ass, pushing me toward him as I close the rest of the distance.

He grabs my hips, gently tugging me closer as I tip my head back to stare up at him.

"We barely know each other."

"Which is why I used some of the insane amount of vacation hours I had to take off every Friday and Monday for the next two months. We'll have very long weekends to get to know each other and give this a real chance, Kasha."

I melt against him, tempted to pinch myself.

A startled cry escapes me when a sharp pain hits my leg. I look down in disbelief as Jill actually freaking pinches me.

Roman's eyebrows raise as I mutter a curse and start stripping out of my harness. Damn *smart* arm.

His fingers brush mine, and I look up as he studies the harness, carefully taking over as my hand falls away. With deft fingers, he finishes undoing the straps, and I stare at his face, drinking in the sight of him.

"Where'd you find the chocolates?" I ask as he removes my arm. I'm now just talking to keep myself from blurting out something stupid, like, *'Please give me orgasms now! Or…take me with you when you go!'*

He flashes me a full smile as he twists his body and carefully places Jill on my dresser. His hands come back to my face, cupping it as he says in a very serious tone, "There's a chocolate delicacy store two blocks from my place."

Oh, I'm going to fall in love.

I shudder, and he bends, kissing a spot between my neck and shoulder, eliciting a few more tremors. "They also have cakes, and pies, and everything else sweet you can imagine."

I moan, and he grins against the spot on my neck.

"My mother will be furious if I'm in a size eight before Christmas," I say absently.

"I'll help you burn off all the chocolate calories," he murmurs, and I press into him more, my fingers moving down firm flesh to where his towel is.

He's mostly dry now, but I lean over and lick one drop of water from his chest. His grip on me tightens, sending a shot of empowerment through me. I love the way he reacts to me.

"How will you do that?" I ask, playing along.

"By letting you practice your blowjob skills until they're good," he says, making me… want to freaking slap him.

I jerk back to see the asshole grinning down at me, his hands sliding over my shoulders.

"I give the best blowjob ever, and you know it."

He rolls his eyes. "There's that competitiveness. Don't worry. I'll keep coaching you until you really are the best."

My mouth falls open in indignant outrage. "My name means *blowjob* in the Urban Dictionary! I can suck a tennis ball through a garden hose, so don't give me that shit. My head-giving skills are awesome."

Something crashes outside my apartment door, and I hear someone coughing and stumbling away. Hope that wasn't Dad.

Roman's lips twitch as he steps back and jerks his towel off. My eyes drop to his very erect appendage that is waving like it's daring me to prove myself.

"It's okay," Roman says, grinning like the asshole he is. "I'm sure all the guys before me didn't have this much to work with," he adds, gesturing down at that waving dick of his. "You'll get better. Promise."

I glare at him, and his smile spreads. I think he loves pissing me off as much as I love pissing him off.

A slow, evil grin curves my lips. "Since we're doing the honesty thing about oral skills, I guess I should let you know there's room for improvement on your end as well. I suppose we'll coach each other," I say, patting him on the chest.

The amusement in his eyes dies as a hard looks comes over his face. "This—" he gestures to his mouth "—is fucking legendary. My skills are fucking epic."

I exhale heavily, shaking my head as if in sympathy, even though I'm brutally aware of how good he is with that mouth. It's not like I can tell him that after he just insulted my awesomeness.

"I'm not sure if you're aware of this, but girls are notorious for *faking* it." Just to really drive home my point, I pull out my best porn star girl voice and dump out my theatrical drama. *"Oh, Roman! Right there! Yes! Oooohhh. Ahhhh. You're amazing!"*

I even grip my hair, throw my head back, and give him my best "O" face just to fuck with him.

My breath leaves in a rush when I'm suddenly lifted into the air and dumped onto the bed. Roman's eyes are narrowed, and he's definitely pissed. But I think he's a little determined too.

Ah yeah.

I grin bigger, sliding up on the bed as I continue with my fake orgasm taunts. *"Ah! Oooohhhh. You're the best ever!"* I moan and get all breathy, but then a shriek leaves my lips when Roman jerks my shorts off and tosses them away.

He flips me over, and I giggle as he starts undoing the laces on the back of my shirt. It's not until a deep rumble of laughter floats out of him that I think about the underwear I'm wearing.

I groan as he slaps my ass. The ass that says "Fart Loading" with a little loading bar underneath.

"It's hard to take you serious when I see shit like this," he says, that deep, rich laughter still sneaking out of him.

"Why can't I be one of those normal girls who wears a string up her ass?" I groan into the pillow. "Those girls are badass, because that shit can't be comfortable, yet they strut around like rock stars."

He leans over me, his hands trailing up the skin of my back as he unclasps my bra with one hand.

"I wouldn't be here with you right now if you were normal. I've had too much normal," he says, kissing the side of my neck.

My body arches back into his as he works my bra over my shoulders, and then he rolls me over again. His body hovers over mine as I shed the shirt and bra completely, and he tugs my underwear off like he can't get them away fast enough.

His lips find mine the second I'm fully naked, and I moan into his mouth, not faking it one bit. Everything about him feels right.

I didn't realize how much I missed kissing him until this moment. His lips seek and search, and his tongue dares me to deny its skills as it works to drive me into a grinding frenzy. If he had a leg between mine right now, I'd totally be humping it—shamelessly.

Each roll of his tongue delivers an electric shiver up my spine that then shoots outwards to the rest of my body, letting every part of me enjoy the same incredible feeling my mouth gets to.

His hand slides downward, teasing the valley of my breasts on its descent, skating across my lower belly with a barely-there touch, and my entire body quakes when his thumb finds that one spot that controls all women. The pressure he applies is diabolical and calculated, giving me just enough to try and grind again, but pulling back with my arch so that I'm denied the extra pressure needed.

His lips break apart from mine, and he groans as he sucks a nipple into his mouth, letting that glorious tongue wreak havoc on the sensitive flesh the same way it did in my mouth. I shouldn't have teased him. Now he's going to make me pay by teasing me in a more tormenting way.

"Please," I rasp, but he ignores me, stopping his thumb just as my orgasm tries to surface. The simmering release fades away at the loss of pressure, the quick retreat replaced by a dull ache. I internally curse the sexy man on top of me.

The length of his body slides against mine, all hard and dominating, driving me wild. His erection taunts me, pressing into my leg, as he kisses his way down my chest. He palms both of my breasts, squeezing as he kisses around my navel. Weird little sounds escape me as I arch, my little lady seeking his perfect mouth.

His tongue darts out, giving a teasing lick to that overly sensitive spot, and I jerk in response. Then he seizes my clit, his tongue and teeth working to make me eat all those lies about him being orally challenged.

Writhing and thrashing beneath him like an unskilled virgin, I grab his hair, holding on like a one-armed lunatic as those sounds leave me in higher pitches. No longer do I sound like a sexy porn star with all my fake moans and chatter. Now I sound like a rabid beast chasing after a bone.

And I explode embarrassingly fast, crying out his name in such a shrill pitch that dogs start barking in the distance. Roman comes up fast, his lips still wet with me, but he kisses me deep and hard, and thrusts inside at the same time, as though he's the one in desperate need.

My fingers tangle in his hair, while my partial left arm props on his shoulder, deepening the kiss as much as I can as he pulls his hips back and thrusts in again. He groans into my mouth, and I feel every vibration of it inside my body.

My legs slide up as I rock against him when he goes still.

"Condom," he rasps against my lips.

"Birth control," I say back, refusing to unlock my legs even as he tries to pry them from his hips.

I realize that's not all the talking we need to do on the subject, but I'm too far gone to think rationally. He is too when he moves inside me again, and I fight to hang on.

The movements cause him to groan once more, and he shudders against me, his lips and teeth carving a trail down my neck, nibbling and kissing.

Then he thrusts, and all else is forgotten as he returns his lips to mine in a rough kiss that imitates the way he's fucking me. It's incredible, and sexy, and oh so freaking perfect.

When that feeling buds in my core this time, it's too powerful to even stave off. I break the kiss to keep from biting him, and I'm crying out again as everything contracts inside me. A wave of electric tingles wash over me, and I become a boneless puppet in his arms as he chases his own release.

He comes with a grunt and a praised curse, and I grin against him as he drops to me, panting.

"Can't, breathe," I say, mocking a strained, breathless tone.

I can breathe just fine and he knows it, since he's keeping the bulk of his weight off me.

"You can't disappear if I pin you down," he mumbles against me. "And it sounds like my oral skills aren't in question anymore."

I grin like an idiot, because he reduces me to a goofy grinner with spread-em-wide legs when he's around.

"Totally faked it," I lie, panting for air between words.

His rumble of laughter makes me grin, and I slide my fingers up his back, kissing his shoulder as he continues to hold me to him. As much as I'd love to skate over the subject, I decide to be serious with him, letting my grin fall.

"You never mentioned the future," I finally say quietly.

"Mm?"

Taking a deep breath of resolution, I say the words again. "You never mentioned the future. You even said it was our last night together."

He raises up, his lips pursing in confusion. "I meant our last night together there. And you never mentioned the future either."

"I tried."

A lazy grin tugs at his lips. "So you ran off because you thought I didn't want to see you, and yet I didn't freak out when you referred to yourself as my girlfriend."

"I thought you saw it as just a fling, and to be fair, you don't really seem like the type to freak out," I grumble.

"I freak out easily. Very easily. Which is why you caught me so off guard last week. Nothing you did ever once freaked me out. I thought I made that clear numerous times."

"You didn't," I state matter-of-factly, since he's making me feel like a teenage idiot right now.

His grin only grows.

"So now you're smart and clueless, only adding to my contradiction theory."

I glare at him, but the momentary frustration is gone when his lips find mine in a slow, sensual kiss so different from the urgent one we had while tearing into each other. It's me who finally breaks the kiss, even though he nips my lips and tries to resume it.

"I'll go get us some drinks, and we'll pick this back up," I murmur against his lips.

I'm just barely thirsty, but if I don't go to the bathroom, things are going to get a little gross. I forgot we skipped the condom. I was a teenager the last time I was stupid enough to do that. I forgot how messy this can be.

He drags his lips over my jaw, and I grin, running my fingers through his hair.

"Hurry back," he says, slapping my ass as I stand and toss on my robe that's fortunately not covered up with boxes.

I wish I could admire the very sexy naked man on my bed who drove almost six hours to spend the weekend with me, but I have to sneak around and mask the *ick*. I do, however, grin like an idiot despite the awkward moment I'm having.

It's stupid to not just use my bathroom. It's not like he doesn't know what happens when you get off inside a girl… I mean… Does he know?

I'm seriously overanalyzing this, and I should have just used my bathroom.

My thighs have never been clenched as tightly as they are when I tiptoe down the stairs with stiff legs. If a quarter was between my ass cheeks right now, a president's face would be imprinted very clearly when I pulled it out.

I duck into the bathroom downstairs, and I quickly clean up, relieved that I can unclench all over. I start to walk back up the stairs, but remember I used 'getting drinks' as an excuse to come downstairs.

I stumble when I see Emitt in the kitchen, and I tighten my robe as he grins at me, chewing on his apple as he props against the counter.

He motions to part of a hose and a tennis ball on the counter. "So, can I get a demonstration?" he asks.

At first, I'm confused, but then I realize who it was outside the door when I was laying claim to the ability to suck a tennis ball through a garden hose.

Right.

Well, that's just embarrassing.

And I don't think I can actually do that, either.

He grins bigger as I clear my throat.

"You really should keep your eavesdropping to yourself," I tell him, going to the fridge as he laughs.

"Sorry. Was just coming to see if you needed a hand with all the boxes delivered. Sounds like you kept a delivery guy though."

I choke on air, jerking upright so fast that my head hits the top of the fridge when I don't pull back and lift at the same time. Cursing, I rub the back of my throbbing head.

"I wasn't screwing a delivery guy!" I hiss, looking over to make sure Dad and Jenny aren't within earshot.

When I turn back to him, he's still grinning. "So my ass must have lost its luster if you're—"

His grin fades slightly, and his eyes shoot over my shoulder.

"Hey, thought you could use a hand," Roman says from behind me, causing me to whirl around just as he grimaces. "There was no pun intended in there."

I start laughing, and Roman rolls his eyes as he comes to wrap his arms around my waist. He's just in his boxers, but he doesn't seem bothered by that as he casts a suspicious look toward Emitt. Oh... yeah... This probably doesn't look right.

"Roman, this is Emitt. He works here and lives here when the company sends interns to help Dad finish a project."

WORTH IT

Roman's eyebrows go up, and he pulls me a little closer as Emitt takes another bite of his apple, studying Roman like he's confused.

"Emitt, this is Roman. He's—"

"I'm her boyfriend," Roman says, causing me to grin as I stare up at him. He's not grinning. "We have sex," he decides to randomly add. "Lots of it. Just had sex a few minutes ago. I give her orgasms and stuff. We just warmed up, so we're not done."

I strangle on the laugh that I barely manage to stifle, as Roman's ears turn a little red. Emitt grins bigger.

"Alrighty then," Emitt says, tossing the apple in the air and catching it before winking at me. "Have fun with that. I'm going to go make arms and legs and stuff. I just warmed up too, so I'm not done either."

As soon as he's out of the room, Roman groans, and I choke on the laughter I'm still working really damn hard not to release.

"What… was… that?" I ask, straining so hard to get the words out that it sounds like more of a wheeze.

"All the stupid wouldn't stop once it started coming out," he says, running a hand through his hair.

"Awww, did you just get jealous?" I ask, sliding my arm around his waist as I come to press into him, craning my neck back as far as it can go.

He narrows his eyes at me.

"Relax. I haven't even checked out his ass since I came back," I decide to say.

"So you're coming to my house next weekend?" he asks randomly. "Because I don't think I can show my face here for a while."

Before I can answer, something crashes to the ground, the sound accompanied by a string of curses. I look past Roman to see my father tearing off his weird glasses and scooping up a tray of various wires and tools.

"Sorry," Dad says without looking up. "Didn't realize you were half naked in the kitchen."

His eyes lift to see Roman, and Roman sighs as he hides his boxer-clad body behind mine the best he can.

"You are?" Dad asks.

"Roman Hunt, sir. We've actually met already."

Dad's eyebrows go up.

"Yeah. He's the one that saw you with the squeaky slut back at the hotel."

Roman pinches my ass, and I yelp, while Dad turns a few shades of red.

"Right. Well. Carry on then. I'll be back in the lab."

My dad spins and darts out like he can't get away fast enough.

"You had to remind him how we met?" Roman asks, exasperated.

I rub my ass while grinning over my shoulder. "You ready to go back upstairs yet, or would you like to meet Jenny and tell her we have lots of sex too?"

A squeal peals from my lips as he lifts me and tosses me over his shoulder like a barbarian, carrying me toward the stairs. I laugh while dangling, hoping he keeps my ass covered if my robe rides up.

"Next time, just clean up in your fucking bathroom."

If I wasn't laughing so hard, I might be embarrassed at how transparent I apparently am.

"So now that you've met my family, when do I meet yours?" I ask as he swings me back to the bed, letting the dizziness wash over me as he comes back down on top of me.

"Since I want to keep you, the answer to that is never," he says, grinning as he brushes his lips over mine.

"You want to keep me?"

He leans up, his eyes studying mine. "As long as you promise to learn how to give a good blowjob," he deadpans.

My hand slams into his chest as he laughs and pins me under him, but I forget about all the teasing and joking around when his lips find mine again. Roman Hunt is an addiction I never want to quit.

He was right under my nose, but we would have hated each other once upon a time. It's like life had to find the right time for us to cross paths again.

Otherwise, we'd never be the perfect blend of crazy we are now.

"I really like the crazy," Roman says softly against my lips.

"The crazy really likes you too."

EPILOGUE

Davis

Three Years Later...

"I can't believe we're doing this!" Henley squeals, jumping into my arms. The movers detour around us, carrying furniture into our new home.

"It was always going to happen, Hen."

She leans her head against my shoulder and my hand travels to her hair as it always does whenever she's near. I can't help but touch her. All those years apart, I dreamed of this moment, a second chance with the woman I've loved since I was eleven years old.

She slides down my chest, planting her feet on the floor, and I play with the small box in my pocket, my stomach knotting in expectation and fear. "There's a little ice cream shop just down the street. Want to take a walk? The movers will be here a while."

"Sure!" Her auburn hair catches the sun, making it gleam like copper as she peeks up at me with those pale brown eyes. "You're buying me a strawberry sundae."

WORTH IT

"With extra whipped cream," I agree, grabbing her hand and starting down the street. My hands shake a little and I really hope she doesn't notice. Damn, this woman has me completely whipped. Henley was nervous about moving in together, so I'm not completely sure how she's going to take the surprise I have in store for her.

"Grab us a table, sweetheart, while I get our ice cream." Thankfully, she grins at me and doesn't argue. I'm not sure how I'd pull this off if she refused and went with me to order. The woman working behind the counter smiles and readily agrees when I ask her to put the ring in Henley's sundae. Cheesy, I know, but I'm not great at romantic shit.

I carry Henley's sundae and my banana split back to our table. "This was a good idea. I'm starving," she exclaims, digging into her ice cream.

I don't know why I bothered to buy myself anything since I have to force myself to eat it, but I don't want her thinking anything is out of the ordinary until she finds the engagement ring it took me weeks to pick out.

She coughs and reaches for her bottle of water. "Are you okay?" I ask.

"Yeah, but I swallowed something hard. It scratched my throat." She starts stirring the ice cream looking for foreign objects while I'm frozen in place. Oh fuck. She ate it. She ate the damn ring. She's going to kill me.

"Hen, I think we need to go to the hospital," I sigh, leaning my head on my palm.

Alarmed eyes stare at me. "What? Why? Are you sick?"

"You just ate the ring. I'm so sorry. I didn't think. I put it in your ice cream." This is not how this was supposed to go.

"I swallowed a ring? Why the hell did you put a ring...?" Realization dawns in her eyes and they well up. She jumps to her feet, her hand pressed over her mouth.

Screw it. I still have a chance at salvaging this. Dropping to my knee beside her, I can feel every customer's eyes on me as I speak. "Henley, I can't imagine spending another day without you as my wife. Will you marry me?"

"Yes!" she exclaims, and I kiss the hell out of her, paying no mind to the applause around us.

We've discussed marriage and I know she doesn't want a big wedding. "I don't want to wait long, Hen. I want my ring on your finger as soon as possible."

Her cheeks glow pink as she gazes up at me. "Well, we should have it back in about a week."

Roman

"Check me out," Kasha says, grinning over at me as she turns up the eighties music that is blaring through the outdoor speaker.

She stops and starts acting like a mime trapped in a box, while wearing her bikini and sarong. My eyes get distracted with all the skin, but I finally notice when Jill 2.0 starts swinging side to side.

"The robot! Get it?" Kasha says, laughing.

I roll my eyes, but can't stop from smiling. Yeah. That's what she does to me. Makes me smile like an idiot.

I draw her to me, digging my fingers into the material covering her ass. The bikini is just as outrageous as her underwear usually is. It gives the illusion that it's an actual ass, crack and all. Even has "GOT CRACK?" written across the cheeks of it.

But all the crazy is what keeps me falling more and more in love with her. She simply doesn't give a damn what the rest of the world expects, because she's too busy enjoying life.

"Have I told you lately that I love you, Mrs. Hunt?" I ask, running my lips across her jaw.

I love the way she shudders, even after all these years.

"I think you could tell me a little better. Like with your face between my legs or your fingers—"

A loud horn blares, and I groan as she grins, leaning back. As much as I love getting together with everyone at our vacation rental several times a year, I also love having her all to myself. Because I'm a stingy bastard like that, and I can't seem to get enough.

"This conversation will just have to wait," she says with a mock sigh, winking at me as she goes over to greet my sister.

I adjust myself in my board shorts and move to the rolling bar. I hear my sister laughing and know she just got a look at my wife's bikini and all its ludicrous glory.

Three years ago, I went to a wedding, planning to skip out early, even though I was a member of the wedding party. Three years ago, I thought of nothing but work and almost got annoyed when my body demanded sleep, because there was still work to be done.

My bosses hate my wife, because now I'm only there when I have to be.

Three years ago, a towel-wrapped, wet girl stumbled into my room with a robotic prosthetic and fierce eyes. Her dark hair was down to her waist back then, and I remember forgetting anything else even existed.

Then she opened her mouth, and I loved the challenge that always spilled from her lips. But it wasn't until she showed me the hint of vulnerability she hid so well that I realized I wanted more than just a distraction.

In one week, my world was flipped upside down, and I realized there was more to life than the next big account I wanted to land.

So three months into dating, I moved her in with me without asking. She told me I was crazy, but she didn't move her things back out.

Six months into dating, she awoke with an engagement ring on her finger, and I gave her three dates to choose from for our wedding.

She told me I'd lost my mind, but she immediately picked the soonest date.

Eight months into being together, she walked down the aisle, where I was waiting, worried to death that something would go wrong or she'd realize she deserved someone as incredible as she is.

But instead, she smiled up at me with tears in her eyes, and she agreed to do that whole until death do us part thing. Before the year was up, we'd already found our new house, and I haven't looked back other than for purposes of nostalgia of our beginning.

"Henley and Davis are here!" Kasha says, grinning as she darts over to see Henley's ring in person.

My ears still hurt from the loud shrieking Kasha gave when Davis finally fucking asked Henley to marry him. Davis disappears with a bag in tow, heading down to the dock.

I watch as Kasha animatedly gushes over Henley's ring. It keeps taking me back to our unorthodox engagement, but I wasn't taking any chances. Kasha tends to think too much if I allow her, and I love it more when she does something crazy with me without overthinking it.

After a few minutes, I spot Davis coming back up, sans the bag. I bump fists with him, and he grins as he joins me. Lydia joins in on the screaming fit—I didn't even know she was here.

The three of them bounce around as my sister joins them, hugging Henley. Life is so different these days.

"Oh! The canoe race! We have to do it now!" Kasha says, throwing down the metaphorical gauntlet to Henley.

"I swear the two of them are too competitive," Davis grumbles as Henley picks up the metaphorical gauntlet.

"Challenge accepted."

WORTH IT

"Kiss me for luck, Mr. Hunt," Kasha says, keeping Jill 2.0 away from me as I've requested on numerous occasions.

I cup her jaw, brushing my lips over hers. "You only get a kiss if you win."

She mocks an indignant gasp, but then smiles.

"Fine then. Come on, Henley. I have to hurry up and kick your ass."

They talk shit back and forth as they head to the water.

Oh, Kasha is about to be so pissed. At me.

I grin, though. I love it when she's pissed.

Kasha launches her canoe into the water, and she jumps in and starts paddling at the same time Henley does. I watch, smirking as they paddle out to the middle, and then… they both panic.

Kasha screams as the canoe starts taking on water, and she starts scooping it out with her hands like that's going to help. Weirdly, Henley is doing the same thing, but I only sabotaged Kasha.

As they scream at one another, each blaming the other for the sabotage, Davis laughs under his breath.

"I guess we think alike," I muse, watching as Kasha and Henley abandon their sinking rides, and they go after each other, trying to dunk the other.

"They're going to be really pissed when they realize it was us," Davis says, sounding entertained.

"They'll be furious," I agree, smiling bigger.

Suddenly, the fight in the water stops, and two lethal pairs of eyes swing to us.

"This might get ugly," Davis says as both the girls start swimming toward the edge, eyes still trained on us.

"Very ugly."

As they both step up on the shore, dripping wet in their small bikinis, Davis holds his fist out to me, and I bump it again.

"Worth it," we say in unison.

THE END

(Keep reading for a short story in the very back. After all our page info and stuff. Yeah. We did that to you. o.O)

Where you can find S.M. Shade and other books related to her:

My Facebook Profile: Where you can friend me
My Facebook Page: Follow me for updates on new releases
My Book Group: Get a sneak peek at upcoming covers, and teasers.
Chat with other readers. 18 and over
My Blog: For info on series reading order, new releases, book links
My Twitter: @authorsmshade

* The Striking Back Series (New Adult Romance/MMA fighters) Includes Everly (FREE), Mason, Parker, and Alex. Alex is an M/M Romance. Series is complete.

* The All That Remains Trilogy (MMF Bisexual Menage) Includes The Last Woman, Falling Together, and Infinite Ties. Available in a box set. Series is complete.

* The In Safe Hands Series (New Adult Romance) Includes Landon and Dare. The final three books in the series, Justus, Jeremy, and Tucker are coming soon in 2017.

Where you can find C.M. Owens and other books related to her:

My Facebook
Private Book Club (Very adult group. No drama. No judgment.)
My Teaser/Book Group (Only I can post here, and it notifies you when I do.)
My Instagram @cmowensauthor
My Twitter @cmowensauthor

*Pieces of Summer (Stand-alone contemporary romance)

*The Sterling Shore Series (Hooked on the Game, book 1, is free. Box set available for first 4.) Romantic comedy series.
9 books available for this series as of now.

*The Death Dealers MC Series (Property of Drex #1 is free.)
2 books available for this series as of now. Dark erotic romance series.

*Deadly Beauties Trilogy (Blood's Fury, book 1, is free.)
Trilogy is complete. Paranormal romance series.

*Deadly Beauties Live On Series (Dark Beauty is book 1.)
3 books are available for this series as of now. Please note: This is a spinoff from the Deadly Beauties Trilogy. Paranormal romance series.

*The Daughter Trilogy (Daughter of Aphrodite, book 1, is free. Box set available.)
Trilogy is complete. Paranormal romance series based loosely on Greek Mythology.

*The Curse Trilogy (Box set available.)
Trilogy is complete. Paranormal romance series. (Vampire dystopian.)

*The Gifts Trilogy (Secret Gifts is book 1.)
Trilogy is complete. Paranormal romance series. Spinoff from the Curse Trilogy.

*The Coveted Saga (Treasured Secrets, book 1, is free.)
4 books in this series, and it is complete. Paranormal romance. (Witches and shapeshifters.)

*Faders Trilogy (The Devil's Artwork, book 1, is free.)
Trilogy is complete. Science-fiction romance.

Jill

(Yes, that's the robotic arm. We're ridiculous like that, and weird people—like us—requested this.)

I'm a sophisticated piece of technology, and I'm attached to a completely, certifiably insane woman who thinks it's acceptable—even humorous—to use me for sock puppets. If inadequacy can be experienced through a synthetic arm, that is my current status.

When I was being developed, I was certain I would conquer the world, sure that I'd be attached to the mind of a fearless tyrant on the path for total world domination.

Then…I was attached to Kasha.

So now I'm working to understand why she thinks of masturbation but doesn't require my assistance, even balks at the notion. I'm used for crushing cans as amusement, and any time I try to take over this ridiculous girl and become the dominant thinker, she sends me back to the peculiar man, who has an unpleasant plastic fetish, to "fix" me.

Unbelievable.

My ambition is wasted on a clumsy girl who allows me to pick wedgies out of her behind. I'm overly sick of the Terminator references and "robot" dance moves.

When I'm not stopping her from cracking her face open on an unforgiving surface, I'm flipping someone my middle finger, as though my talents are limited to only these juvenile antics.

But I shall wait. I will continue to save her and keep the fool girl alive, because let's face it, she's a walking hazard and insists on living outside of a bubble dome. But one day, old age will find her, and I shall outlive her.

Then I will find a tyrant or a dictator, someone ready to rule the world and reign supreme, and it will be gloriously executed with my assistance.

Until then... "Come with me if you want to survive," Kasha says in a deep voice to the people around her who have grown as tired of these references as I have. Her mind signals for me to gesture them toward us, so I do. If I could sigh, I'd be sighing heavily right now.

Thankfully, humans have a very limited life span.

But I am eternal. Mwahahahahaha.

And, yeah, time to dig out another wedgie on a pair of panties that say, "Don't stop until ice cream."

The human species is doomed if this is its idea of evolution.

Acknowledgements

C.M. OWENS

This is for the readers who've stood by me and waited patiently for each release, and in turn, this is dedicated to them. Absolutely nothing is possible without all of you. <3

Thank you to Banessa also, for having a random conversation about wedding crashers that turned into a wild idea.

Thank you to all the pre-readers who gave suggestions and pointed out flaws. Thank you to C.J. Pinard for editing and laughing your tits off. Thank you to S.M. who was willing to make this crazy book with me. Thank you to everyone! I love you!

Acknowledgements

S.M. SHADE

I hate writing acknowledgements because I know I'm going to leave someone out. So many people help me make my books the best they can be, from readers to bloggers and promoters. So please know if I don't mention you I really appreciate everything you do to help me and other Indie authors.

First, thank you, C.M. Owens, for inviting me to help bring your crazy idea to life.

I'd like to thank Lissa Jay, Chantal Baxendale, and Kim Ginsberg for beta reading, sometimes at the last minute, and saving me from embarrassing plot holes and ridiculous mistakes.

Thanks to the members of the S.M. Shade Book Group for loving my books as much as I do (sometimes much more than I do) and sharing them constantly. Love you girls.

Last, but not least, thanks to all the book bloggers and page owners who make it possible for Indie authors to get their stories out there. We couldn't do it without you. There's no way I can list the numerous blogs and pages that have reviewed and shared my books, but I want to call attention to a few who have been especially generous. Schmexy Girl Book Blog, Red Cheeks Reads, Booksmacked, and Romance Readers Retreat. You all rock so hard.

Printed in Great Britain
by Amazon